The Witch

Healer Part II

The Witch
Healer Part II

Magdalena Kułaga

WRITTEN BY MAGDALENA KULAGA

PUBLISHED BY ROYAL HAWAIIAN PRESS

COVER ART BY TYRONE ROSHANTHA

TRANSLATED BY RAFAL STACHOWSKY

PUBLISHING ASSISTANCE: DOROTA RESZKE

***

FOR MORE WORKS BY THIS AUTHOR, PLEASE VISIT:

WWW.ROYALHAWAIIANPRESS.COM

***

VERSION NUMBER 1.00

From the editor

The healer gifted with extraordinary abilities is able to heal not only physical wounds, but also sadness, worries and slow down the aging of his loved ones and the inhabitants of his village. Everyone loves him and are grateful to him, treating him as a holy and untouchable person. He has just returned from a long journey from the capital, where he almost lost his life while treating courtiers and royalty. The healer skills are appropriated by Mayene - the demon, the titular witch - indestructible, without a heart. The healer stands up to fight her, and the life of his loved ones and those around him is at stake. He can not allow anything bad to happen to them, to which his above-average sensitivity suffers. However, he is not alone. He is assisted by the reliable friends we met in Part One. Everyone is engaged in a hard and ruthless fight against evil, which involves many victims.

In the memory of my Grandfather

Chapter I

Kidnapping

"What the hell is wandering around in the bushes on the edge of the woods?" Alesei asked. "Our little forest friends or some other evil?"

The blacksmith Azylas followed his gaze slowly.

It's a troll," he remarked upon reflection. "They won't come any closer. We burned their asses a month ago. See how it hides, scumbag? It must be one of those seared ones, like a whipped dog!"

Do not offend my dog," Alesei warned him, glancing meaningfully at his favorite, who was now standing next to them on the town walls, "He does not like it very much."

The blacksmith met the dog's eyes, and a faint growl reached his ears.

"Yeah..." he muttered under his breath, looking like a philosopher.

Alesei studied the hairy creature. His body flashed every now and then in the thicket of bushes near the walls.

"Maybe end it with an arrow?" He suggested calmly.

"Then more of them will be here to take revenge," the blacksmith replied confidently.

"Don't touch them, if they don't touch you.

The golden rule in the town?"

And so it is."

Alesei stamped his foot on the spot again, rubbing his massive shoulders hidden beneath a thick sheep's wool jacket and a fur cape. Dressed in a modest blacksmith, he looked very funny; as if he was about to move north to the Frozen Lands. That's what Azylas thought with a half-muttered smile.

It's cold today," the disgruntled bully remarked in the meantime.

"Still not used to it?" The blacksmith muttered with a smile. "I told you to take a bath in the river when the first frosts hit. You would have toughened up!"

"You take it..." Alesei began but ending his argument with indistinct mumbles masking a few ugly curses.

The Count has already done that… your friend Sel has already done that. Only you, Ross and the ladies," Azylas enumerated, grinning at Alesei's face, "didn't even get your finger wet.

Even the soldiers who were here bathed in our cold water. We always have stiff dicks and yours are hunching like old leaves."

"Heard no complaints," Alesei grimaced in response. "Mine warms up quickly in good hands."

"So," smiled the blacksmith, "tell Sel to heat up better, because his friend will die."

For these words Alesei glanced at the blacksmith but saw only sincere merriment without a trace of prejudice. This continued to amaze Vivan's new friends, from the very first days of his stay in this place. Nobody mentioned their past, although he saw that due to his and Sai's appearance, they were recognized in the town. No one has ever harassed them or pointing Ross's orientation out, which is definitely more conspicuous than Sel, who happened to look round a pretty girl. Maybe because they were friends of Vivan now? Or maybe the people here did not look at the tastes of their neighbors, but at the value they represent?

"I'll tell Sel you're worried about Ross," he said, seemingly casually, hoping for an appropriate response.

He didn't miscalculate.

The blacksmith grunted in response, clearly confused. Alesei, laughing revealing his beautiful white teeth, gave him a friendly nudge.

However, some things don't change just like that.

* * *

For the next three weeks, right after his return, Vivan went into hiding. He was too weak and, which he could not hide from his relatives, too scared to face the crowd. However, after a few days, an irresistible urge to help made him go on secret expeditions each night to surreptitiously save at least a few lives. And nothing could dissuade him, not even the fear he fought every day. Alesei, Sel, Ross, and even several times Oliver still in a woman's disguise, went out with him and two plainclothes soldiers for protection, also hiding their faces. However, rumors soon began to circulate about his return, especially as miraculous healings began to multiply. They were no longer safe. Oliver had to withdraw from the night expeditions after someone pressed a piece of paper with the address on him, whispering pleading for help. Julien claimed the dresses had betrayed him. Women have an eye for such things. Probably one of them noticed a detail or material that did not escape her attention.

From then on, Selena became an intermediary between the needy and the healer. Ross also had to back out, though the reasons for his actions were not up to clear end. One night, his hood was deliberately opened. His face and a strand of white hair were seen. For a week while they were still with the queen's soldiers, Ethan, eager to redeem himself a bit for his earlier behavior, replaced him on these secret missions for reasons he knew only. But he stopped after he was attacked, and then unexpectedly left without any harm. Until the last day of the soldiers' stay, the strange incident was a mystery to everyone. After they left, Ross almost stopped leaving. Not only because his hair made him too distinctive. At that time, they had moved to winter from the carriage in which he, Sel and Alesei lived together, to the estate of Vivan and his family, vigilantly guarded by volunteers recruited by a blacksmith.

There was something else that only he and Vivan knew.

A month earlier, travelers who had come to the town joyfully announced that the plague had passed. The world began to return to normal. Many left Barnica to return home. Others have decided to stay here permanently. Vivan could leave without fear that the crowd of needy would surround him on all sides. He was properly protected, made up of people ready to defend him with their breasts, so that no one would ever lay a hand on him again. Or no one wouldn't try to kidnap him. Even if they were the soldiers of the king himself again.

However, the fear of the lived nightmare was never to leave him again. Especially when more than a few people gathered around him. He was afraid of the crowd.

On that day, when Alesei and a blacksmith were voluntarily serving on the town walls, a woman who was injured in the hand came to Vivan. She claimed to have fallen over during cleanup. A healer who with his supernatural gift saw the cause of all wounds, abrasions, beatings or even diseases could not be fooled in this way. He knew she was hurting herself on purpose to show up to him. He also knew the reason why she had come, and he almost dismissed her angrily.

From behind an upstairs pillar, Ross watched his mother and friend.

Vivan did not refuse to help her. With difficulty controlling her agitation, he healed her injured arm, while she surreptitiously, with greedy, alert curiosity, looked around at her surroundings.

She was looking.

Ross was sure of it, like his own terrified heart beating.

She watched the healer's movements attentively, the expression on his face, the eyes that looked at her, trying not to reveal any secrets. With every nerve, Vivan felt the tension in the hall between the disgusting mother and her son hidden in the shadows. It was difficult to maintain the neutrality demanded by the game of appearances the three of them were leading.

Moreover, she was sniffing! Like an animal catching the trail of its victim.

She listened...

Ross saw Vivan's face grow serious; as he becomes more and more tense. It was thanks to the behavior of his friend that his suspicions were fully confirmed. He felt a chill sweep over him. A fear he had managed to suppress, an old fear from a gloomy age, a child's fear of being beaten, of an undeserved, unfair punishment - reappeared in his mind.

The mother looked at the healer with the watchful gaze of a born predator. Oh yeah, Ross knew that look...

She had always had it... This sense, this instinct... This cunning!

She thanked him, still staring at him.

A smile of satisfaction twisted her face as she walked away.

She knew.

She came to see if the rumors turned out to be true. The healer was betrayed by his unusual sensitivity.

"Don't tell Sel," Ross asked quietly shortly after she left.

Vivan looked at his friend carefully, genuinely surprised by his request.

"Why?"

"I asked Oliver for help after someone attacked Ethan. Something was wrong for me. As if the attacker didn't mean him, as if he were just a warning. I was right. Oliver discovered that the mother and her bastard, Ramsey, this..." Vivan nodded his head in agreement, to show that he understood, to spare him further, painful explanations, "...they have a ship in port and are going to leave soon.

Do you know what they called him?" He asked regretfully. "CADELIA! They used my mother's name. The ship's galion has her features! And Ramsey is the captain! Vivan..." He broke off suddenly, feeling hurt. "They... They don't know anything about Sel, do they? Or they don't care. And let it stay that way. Let them go! Let them disappear from my life once and for all! Because if Sel finds out... I don't want him to do anything about it! I don't want anything to happen to him! Let them finally go away!"

He uttered the last words with a strange vindictiveness unlike him. After all, he was usually cheerful and kind to the world, especially recently, when he had mated with Sel for good.

Vivan watched this strange change in silence for a moment. No one would have guessed at this point that, deep down, he himself sometimes struggled with a similar anger at people who were ready to tear him alive without hesitation. He didn't let these feelings take over his heart. Just like Ross did, with whom the healer found more and more in common. Maybe because they both wore the same pendants in the shape of a hand embracing a ruby? Ethan gave his copy, which for obvious reasons went to Vivan.

Or was it just about the kinship of souls?

Finally, hesitantly, he nodded his head in agreement.

"I hope I won't regret it," he said softly.

* * *

Another trip to the shores of the bay, where Sel was eagerly trying to capture the beauty of the fjord overlooking the town, was a success. They were surrounded by mountains on all sides, and numerous waterfalls made this place majestic and uniquely beautiful. For a man who spent his entire life within the walls of the capital, hoping for nothing else, it was a truly priceless and moving sight. It happened more and more often that help was necessary. It was like that today. The people with whom he usually spent his time drawing on the porch willingly let him do so. In return, Sel helped them on the farm and brought their purchases from the market, which really earned them their gratitude. It was a nice couple of rather old people, in good health, like most of the inhabitants of the healer hometown. The old couple, however, were lonely, so they welcomed Sel's visits with gratitude and treated him as a good friend of the house. For most of his life, Sel was eager for such acceptance and accepted their friendship with gratitude.

He was just holding in his hands more sketches for his small exhibition, which he was preparing in the carriage, intending to hang them soon on an empty piece of wall.

At that moment he noticed a broken glass in the window.

In the blink of an eye his good mood faded. Filled with foreboding and learned from previous experience, he drew his unicorn-hilt sword as he carefully approached the carriage.

However, the tracks in front of the vehicle did not reveal anything. There were always a lot of people hanging around in the square in front of Oliver and Julien's aunt and uncle's house, and it hadn't been snowing since yesterday. But he felt that an unpleasant surprise awaited him inside the carriage.

He was right.

There was a piece of rock on the floor, sloppily wrapped in a roll of parchment, which was clearly of a hurry. He felt his heart pound as he began reading Ross's familiar handwriting. It was a bit childish because, as he had once revealed to him, he could not read or write until he was taught it by his wonderful guardian, Valeri, when he moved to the House of Pleasure. However, not only the content evoked a bad feeling.

For the words were written with human blood:

RAMSEY CADELIA SLAVE BAY

Underneath, Ross had written one name in huge bloody letters:

MAYENE.

Chapter II

Panic in the town

For a moment, a very long moment, Sel stood still, silently clutching the parchment with his lover's handwriting. The sketches had been so adored just moments ago now littered the floor completely forgotten. The wind was pouring through the hole in the broken glass of the carriage, and the muffled sounds of everyday life could be heard from outside.

As if nothing bad happened...

Thoughts swirled in his mind like mad. Why? Who could want to kidnap him? And what would his purpose be?

"Ross..." he whispered, pain in his heart.

As if the name becomes a spell. He slowly returned to reality. The wind intensified. A breeze of snow hummed softly. And from the outside you heard no sounds of everyday bustle, but louder and louder calls and shouts.

Something was wrong in the town, he was sure of it.

He stood on the steps of the carriage to look at the market square just beyond the fence. Soon the twins' aunt, who had made all Vivan's new friends call her by name, stood beside him.

"Sel?" She asked. "What's going on there?"

Dressed in accordance with the local highlander custom, she quickly reached the fence to observe the events outside with amazement. Several women were just walking around calling for their husbands or sons. In the case of the latter, there were also fathers. She also heard the names of the women.

"Laysa!" She shouted to one of Semerald's women. "What's happening?!"

"I haven't found my son since this morning," replied the old woman, wringing her hands. "He was supposed to get married in the spring. May, my future daughter-in-law is also not there. We're all looking for them. And Maryta is looking for her man, because he has not returned home for the night. Apparently, the blacksmith's wife and the innkeeper with their sons are also missing. What's going on here, Seme? First, we were threatened with death, and now ours are gone!"

She walked away, wringing her hands and still calling for her loved ones. Semeralda, or Seme, as her friends called her, looked at Sel. The man stood next to her with the parchment in his hands.

"Sel..." She looked at him, and then saw the expression on his face. Touched by a hunch, she whispered:

"Ross?"

"Oliver?" He asked.

"I'll check right now!" She replied nervously.

"The strongest ones are gone," he observed. "Or the smartest. Those who were unlucky and were just outside the house when the round-up began."

"What are you talking about?!" She asked in horror.

She knew these people, so she couldn't disagree with him. The blacksmith's wife was a great archer. The innkeeper and his sons were able to bring order to the newcomers.

"And Ross…" added Sel softly, "he has a Hope Jewel. Someone wants that the town was in chaos."

"What is written here?" She asked, pointing to the parchment in his hand.

"Later, Seme," he replied, touching her shoulder. "Don't let Oliver and the girls leave the house. I'm going to Vivan."

"And if they take you too?"

He did not answer.

He walked past her and leapt over the fence with his newly acquired dexterity.

* * *

Vivan and his brother only needed a glance at the parchment Sel had brought to clear some of Ross's mysterious message.

"RAMSEY," said the concerned healer, looking at Sel. "Ross didn't tell you?"

At the mere mention of that name, he had a nightmarish vision of what he had experienced with Ross. He remembered Ross's mother urging her lover to beat the boy with a fire poker...

"Was that the same bastard that...?" Sel didn't dare to finish, and Vivan just nodded.

"He was in town," he replied. "Together with his mother. But Ross asked me not to tell you about it yet. He hoped they would go away. As far as we know, they were getting ready to go to sea."

Sel pursed his lips in anger.

"SLAVE BAY," Paphian drawled slowly. "That bastard must have been sailing there! A gloomy place. Name corrects with destination. This is where they trade slaves, and on a large scale. And CADELIA..." He snapped his fingers. "It's a ship! I saw it!"

"Probably set out at dawn today!" Sel called. "Together with Ross!" He groaned and fell silent away with tears in his eyes."

"And Ramsey," Vivan added grimly. "And, as you say, also a few or a dozen inhabitants of the town."

"Mother decided to sell him at the slave market!" Sel hissed angrily. "They wanted to make a pile! Ross has a magic gem!"

"And he's not ugly," added Paphian ominously.

Sel felt a sudden chill seize his heart. He was afraid to even think about it...

"But why now?" Vivan asked. "And why these people?"

"Because they are in their prime of life, Vivan," replied the Paphian. "And the plague is over."

Vivan was devastated by the news. But something was bothering him. Nevertheless, such sudden anxiety was too little for him to share with friends now. He had to wait for events to unfold to support his grim suspicions.

And that was just the beginning.

"I'm going to the port," Sel said firmly. "I'll take Alesei with me. I have to find Ross, Vivan. If you're right…" He bit his lip, too consumed by the gloomy vision to finish the sentence.

Vivan nodded his head in approval. He touched the bloody ink with a heavy heart.

"What you see?" Paphian asked him.

"Ross cut his finger to write this," the Healer replied intently, touching the handwriting. "He was scared…" He paused, staring thoughtfully at the words. "He was afraid that no one would find out…"

They looked at him with concern.

"Who is this Mayene?" Sel asked.

The brothers exchanged glances. Paphian shook his head and replied:

"I have no idea, Sel, but she's definitely behind it all."

* * *

Pressing against the wall of one of the huts, Ross tried to calm his heavy breathing. The run between the buildings in the port, fences and walls to escape the pursuers was quite a test for him. He had not been forced to such physical exertion for a long time. The neglect of form turned out to be a serious mistake.

She discovered him!

Hours before Sel began his search, Ross discovered the intentions of Ramsey and his pirate gang. He only wanted to make sure after the news from Oliver that they would indeed leave that night. It would never have occurred to him that they had such plans. Apparently, Ramsey hadn't talked to anyone about it when Oliver was hanging around here. He delayed the decision until the last moment. SHE led the demonic plan: the redhead, who handed a large pouch to Ramsey. Ross's mother was at his side.

"You have to catch him," the redhead ordered them. "He has to leave town!"

"We'll take care of it," Ramsey replied in a sloppy tone that was meant to make it clear that he didn't like to obey someone else's orders.

At the sound of his voice, Ross felt an involuntary shiver run through his body and his hands tremble like an old man's, unconsciously sweating. He was glad no one saw it. Nobody knew how much trouble it took him to shake off their last meeting. Only Vivan guessed the truth.

"I sense the Jewel," said the woman. "He's nearby."

"We'll find him, Lady," Ramsey replied confidently.

She took him by the chin with a firm, quick hug, then hissed angrily:

"I hope so. Otherwise I will kill all of you...".

Unexpectedly and too abruptly, she looked to where Ross's hideout was now located. As if she smelled him! Her eyes flashed with a strange iridescent glow. They seemed inhuman, greedy.

He was terrified and started to flee before she ordered a chase. In this way, he gained some time.

It was then that he heard her name in the port.

MAYENE.

As he fled again, weaving through the narrow streets of the port town, in one of the hiding places, on a scrap of parchment, he wrote the words that had upset Sel so much. In the alleys he noticed how Ramsey's people and his mother grabbed residents who, for various reasons, were still leaving asleep and sleepy with the light of a waking day.

They had to hunt him for a long time.

The sun was peeking out from behind the clouds as a passer-by threw the stone and parchment at the window of the carriage.

They did not notice.

But one careless maneuver was enough.

They seized him.

* * *

"Don't let him wake up," he heard the red-haired woman's voice. "If he is aware, he will use the Gem to break free. Don't kill him! The gem is closely related to him. Without him, it will be just an ordinary ruby. Don't be too harsh on him and you'll get a good price. Sorcerers will know his worth, believe me!"

Suddenly he felt that someone was holding his head and trying to pour some hideous liquid into his mouth. He struggled, ready to defend himself at any cost.

"Hold him!" The woman shouted.

"Stand politely as you are told!" He heard his mother's low voice, hoarse from many years of drinking, and felt her give him a strong cheek.

The wound pulsed where he had been hit with a stick. His legs buckled under him at the sound of that voice.

But he didn't give up.

He jerked and looked for her. She was standing right next to him. Dressed in a men's leather outfit, you can see that it is comfortable, but also expensive. She must be doing well now. He pushed her until she fell. Someone redoubled his efforts to hold him down. He was immobilized. The smirk vanished from mother's face, however, and it was replaced by grim anger.

Taking advantage of the fact that two people were holding his head, Mayene forcibly poured a few drops into his mouth.

"Three is enough," she told his mother, handing the bottle. "From more than that, you can permanently damage his head or even kill him."

"I wonder..." Ramsey said with a sullen smile, but Mayene snorted at him angrily.

Ross felt terribly helpless and heavy. Helpless. He hated feeling vulnerable so much!

"Darling," he heard the redhead's voice in his ear suddenly. "Have fun far away with your new masters. You don't even know what you have, do you? How much power do you have? You could do so much with it... You could be more powerful than the most powerful pillars of this earth. And you waste that power, you keep it on a tether. So pay for your stupidity! Your friends will be looking for you and will follow you to the Slave Bay. Let them sail. In the meantime, I'll take care of the one who stays here."

"Vivan!" He thought in horror.

"Slut!" He said to her, not playing with any pleasantries.

He heard her hoarse laugh, some voices, and confusion.

He was dozing off. He was losing the sense of reality. All the sounds rose strangely in his head. They distorted. The world was blurring.

"Sel..." he whispered softly, before the awareness of time and place stretched, swayed and distorted for good.

As if he was falling somewhere in infinity... "Find the message," he thought pleadingly.

He remembered his face with pain and longing. Right now, when they started to make their own lives... When Sel was healthy...

They found themselves in serious trouble.

* * *

"Sai," Julien asked. "How does it all look like?"

Sai awoke from her thoughts to look at her. She was flawless. At first glance, the deceptive similarity could confuse anyone.

"Hear me!" The door to the room opened suddenly as Semeralda burst in in apparent rush. "Oliver is not in the room! Is he maybe...? Ah... you are here!" She shouted with relief. "So now I have to look for Julien. Something terrible has happened in town! Someone kidnapped a dozen of ours! Oliver," she came closer. "You have to tell Julien... If only she was here somewhere..." She paused to catch her breath.

"What happened?" Julien looked anxiously at Sai. "Aunt!"

"Ah..." the woman hesitated suddenly, as if a thought had crossed her mind. However, after a while she replied impassively, "Ross was probably kidnapped!"

"What? How is that? He too?!" Julien shouted, and this time her aunt looked at her more closely, her eyes widening as she realized in an instant what had really happened.

"Sel said so..." she informed slowly, staring at her face. "Great Mother, it's you, Julien! And I was already thinking..."

Deceptively like her brother, Julien became Oliver thanks to the Sai characterization. For all those who did not know their siblings like friends and family, she could safely pass for them. The wig reflected the color of Oliver's hair. The slight line of a sagging beard and a thin line of mustache were identical to the boy's. The face looked even more like it than before, the delicate web of details that helped distinguish the twins disappeared. While disguised as a woman, Oliver almost completely resembled his twin sister. Disguised as a man, Julien used tricks to bring out what usually distinguished her brother from herself. In this form, they almost became one. Like him, when he had to use his disguise until recently.

"What are you guys doing?" Semeralda whispered in shock. "What is all this supposed to mean?"

"Don't betray us, Aunt," Julien asked gently.

"Aunt..." Semeralda repeated reproachfully. "I knew it right away. Oliver always calls me Seme, because I let him that way. I knew something was…"

"Please…"

"Why are you doing it?!" The nervous woman shouted.

Julien gently placed a hand on her shoulder. Sai stood next to her.

"Please listen to me," Julien said. "Don't say what you saw. Officially, Oliver is at home. Julien too. Nothing has changed…"

"How is that...?"

"Oliver is home, Seme," this time Julien emphasized the way her brother addressed her aunt. "Julien too," she repeated emphatically.

"Your uncle must know," Seme whispered to it, though she didn't quite understand what it was all about.

"Only he," Sai said calmly. "And our friends."

"Where is Oliver? Will I finally find out what all this is for?"

Julien, now completely transformed into Oliver, leaned towards her. Sai smiled slightly, though she mentally worried about her lover's fate.

"What do you think?" Julien asked, the corner of her lips twitching. "Where is my crazy brother now?"

* * *

"Don't panic!" Erlon, Earl and Lord of the surrounding lands centered on a harbor town on the shores of the gulf, stood in front of the agitated crowd gathered in front of his palace.

His family accompanied him with a small volunteer guard. Even Vivan's maternal grandfather, standing by his beloved grandson, carried a sword at his side. Fit and strong more than his age he was accompanied by his wife. A war veteran from his mysterious world, symbolized by the cross around his neck worn in his family. Vivan tried to keep pace with him, though his heart was pounding in his chest like mad, fueled by the fear he had tried to fight with himself since the tragic events at the marketplace in the capital. But fear was still with him when there were so many people around, most of whom he had known almost from birth. Even the presence of brother and friends did not help much in this situation. But today he was afraid not only of the crowd. He knew it. He looked around slowly, hoping that he might see the source of his anxiety.

On the edge of the crowd, he noticed Sai and Julien, hidden in the shadows, who disguised herself as her brother.

Judging by the faces of the family knowing his new friends, no one else noticed.

"Where's Julien?" Paphian asked quietly, thus confirming his suspicions.

"She must have stayed with her aunt and uncle," he replied without hesitating. "Oliver is afraid for his sister."

"And not about yourself?" Paphian was a bit surprised, while his father tried to convince upset people to stay calm and take reasonable actions.

"I'd sooner guess he's at Sel's side in the harbor."

"Maybe," Vivan agreed, looking Julien in the eye.

She shook her head slightly, which meant "Don't tell anyone you know."

"What is it for?" He wondered.

"Paphian," he whispered to his brother. "This is just the beginning."

"I think so too," he replied calmly. "And I think it's about you again."

Vivan felt a chill penetrate him. He shared his brother's concerns.

Things had gone weird around him lately. He was worried, paying less attention to his habit. His relatives and friends had suffered once when it came to him. Now they too were in danger. Ross has already fallen into the hands of people who once hurt him cruelly.

Was the gift of healing still a gift?

"Lord Count!" the blacksmith Azylas, who found a replacement for himself on the walls, quickly appeared at the meeting. "We can't leave them! My wife is there!"

He was looking directly at Vivan, expecting his help. The words of others began to come out immediately:

"And my sister!"

"My wife too!"

The call of many echoed through the palace courtyard.

All concerned now looked at the healer as a sure rescue and a rock, as if he was to restore order, thus excluding his stepfather asking everyone for consideration. Vivan was their support in every misfortune.

During the plague, he did not hesitate to come to their aid, they could always count on his gift. And now, though it would be of little use here, they turned to him again for help. Even respect for Count Erlon, to whose line these lands belonged, could not win this time with the authority of a healer. Vivan met his adoptive father's gaze. As always, in hard times, he could see the reflection of his mother's feelings in his eyes. Support and understanding. The count stepped back to give him his place in front of the crowd.

Recently, moments like this made Vivan want to run away in panic.

His family knew about it. They sincerely felt sorry for him.

But he couldn't run away from it forever...

He swallowed nervously before reaching out to the worried people.

"You can't all leave," he said.

He even managed to keep his voice under control: he only trembled at the beginning of his speech. Then he felt more confident.

"What about our loved ones, my lord?" Azylas called again.

Vivan did not hesitate to answer, although the decision was not the easiest one:

"Choose the people. The city needs protection."

"Hydra is at dock in port!" A man exclaimed. "We will leave!"

"Azylas!" Vivan's voice, when he chose, was able to break through the others without difficulty, giving it the right strength and melody. The crowd fell silent at once, as if the healer had lashed the air with a whip instead of a word.

"Yes, Count?" He replied with some apprehension.

"You choose volunteers and send them out with my friends," Vivan told him. "You will stay here..."

"Lord Count!" The blacksmith protested, but Vivan silenced him with a gesture and continued. "You will stay, otherwise there will be no blacksmith in town. Ask the high elves to come to me, gather the people. Arm yourself!"

"Should we arm ourselves?!"

"We have to be prepared. Everyone else," he turned to the crowd, "beware. Be cautious! Don't go anywhere alone. Keep your weapons in your homes. Don't trust strangers!"

His words caused a real stir among the people.

"What's going on, my lord?!" someone exclaimed. The healer's keen senses, which had grown considerably since he returned home, finally sensed the presence of enemies. However, he did not know how many there really were. He was being watched.

"I hope I can surprise you," he thought to them.

"We may have to defend ourselves," he replied seriously.

The crowd became even more agitated, discussions flared up. The blacksmith Azylas loudly decided who was assigned to the rescue mission and who was to be left. He was doing very well in this role.

"Isn't it too early for that, Vivan?" Count Erlon asked. "You have no evidence that we are in danger."

"When my forebodings were not believed recently..." Vivan looked into his adoptive father's dark eyes, "the viceroy grew in strength and organized a coup d'état."

The Earl of Erlon looked at him closely, considering the right choice of words. He felt that behind Vivan's actions there were echoes of recent events, including those from his worst nightmare, even before he spoke the words. This case was still an extremely painful topic. And maybe it will never stop...

He got it.

"Then it will be better if we return to the palace," he said, glancing at the gathered people.

Azylas chose a group of daredevils who went to the port. In the courtyard there were still those who did not like his decision. The dispute was in full swing.

* * *

"You went white," the mother said to her son as the family headed for the palace.

She took his arm. She, not so long ago, radiant beauty has been marked the hallmark of painful experiences of recent months. Girlish innocence gave way to female, motherly maturity, despite the still young appearance. For days after her son's return, Lena Beckert cried in secret in the darkness of the night or lay awake.

She often sat by her son's bed, excited and terrified by the boundless cruelty of people towards her beloved child. She woke him up from agonizing nightmares and drove his gloomy thoughts away with motherly tenderness. When she was not with him, when he set off on one of his secret trips with friends, she indulged in a regret that he could not see at the time. Still, he knew. And then, instead of comforting him, she listened to his soothing words, calmed down under his touch. He couldn't bear her distress, he was worried about her, so in order not to worry him, she ordered herself to calm down. To give him strength, she became strong herself. She had to find it within herself not only for him. The whole family was shocked to learn about what had happened; when they saw the pale and thin Vivan, so different from the one he once was. She was strong for them too. She didn't want them to see her tears. Even her second son couldn't see them. He, too, experienced what befell his brother, albeit in his own way. Their sons' new friends, whose kindness quickly earned the trust of the Beckert family, became a great consolation. Ross, in particular, became the favorite of a troubled mother and grandmother for his warmth to the healer and his willingness to help in times of need. She was surprised he wasn't here now, and neither was Sel. This prompted an anxious question as a sudden thought flashed through her:

"Vivan," she said to her son. "Have any of your friends been taken?" Everyone paused in the hall awaiting a reply. Vivan looked at Paphian before his eyes met his mother's, as blue as his own.

"Yes," he replied, trying to make it sound calm. There was silence after these words.

"Who did they take?" Mother asked.

The healer's grandmother approached them. Both women almost sensed the answer.

"Ross," he replied in keeping with their apprehension.

"Someone else?" Asked the Countess in a trembling voice, while her mother glanced nervously at her husband, curious about his reaction and at the same time terrified of the news.

"No," Vivan replied softly, hoping he was right.

He did not see Oliver in the crowd, though the others were convinced they had seen him.

"Well, he lived to see it," Vivan's grandfather muttered under his breath, rubbing his hands together nervously. "He always went where he didn't have to!"

"What are you talking about?!" Indignant grandmother shouted at him. "The boy had a terrible misfortune! How can you be so cruel?!"

"Grandma..." Vivan began, but his mother reassured him with a gesture.

Knowing both elders for a long time, he agreed with his mother in silence. Grandfather departed soon after his grandmother's rebuke, which he ignored in silence. The younger members of the family followed them with their eyes.

"I see your father still hasn't changed in some respects," Count Erlon smiled slightly at his wife. "Whatever Ross did, he would still not be good enough for Grandpa."

"You are wrong," the Countess returned the smile tenderly.

They have already conducted many similar conversations. Her father's views, drawn from the world he came from, were a source of indulgent conversation among the rest of the family. The quarrels between the elders were no longer concerned. As quickly as they argued, they reconciled so quickly, which always surprised Count Erlon: his parents were extremely quiet. And cold.

"Yes?" He asked with a hint of surprise.

"He'll never admit it," Paphian shook his head. "But Ross is his favorite."

"How's that?" The count asked, surprised. "He always made him understand that he barely tolerated him. He even pretended at first not to see or hear him, if I remember correctly."

Vivan felt regret squeezing his heart slowly. Slowly and painfully. He did not participate in the conversation, he was concerned about his friend's fate. He still remembered that nightmare vision...

Now he was with them on the ship...

"Yes, it was like that at first," Paphian explained. Grandpa really barely tolerated Ross and Sel. Sel quickly gave up and stopped talking to him. He kept his distance. But Ross persisted. I think that despite everything, he liked grandfather very much. An old war veteran from an unknown land, so full of dignity, so proud, inspiring authority. Ross must have never met anyone like him in his life and he was very anxious for grandfather to convince him. In some ways, he even resembled him..." He broke off as suddenly he felt a firm hand grip on his shoulder and saw the look in his brother's eyes. "Vivan?" He asked surprised by his behavior.

"He's not dead, Paphian," Vivan said softly. "Don't talk about him in the past tense."

Paphian fell silent, absorbed by this remark.

"He really got upset about it," Vivan added, thinking of his grandfather. "He rubs his hands when he really cares about something. And he is silent because he is afraid to make a fool of himself. He prefers to be silent rather than admit that he cares and thus expose himself to possible silly jokes. He hates it."

"I don't…" Paphian began awkwardly.

"I know," Vivan's gaze softened. "I'm just worried. Excuse me." He passed them all and went to the library. After a while, they heard a faint crack of closed doors.

"I'm a master at making idiotic mistakes!" Paphian got angry at himself.

"Oh, no," his father soothe him. "If it wasn't for your perceptiveness, I would never have believed Grandpa and Ross really liked each other. In a few sentences you made me realize how their acquaintance grew. Now I remember Ross listening to the stories of the war with us and just… yeah… your grandfather's efforts not to show him he was glad to see him." He laughed softly, looking at his wife and son. "It was beautiful. The old man was eager to show him something, but he hid it so carefully…" He shook his head in disbelief.

"And Ross saw it," said mother softly. "And he did not say a word." They felt a strange emptiness in their hearts and a sudden fear overwhelmed them. Only now they realized for real how much the presence of an extraordinary man and his magical Jewel of Hope had given them. Paphian was sure that the encouragement Ross brought into their hearts was not only due to the magic object worn around the neck.

The life force that helped him face adversity, Ross has always had...

* * *

"Please come in," he said softly, seeing the red-haired Vashaba and her companion.

He silently returned to his desk. Vashaba looked curiously around the imposing library of the palace. There were several books on the desk. She had never seen such magnificent volumes in the entire kingdom before. She stood in front of the healer and looked at him for a moment. However, he did not respond to her extremely shy smile. He was engrossed in other matters.

"You need our help," she said more than she asked.

"Yes," he looked at her.

He never looked away when he was talking to others.

He was honest.

Nor had his eyes strayed casually over her body, never followed her movements, as did the eyes of many men she knew. Similar thoughts were either alien to him, or there was a different reason behind it. She suspected the latter. Ever since he showed up, and she didn't know him before, women treated him more like a brother or a friend. As if neither saw him as a man. They were really so blind, or did they just prefer to see him as extraordinary but unavailable? Did they not see his beauty, his merits in any other way? It must have never occurred to them that Vivan was a flesh-and-blood man like the others. The respect for the healer, instilled by the elders, pulled him away from people to such an extent that he also lost interest in it.

She didn't believe it for a moment. There was definitely a way to get to him.

She walked around the desk and perched on its edge, just one step away from Vivan that his eyes would have to rest on her voluptuous figure and slender legs, even for a moment. She had no evil intentions, she did not want to seduce him. She just wanted his attention.

At the beginning of.

Silent, he followed her actions with a straight face.

"Why the elves?" She moved, but the healer kept looking into her eyes as if he hadn't seen anything else. "Why would they help people living in a small port town?"

"Because it's the first time I'm asking you to do so. I have helped you many times."

"And that's why we have to pay back now?"

He looked at her with a look that saw regret. He got up. It made him even closer to her.

She finally lived to see it: his eyes rested on her full lips for a moment. Just for a moment. Whatever was going through his mind now was quickly gone. However, it was enough to make her feel a little shiver.

"I'm just asking for help. I do not demand gratitude or payment," he replied softly reproachfully.

The conversation was going in the wrong direction.

"Sorry," she smiled gently. "I didn't want it to sound like that."

Her heart skipped a beat as she felt his closeness. She felt the legendary warmth he radiated. She could see his eyes up close. She hadn't been this close in a month. At your fingertips.

She swallowed hard. She got up. She was his height.

"There are only two of us, but we'll be happy to come to your aid," she said softly, giving her voice a slightly voluptuous tone that worked on men.

Apparently not at Vivan, at least, not as she had expected. Though he undoubtedly noticed her advances, he remained calm. She wanted it to be otherwise. Men generally undressed her with their eyes. The healer treated her quite simply, in a friendly way, like an equal partner or one of his friends. When she discovered that he did not adore her as she expected, she was surprised. Until now, she had loved to provoke, especially those who caught her eye. And suddenly there was a man, young and attractive after all, who treated her as an equal, with respect and sympathy. And then she became angry at the thought that he was treating all the procedures with peace. The man whom she wanted to like her did not exceed certain limits, he was understanding, composed, and he deliberately ignored her advances, as if passion were alien to him. She could puzzle over the reasons behind Vivan's behavior, furious with herself. He did not want, he did not desire, he did not flirt. And that was what made her notice him. Now it alternately drove her to anger and despair.

Someone knocked on the door and after a while she saw the dark-haired brother of the healer in the company of two other men. An almost involuntary habit made her focus her attention on them. The silent one bowed politely to them, to which they responded in a clear haste.

"Forgive me, Vivan," Paphian pleaded. "But time is running out!"

"We came to say goodbye," Sel said nervously. "The ship was originally supposed to leave tomorrow, but luckily it didn't take much to get it ready today. Volunteers say goodbye to their families."

Dressed for the trip, Sel and Alesei were a sight to behold. Vivan hurried over to shake their hands.

"Bring him home!" He asked, hugging Sel tightly in a friendly embrace.

"Even at the cost of my life," Sel replied, agitated. "If it were possible, I'd go right now!"

Vivan met his eyes, hands on his shoulders. Vashaba watched them both in silence, sympathetically looking at the more and more handsome Sel, a brown-haired man with long, thick eyelashes, beautifully framing his eyes with a dark frame. When he arrived here, he looked thin and weak, as if he had suffered a serious illness. As time passed, the hospitality of one of the friends' aunt and the training of the queen's soldiers made his body look pleasant to the eyes. Unfortunately, his heart was surrounded by an impenetrable wall. However, the rumor that although he was faithful to his partner, he was not completely indifferent to the sight of women. Many people in the town would gladly turn him back to the "right" path. The possibility itself was exciting.

"Do you have my blood?" The healer asked seriously.

Sel nodded.

"We have. You don't have to worry about that."

Healer blood. It was a rare and very welcome delicacy. She healed every wound, every disease, even if someone was close to death.

The friends looked at each other in silence for a moment. They were consumed with concern for the kidnapped one. They pained the thought of what might be happening to him now.

They were afraid to express their fear aloud.

"Can you do it?" Sel worried at the thought of Vivan's fear of people and nightmares.

Today his friend's eyes also had dark circles under his eyes. He wasn't sleeping well again.

"Yes," Vivan replied, looking away. "It had to happen sometime anyway." Sel looked at him seriously. He knew a lot about his suffering and how Ross' help was very useful. He embraced him in a firm, comforting embrace.

"We'll be back," he said straight into his ear. "And you make sure we have place to go back."

"I will," Vivan replied.

"I'll make sure he keeps his promise," Alesei said, flexing his muscles under his thick jersey.

Vivan smiled at him seriously.

"I'm sure you will," he replied. "Just don't forget about yourself."

"And about my brother!" they heard the voice of Julien, who entered the library with Sai and the Beckert brothers' family.

She smiled knowingly at Vivan. The silent man approached Vashaba, looking at the girl entering with interest.

"But I saw him," said Paphian.

Julien, now in her dress with a short sword and leather armor on like Sai, smiled and revealed her trick to the audience.

"Only you and my uncles know about it," she said.

"And Oliver...?" Vivan's grandmother asked.

"He's on the ship. He signed on there. That was the plan in case something went wrong. They thought someone might kidnap Ross, or even you," she looked at Vivan closely. "What really happened, nobody foresaw. The captain did not say a word. The witch was careful. In the rooms, she drowned out conversations. Outside, she did not speak of her plans."

"A witch?" Count Erlon inquired immediately.

"Yes," Julien replied, shaking the storm of her dark curls in the process. "She's using magic."

"Honey," the old woman said again. "Oliver did noble. And very recklessly. For both of you."

Julien looked at her meaningfully.

"He couldn't have done otherwise," she replied calmly, though she shared those fears in her heart.

Vashaba and the Silent One approached them.

"It makes the case more serious," Vashaba said.

She was close to Vivan again, but the importance of the information she heard was now more important. However, inadvertently, she came a little more, and the body took on a trained defender posture, slightly moving in front of the healer.

"We'll be your guard," she told Vivan.

Her every move was marked with feline grace, so this one emanated sensuality, though unconsciously. It was just her nature. From his gaze, she was relieved that he understood her good intentions.

"An additional sword will always be useful," said Paphian, looking at the interlocutor.

He would be an easy target if she only wanted to. But she cared less and less about it. Especially in the presence of Vivan.

"I'm calm now," said Sel. "I know that I leave my friend in good hands."

Paphian cleared his throat significantly. Sel smiled slightly.

"I mean you too."

He bowed to Paphian and the elves. The silent man responded with a similar bow, a slight, cryptic smile on his face. Vashaba knew that her companion respected Sel for his perseverance and extraordinary talent.

Sel allowed himself a brief contemplation of the beauty of the unusual red-haired girl. She couldn't help but smile. So, the rumors did turn out to be true.

It only took a moment. As if he gave the impression that his thoughts wanted to distract for a moment from the gloomy visions in his head. It was evident that the concern had already left its mark on his face. Nobody doubted that Sel had been badly affected by Ross's kidnapping. More than he showed.

There was silence.

"Come on, Sel." Alesei lightly tugged his friend towards the door. "Time to leave."

Sel nodded his head in agreement. He pulled himself together and said goodbye to everyone again.

Vivan looked after him with concern.

"Alesei!" He called, before the four friends had left on their rescue mission. Four, because the girls decided to accompany them.

The muscular young man turned. His long brown hair was pulled back into a ponytail for comfort. His dog, who followed him everywhere, also stopped, as if connected with his master by some strange bond.

"Take care of yourself," Vivan asked. Alesei nodded solemnly.

"You know me," he replied. "Nobody will die on my watch again. We'll get him out of there. We'll get them all out."

He rested his hand on a sword with a unicorn hilt.

"Ah... Vivan!" He called, before the man left. "Keep an eye out for the trolls beyond the wall."

Vivan looked knowingly at his adoptive father. Erlon touched Lena's hand in a comforting gesture. A light and warm smile gave her a concerned about this information mother, whom he loved more than his own.

Vivan knew the reasons for the anxiety of both women. He heard, like his brother, the history of the town's founding. It was then that his stepfather received these lands from his family.

"I won't forget," he replied seriously.

His stepfather was close to Erlon's age when the trolls attacked them. It wasn't just a handful of feral creatures that began to appear again against the wall.

There wasn't even a wall then...

Alesei indulged in one more smile, bowed to everyone and left the library.

Vivan stood silently, listening until the front gate slammed behind his friends. There was a growing fear in his heart about the future that probably none of those present had noticed yet. A dozen resourceful and talented people were kidnapped. Ross and his unusual gem were taken. And now, in the wake of the kidnapped, others followed, which again depleted the number of people in the town. Other friends of his left with them. A brawny and talented constructor whose ideas were willingly used in Barnica. Was he the only one who saw it as a deliberate act?

"A witch," he said, neither to himself, nor to his brother Paphian. "It's worse than I thought."

He looked into his eyes and saw the same fears that tormented him.

"What's next?" He asked softly.

Their grandfather stood by the window. He silently stared outside at the distant harbor that Sel and his friends were now approaching. True to his relentless nature, he took care not to show concern, but the expression in his eyes and a soft sigh betrayed him.

Vivan knew he wasn't just worried about his favorite. He lived to see the times when he again had to worry about the fate of his loved ones.

He shared his fear.

Chapter III

Cadelia

Oliver looked up at the mountains once more before resuming scrubbing the deck. They had left the fjords, leaving the bay and port town behind a few hours ago. He did not know that access to the open sea would be available to them only now. They sailed for a long time among picturesque mountains and valleys, bidding farewell by the quiet roars of dragons and the sounds of wild animals. The morning was full of extraordinary impressions that he would have enjoyed under other circumstances. The sunny day contradicted the gloomy events aboard the Cadelia. He watched in horror how badly the imprisoned people were treated: they were placed in the hold, chained and gagged. He had already inquired about how long it would take to travel to the Slave Bay.

Two days.

Two days in such conditions, only bread and water, if the kidnappers show favor, or hunger, if they do not. Tied up, chained like animals under the watchful eye of pirates.

Two days for Ross, who was now lying below deck, unable to point consciously at the mercy of his cruel mother and her lover, the ship's captain. It's been several hours now, and neither of them took any interest in him. They just checked to see if he was still alive. Ross's mother said maliciously to Ramsey that he would probably lie down like a log until evening at his own request, since he had drunk not three, but at least five or six drops of the witch's potion. At his own request because he struggled when it was first given to him.

Ramsey replied that at least now Ross had closed his mouth. He advised her to do the same, because he doesn't give a shit what her baby boy is doing.

Oliver noticed that Cadelia Hope had actually preferred to remain silent rather than expose herself to the wrath of her lover. She clearly did not want to lose his favor, ready to agree to much, through diplomatic efforts rather than fear. She was a tough woman who would not be easy to intimidate.

Ramsey did not seem to be forgiving or indulgent, but he was devoted to her. Ross's mother's action was dictated not by fear, but by prudence and a blind feeling that Oliver, for his friend's sake, genuinely despised. Ramsey was strict with his workings, but he loved her. Together they were capable of everything.

Oliver sincerely hoped that he would be able to reach the imprisoned people and an unconscious friend as soon as possible. After hire the volunteers as a crew member and confusing the imprisoned, the cruel couple went to the captain's cabin and did not leave it for long hours, in the meantime deigning everyone on the ship with the sounds of their disgusting amorous frolics. Fortunately, for an hour or so, Oliver's ears did not hear the groans of pleasure. The Bo'sun ordered him to scrub the deck along with some new ones. It was better to agree than to go around aimlessly.

Finally, Ross's mother left the cabin fully clothed. He guessed that the animal with which she had spent the last few intoxicating hours was sleeping in its lair now, tired of the effort. Faking his scrubbing spot, he moved closer to the stairs that led to the deck. Cadelia, slightly drunk, straightened proudly, straightening her hair in a bun. She was upright, though her head must have been buzzing with the drink she had drunk. She looked around as she watched the sailors at work. Oliver pretended to have to stretch himself before continuing to work, to which the boatswain, urged by the sight of the captain's lover, yelled at him to go to work. The scream drew him the unwanted attention of the woman. She raised her eyebrows in surprise at the sight of him, then smiled slyly.

Oliver lowered his gaze, then immediately returned to his activity, diligently applying himself to him and pretending that he had not noticed anything but felt her gaze on him.

This time not a female disguise, but his real form attracted attention.

He was sure she would come over to him soon.

He was right.

"Mr. Lean!" She screamed at the gray-haired boatswain, stopping by

Oliver.

The toes of her shoes were about two centimeters from Oliver's hand on which he was leaning.

"Yes, your first mate?" The summoned responded, and several of the sailors looked at them curiously.

"Since when do we employ porcelain dolls with us?" She asked, looking at Oliver with disgust.

"He has arms and legs, that's fine," replied the boatswain. "He won't have a pretty face as long as he stays with us!"

The rest of the sailors chuckled at the comic remark.

"Get up!" Cadelia demanded softly.

Oliver stood up slowly, brush in hand, not meeting the interlocutor's eyes, so as not to reveal his true thoughts. She looked at him for a moment in silence.

"You got a name, doll?" She asked harshly, which caused a little laugh here and there.

He lifted his head, revealing his face beneath the battered hat. For a month, he only grew a little stubble. The feminine qualities that made his beauty so ambiguous did not allow for a real beard.

"I'm Delen," he replied.

As he spoke the name, he bit his lip a little, trying to hide the tension and emotion that was tearing him through.

"You're young," she said with a smile. "You barely got any stubble. How old are you?"

"Almost eighteen," he lied.

"First time on the ship, right?" She reached out and grasped his brush hand with her long, black-painted fingers. "Skin delicate like a girl's," one of her hands ran over his reddened skin on the cheek. "You've never worked hard. The son of a rich man looking for adventure?"

"Yes, Officer," he replied, struggling to keep from tearing his hand out of her grip in disgust.

She nodded with a lopsided smile.

"Can you look after others?"

"During the plague, I helped in the city to look after the sick ones," he replied, seemingly calm. "I washed them, cleaned up after them, fed them, watered..."

"Yeah..." she looked at him thoughtfully. "You would be perfect. You're done here."

She took the brush from his hand and tossed it in the corner.

And then, for which he warmly thanked Mother Earth, she uttered the words he expected:

"There are men destined for the slave market below. You will make sure they arrive there in good condition. There is also a sorcerer. Take care of him, but make sure he does not fully regain consciousness. You are responsible for this with your head. If he wakes up, notify me immediately, understand?"

"Never," he thought angrily. He replied, trying to make it sound as honest as possible:

"Yes, officer."

"Come on," she moved a little unsteadily, close enough until he could feel the booze on her breath, then he backed away a little reflexively. "I'll show you what to do."

He followed her in glum silence.

"Everything has to be as it should be!" She finished as she explained to him how she imagined him caring for the prisoners. "Mr. Lean!"

"Aye aye, officer!" The summoned called, now standing by the two seamen assigned to guard.

"Give him what he asks for as for the sorcerer!" She ordered, having merely graced the gaze of her unconscious son, who lay on a pile of straw facing the bound highlanders. "Within reason, of course!"

"Aye aye!"

When the boatswain went upstairs, she finally approached the unconscious. Oliver looked at her with a mixture of disbelief and disgust. The woman had an expression of such unconcealed contempt and malice on her face that he would never have expected of a mother looking at her child. He wished she would go, as if her reluctance alone could make his friend's condition worse.

Ross has almost become a vegetable. He was alive as his heavy, jerky breathing testified, as if it took an enormous effort to inhale and exhale oxygen, or he was suddenly silent, almost inaudible, his chest barely rising and falling. The ruby glowed with a muted red light. Oliver was almost certain that it was only thanks to the jewel that Ross was still alive, despite too much of the potion.

His mouth was dripping with saliva, and his half-closed eyes showed no sign of any consciousness. He alternately mumbled or remained silent, shaken by nervous tics. Everything that constituted the essence of his character, the strength of his spirit, all the vitality and energy that he emanated, disappeared. Ross no longer looked like himself, didn't even look like the village idiot Oliver had read about in his stories. He was a denial of everything he was previously thought to be. He aroused pity and horror at his condition.

"Hope he just pissed," his mother muttered contemptuously, touching Ross's pants with the toe of her shoe where the stain was visible. "How bad it would be if he knew what he did! He, such a stickler for cleanliness! So neat!"

Oliver felt that he was very close to the breaking point. He wanted to get her here and now, to take revenge for treating his friend like that. Fortunately, neither she, absorbed in getting satisfaction from Ross's plight, nor the guards guarding the prisoners noticed the expression on his face, because then his deception would be useless. He would be executed quickly. He knew about it. And yet the hatred for this woman so burst his heart that he could hardly refrain from hitting her.

"And what?" She asked the unconscious. "Now you're not so smart! We can do anything with you, and you can't do nothing!" She crouched beside him. "I would find those who would please you, if you like it so much, that you could not walk. They could shit on your face, little pervert!" She hissed with hatred. Oliver clenched his fists, barely controlling himself. "What do you say now, huh?!" She cried, and the shocked prisoners stared at her in horror. "You will not do anything! Nothing! You will not come forward! You will not run away! You're not gonna do anything, you wicked guy! Duke, who felt he is better than others? So clean, so tidy. So noble!" She got up to kick him angrily, and Oliver twitched nervously. "Simple, cheap, perverted whore! Here's how you finished! I," she pointed at herself with a trembling finger in drunken anger, "I'm somebody! You hear that?! I'm the first officer on this ship! It bears my name! It has my face! And you? You are NOTHING!" She hissed angrily.

Angrily she turned to the shaken Oliver, who in his mind's eyes was already hitting her face. She gasped, swallowed hard and snarled at the boy who was barely in control:

"Clean him up! I will sell him to one who will give just a denier! I will even give him for free, so that he just gets out of my sight, do you hear?!"

"Yes, Officer," Oliver replied with difficulty, swallowing loudly, but luckily Ross's mother did not notice or simply ignored his agitation.

"Come on!" She waved her finger in front of his nose. "You are to call me anyway! You got it?!"

"With hate?" He contemptuously asked her in his mind.

"Yes!" He replied, trying to pronounce the words as calmly as possible, without showing any emotion.

Cadelia was satisfied with this answer, because she interpreted it her own way with drunkenness.

She smiled with satisfaction.

"Let's do it!" She screamed, and on the way out she unexpectedly slapped him on the ass, probably harder than she intended.

Anger and a sense of humiliation flared up in Oliver's mind. He could barely keep his hands to himself. He had not felt so fiercely angry towards anyone for a long time; since he had fought for his life in the viceroy's chamber. Even then, it seemed to him that his sensations were weaker than those present, which now burned him with fire.

Then he looked at his unconscious friend.

His anger, like a burning fever, faded in him, replaced by pressing tears. With his back to the guards, he slowly imposed composure on himself for Ross and the other captives.

For all the gods he knows, he must help them! He must save a friend from this horrible state! He must! Otherwise they will be lost! Everybody!

He knelt by his friend to examine him closely, terrified by the effects of the potion and envy. What he saw simply did not fit in his head. In his home, no one would ever treat another person this way, especially a loved one. At the moment he understood very well and, in a way, accepted the behavior of his friend in the past, his choices. The House of Pleasure was an extremely welcoming place to Ross compared to his own.

Where was the source of this hatred? Because it couldn't be just a friend's orientation. There was something else in it, he was sure of it.

"You there!" He called to one of the guarding men. "Take a buddy and get some water, some clean clothes and rags!"

"I'm your maid or what?!" The sailor's voice rose angrily. "Bring it yourself, that's what you are for!"

He had expected such an answer, and he had a way of doing it, although he felt weak at the thought of how much he was risking, and not only with his life.

"Listen!" He quickly found himself next to the bearded individual. "Didn't you get to know what she was saying? You are to give me whatever I ask for! If he wakes up," he pointed to Ross, "with one thought he'll make you do what he wants! He makes you dance, you will dance. Kill a friend," here the man looked nervously at his companion, "why not?!" Continued Oliver without mercy. "Jump into the water? Even now! Therefore, do what I say! The sorcerer has to feel like down to sleep like a baby and not wake up to the port! And the prisoners are fit for sale, otherwise no one will buy them, okay? Do what I say, otherwise I will report how you follow orders. And you don't want this, do you?"

The sailors glared at him and cursed under his breath. Oliver was aware that he had just gained additional enemies, but he could see how devoted they were to the captain and his mistress, without any qualms. Neither of them bothered to relieve the prisoners, and it was not dictated by fear.

"And who will watch them?" Asked another sailor with a scar above his eye.

"I'm responsible for them," growled Oliver shortly.

They smirked at the thought that he, too, had reason to fear a malicious first officer.

"You better get on with it!" The bearded man said to have the last word, before they both finally left.

Oliver did not care about their irritability at all. He felt that his struggle for a better life for prisoners was just beginning. He stopped thinking about the consequences. He silenced the fear.

"I'll take care of you," he said to the people staring at him, squeezed on the opposite side. "I promise."

The innkeeper, the oldest in the group, nodded his head approvingly. They couldn't speak, but their eyes could express a lot.

He knelt by Ross again and reached for the little vial about his neck containing the healer's blood. Of course, the gloomy thugs from the ship robbed his friend of a similar vial, still completely ignorant of the magic of the gem. He lifted Ross's head and carefully poured half of the contents into his mouth. Then he wiped it quickly with the hem of his sleeve to keep as few marks as possible.

"Swallow," he whispered.

He didn't know if Ross heard him, but after a while he saw, perhaps reflexively, that his request had been granted.

"It'll be okay," he whispered, leaning close to his ear. "You'll get out of this." Upstairs, the sailors rolled a barrel of water to the entrance. He heard their voices.

"Ross," he whispered. "Be careful. You are our only hope." He looked up as the conversation grew louder. "I heard her. She said you can be stronger than the foundations of the earth. Don't show that you feel better..."

Footsteps on the wooden steps made him silent. Time is up. He sprang to his feet as he saw the sailors returning and the boatswain.

"Finally," he said grudgingly. "Show me what you got!"

On the wooden floor, his friend woke up from deep unconsciousness, while Oliver gave orders to the prisoners, ordering them to take off their gags, tie them differently (for a few hours they had their hands tied behind their backs), and divide the water. He wished he could order their release, but he could not overdo it, as he would have made him suspicious. And so he risked being accused of undue concern and tying him up with others or throwing him overboard.

Most importantly, he gave Ross the gift of a healer. He clung to that one thought. The eyes of the prisoners communicated with him in fear whenever they heard the faint groan of the man lying down. They feared what might happen now. They were afraid that the kidnappers would find the "sorcerer" conscious and all would be lost, especially since they had seen visible changes. However, for now the sailors were busy following orders, while Oliver took care of his friend. Covering him with himself, he changed his clothes. It wasn't just the pants that needed replacing. He told one of the sailors to bring a blanket and straw because Ross was lying on the cold floor. His winter katana was wet with sweat inside, as were his shirt and jacket.

For the first time he saw his scars up close...

It seemed to him that when he saw Vivan he had become accustomed to the sight of cruelty towards another human being.

But it was not in his nature to be insensitive to harm. Some of Ross's scars were old, probably from childhood...

He had struggled to shut his mind to the visions of what had happened, otherwise his anger would have clouded his mind. Calmly, as when he was helping a sick girl from the castle and later nursing the sick he and Vivan visited, he took care of his friend, closing other feelings within himself. Finally, when he was done, Ross opened his eyes and looked at him half-conscious. Well, it still takes some time to remove the effects of the poison in his body.

For a moment Ross looked at him as if he couldn't believe his eyes. And when understanding came, the lids opened wider. Oliver discreetly shook his head, feeling his heart beat faster. Ross closed his eyes as the sailors leaned over him curiously.

"And what?" The bearded man asked "He woke up?"

Oliver reached for the prepared cup of water with a slightly trembling hand and held it to Ross's mouth. In keeping with his quiet hope, Ross took only a small sip, the rest dripping down onto his shirt. The reassured sailors took it for a normal reflex.

"I suppose you can see that don't," replied Oliver, setting the cup aside.

"She would cut our heads," the bearded man said grimly.

Oliver looked at both men. Despite their earlier quarrel, they sought agreement with him, rightly knowing that they would share the same fate in the event of defeat. His gaze, a bit confused and full of fear, must have pleased the sailors, because the bearded man patted his friend on the back.

"Well done," he praised.

Chapter IV

Hydra

Julien and Sai watched the last hurried preparations. There were affectionate goodbyes and final talks were held before the expedition. Most of them were already on board, saying goodbye once again to their loved ones and gathered people on the pier and the beach. Sel and Alesei brought their little equipment and helped move the rest of the food. Julien smiled fondly, proudly. Sel was overjoyed at his regained health and overwhelming energy. He willingly took on any work that he could not do before. He liked to work physically and enjoy the effects of his work. It pleased him, mostly because he no longer felt useless. He was eager to learn new skills and it was obvious that his diligence had already gained some respect from the locals. If he did not know something, he was treated with understanding. The news that he was one of the healers torn from the paws of death by Vivan undoubtedly helped him gain sympathy as well.

For the last time before his journey, he approached to say goodbye to the women on the pier.

"Take care of yourself," Julien said, looking him in the eye.

Regardless of what they were doing in their lives now, their childhood bond would remain with them forever. Any feelings that might have hurt were overshadowed, though the decision was largely due to the fact that they both loved Ross, although each otherwise. The warm that developed between them was impossible to suppress. Time strengthened friendship and extinguished inconspicuous love, unnecessary and destructive. They cared more about friendship, although there were times when feelings tried to lead them astray. Just like now.

"Come back as I see you right now..."

"I can't promise you that," Sel replied seriously. "But I'll try to come back in one piece." He smiled slightly.

Sai tiptoed slightly to kiss Alesei on the cheek. It was like a brush of wind and a drop of rain, but it gave him much more pleasure than the many caresses other women gave him. None of those were his friends, they didn't know the world, which they left together.

"I'll bring him," he promised her in an extremely serious tone, without the confident, strongman mask he used to wear.

He wanted to say so much to comfort her, but words were never his forte. So he embraced her gently, as if she were a fragile eastern flower, for fear of crushing her in his firm embrace. Now her concern made her look fragile and delicate indeed, but he knew her steadfastness and the strength that had helped her endure. She hugged him without saying a word. Her black hair smelled like jasmine. He carefully sniffed the smell, wanting to remember it for the duration of the journey.

Julien didn't have to tiptoe to kiss Sel's cheek.

"Tell Ross that his sister misses him."

"Sister..." he whispered. "Yes, I will tell him for sure. He will be glad," dangerous eyes started to sting him.

"And tell Oliver..." she added, "tell him that I love him. Always. Forever."

"Fine," he replied.

"And one more thing," she smiled fondly. "Give them this for me."

She brought her face close to his and lightly kissed both cheeks. At

the second kiss, Sel jerked, causing their lips to touch each other before she brushed his face.

As if time had stopped suddenly, holding her breath between touching her lips and kissing on the cheek.

They agreed to let this moment pass.

When she pulled away from him, she felt some change in their lives. The heart changed its rhythm. Peace overwhelmed her.

In his eyes she read similar feelings and suddenly, full of relief and calm, she hugged him tightly, to which he replied, laughing softly. He sensed it too. Two tears ran down his face.

The love that shouldn't exist has just gone away.

Alesei didn't play with subtlety.

"It will be damned hard to convey this to Oliver," he observed with a smile.

There were other feelings in his eyes that he didn't reveal now. Sai looked at them both, but after a while she smiled kindly. Julien looked at her gratefully. The tension was gone.

They stood on the pier as long as the ship was visible on the horizon.

As it passed the fjord and out of sight, they held hands in a sisterly embrace.

"When we start?" Sai asked calmly.

The wind ruffled their hair, moved the delicate material of the dresses.

Julien raised her head a little, closed her eyes to rest from the lash of her hair.

"Now," she said softly.

* * *

Captain Noren Englehon, the man with the wind-blistered face and the gaze of the royal escort officer, was a man who had survived many times in the stormy waters of the seas and oceans, although he was not yet forty. It was not easy to surprise him, and he valued discipline and obedience among his crew above all else. In return, his men could be sure he would do whatever he could - even more, it was said - to save the ship and crew. The little three-masted Hydra was undoubtedly his beloved child, and nothing would have jeopardized the captain's anger more than breaching his ship in danger.

He appraised a handful of local representatives, that is, the townspeople, making sure that not a single muscle twitched on his face; so as not to bring up a slightly contemptuous smile. These people wanted to get their own by fighting Ramsey and his gang? Well, some people had a chance. The others were driven onto the ship by strong motivation, and apparently only that, because they didn't seem to have ever held a sword in their hand. However, he knew that the world was constantly changing, and weak people, who would not be accused of courage, often saved the lives of others. And those considered strong fell sometimes quite bloody and painfully, taking many lives with them. So, he never foredoomed the matter by the first impression.

"Whoever wants to quit, we will send him ashore. While there is still time," he said to the highlanders lined up and members of his own crew, nodding at the surrounding fjords between which they were sailing.

They would be out at sea in an hour.

The eloquent silence after these words meant a lot to him. The captain looked at them in turn, looking for fear in their eyes, but their gazes were steadfast. At the beginning of the front row were two friends of the healer, according to information from boatswain Nat. He had heard rumors of why they were aboard the ship. The most important thing is that they should follow his orders without unnecessary discussion. The rest, so far, has been less important.

"From now on," he said to the newcomers, "you are my crew. You are to obey my orders. I'm in charge here. I understand your motives

I respect them, but if you jeopardize the lives of my crew…" He lingered at the healer's friends for a long time, looking them in the eye, "…I won't hesitate to give the order to throw you overboard. Hydra is not your toy. This is my ship. Who will not listen to me… will regret it!"

He walked down the line again, as if checking that everyone understood his words. When he turned back, he met the gaze of one of them.

"Fall out!" He ordered.

As the group fell up, the captain nodded to his boatswain and nodded at the man who looked at him with such determination as he spoke.

"Who is this?" He asked.

"Sel Andilo. It was his lover they kidnapped, the one with a glorious…"

"I didn't ask for it, Nat!" The captain interrupted briefly.

The Bo'sun stopped immediately, only to say in a calmer tone a moment later:

"Sorry, Captain."

"These people don't know about sailing. I want you to teach them certain attitudes. They won't be wandering around the ship aimlessly until we're in a fight."

"Yes, Captain. The fight is sure?"

"It seems that. Weapons and cannons ready?"

"The arbalest mechanism is broken. It does not release the rope, it is difficult to turn."

"Why wasn't it fixed?"

"We have no idea what's wrong there. Everything looks fine at first glance."

The captain lifted his hat a little nervously, immediately setting it back on his head, adjusting the brim with the last movement of his hand.

"Not good," he said dissatisfied.

"Aye aye," the dark-skinned petty officer agreed. "Not good."

"Mr. Andilo!" The captain exclaimed, touching his hat reflexively.

Sel broke off his conversation with Alesei, rubbing his hands with cold, and approached the sailors.

"Excuse me, Captain?"

"Are you supposed to be a constructor?"

"You could say that, although I have not done much so far. Mainly I brought water to the palace, improved the kitchen. People use my ideas."

"You know the mechanisms?"

"Better than the others," Sel replied with a modest smile, not going into the details.

Mechanisms and their operation were Sel's second hidden passion, who, if he did not sketch from nature, silently designed his own ideas and constructed models in one of the utility rooms of the Beckert Palace. Helping the victims of the plague and the resulting lack of time was holding him back for the time being. But as the world was returning to normal, Sel had more and more times when he could develop his passions between duties. Ross, sensitive to aesthetics, took care of the visual form so that the whole thing was not disfigured. It foreshadowed a rather dynamic future, especially with the support of the healer.

"Will you take care of our arbalest?"

Sel looked at the indicated item and smiled slightly at the display. Concern constantly occupied his thoughts, despite the appearance of peace.

"I will deal with. I don't like waiting idly, Captain."

"Excellent," the commander held out his hand, which the other shook, he motioned to the bo'sun to bring Sel to the details.

The captain studied them for a moment. Sel seemed to know his stuff because after a long investigation he found out where the problem was.

"You have to disassemble," he said shortly.

"What happened?" The captain inquired.

Sel motioned for the three men standing next to him to get a better look at the modes winding the arbalest bolts. Even the dog showed some interest in their actions. The Bo'sun caressed him as the animal passed him.

"The inner gear is broken," he said matter-of-factly. "They have to be replaced. Fortunately, I can simplify the mechanism, fewer wheels will be needed," he explained so that they understood. "I need some tools and one hour of time."

"Will you do it in an hour?" Alesei was surprised, because, like the others, for him the rules of the arbalest with the use of gears and cranks were almost like magic.

"Maybe less than that," Sel winked at him. "If you can help me."

"Do what's necessary!" The captain ordered, genuinely surprised at Sel's skill.

Sel saw his hidden admiration but pretended not to see anything. He was already beginning to like this captain, who was seemingly demanding, but inside he had the spirit of a true adventurer. This was evidenced by his immediate consent to participate in the dangerous expedition and the ridiculously low payment he accepted for it. The Bo'sun excused himself to help and sympathize with the healer, but Sel knew otherwise. He felt they would make a good duo.

Chapter V

Under the Unicorn Inn

It was noon on that fateful day. Apparently, life went on as before, but in every house or yard, every newcomer's tent that remained in the settlement, weapons were kept at the ready. The sight of the sword did not surprise anyone anymore. Mothers scolded the children to stay alert and stay away from strangers. The highlanders carefully eyed the people who had arrived for the healer, whose camp was still located in the center of the town, although their number had drastically decreased.

Frost still held firm, although the first signs of spring appeared timidly in Wermoda. It was always felt late in the mountains. The bright, exceptionally sunny day belittled the gloomy mood in the town.

He was standing silently outside one of these tents along with Vashaba. Vivan, despite the feeling of danger, decided not to ignore the pleas for help from people in need.

Paphian accompanied him inside.

"Sister, but honestly..." he turned to her. "Do you feel something for him?" Vashaba looked at him. This way of addressing her for years

it was affectionate, not linguistic error. Under the supposedly arrogant silence and pride, her brother hid his kind heart.

"I don't know," she replied, "but I know that my brother liked these people."

"You know that I..."

"I know, Solai, my brother," she smiled warmly. "You do not want to get involved."

"They are dying," the blonde-haired elf observed gloomily.

Vashaba knew the cause of this mood. And the painful longing that comes with it.

"Time cannot be stopped," she whispered.

"Unnecessary talk!" He snorted angrily. "Empty words!"

"That's the only way we'll survive. If you are only a spectator, life will take on a bitter taste. You will suffer more. Nothing can soothe this pain until you decide to die."

He was silent.

"Only other people will soothe the longing for those who passed away," she added. Again, only silence answered her.

"Allow yourself to do this. Enjoy the times you spend with them."

"And let them die..."

"If such is the life of mortals..."

"They don't like me," he said softly. "No one but your healer likes me."

She ignored the hitch.

"You don't allow it," she replied. "You don't allow anyone to you. Tell them your real name, hold out your hand. Help them. Mayene is hiding somewhere nearby. You can help find her. You can do it."

She could see him deliberating on her proposal. She knew she had to be patient. She must wait until he stops struggling with himself.

Finally, he looked back at her.

"Agreed. I'll take a chance again."

"So, what are you waiting for?" She asked. "Go. Find Mayene." He sighed heavily in mock resignation.

After a while, he was gone.

* * *

Vivan smiled reassuringly at the recumbent woman, his hand on her swollen belly. She was very young, and so was her husband. Concerned parents both stood next to Paphian, worried.

From the beginning, since he had entered the tent, he had established a thread of understanding with the young man's mother, a woman whose eyes revealed some life experience. Now he has made eye contact with her, seeking communication in a difficult situation. She understood his gaze. With concern and compassion, she approached her son, waiting silently for the healer to reveal the truth. The young mother also sensed something. The healer made the pain go away and she could finally think clearly, so she was fully aware that something bad had happened to the baby. She was afraid of this truth. Her eyes looked for comfort in those of her mother, who was holding her hands to her face, ready to burst into loud cry.

Vivan felt it was the last thing a girl and her gathered relatives needed now. This hysterical sobbing would not help, it would only provoke irritation and would scratch the wounds on his soul even more, so he delayed his reply. He took the young mother's hand as if to give her strength. She hugged her tightly. Her eyes were already full of tears. She already felt...

He closed his eyes and let the soothing images of his memories come alive in his mind. Common conversations at the table. Evening family meetings on the terrace. Grandfather's stories and the listeners who were excited about them. The night when together with Paphian they were walking on the roofs because of a crazy idea. Sai and Oliver. Ross laughs. The last evening, as they returned home with the royal escort. Alesei and his dog, so far called simply dog...

The good mood evoked by these memories slowly influenced the people accompanying him in the tent, like vapors of perfume extremely pleasant to the nostrils. The mother of the young pregnant woman calmed down. Her father, like her father-in-law, straightened up, ready to accept whatever fate would bring. The young man sat on the other side of the bed and hugged his wife, holding her other hand.

"What's your name?" Vivan asked softly, and the man's mother sat down next to them.

"Nelsa," the girl replied softly, bravely trying to hold back her tears and squeezing her husband's hand.

Vivan waited a moment longer for sorrow to replace despair. Paphian always admired the strength in him that allowed him to convey bad news with calmness and care at times such as these, without being overly compassionate.

"Nelsa," Vivan began, his melodious voice soothing the thoughts of the assembled family. "Unfortunately... your child is dead. The umbilical cord twisted. I must take them out or you will die. Let us bury them."

Nelsa looked at him in horror, then at her husband and the others. The woman with her stroked her face reassuringly. Mother, much calmer thanks to Vivan, silently hugged her. He felt someone's soft touch. The woman with the wise eyes touched his hand. Paphian sighed softly.

"Gentlemen," Vivan said softly to the men while the women cried. "My brother will take you outside. Wait there. I will meet you again," he looked warmly at the young man.

The man nodded understandingly and kissed his grieving wife. They whispered words to each other, full of tenderness and devotion, before he followed Paphian as the last.

"Do you need anything, Count?" The girl's mother asked softly.

"I don't use any tools," he said, first of all, to the terrified girl. "I need the same thing we use in childbirth. Hot water. Towels…" He didn't mention that it wouldn't be of much use to him. It was more about keeping them occupied. "It won't hurt," he assured all of them as they looked at him with a mixture of regret, horror, and amazement. "And it won't be long."

"It means?" The young woman asked.

Vivan nodded to the elders who had begun their preparations. Nelsa's husband's mother left the tent to bring hot water.

He touched her forehead with a tender gesture.

"Fall asleep," he whispered to her, and when her eyes began to close under the influence of his touch, he added warmly, "I'll make sure you can have babies again someday. As much as you want. Now everything will be alright..."

Before she could say a word, she fell asleep.

When everything was ready, he asked again:

"Who's gonna take the boy?"

The concerned women looked at each other, surprised at the sad news.

"Me," the woman with the wise eyes replied. "I'll take care of him. You take care of your daughter." She looked at the other.

Nelsa's mother nodded silently. If Vivan hadn't helped them, she would have certainly acted differently. She wouldn't have that strength.

Vivan kept his hand on the pregnant belly the whole time to protect her from pain. His only regret was that no one could save him from this monstrous sight. He forbade Paphian from entering the tent.

He ran his hand gently over the skin. Then, with his index finger, he traced what a knife or a dagger would probably follow. Energy pulsed under the other fingers of the hand, protecting the body of the would-be mother, taking control of the entire life process. The whites of the healer's eyes glowed bright white under the pulsating power, like a volcano waking up.

The women stared at him, not daring to break the silence with a deeper sigh. The body felt the touch of his hand. He turned it to the side to gently run his little finger along the path he had marked out for himself, and then, in the unusual silence, the hand plunged slowly, as if it were entering the dough, not the throbbing body. The slit opened wider due to hand movements. But there was no sign of blood.

Vivan held his breath. He felt the delicate body of a dead child under his fingers. He took control of himself with effort, for the sake of the women who watched him with tension. He felt sweat beating his skin.

And then again, the gentle touch comforted him. The woman's wise eyes looked at him with understanding, her affection like a soothing balm.

He looked at her gratefully.

"Get ready," he said softly.

* * *

"After three months, because we know each other so much, you come by all of a sudden and offer to help find Mayene as if nothing had happened, and you say more words than I ever heard from you!" Julien blurted out from behind the screen she was disguising herself, "what happened? Have you been drinking?!"

Sai noticed that hearing this stream of words, the elf started to smile slightly.

More than one man liked her friend's temperament.

"I was reticent," he said, deciding to be honest, "and a bit dry as a result..."

"A bit?"

"Yes. This is because I become attached to friends... people. And when their time comes, they die... It hurts," he added after a moment of silence.

Sai became sad. She understood his words well. The longing for Lena still hurt, despite the fact that she was happy with Oliver now, and his presence was a real relief for her.

"When did they leave?"

"My best friend died last spring," he replied. "He lived to a great age."

"He had a good life?" He nodded his head in agreement.

Julien emerged from behind the screen, disguised as her brother, breaking the gloomy mood.

"I will find her by the traces of magic," he said to her, "and let you know immediately."

"I will go with you."

"Remember that two hearts are beating in you," he admonished her gently. "Let me do this. I'll be back with the news. I know some magic tricks. You'll have your chance, I can feel it. But not now. Not yet."

She looked at him, torn by the sudden memory. Ross said the same.

"I have another assignment for you. It's about the man. I don't know what he's doing for her yet, but they're definitely meeting. He lives in the Under the Unicorn inn."

"What does he look like?"

"Tall, dark haired. He has gray eyes. And a magic bracelet on his left wrist. I don't know what the spell engraved on it is about, but it certainly has power over it. His disobedience causes him pain."

Julien looked anxiously at Sai who shared this feeling. They both recognized him from the description.

"What is going on?" Asked the elf, concerned about their behavior. "Do you know him?"

"Yes," Julien whispered. "It's Tenan."

"For sure?" whispered the elf still called the Silent as they discreetly looked at him through the inn's window.

Julien nodded her head in agreement. Tenan hadn't changed much. He was still wearing overly clean clothes, and his eyes were icicles. They seemed even brighter than she remembered them, which kept the rest of the inn's regulars and travelers at bay. The look he gave people did not encourage him to make friends. Since the girls had briefed him on the story of Tenan and his affiliation with a gang of thugs, whose leader had a special fondness for Oliver as a victim, before their arrival, the Silent had a better understanding of the dangers of his contacts with Mayene. He had noticed them recently. He hid a dark secret, the disclosure of which was only a matter of time.

Tenan is a bandit and a cruel killer, so he surely hasn't met the witch for fun.

"Mayene isn't here," Sai and Julien said as they hid in the rear. "But she's nearby. At the marketplace."

Before the outbreak of the plague, the square in the center of the Healer Harbor town was a marketplace to which more and more merchants from all over the kingdom and the sea attracted.

During the plague, the market ceased to exist and the tents of people who came for help were erected in its place. Gradually, the migration of newcomers meant that tents were set up in almost every free spot in the city. For a month, their number has once again shrunk to a dozen at the market square.

"Do you feel it?" Julien asked curiously.

"I said I fell magic."

"Usually at this time of day Vivan treated the needy in the marketplace," Sai reminded anxiously.

Both looked pleadingly at the young elf.

"Yes," he replied to their silent plea. "I'll go now," he glanced at the three-pronged, cloaked weapon with a strangely elongated central spike, which Sai named after her name. Sai knew what he meant by that.

"Wait!" Julien grabbed his arm before he left. "We still have to call you Silent? I admit, after your confessions today, it just seems silly..."

"Julien…" Sai shook her head at the words of her friend. "I don't think it should be…"

The blond-haired elf bowed slightly, soothing her with a gesture.

"I'm Dinnaroth," he smiled politely.

The disappointment on the girls' faces was meaningful. He almost burst out laughing.

"Just call me Dinn," he said softly. "I don't like that name either. Father wanted to stick to tradition."

"Dinn," Sai said, reaching out first for a hug. "That sounds so much better."

He felt the corns on her hands, seemingly so delicate. Sai's weapons were not merely ornaments.

"Should we just stand here and wait?" Julien asked after he left "It may take time!"

"How else do you want to find out what Mayene wants?"

"I'll go crazy if it will last to the evening!" Julien was angry. "Maybe I'll just go in there and…"

"And what?"

"I'm a man, no one will know me!"

"Yeah. Whether I'm Oliver or not, he will recognize me." Sai thought for a moment.

"Tenan doesn't reveal his emotions in bed," she noted thoughtfully, as Julien looked at her. "That's what I heard," she replied calmly, with a smile that carried traces of her former life. "He has a weakness for you."

Julien shrugged.

"Paphian said the same," she replied, glancing at the walls of the inn as if she could see through them and see him sitting alone at the table, as just moments before. Suddenly she found herself thinking that she felt regret. *It's a pity that he is sitting alone now and people are afraid to approach him...*

"Are you out of your mind?!" Sai was surprised seeing her gaze. "He's a murderer. He killed your best friend, Sel's wife! Then two servants whom you have known since childhood, and who knows who else! He wanted to have you like a thing, and believe me, if it hadn't happened for what happened, you'd definitely be his whore! How can you even think of him that way?!"

"What, Sai?" She tried to defend herself. "I didn't think anything..."

Sai fell silent. She looked at her with a gaze that contained life experience.

"He's a murderer," she whispered. Julien avoided her eyes.

"I remember," she said, trying to keep her tone of voice confident.

She had thought about it more than one night. She remembered his actions when he was in Moren's gang. This chill, no warm feelings.

And Milera. Milera, which he hung the noose around her neck and pushed out the window without hesitation.

Milera, who was lying with her head smashed on the pavement in front of her house.

She covered Sel's eyes to ward off the sight of his dead friend who had become his wife only a month before.

How could she anyway...?

Why was she thinking about it?

He gave her the Jewel of Hope, then still belonging to Vivan, and he had ripped it from his neck.

Paphian said the feeling had to be real, otherwise the Jewel would have no value now. Love, though not only Tenan, endowed the gem with power.

Tenan handed it to her out of love.

Dinn confessed that disobeying the bracelet made him hurt.

What if it was feelings that made Tenan disobey the will of the bracelet?

"I wanted this for you." She remembered the words.

She remembered...

Even Sai did not question these feelings. She said Tenan had a weakness for her. His feeling was sincere. That sadness in his eyes...

"Sai," she summoned her to the world of the living. "Tenan is a bracelet prisoner. Think. He gave me the jewel back. He said he wanted to keep it for me."

"He ripped it off Vivan's neck!"

"He," Julien was sure of the confession that was about to come out of her mouth. "Shouldn't want anything for others. He should not. A man who does not have human feelings in himself does not desire but is guided by the satisfaction of his own needs. He's a man like the others. When he came to the House of Pleasure, he satisfied his needs and left, right? He didn't even use the word thank you."

"You don't understand..." Sai began, but Julien interrupted her nervously.

"Wait! He always did Moren's will. He killed on his orders. He also killed Milera on his orders. That was Moren's will. He wanted Sel to be free again. He killed Sel's father on his orders as well. He carries out orders, even the cruelest because he has to! But he took the jewel himself. He did not return to Moren with it. He gave it to me!

Sai, the jewel follows love. Ross says the jewel is aware. Tenan loves me."

"It's not a good feeling," Sai replied. "He's a bad man. He will kill you. He will rape and kill. Here is his love!"

"It's very easy to check," Julien replied with deathly composure. "We'll find out what Mayene wants from him, and what he really feels for me. I'll provoke him."

"Are you crazy?!"

"You'll be nearby," Julien looked at her. "If he wants to hurt me and kill me, as you say, then you will kill him!"

* * *

Under the Unicorn inn offered guest rooms on the first floor. The last one, quite small, with a view of the stables, was occupied by Tenan. Apparently, he didn't care to see beautiful fjords or a bay, or even to see a healer's palace on a hill. But he probably missed the company a bit, which would explain why he had eaten downstairs instead of in his solitary room. Though people stayed away from him, their presence was enough for him. Julien and her distrustful companion, leaning towards her theory, seemed plausible.

"And Dinn was worried that you were in greater danger with Mayene," Sai remarked as they entered Tenan's room thanks to courtesy of the innkeeper. Sai, whom Tenan knew poorly and did not even notice in the crowd, spoke to the benevolent innkeeper, who obviously knew her as a friend of the healer, and then pulled Julien through the open window.

"Just in case..." Julien reached for the healer's blood vial hidden on her chest. "I'll use it when he comes..."

"You're crazy," Sai remarked.

"I think it runs in the family."

They smiled to each other.

Julien touched her friend's arm gently.

"Don't worry," she said warmly. "My brother is like a cat. She can't hurt himself. Maybe you even heard something about him. He was called the Cat of Vermod. He cleverly escaped over roofs and walls right in front of the gang's nose."

"He's the boy who would even climb a glass mountain?! That was what it was said about the Cat. I heard about him. The girls from the house wanted to see him closely. Apparently, he used to sit on the rooftops near the House of Pleasure. So that's him..." Sai shook her head in disbelief. "He didn't mention it."

"Because he went there to watch you and Lena," Julien thought to herself. It was at a time when they had no secrets yet. Julien knew a lot about her twin brother's secret longings. But she also knew why he hadn't gotten close to these women then. Until now, she had lamented his loneliness all these years. Fortunately, Vivan's help stopped this torment. Sometimes she thought how strange their fate had been so far. Her brother surreptitiously watched the two beautiful women in the House of Pleasure while their friend Sel met them in the morning as they finished serving customers. Then he slept between them in the bed. He even drew their portraits. It would take so little for Oliver and Sai to get to know each other sooner. But what would their fate be then? Wasn't it easier for them to live now?

The whistle from the side of the stables made them realize it was time to prepare. The stableman only whistled once. It meant Tenan was walking back into the room alone. Sai quickly looked at her nervous friend.

"Remember what I told you about men," she reminded her of a conversation they had at home once. "Touch is magic. Don't be intrusive. Touch him, but mostly look him in the eye."

They heard footsteps in the corridor.

"I'm here," she whispered reassuringly, and hurriedly hid under the bed, pulling the bedspread a little. Julien took off the slight stubble and hurriedly picked up the bottle of blood. She took a long sip as if it were rum to encourage herself.

"It'll be okay," she whispered to herself.

The door swung open and Tenan, Milera's killer, stepped in...

* * *

Seeing the surprise on his face and the gleam in his eyes when he discovered the identity of the man in his room was an invaluable experience for Julien, for for that one moment in Tenan's eyes she did not see the usual coldness and calculation, but a spontaneous joy. It was short-lived but confirmed her theory about him and the connection to the bracelet on the hand. Before Tenan regained his composure, the corners of his mouth curved up in a welcoming smile, but it was not a perfidious smile. Unfortunately, right after that, his mouth tightened, and his body tensed.

Pain shot through him like an arrow. She could see it clearly.

Why had she not noticed it earlier as he followed Moren?

Because then he disgusted her. Ever since she suspected what was behind his coldness, he had awakened completely different feelings in her.

She reached for her wig and took it off.

The cascade of black, long, waist-length hair did not escape Tenan's attention, though he tried to control himself. Sai was right. If a man likes a woman, he involuntarily follows her every move.

The men's clothes made him raise his eyebrows slightly.

"Come on," he said, seemingly calm, "I'm more interested in what you have under that jacket," he walked past her to lean on the table. "Start undressing."

A spark of anger crossed Julien's face. "What else!" Her eyes told him.

Tenan's face returned to its old indifference for good.

"What are you here for?" He asked.

"Have you been in town for a long time?" She asked bluntly, pulling back the delicate stubble stuck to her face. She only hesitated for a moment whether to approach him. Sai was right. She lacked familiarity with men. Maybe because she had only kissed them so far. Sharing a bed with Ross was by no means not an intimate relationship. He was like a brother to her, despite one kiss that happened in rather unusual circumstances.

"I don't think that's your business," he replied coldly.

She stood beside him.

"Why did you come here?"

"And why only now?" She added in her head. "Where have you been before?"

"The ships go out to sea from here," he replied laconically.

"Vermod is not far from the sea," she replied mentally, tilting her head defiantly. "You could have come out of there."

"Not true," she said aloud before considering her answer.

"Isn't it true that the ships set sail from here to the high seas?" He feigned surprise, clearly mocking her.

"This is not why you are here," she was not provoked.

"You're right, not that."

"What are you doing for Mayene?"

He showed no surprise. If it were possible in human nature, he would rather show nothing of himself. But being away from

Moren, alone, on his own in this room, he showed more freedom of behavior.

He was silent for a moment, looking at her. She bravely held the gaze of his gray eyes, so strangely inhuman.

"He's been coming here since I came," he replied. "She fucks me every night." She could almost hear Sai's voice in her head. These words were supposed to move her somehow, maybe even hurt. Yes, she figured it out.

"Have you been here for a long time?" She calmly repeated the question.

"For three days."

"That's all what she wants?"

"No."

"So, what else?"

"I'm a killer, Julien. I can't believe you have forgotten."

He said her name strangely softly. As if he was admonishing a little girl.

As if to tell her, "Be careful who you talk to. I'm dangerous. Get out of here while you can."

"Who are you going to kill?"

"She hasn't told me yet."

"Will you do it?"

"I always do that. It's my job."

"Even if it's about my friends?"

"They mean nothing to me."

"And I? Will you kill me too?"

"Of course. By entering here, you signed your own sentence. I'll kill you here." The chill of his words made her shudder.

"They know I'm here."

"So what? You'll be dead by now."

"They'll kill you for this."

"Good luck."

"You gave me Vivan's pendant."

"That won't save you from dying."

"Tenan..." She reached out and placed her hand carefully on his palm. "I'm not asking for a grace."

"Or maybe you should? Your sudden death will kill Oliver."

"It's all meant to scare me," she thought. "So why am I not afraid?"

He didn't take her hand off his. He didn't even move.

She looked into the killer's eyes.

They already knew some of what they wanted to know.

How is he to break through his cold gaze and prove to Sai that Tenan is a bracelet slave? Seeing his behavior and remembering what Milera had done, she began to doubt herself..."

He will kill her. He won't have a choice. Unless Sai anticipates him. Then she will kill him. And no one will ever know the truth...

She felt tears. She blinked in surprise as it ran down her cheek. Tenan's face changed from indifferent to surprised and shaken. He reached out and touched the falling tear. She held her breath.

Then suddenly a pain shot through him, greater than before. Pain that caused anger. "Be careful," Sai had told her as they discussed the plan of action. "If Tenan finds out you know about his link to the bracelet and thinks you are doing it to make him suffer," he might even kill you."

Tenan thought about it.

In the blink of an eye, he was no longer reserved.

"You think you have me in the palm of your hand, huh?!" He shouted. "You got something on me?"

He stood up sharply at the words, grabbing her by the shoulders. He jerked her off to the side of the bed, then brutally tossed. The pain had apparently passed in a time of anger, but the memory of it made a violent eddies still within him. He tore off his jacket and tore his immaculately clean shirt.

Julien was terrified. She had not expected that he would have such strength. He lunged at her and with both hands he held her hands, pinning them against the sheets. She felt his weight on her body. In the struggle, she could see his muscular torso and the hair on his chest. She smelled a scent that had a very different effect on her than it should have under the circumstances. He was intoxicated. She realized that it was a serious mistake to drink the healer blood before meeting the man who had acted on her in some way. Vivan's blood showed itself when Oliver took it. She, too, was not free from its actions, as she had already found out. Her own blood began to rush, her body awoke to previously hidden sensations. Tenan's movements, who sought to intimidate his victim and enslave her by force, aroused excitement instead of fear. She stopped being afraid. After all, she will not suffer when

Vivan's healing blood circulates in her blood. Her body was reacting against all reason. Her cheeks flushed.

"Woman," Tenan said through gritted teeth. "You'll wish you had died right away!"

She waited until his lips were close enough. She jumped up and provoked a kiss herself.

Thinking that Julien was playing a game with him to win his favor, he picked her up and parted his lips to kiss. She could almost hear his thoughts. If she wanted to kiss him, why not take advantage of it?

Tenan did not know that there was one man in Julien's life who thought he would never succumb to a woman's kiss...

Vivan's blood made him drunk as wine. He clung to her body with a soft groan, thirsty for her mouth. He succumbed to her kisses like Ross, unable to resist it. Finally, with an effort, he pulled away, releasing her. He rose a little, and then in the light of day from the window overlooking the stables, she saw his eyes up close.

They were amber.

She had not seen eyes like that before. It was sometimes said that the color resembled old gold, but all those who traded and made jewelry from it, like her father did, said that the lucky ones had that color.

Amber.

She stared, she was lost in those eyes...

"Amber..." she whispered in delight.

He was amazed at these words. Out of the corner of her eye, Julien saw a movement just behind his head. She glanced at it.

Sai was standing behind Tenan.

One of her reliable blades was inches from his neck. Supported by her knee on the bed just behind him, the other hand with the blade raised slightly, preparing to deliver two blows.

Time and time again.

Tenan was separated from death only by the words Julien spoke about his eyes. They stopped Sai from the blow.

Tenan looked at her as if he was desperately trying to penetrate her thoughts, to guess her feelings. She felt his body tremble.

"It's revenge, isn't it?" He asked softly, with resignation and sadness. "You want me to pay for Milera's death?"

He waited for her answer. He was sure of it. Maybe he even expected Julien to scream it in his face with a cruel laugh?

She touched his cheek.

Sai lowered the weapon and looked at his hand. Gold gleamed under the sleeve.

Bracelet.

"How to free you?" Julien asked quickly. "Tenan! I know about the bracelet! How to help you?!"

Tenan's forehead glistened with sweat. He struggled to keep from groaning at the pain that was slowly building up. If warm joy made pain penetrate him through, if tenderness caused suffering, what could an affectionate, passionate kiss do with him?

It will probably make him beg for death, twisting in terrible convulsions...

"No..." he replied, struggling to sit down on the bed. Sai's presence was barely noticed, too engrossed in what was happening to him. "I deserved it."

One serious word touched both women. It was Sai who knelt beside him and spoke softly:

"Say..."

Tenan's eyes were still amber, as if there was no point in hiding behind indifference and coolness. He broke the terms of the curse.

His head throbbed with pain.

Julien reached quickly for the handkerchief in her straitjacket pocket when she saw the blood pouring from his nose.

In a moment the pain will be unbearable. Then he will even be ready to kill them to stop it.

"The spell will continue," he recited softly. "Until the sign of love breaks it."

"Sign?" Julien asked. "A kiss?"

"Get out!" He exclaimed in anguish.

"Tell me!" Julien pleaded him.

He looked at her. His eyes glowed again. The color was fading away.

"Get out!" He gripped her arm painfully hard and yanked towards the door. "Get out! I'm lost because of you!"

"I will not leave you!"

"Don't imagine that I have feelings for you!" He pushed her against the door until she groaned painfully.

"Julien!" Sai warned her. "We have to get out! Pain takes his mind!"

She wanted to run away, but he held her down like a cat trapping a mouse and getting ready to eat. She couldn't get away from him. Rage filled Tenan's eyes. They were white.

Inhuman.

The bracelet pulsed with light. Blood began to drip from his ears as well. Sai groaned and looked around quickly.

Julien tried in vain to free herself from his grip. On the other side, someone pounded the door with a fist and called to be opened. Probably a concerned innkeeper.

Sai grabbed a water jug and hit Tenan on the head with it. The copper pot tapped hollowly against the skull. Tenan staggered and fell, knocking out.

They stared at him for a moment, trying to calm down. Then Julien opened the door and reassured the innkeeper and his men with a few words that they were in control of the situation.

"What now?" She asked her friend, anxiously watching the man lying down.

"You still think he can be saved?"

"Yes. Why didn't a kiss release him?"

With an eloquent gesture, Sai reached for the flask of Vivan's blood visible on her friend's neck with half of its contents.

"It was supposed to be a kiss of love," she noted. "Come on, we have to drag him to the bed and tie him up. There I see a rope in his bag."

"Should we tie him up?"

"Want to finish an interesting conversation from a moment ago?" Sai asked ironically, taking the unconscious Tenan by the armpits. Julien grabbed his legs and, somewhat awkwardly, knocking him against the floor and the bed, managed to pull him in. "We'll get out of his sight and he'll calm down."

"Where do you get that confidence? What if the bracelet gets the job done?"

"Tie his wrists to the bed frame," she ordered. "It is your presence that causes his torment, your kiss. In this respect, he is right. It'll be easier for him without you."

"This way I won't free him."

"You'll try again when he'll be calm again. Otherwise you will eventually kill him before you break the curse. Can you see the blood? Julien looked at Tenan's face.

"Let's wash her off," Sai said. "When Mayene comes back here at night, she'd better think he was just having fun."

"Mayene," Julien whispered, finishing tying him up, "Will we leave him there for her?"

Sai was still calm and foursquare.

"Honey, your Tenan hasn't been a virgin for a long time."

"But they will..."

"Distracting from you will only help him."

"How can you be so...?"

"He'll be grateful for not killing you, you'll see. He would certainly regret that. He's crazy about you. I can spot it."

Julien looked at her, eyebrows raised.

"You think..."

"I can't believe I'm saying that," Sai smiled warmly. "But this madman really loves you. Let him find out who Mayene is ordering him to kill. We need to know that."

"What if he tells her about us?"

"He won't," Sai assured her confidently, looking at Tenan. "I'm sure."

Chapter VI

Mayene

Vivan left the depressed by the loss people who said goodbye to him despite their overwhelming sadness. Burdened by the still gloomy images from the tent, he looked around the makeshift camp. Paphian was just crouched next to one of his white tigers. As if on command, he and the animal looked at Vivan. Concerned by his expression, his brother approached quickly, and the tiger followed at his side. Vashaba continued to watch the area. She could feel the healer's mood. She wished he had time to soothe his nerves. Unfortunately, his brother's concern did not allow this.

"Are we going back to the palace?" Paphian asked with concern in his voice.

Vivan would be grateful if Paphian had tried less sometimes. Ever since his memorable events at the marketplace, he had worked diligently to protect him. His zeal and mother's grief sometimes tormented the healer, who also had to struggle with nightmares. Knowing that he worried his loved ones with bad mood did not help him to improve his mood. Vivan wanted life to go on as normal and the nightmares fade away. Unfortunately, his mother and brother did not allow him to forget about the past for a moment with their care and sorrow, although he tried to make them understand what he expected of them. The rest of the family was trying to understand him. Just like friends. It was his consolation.

"There are two more in need," Vashaba interjected to distract both of them. "There is a girl in that tent, who has a headache, nausea and often passes out," she pointed to the tent on the right. "And in this," she pointed to the one next door, "there is a stonecutter. An accident during the construction of the miller's house left his leg broken in three places."

"There have been cases of plague?" Vivan asked, grateful to be kept busy.

"I would say."

He met her beautiful eyes and looked down before she could make his blush.

He closed his eyes. Through the palette of the colors of his feelings, he focused on the two mentioned by Vashaba. A dark aura around the girl's head. Black around the stonecutter's leg.

His suffering. The courage he tried to show his companions despite the pain.

Help is here soon.

"I'll visit the stonecutter first," he decided, walking towards the tent.

"I'll come with you," Vashaba said, interrupting Paphian, who obviously wanted to propose the same. "Stay on guard!" She ordered him firmly.

"Semen." Vivan briefly touched the fur of the tiger accompanying them. "Don't go away."

Semen muttered softly.

"What's up?" Paphian knew Vivan hadn't given the order just like that. He knew him too well. Vashaba also became alert, not only under his words.

"She's here," Vivan replied quietly, and without waiting for his brother's reaction, he entered the tent with Vashaba.

The colors of Mayene's aura could not be mistaken for anything, though he merely touched her presence with his senses. Silver and black. Unnatural.

Inhuman.

He nodded slightly to Vashaba in silent thanks for helping with Paphian.

"He means well," she said gently.

"I know," Vivan smiled warmly before greeting the wounded stonecutter's two companions and himself.

"I remember you," he smiled at the sufferer, placing his hand gently on his broken leg. "You're Bert. Last year you won the tournament of the strongest men in our city!"

"A whole bag of gold!" Cried a pleasantly surprised man with a curly beard. "It helped me build a house here, Count! I'm glad you remember me!"

"What happened to you during the plague?"

"Fortunately, she missed me and my family, sir. And now I help those who decided to settle here. I'm making a nice profit from it."

Vivan listened to the chatter of the man and his friends, still keeping his hand on the stonecutter's leg. The pain subsided as soon as the energy spread from his hand to the broken leg. Moved by the meeting with the healer, the man talked about the accident, looking at Vivan with pride and joy.

During this time, the leg was returning to its original state. The bones joined with a soft click that made the men silent and watched the changes with fascination. Blood circulated slowly.

Second crack. Second fracture fused.

And finally, the third.

Here the bone had pierced the skin, and thanks to the slit of a trouser leg, everyone could see the bone plunging slowly into the body and returning to its place with a soft click, without pain. The wound closed slowly until it disappeared as if nothing had happened. Only the traces of blood and sweat on the stonecutter's body were evidence that something was wrong after all. The stonecutter got to his feet hesitantly and thanked him profusely, and his comrades threw a few pieces of silver into the surprised Vashaba, although both she and the healer refused to be paid.

"I'm very sorry, Count," said the stonecutter Bert gravely after the euphoria, "because of what happened to you. Know, my lord, not all people in this world are scoundrels. For my health and happiness, Lord, I will adore you until I die. Say the word and I'll go anywhere and do what you want. With me, no one will raise a hand against you."

Moved, Vivan hugged him briefly and tightly, unable to utter a word. He knew, with all the certainty his keen senses gave him, that the stonecutter was honest and ready to put his words into practice. Such sympathy always made his heart warm with love for people. And even that cruelty seemed to fade in his mind then.

In good spirits, they left the tent. Stonecutter Bert was just inviting everyone to an evening treat at his place and a barrel of beer, when suddenly the tiger snarled malevolently and before anyone could react, Vashaba stood in front of Vivan, shielding him with her body, and then swiftly threw the dagger...

A female figure with fiery red hair flashed past like a flash of lightning.

"Paphian!" Vivan shouted, seeing the sword in his brother's hand.

"She walked by. She wanted to cast some spell!" Paphian's long, dark hair came out of the buckle. "I think she wanted to set fire to the tent! I've hurt her, and your brother," he nodded to Vasheba, "seems to be after her. I had no idea she is so fast!"

"We didn't know she existed in the morning," Vivan remarked.

A blast hit their faces. The stonecutter and his friends joined Vashaba and sheltered Vivan. The tiger snarled again and ran somewhere to the left.

"Semen!" Paphian called after him, but to no avail. Vashaba drew her bow and arrow.

"I have to go to that girl," Vivan whispered in the silence.

Only the crackle of a burning fire in the middle of the makeshift camp disturbed the silence.

Vivan closed his eyes.

He barely touched the witch's aura...

The tiger snarled somewhere on the other side. A second voice answered him. Reeba, the tigress, appeared beside them and stood defensively in front of the people.

Suddenly they heard screams in the tents, and a moment later the tent with the sick girl inside burst into flames. A frightened family ran out of the tent. The father carried an eight or nine-year-old daughter in his arms. The mother pointed at the tent.

"The witch," she just said.

A female voice shouted as Semen ran past the burning tent. The gathered people stood beside Vivan's group, staring at the spot where they had just flashed white fur and a scream.

And then, in the open space on the other side of the square, she appeared. For the first time, Vivan had seen her inhuman, iridescent eyes. She was much older than him. She had sharp features. Her wrists were adorned with numerous bracelets and rings, and her clothes shimmered with orange, red, and yellow. Her hair was of such a mesmerizing shade that the crowd couldn't look away.

Her clothes were stained with blood. She held one arm a little stiffly. She raised her efficient hand in a winning gesture and threw the object she was holding, which she had hidden earlier for better effect. Reeba growled furiously.

Mayene threw the head of a white tiger under the feet of the crowd... Vashaba lifted her chin a little.

Dinn was standing behind Mayene, and his hand had just released an arrow. The bow's string groaned.

But Mayene was gone. Vashaba stepped forward and deflected her brother's arrow, striking her bow before it accidentally killed someone.

Vivan stood among the people, next to his next charge in the arms of his father.

"It was a show," he said gravely. "A trick that was supposed to show us some of her skills."

"She's fucking fast," said someone in the crowd.

"But not enough," Vivan looked seriously at his brother and the elves. "We can hurt her."

A thought crossed his mind. A memory of what he had accomplished, though he was not proud of it. It would be best to get the event out of his mind. From Paphian's glance, he guessed his brother was thinking the same.

About their conversation at Sel's house...

"If necessary, are you able to repeat what you did then in the marketplace?"

He looked at the people around him. The stonecutter was still vigilant, looking around. Vashaba stood at his side. Paphian walked over to the head of the slain favorite. The little girl looked into the eyes of her healer, now held by her father's hand. He felt a familiar chill sweep over him.

"What if I have to do this?" He replied mentally to that question. He extended his hand to the sick child....

Chapter VII

Mutiny Aboard

Ross lay with his eyes closed, gathering his strength. He heard the sounds of other prisoners' conversations, the sound of the waves and the boatswain's commands. He could feel a soft pillow and a lot of straw under his head, and the warm blanket warmed him pleasantly. For some time after awakening from a narcotic sleep he felt a bitter cold. The trembling was unstoppable. Oliver dismissed the anxiety of the accompanying kidnappers by saying that it was nothing. Before, he was moving restlessly and mumbling or drooling, and now he's just shivering. This was not only to suppress suspicions. In this way, the friend gave him directions on how to behave so that it would look natural.

Once again, he mentally thanked the fate of Oliver and his courage to maneuver among Ramsey's thugs. And at the same time, he trembled mentally at the thought of what would happen to him if they guessed the truth.

What would happen then with Julien...

Why would he allow him this crazy idea to recruit himself onto the ship while Ramsey was looking for adventurers?!

But if Oliver had not done it then...

He was very thirsty, but Oliver did not have a chance to give him water. All he had managed to do was wet his lips an hour ago, under the pretext of wiping his sweat off his lips. If he had just watered him, the sailors would have told Ramsey that the wizard was obviously waking up because he was drinking water like the others. The two who had accompanied Oliver from the beginning were constantly hanging around. To somehow kill time, they played dice in the corner, they even tried to get Oliver into it. For peace of mind, he sat down to watch the game.

Probably wondering about his next move. It was already noon.

"What now?" He thought frantically. "We have to do something."

"RAMSEY," the Hope Stone whispered.

It was not the first time a stone had spoken to him, though Ross had not disclosed it to anyone yet.

As if guided by this hint, he listened more to the sounds on the ship. It was so natural, so simple. Through sounds and waves, he reached the mind as if it had been doing it for a long time. He didn't even feel scared.

Ramsey finally got up from the bed, scratching his crotch. He would have been quite an interesting man if he hadn't smelled of sweat and rum now. Ross knew that when the man sobered up, he would take care of himself, or rather make sure others took care of him. He hated smelling like a pig. He approached his mother from behind and held her breast in a little subtle way.

"I don't want to see it," he told the Jewel in his mind.

Ramsey and Cadelia smooched sluggishly until he sobered up. He decided to get some cold air. As he greeted the crew, his eyes fell on the door leading below deck.

"How's our stuff?" He asked his woman who followed him.

"They are to eat and drink," she replied shortly.

"And your baby boy?"

"He sleeps like a dead man."

Ross flinched as he realized Ramsey was going here.

He was more afraid of him than he would like to admit.

Ramsey went downstairs. Apart from the prisoners and his men, he noticed Oliver immediately, and it did not escape his notice that he did not remember him at all.

"Who the fuck are you?" He asked.

"Your first officer has assigned me to look after the prisoners," replied Oliver calmly.

"Did you give them a babysitter?" Ramsey made a face at his mother.

"Not otherwise," she replied with a shrug.

"Where's your dress and cap, lady?" He sneered at Oliver, to which his sailors chuckled, and several others began to peek in from the deck in an interesting way. "He has a mouth like a girl, only give him a dress," he grimaced in a smile, not in some anger.

Ross heard his thoughts. After drinking, Ramsey was able to get angry in an instant. He has already found out about it. Sometimes one thought was enough.

Now he thought that Oliver's face was definitely too pretty for a sailor, and his mistress had chosen him herself. Twisted logic told him the rest.

Oliver was in danger.

Such thoughts on Ramsey's face threatened to explode instantly.

"You chose him?" He asked ominously.

Cadelia sensed what was going on, and so did her son. Everyone fell silent, waiting for the continuation. Ross sensed his friend's fear.

He was starting to fear for him.

Ramsey was apparently still in a good mood, but his eyes denied it.

Ross could see it through open eyelids.

"Why did you choose him?" He asked with drunken seriousness. Cadelia hesitated only a moment.

"If you want, choose another one," she replied, shifting discreetly to cover the source of the trouble. Oliver was cautiously silent.

"Would you like to try both ways?" Ramsey continued stubbornly. "Are you looking for the younger ones?!"

"You're in trouble," Ross thoughtfully turned to his mother.

"LET'S DIVER HIS ATTENTION," said Jewel. Ross considered it.

"Better not see you here with him," he whispered into Ramsey's mind.

Like a stranded puppet, Ramsey almost repeated the word:

"Better I don't fucking see you here!"

Ross allowed himself a soft sigh. Now, no one paid any attention to him.

"He's to sit here below deck all the way to the harbor in the Bay," he whispered his mind into Ramsey's consciousness.

"Forgive me, Oliver," he thought to his friend. "It's for your own good."

It was a bit strange, but Oliver seemed beyond his actions.

He hardly heard him...

"He's to sit below deck all the way to the port!" Meanwhile the captain shouted to his mother's face.

Oliver looked suddenly at his lying friend. Ross's heart fliped. He closed his eyelids.

"Let him sit," Ross's mother shrugged with apparent indifference, in perfect control of herself.

But Ross knew she was still afraid of his lover's anger. He could feel her tension. He felt the emotions of others more and more strongly. Like circles in the water when a stone is thrown.

Oliver suspected something.

Ramsey was reassured for the time being by Cadelia's reply. He looked at the crew's familiar faces and glanced at the prisoners.

"This is how a woman is supposed to listen!" He called to everyone, putting his arm around her, then his gaze fell on Ross. He walked over to him, curiously examining the bed and the lying one.

"He has good here. Like the prince!" He remarked with a smirk. The crew chuckled softly, silently accepting the change of subject. "Is that your job?" he asked Oliver.

"Yes, Captain."

"And who smashed his nose without my orders?"

"What are you talking about?" Cadelia looked at her son carefully. "Nobody hit him. His nose is bleeding and that's it."

"Blood?!" Ross wondered. "IT'S BECAUSE OF ME," said the Jewel.

Unconscious, according to Ramsey, Ross wasn't interesting yet.

So he walked over to Oliver, still more preoccupied with than anything else. He shook his finger in front of his nose.

"Do you fucking understand what I mean?" He asked him.

"Yes, sir," replied Oliver, and Ross mentally envied his composure.

"Ok!"

"Gentlemen!" He exclaimed. "We should celebrate today for our hunting! Bo'sun, get me some music and a barrel of rum! We are going to make a pile tomorrow!"

The crew chorally shouted with joy.

The two sailors who had accompanied Oliver so far followed the captain, ordering him to stay as ordered. The door slammed shut.

They were finally alone.

Oliver took a dagger from his belt and approached the long-haired girl, the first prisoner.

"What's your name?" He asked quickly.

"Maia," the girl replied.

"I'm Oliver," he cut her bonds. "You know what to do."

"Yes," she nodded and freed her legs. After a while she came up to the young boy who looked at her fondly.

Meanwhile, Oliver poured water into a small bowl and soaked a piece of cloth in it, which washed away the blood under his friend's nose.

"Slowly," he gently helped him sit up against the wall, then poured water into a cup for him. "Drink. Just not too fast."

Ross felt sick.

"Do you like sea travel?" Asked Oliver with a smile.

"So far I have not had the chance..."

"When they come back, pretend to be tied up," Oliver instructed the kidnapped. "Let them get drunk first!"

They nodded in agreement, releasing each other from the bonds.

"Did you use it?" He asked his friend bluntly, gesturing at the jewel. Ross looked at him with interest.

"IT'S A TWIN. THEY ARE EXTREMELY SENSITIVE", said the Jewel in his mind.

"I've tried," he replied.

"Are we taking over the ship?" One of the innkeeper's sons asked them softly.

"We have no other choice," replied Oliver. "Unless you want to be sold into slavery."

"Will you help us?" Maia asked, looking at Ross, "You and the Jewel?"

"This Jewel does not have such mighty power," observed the innkeeper with a hint of regret. "Put your hand up," Ross thought mentally.

Before the man considered his wish, he obediently raised his hand. Someone asked him what he was doing, and the innkeeper suddenly looked at Ross in amazement as if he had rediscovered it. After a while, everyone guessed the truth.

There was silence.

"I'll help you," Ross replied seriously.

* * *

"The tub, Captain!" A young boy broke out of the crow's nest.

Sel twitched and looked in the direction indicated. Alesei and the village volunteers followed his gaze.

The ship was sailing far ahead. Hence, of course, it was impossible to tell if it was Cadelia, but the mere sight of him, though so distant, made the heart in Sel's chest pound uneasily. It had to be the ship!

The ship that carried Ross and his tormentor on board. The one who almost tortured him to death. And Oliver, probably unaware of how serious trouble he got into.

The ship's bell rang in the sailors' ears.

Once.

Seeing the captain holding the telescope to his eye, Sel ran from the bow to where he had finished repairing the arbalest, then stepped onto the bridge. The Bo'sun tried to stop him, but the captain's gesture allowed him to stay.

"Is that them?" He asked softly to hide the tension.

The captain glanced at him, masking his curiosity better than the boatswain, who was obviously fascinated by Sel's devotion to his friend and lover. Sel was used to such looks a long time ago, making no difference to them. He took the telescope from the captain's hands and looked impatiently.

He saw a little, but his heart gave him unwavering confidence.

It was Cadelia.

"How soon will we catch up with her?" He asked anxiously.

"Less than two hours," replied the captain. "Unfortunately that's bad news, Mr. Andilio."

"Why?"

"Storm," the boatswain gestured to the west sky. "In an hour the clouds will cover the sun. In two - all hell is going to break loose."

Sel looked in the direction indicated. He barely noticed the blackout in the sky on the horizon line.

"That's for sure?" He asked them. "I can hardly see any change because of this sun."

"Changes are in the air, Sel," Alesei told him from aboard. "It's going fast," he added. "It'll even be here sooner. The wind favors it."

As if summoned, the wind suddenly burst in a sharp gust, slapping their faces.

"Have you been to sea before?" The captain asked curiously.

Sel looked again. Indeed, as they talked, the skyline darkened noticeably and the clouds filled more space.

"We were growing grapes on the slopes of Herna, beyond the Terinas," said Alesei thoughtfully, looking at the horizon. "Father taught me to recognize changes. To know was to survive."

Sel looked at him. The open-minded and outgoing Alesei, who has already managed to arouse sympathy for the crew, he told little about his life, both when they knew each other in the House of Pleasure and now. As if it had cut itself off from the old days. However, Sel knew what was behind it. Reveler and a womanizer who lived carelessly on his father's goods, and his best friend once left their family homes, after a harvest disaster devastated the plantations. His father got angry with his son and drove him out of the house for bread, and Alesei, after many adventures, set up a comfortable nest in Mother Rebecca's house. From there, he sent money to his family. The death of Darmon, killed at the hand of the bandits, whom Sel was also very fond of, and the subsequent events of the day Vivan was led out of the castle for certain death made Alesei considerably more serious and mature, though some habits continued to work well with him. However, everyone knew that this bully, although he liked to play and was an incorrigible womanizer, friends could always count on.

"It didn't even help us," added Alesei. Though it sounded puzzling to others, Sel understood his friend's words.

"Call the crew," the captain ordered to the boatswain.

After Nat did so, the captain delivered the news to the people, especially to the highlanders from the town who were involved in this little gathering.

"There's one more you must know, too," he said to them at the end. "These smugglers and the storm aren't our only concerns."

Several of the ship's sailors smirked. One of them, with an earring in his ear and spiky hair, walked past the innkeeper's wife, muttering to his white-fish dagger as if it was going to be fun.

"Where we're going, it's swarming with sharks," said the captain, to which Alesei swore in his own way. "This area has often become a place of clashes. Sharks like human flesh."

"In other words, people..." cried the petty officer, grinning at the surprised volunteers perfectly white teeth, so contrasting with the color of the skin. "Don't invite the sharks over here for dinner, okay?"

"Excellent suggestion, Mr. Willon," the captain said, refraining from smiling at the surprised and frightened faces of his guests.

Sel looked at Alesei, who grinned in response. Someone from the crew gave him a friendly pat on the back. The Bo'sun laughed favorably at the sight of his expression.

If he couldn't help it, it was better to focus on what he could do.

This is just another complication.

He glanced at the ship in the distance. The captain gave the orders, and the Hydra increased speed as the sails were adjusted to a different position. She drifted the waves, racing the wind, the storm, own destiny.

"I'm opening a can," Sel whispered softly to himself in his old habit.

"A silver spoon, a flowering twig, a blade of grass between the stones..."

He felt calm overcome him.

Chapter VIII

This is just another complication

On their way back, they encountered Sai and Julien, who dragged them together for a meal. Julien was in disguise again. The innkeeper promised discretion regarding the events in Tenan's room. She was sure he would keep his word. Mayene had no reason to question him. Seme welcomed unexpected guests with open arms. She hugged the visibly tired Vivan heartily like a natural son, studying him with concern. From childhood, he and Paphian often came here as neighbors, played with her sons, now living in another kingdom overseas, from where she often received letters when ships from Alinor called at port. She had forbidden them to come in the time of the plague, and now that she was quiet she watched for their arrival. Her sister's children, whom fate had given her, were now a sweet tooth for her longing for her own, and Vivan and Paphian evoked so much memories and maternal affection in her as if they were also her children. After all, she knew them. The sensitive healer was both a concern of his own mother and Seme herself, so it is no wonder that she was also troubled by the haunting nightmares she had heard about from the Countess. However, unlike her she didn't make that much fuss. She wanted to give him as much peace as he needed, although as a mother she understood the grief plaguing her friend. There was always warmth and love in the home of Seme and her husband Kirst. For these reasons, afraid that the healer had been taken to the castle of Seme, she ordered her sons to go by ship to another kingdom. Now she quickly enlisted the girls to help serve the meal, convinced that the hot soup would help Vivan bounce back. She hadn't forgotten about Paphian either: she'd asked him what he'd rather eat and drink afterwards, stroking his head as if he were still a little boy. Paphian was very fond of his foster aunt, allowing her to be treated like that without anger. Surprised by the slightly warm atmosphere, Vashaba and Dinn quickly got carried away. Only Paphian's gesture, sadly feeding his tigress at the table, reminded of the unpleasant events. Seme agreed that he would bury his favorite by the river, in her garden, where winter darkness was already falling. It was moving to think that the witch had ripped off Semen's head without using any weapons. When they finished eating their late lunch and started talking about what was happening at the marketplace, the good mood simmered down a little.

Together, they began to think about what to do next. It was clear that Mayene wasn't going to stop there.

Vivan wanted to be part of this conversation. But the weariness, mainly caused by a bad night's sleep and the very intense day which was behind him, were already felt. Though some things bothered him about Mayene since he touched her aura, though he felt he was on the verge of discovering something important, he couldn't focus enough to share his insights with his friends. His eyes were closing. A warm meal and the sympathy of his adoptive aunt and uncle made his thoughts shrouded in a cozy quilt. Involuntarily, his body began to tilt towards Vashaba, as if he was subconsciously seeking support from her. Seme smiled at the red-haired girl as she looked with emotion at the healer falling asleep on her shoulder. There was something between the two, still shy and wary, but already visible to the others. It would be good if Vivan finally found someone. Seme wished him this with all her heart.

"I'll wake him up," Paphian said softly. "We still have to go home."

"No need!" Semeralda waved her hand. "I'll send someone. Let him say Vivan sleeps at my place today. You stay with him, right? A big house, there is plenty of space in it since the travelers moved out. Will be a lot of place to sleep. There will also be a place for you, little soul," Seme looked at the beautiful woman-elf and her brother. "We'll put Vivan in the guest room, let him rest. He always sleeps well with us. Nobody bothers him. And since it is not a temple, you will lie down next to him and make sure that he sleeps really well. Just don't bother him today, he's so exhausted he hardly got here."

"I don't…" Vashaba stuttered, aware that everyone was watching her, and Dinn almost burst out laughing. "I'm his guardian! I have to keep an eye on him, that's my job! I promised."

"Well, I just said that." Seme feigned surprise, though her eyes were laughing.

"Take care of him, take care of him, because he's our only treasure. And you don't bother him anymore," she told Paphian. "Just lie down in the other room with her brother, each in his own bed, because there are two. You don't have to warm each other like Ross and Sel, do you?"

Paphian opened his mouth, not knowing what to say, and everyone laughed softly so as not to wake Vivan. Dinn shook his head in amusement, which was a really nice sight to see after all his serious expressions.

"I'm warm enough," he replied.

If he was wondering whether to really risk again with new friendships, he was sure now it was worth it. Nothing warms the heart more than kindness.

"Well! You see you're a hot boy! Only this unnecessarily grave face you put on. The moon could be sold for such a smile!"

Krist cleared his throat significantly. Amused, Seme kissed him loudly in the cheek.

"Come on, children!" She called out to the young ones. "It's a long night. Vivan needs to be put down. And tomorrow it isn't known what else will happen with this witch."

"Who knows if I will do something at night..." her husband said for the first time that evening.

"No, uncle," Julien replied, glancing at Sai, "she will be rather busy today." With her keen eye, Seme also noticed that her niece was strange sad at the thought. She hoped to find out what was causing it later.

"We have something to tell you," said Sai as they got up from the table. Paphian and Vashaba tended to the sleeping Vivan, leading him up the stairs.

Paphian silently nodded.

* * *

In the middle of the night, Vivan opened his eyes.

He was lying in a familiar room, at Seme and Krist's house. So he did not abandon it. The night was quiet. Everyone was asleep.

A heart was beating beside him. He heard the pulse.

"Bad dreams again?" the sensual voice could only belong to Vashaba. He held his breath for a moment.

Her hair was loose, and it was now cascading onto the white sheets. White shirt emphasized her perfect complexion. She was propped up on her arm, clothed next to him.

She only took off her winter coat. She was still wearing her high leather boots.

She had a dagger and a sword with her.

She was so beautiful in the candlelight....

He had never been so close to a woman, he had never been lying next to woman. He did not allow himself such thoughts, dreams of closeness.

He had several reasons.

He did not consider himself worthy of a woman like Vashaba.

In the castle, people showed him how to disgust something that he may have been a bit naively associated with feeling so far.

And here in his hometown, women treated him like a special kind of medic or even a priest. Untouchable...

"She just watches over me," he reminded himself with a hint of sadness. Even the fact that in her thoughts he sensed the denial of these words, he hid it deep within himself.

He probably couldn't live that way. He wanted to love reciprocally, but was afraid that after a while his character would be the biggest obstacle. He would start to irritate with his sensitivity or make a loving person applaud him with his protectiveness, convinced that this is what he needs. He didn't want that to happen.

Vashaba touched his forehead with concern. She had a cool hand.

"You must have a fever," she said.

"I'm always so warm," he replied softly.

For a moment she just stared at him as if she wanted to do something else, but was afraid to upset the delicate balance between them.

"What woke you up?" She asked finally.

She was so close... Even her slightly pointed ears seemed beautiful to him.

He thought back to his dream feelings.

"She's not a human," he replied in a whisper, as if afraid the witch would hear him. "Her aura is not human. There is nothing human about her."

"So, who is she?"

"I don't know. But she does not belong to beings…" He broke off suddenly, touched by a terrible thought, "of our world," he finished in horror.

Suddenly he was struck by a thought, a memory terrifying in its detail.

"Black," he said softly. "Black means disease. The evil that engulfs the victim's body…"

Vashaba listened patiently, eyeing the windows carefully.

"Black is impending death," he whispered. "It's death."

"She is dying?" She asked.

He looked at her, stunned by what he wanted to say. He could feel her. He felt her pulse quicken. She was worried.

"It means I won't be able to do it…" he whispered to himself.

"What? What do you mean?"

He remembered.

A feast of colors and taints of the aura of living creatures. Black and Silver of Mayene. Black and gray in a stonecutter and a sick girl. Death stretched out its hands. She had already pointed at them.

Iridescent eyes.

Colors that were supposed to disguise the mystery.

Death cannot take away what is not alive.

Death is about the beings of this world. It touches everyone.

But she will not touch what is not alive, although the colors she wears are supposed to suggest. Vivid, eye-catching colors.

"She has no heart," he whispered, turning pale.

"She's cruel," said Vashaba. "Yes. My guess is..."

He looked at her with deadly seriousness, making her fall silent.

"No, Vashaba," he said. "Her heart doesn't beat. She isn't a being of our world. In our world, everything that is alive must someday die. Our laws do not apply. Which means I can't kill her by stopping her heart. Because she doesn't have it."

"Paphian hurt her."

"Paphian..." Vivan felt the fear clench his heart. "Paphian will be dead soon. I bet she already took care to heal the wound."

Vashaba remembered what Sai and Julien had told them before she went to bed with Vivan.

Tenan is going to kill someone.

She didn't tell him. Julien explained to her who Tenan was and how Vivan might know him. She said she would tell him about everything herself.

"Something's got to kill her," she said.

"Something must feed her too."

She looked into his eyes. Vivan was suggesting some cruelty to her, something beyond comprehension.

She saw that he was trembling as if he was suddenly cold. She touched his hand. It was cold. Even though Vivan lay under the covers, he trembled as if suddenly in an ice cave. She took the bedspread and covered him as best she could. He thanked her with a look. She wrapped her arms around him to keep him warm. Her face was close to his.

She kissed him lightly on the cheek.

"And that for what?" He asked, slowly calming down and warming to her touch. "I just gave you some terrible news."

"Just like that," she whispered.

They stared at each other until she felt under her hand that he was warm again.

She felt calm overwhelming her. Vivan wrapped his warmth around her, soothed her senses.

He smiled slightly, touching her nose playfully with his finger.

"Don't worry," he said with his former calmness, his melodious voice sounding like wonderful music in her ears. "We'll find a way."

* * *

When dinner was being eaten in Barnica, Ramsey cursed about the world and rushed his people. He threatened the sky and every god he remembered. His face, covered with hair and splashed with rain, twisted stubbornness.

Attacked by the furious waves flooding the deck, Cadelia slipped by guided by his skilled hand. Whatever could be said about her captain, one thing everyone was sure of: there was no greater madman and no more courageous captain than he was. The whole world could sink into the depths of the waters, the sky could burn, and Ramsey would face it fearlessly, even if the elements were controlled by the devil himself. Lightning bolts beat around and the wind whipped people and sails. Ramsey mocked this and threatened the elements. His people, staring at him like a deity at such moments, obeyed orders without murmuring, quickly and precisely, as much as their raging nature allowed them. It is known how a captain can get angry when something does not go his way.

"Come on, rats offspring!" Ramsey called. "My mistress is not afraid of the waves and thunderbolts!"

He pulled his mistress closer to him, to contemplate her face in the flashes of lightning. She adored him in his element, though she feared the extent of his madness at the same time. Though completely soaked, she stood by his side, ready to face the worst, devoted to his courage, staring at his face and eyes, visible despite the thick stubble and long hair. It was at such moments that she loved him most.

And he loved her.

"Are you afraid, my queen?!" He shouted, shouting over the sound of the waves and the thunder, as if there weren't enough reasons to be scared around.

"Not with you!"

She saw tenderness and devotion in his eyes, though only for a moment. He shouted at his sailors again, but he didn't let go of her, still hugging her waist.

He wanted her with him.

Sometimes it was a bit overwhelming.

"You're not afraid of anything," he said proudly, as if he had contributed to it. He looked around. A raging storm tossed them, waves flooded the deck.

But that didn't spoil his humor.

In the glare of lightning and rising waves, he suddenly saw the hull of the smaller ship, and on the sails he noticed the familiar mark of a furious beast from the dark ages that the sailors trembled at.

The ship was quite close now.

"Caddy!" He screamed inhumanly. "Check with people what your baby boy is doing. If he will be bad... you know what to do!"

"What's happening?"

"It seems to me..." Ramsey was shouting over the roar of the storm's effects, "that his fucking lady is coming to us!"

Cadelia followed his gaze.

"Hydra!" She snapped, seeing the mark on the sails.

"I'll give him a proper greeting!" Ramsey assured her. "You can be sure. I will tear his legs off his ass!".

She grabbed him by the skirt of his doublet and kissed him fiercely.

"Whatever you do to him," she said, "do it in front of Ross. Like then with Nim, remember?"

Ramsey smiled at her anger, excited at the prospect of cruel play.

"What a devil you are..." he said with satisfaction, pressing her waist closer to him.

* * *

In order not to feel the effects of sea sickness, most of the kidnapped highlanders had to take some of the already depleted portion of Oliver's gift from a healer. Though he worried that the gift might be needed for the coming fight, he had no choice. Most of these people have never even ridden a fishing boat, including himself. There were only four of the fifteen abductees who were engaged in fishing. It was a blind fate that allowed Mayene to kidnap representatives of the professions associated with the mainland.

"There is nothing here that can be used as a weapon," said the innkeeper. "Purely like a temple."

"They are ready, damn them!" The wife of the other innkeeper who remained in Barnica swore. "If only I had a stick, but nothing of that! You have to go out empty-handed and catch them so quickly that they don't even have time to catch their breath! I don't see any other way out!"

A few nodded at the words. Once it was certain that the raging storm was effectively distracting the hijackers, pretending was stopped. There was no need to stay tied up anymore. Time was running out.

Oliver was silent. He was aware of the risks when he boarded the deck, but the closer he got to the fight, the more disturbed he was to face enemies without weapons, only with the inherent slingshot and dagger. He knew Julien and Sai didn't condemn him for this madness, but he hoped fate would be on his side. His unbreakable bond with Julien, his love for her and for a woman dear to him, perhaps even more, was his constant source of anxiety. But he knew anyway that he couldn't have done otherwise. He liked Ross, who meant a lot to his sister. He was like a brother in suffering as he struggled to survive at the king's court, a true support and a friend who did not hesitate to risk his own life when the carriage fell over to protect her.

He understood how much their shared experiences had brought them together. What else had gotten to him, bits of history from his new friend's life, even a love for Sel, also made Oliver not hesitate to come aboard when Ross was dragged there.

It's good that he wisely hire as a crew member earlier.

Without it, these people might not have even the slightest chance of being free now.

He was glad that he did so, and that is here now with them.

At the same time he was afraid. Perhaps more for the women who loved him than for himself, but still.

Ross touched his shoulder with the shadow of a smile. Being so close to his mother and her cruel lover, he could not face the danger with the old strength, but still he did not lack courage.

Oliver felt uplifted by the Jewel, and he took in the people who accompanied him with a new gaze.

The innkeeper hugged him tightly.

"This boy needs to be protected. He has two lives in him, and yet he put himself in danger for us and for his friend!"

"Stand behind us, Oliver," said the stocky alewife, which as most of them he known beforehand, but he was mostly Selena back then, which he didn't want to look like now. She had obviously heard his name when he introduced himself to Maia, who smiled kindly at him. "Don't let them reach you there."

"Let's get out of this hole, father," said one of the sons of the innkeeper with hair as curly as his parent's. "Be that as it may!"

"Wait!" Ross looked up. His focused face paled visibly now.

"My mother and some people are going here," he explained gravely.

Maia spoke first, before the others, still unused to Ross's new skills, cooled down with surprise.

"How many people?" She asked consciously.

He looked at her, surprised by the hard sound of her voice, which marked courage and determination. He admired her attitude.

He couldn't let these people down by letting fear reign over him. So, although his heart was beating restlessly, he replied, assisted by the girl's strength:

"Six."

"Okay, not bad!" One of the hunters exclaimed. Ross looked around quickly.

"Get in!" he commanded. "They have to come in here!"

When they all sat down again, pretending to be still bound prisoners, except for Oliver nonchalantly leaning against a barrel of water, the wizard of the Jewel added:

"But they don't have to get out of here..."

The abductees spilled out sinister smiles on their faces.

* * *

Cadelia stepped below deck, eyeing Oliver and the bound ones sharply. The son was lying on a cushion. Her cunning soul sensed the change in the air, something unsettling, but before she could figure out where the cause was, her people followed her and closed the door. She motioned for them to keep an eye on everything.

Something was wrong. She felt it.

Oliver looked at her calmly. Ross removed the fear from his companions' hearts, which was both a blessing and a madness to them, but they were mentally grateful to him. Now each of them was slowly beginning to feel his influence.

"This boy is dangerous," thought Cadelia, looking at Oliver. "You will not leave this place alive" suddenly her companions heard in their heads.

They felt fear. Shocking fear of the voice and what the message conveyed. Six strong people, who knew many dangers in their lives, who had quite a good chance in the fight against the kidnapped, suddenly became terrified, hearing voices in their heads, like an oracle of fate announcing their doom.

They got mixed up. To Cadelia's surprise, they drew their swords in superstitious fear, looking around carefully, checking the faces of the captives. Only Oliver raised his eyebrows slightly in surprise. The others remained on the floor, seemingly avoiding the gaze of the sailors.

It wasn't for nothing that Cadelia was the first female officer in this gang on the ship that bore her name. She might have feared

Ramsey a bit, but that didn't mean he had full power over her. Only what she allowed him through his blind love.

"What the hell?!" She yelled, feeling a slight twinge of panic. "Something happened to your head, you damned dogs?! Why are you drawing your swords?"

"Voice..." one of the sailors whispered.

Cadelia immediately looked at her son. He was still in the same position as she had seen him at first, but she was no longer sure he was unconscious. She thought stabbing her sword in his ribs would explain the matter immediately. She can't be fooled by his tricks. The witch ordered to watch out for him. She knew very well that the other was right. Surely he would have been eager to cut her throat for her previous actions, chip off his father!

She didn't know him at all. She never wanted to know him. She did not even want him to be born, but the fetus did not get spent. It was beyond comprehension how the monster's son had clung to life until now.

She knew that one day he would make her pay for all the crimes she had committed. So it would be better if he was still unconscious now. Just in case, she took out the witch's flask and gripped the sword tighter in her hand.

When she was right next to him, he sprang from the bed, grabbed her by the leg, and pulled her until she hit the floor, signaling the others who had fought the sailors.

Ross would have been happy to help his comrades by influencing the sailors to make them lose their will to skirmish, but the mother turned out to be a woman with a truly remarkable survival instinct. As the highlanders overpowered and restrained

Cadelia's men, she released her sword and scratched Ross' face with her sharp nails, making him step back so as not to lose an eye. Despite the pain of the fall, she threw herself at him furiously, screaming, pulling him to the floor to crush him with her own weight.

Oliver jumped forward to help, but the highlanders who wanted to protect him pushed him back, still struggling with the sailors, because two of them fought really well. Maia reached for the sword of one of the defeated, but the fear of dying prevented her from delivering a blow. The boy by her side took the weapon from her hand and, full of revenge, thrust it into the enemy's chest as if he had been doing it all his life.

Others, however, did not die. The highlanders tied them up and gagged them, stunning some of the reluctant ones, and treated his act with a mixture of horror and forbearance, leaving the judgment to Maia, who would soon become his wife.

The mother managed to crush her son by sitting on him. She painfully twisted his right arm, wanting to implement her rescue plan and pour even the entire contents of the witch's bottle into his mouth to prevent his desire for revenge, which she suspected him of. If it had been someone else, not her, Ross might have defended himself more fiercely. But it was his mother who had betrayed him more than once. More than once she was a source of suffering for him and almost ruined his life. The panicky fear that had arisen since childhood, the same one that made him afraid of coming home, that made him wake up at night convinced that he was going to him to punish him for the unfulfilled deeds and mistakes of the child - weakened his will to fight.

"You will not take revenge!" She screamed over him, struggling furiously with him. Several people looked at the scene with horror. Oliver finally broke away to front.

"You should love me!" He shouted, his voice so full of regret that they all looked at him now. "You should love me, mother! Why do you hate me so much?!"

His words made Oliver freeze.

Everyone seemed to be waiting for an explanation.

Though Oliver followed Cadelia's hand with the bottle and Ross with his eyes, he refrained from helping his friend, as did the others, who stood uncertainly, waiting for a reply from the degenerate mother, which might otherwise never happen again.

"The son of a murderer, a degenerate, who didn't care of a human life!" His mother screamed in his face. "A pervert like his father! A dirty pig that hides under decent clothes and thinks his shit doesn't stink! You shouldn't exist! Neither you nor your father - butcher and rapist! None of you!"

The strong alewife gasped at these words, walked over to Cadelia, who was sitting on her son, and punched her in the face. Then, as a startled and darkened Cadelia felt her sore cheekbone, she disrespectfully twisted her hair around her hand and pulled her to her feet, facing her face.

"You blame the child for the crimes of his father?" She hissed furiously. "Look at the mirror, only there you will see the devil!"

She pulled her towards the stairs, tearing the bottle from her hand.

"Don't stare like that!" She ordered her stunned companions. "Come on, separate. Some watch the prisoners, others follow me! Oliver!" She screamed, but Oliver had given her orders and he was already with his friend, so she only nodded her head at the sight and added aloud: "Tell him to buck up now! At home, I'm going to give him a bread with pork dripping and he will get a pot of the best beer, but now we have to act!"

Ross looked at her and his mother with a bloody nose, feeling warmth and gratitude warm his heart for the alewife. For the second time in his life, a foreign woman stood up for him in a fight with his mother.

Once, Valerii took his side...

The mother jerked, but the pain and the threat of the hair being torn in a tight grip of the alewife stopped her aspirations.

"I'm not done with you!" She screamed to her son.

"You can see that you are done!" The alewife glanced at the door, hearing more lightning bolts. "And now I'll talk to your man! We'll see how he cares for you!"

"You are holding on?" Asked Oliver with concern, examining the scars on Ross's face.

These, however, are already starting to disappear due to Vivan's blood circulating in his veins. Oliver was relieved.

Ross looked at him without saying a word. His friend saw tears welling up in his eyes, but the latter shook his head quickly, clearly ordering composure. He glanced at the stairs that most of the abductees were already climbing. Even Maia shook off the momentary lethargy.

Ross leaned on Oliver to get to his feet, pushed any feelings away for later.

Oliver saw how much his friend had cost to meet his mother. Despite the appearance of calm, his hands trembled.

Ross looked at the trapped sailors.

"Do not oppose," he said suddenly in a tone that made even Oliver feel chills down the back of his neck. "Otherwise I will make you all jump into the sea and you will not fight for your life..."

How did he manage to stay cool after what happened? This Oliver did not know. He saw that the Jewel glowed red for a moment, then went out.

Show to intimidate. Even the prisoners knew it. Despite this, they gave up their resistance.

Ross didn't want them dead. He just wanted them to sit still and not disturb.

Oliver quickly looked away so that his friend would not see tears of emotion in his eyes.

Anything the degenerate mother suspected her son of was not true. Ross was not a bad man.

"Mikela!" The innkeeper suddenly shouted.

The stocky woman staggered on the stairs, and had it not been for her smuggler and other companions of misery, she would have fallen to the floor. There was a distinct cut and blood on the temple.

Ramsey stood by the door, a wooden hammer in his hands. He wiped his face carelessly in the driving rain and wind, doing nothing to himself about the raging weather.

"Caddy!" He called to Ross's mother, who took advantage of the commotion she broke away towards the door.

In a gesture of unusual courtesy for him, he extended his hand to her to help out, and then positioned her behind his back.

Fear seized the hearts of the kidnapped.

"Get them!" Ramsey shouted.

It was that short moment, one heartbeat, as fear gripped the rebels and their hope faded in hopelessness.

Then Ross took a deep breath and shouted:

"Close the door! Defend yourselves!"

"He's awake!" Cadelia assured her lover, fear in her voice.

The innkeeper pushed his sword clumsily. Ramsey caught his hand. A short scuffle ensued, as a result of which the brave man and two other people managed to get to the door handle and pull it towards him. Managed to use Oliver's handle and dagger to block. However, it was clear that this makeshift would not last long. Nevertheless, the little success made the highlanders cheer happily.

"They'll massacre us here!" One of the girls, who during the plague distributed food to the needy and organized supplies, shouted.

Her words, despite their meaning, sounded more like a statement than a symptom of fear. Courage was back.

Meanwhile, Maia was washing the temple of the alewife on the floor, whom Oliver had poured a drop of the healer's waning blood into her mouth.

"What about her?" Ross worried.

"It will be all right," replied Oliver.

The innkeeper stood at the foot of the stairs, a sword he did not allow himself to be torn off. He grimaced at Ross in satisfaction.

"Good job!" He exclaimed. "We all started shitting our pants instead of acting. If I stand like a stupid goat again - kick my ass!"

"You got it!" Ross smiled.

"It won't do any good," Ross said emphatically, looking up. "Let's quit. Even if we open them, they will kill us one by one..."

"What he is doing?!" Maia's fiancé asked in amazement.

"What he does best," he replied mysteriously, looking at the glowing Jewel of Hope.

The sounds stopped.

"Mother Earth!" One of the highlanders whispered, looking at Ross with superstitious dread.

* * *

"Set fire to?" One of the sailors asked, and Ramsey shot him in the face without warning.

"You'll burn the ship, idiot!" Cadelia shouted, and to her lover in panic she shouted: "He will make us do everything! Mayene warned us!"

"Not about everything, Caddy, not about everything!"

"He'll kill us or make us kill ourselves!"

"That," Ramsey grimaced at her, "he cannot do. He knows it well."

"Why?" She asked, to which the sailors waited curiously for an answer.

"Because what's dangling around his neck is the Jewel of Hope," he explained to them. "Supposedly born of love," he pointed out with mockery, giving these words a second meaning and causing mocking smiles on the faces of the crew. "And no fucking love gem will let you kill. It cannot use it for this purpose. That's what the witch said."

They were relieved to hear the news, but after a while one of the sailors asked:

"What can he do?"

"Ross!" Ramsey yelled at the closed door without answering. "Your sunshine has come! I'll personally cut his balls off! I'm starting to get used to it!" He smiled maliciously. "Do you remember Nim, your lover?"

There was no answer, but he smiled at Cadelia and the crew with satisfaction.

"This will burn him off," he said.

Meanwhile, the highlanders stopped Ross before he could reach the door, torn by grief and anger.

"This is crazy!" The innkeeper called. "Most of us have never fought! They'll kill us before help can get on board!"

"If you want to defeat him, use that magic of yours!" One of the kidnapped hunters shouted.

"I'm not good at manipulating people!" Ross admitted irritably. "It's not that easy!"

"Then make them kill each other!" The hunter replied.

"I can't," Ross replied, briefly explaining how the jewel worked.

"A jewel born of love..." the innkeeper scratched his head thoughtfully. "Then why not make them fall in love with you?" He suggested uncertainly.

A few highlanders chuckled softly.

Ross looked at him with an unreadable expression...

* * *

"It was stupid from the beginning," thought one of the sailors, looking at the approaching ship. "Why did we push ourselves into human trafficking? We felt good earlier…".

"Cadelia's boy is not so bad," thought another. "He has a jewel of love…"

"Who said we had to push ourselves into it when it's between a mother and a son?" Meanwhile another old sailor wondered.

* * *

"What is he doing right now?" Oliver asked the innkeeper softly, seeing Ross closed his eyes in concentration.

"Shhh..." the asked one only put a finger to his lips.

"Caddy..." Ross whispered in his mind to Ramsey's mind. "Why are we playing this?"

He tried to word the words the same as Ramsey used. He was afraid he would discover manipulation. This ground was still uncertain for him, largely because he feared the anger of his pursuers. Fear would not leave him, it was too deep in him. That's why Ross didn't even try to penetrate his mother's mind...

"Caddy." Ramsey wrapped his arms around her waist as he gave the orders to get the weapon and guns ready. "Why are we playing this?"

"Stop it," Ross whispered softly, also after his heart's whisper. Oliver looked at him sadly.

"Get it over with," Ramsey repeated. "Why the hell are we need it all?" "He agrees with me," said Ross silently.

"Let's leave these people and go back to our business." Ramsey watched the Hydra struggle against the waves as it moved toward them. "We were fine with it."

Ross sensed the hesitation in his mother's feelings. Something twitched in her....

She wondered, suddenly touched by the thought that maybe there was something to it. But she was still tormented by fear. She has gone too far...

"He will not forgive me," she said, looking into the eyes of her love, looking for understanding in it.

Ross's heart was beating fast. Driven by the desire to gain at least a hint of acceptance by a wounded love that had waited all his life for reciprocity, he was tormented by regret, not knowing what to say. What words to whisper. He couldn't argue with Ramsey's lips. There were things that would be hard to forgive, if at all possible...

He made a mistake...

Chapter IX

Storm

Barnica was going to sleep. Paphian gently adjusted the pillows under his brother's head. He smiled at Vashaba. Sai waited next to him in silence, looking with concern at the tired Vivan.

* * *

Mayene entered Tenan's room. She saw him asleep with his hands tied to his bed...

She smiled crookedly as she sat down carefully next to him. For a moment she contemplated his beauty, staring with iridescent eyes without whites, like a being from an alien planet examining its prey. That's what he was for her. A toy, a victim... nothing more.

She sat down on him and grabbed his bound hands. He shuddered, awake suddenly. His amber eyes met her inhuman gaze.

She kissed him.

He felt himself losing strength. His entire existence protested this, defending itself against extinction.

But he had no choice...

* * *

In the sea, Hydra danced on the waves. The captain shouted orders over and over. Sel hadn't seen the sharks announced, but he was sure they were hiding somewhere in the depths of the waters, waiting for opportunity...

Cadelia, a beautiful galleon adorned with gold, glided in front of them on the waves.

"Are we going to lose them?" Asked the bo'sun with concern.

"No way!" Nat shouted back, giving the impression that wind and rain were commonplace.

"Hold on..." Sel whispered his mental message softly ahead to Ross, though he knew the other couldn't hear him.

Alesei tossed back his heavy, long hair, wet from the rain. He glanced at his friend.

"He can do it!" He shouted to cheer him up.

However, he himself was worried about his friend, cursing the passing moments without knowing his fate.

Some of the highlanders took refuge below the deck, but when they approached Cadelia, they went outside despite the storm and nausea. It never occurred to anyone to improve this condition with Vivan's precious gift, which two of his friends carried with them. He was precious. They did not want to waste Vivan's blood on such trifles as seasickness, although Alcsci had offered it to the highlanders. They replied proudly that it was not water, but the life of a healer, so they would manage without the intervention of magical powers. So the friends did the same. Out of respect. The highlanders' proud refusal told them a lot about their devotion to Vivan. They attached increasing importance to the gift of a friend and the impact it had on people. Also on themselves.

Sel was completely wet. Terrifyingly great waves filled him with dread, which, however, he tried not to show bravely, since everyone had made such a decision. He has never been at sea. He had never imagined that this would change one day, and in such horrible conditions. He just wanted to be with Ross as soon as possible; know that he is safe and sound.

Then he could even endure storms and thunderstorms.

"Get ready to board!" The captain shouted.

Even the highlanders were familiar with this word. Some of them nervously checked the sword and knife at the belt. The alewife, whose husband and sons had been kidnapped, took a deep breath twice and pushed back the wisps of wet and sticky hair away from her face. The sailor with an earring in his ear, smiled at her, showing off his kit. Maya's father, whom Sel had known recently assisting travelers seeking help from a healer, nodded to Sel. He nodded his head for reassurance, then both looked ahead at the beautifully carved galleon that was the prison of their loved ones. They all had the same determination written on their faces.

Hydra was catching up with Cadelia.

"Come on!" Alesei shouted.

"Blades!" Captain Noben shouted amid crackling lightning.

Alesei jumped to the lever at the front mast and pulled. The sickle-shaped blades slammed from the fuselage.

Hydra showed her teeth.

The dog stood in the bow, barking at Cadelia with short single barking.

They were so close that they could see the hull of the mighty ship, which made the Hydra look like an ordinary fishing boat and could see guns ready to fire and armed sailors threatening them from the deck. However, they gave as good as one gets.

The lamps on the ship shone in the dark like lanterns over the captain's cabin. The beautiful female figure gracefully crowning the prow of a sailing ship with flowing hair, similar to its prototype, looked with the utmost contempt with a cloudy expression on her face.

Sel watched the woman deliver Ross into the world.

He remembered her image in his artistic memory.

Captain Noren's face turned white. Nat froze as he stared at the guns ready to fire.

"Captain!" He exclaimed. "They'll rout us!"

"Mr. Andilio!"

"Yes, Captain!?" Sel shouted instinctively.

"It's time for you to demonstrate how the crossbow works!" He called to him. "Right now!"

Sel looked at him unreadable as he considered the possibilities.

"Aye aye, Captain!" He replied after a moment.

"Stern left!" The captain exclaimed.

"Stern left!" Was the steersman's quick reply, as swift as his action.

"We'll get the gold elsewhere," Ross whispered to Ramsey's mind. "Why takes the risk?"

Ramsey, as before, repeated the sentence almost word for word. But suddenly something creaked inside him. He felt disgust as soon as the words came out from his mouth. As if someone else were saying them.

His people were threatening these on Hydra. He promised himself to look out for the captain and look for dear Ross, who might be standing by his side, but what his mind told him distracted his attention. Forgot to order an attack...

Something was wrong here...

"Ramsey!" Cadelia tugged at his doublet. "We have them! What's going on with you? Why aren't you giving the order?! And since you are afraid of risk, you give up gold, huh? Suddenly you are scared?! I'm talking to you, listen to me!"

Cadelia stared at him, surprised and furious. It didn't look like him. She loved and feared him at the same time as he pushed himself into danger with a twinkle of madness in his eye. Ramsey was not afraid. He never gave up. Even if he risked it all.

He knew it perfectly well.

"Shut up, woman!" He shouted suddenly, frightened by his unexpected earlier behavior.

He hoped none of the crew noticed it. He wondered as the Hydra… turned back.

"We lost her!" One of the sailors shouted angrily at the captain.

He will also lose respect of his people in a moment.

"Go to hell!" He shouted furiously. "Follow them!"

"Captain, the water is breaking into the ship!" Another called, hurrying from beneath the deck.

The raging waves caused the water to flood the cannons in the cannon decks and the people standing next to them, breaking into the interior through arrowslits.

"Shut down!" Exclaimed Ramsey, a little distracted.

The sailor hesitated but assumed that the captain was most likely interested in the cannons, so he ran back below deck. Meanwhile, the Hydra lined up behind them.

"Load the onboard guns!" Ramsey shouted.

The sailor stopped mid-step. They all looked at the captain uncertainly for a moment, until he looked at them askance. Then they rushed to obey his order. Ramsey cursed angrily.

"Your son is confusing my head!" He hissed at Cadelia. "He's telling me things I don't want to say."

"Talking…"

"Look at me, woman!" He shouted. "Have I ever hesitated?!" Well, she had to admit never.

Ramsey reached for his sword. He summoned a dozen people before entering the deck hatch where prisoners had barricaded themselves.

"Enough of this shit!" He called out to them. "Get them out of there!" But there were unexpected complications.

"And for what?" One of the sailors suddenly asked. "Why should we risk our lives? Because mommy couldn't spank her son?"

Ramsey and Cadelia looked at him, surprised by the audacity.

"We will die in battle for nothing!" Another cried, before the captain decided he would punish his man for insubordination by beating his face properly.

The boy has a love gem!" The old sailor called. "He will do us nothing!" Ramsey understood. Another manipulation. He knew his people. It can't be that they suddenly got so sensitive...

"Ramsey..." Cadelia said hesitantly, watching people around them.

"I can see," he replied grimly.

The final proof that the sailors had succumbed to Ross's suggestion was the words of the boatswain, a man who had once been a whaler.

"They just want to be free. Why risk yourself?"

и и и

"Ross," Oliver became concerned as he watched his friend. "Your blood is flowing from your nose..."

Ross looked at him, half-consciously touching the indicated spot. Oliver reached for a piece of cloth from the dressings he was carrying with him.

He had to win this fight of will against Ramsey. In a moment, the latter will intimidate people with his style. He will bring order among the crew by the strength of his authority. If he didn't stop him, he wouldn't riot the crew.

He had never done anything like this before. He didn't even know he could... Until he decided to use his power. Jewel said they should try...

* * *

"We are not going to fight them!" The sailor called, and several others echoed back.

Ramsey was furious. He faced his men with cold fury. He saw the fear in their eyes. However, they were afraid of him! He was shaking with an anger they had never seen before. His blue eyes almost shot lightning. He jumped to the first who spoke, then without hesitating, plunged the dagger from his belt into his heart.

The crew froze in horror, not daring to face him. He was heard so strong. Cadelia pulled out her dagger.

Ramsey let his body slide over him with apparent composure. And then he looked at his people...

* * *

Ross realized he had lost.

Now all the sailors trembled in fear of the wrath of their captain. He had underestimated the strength of his authority. And people's fear of his madness.

He wanted to do too much at once, without practice. He could hear the constant buzzing in his head, and he felt sick.

"They're coming here," he said with difficulty. "Sorry... LET'S GIVE THEM THE WILL TO FIGHT," the Jewel whispered.

Ross closed his eyes...

* * *

"Pry away!" Ramsey ordered shortly, no longer trying to explain. His men eagerly proceeded to obey the order.

Suddenly a clap broke through the thunder.

Out of nowhere appeared a huge arrow tied with a long rope, which impressed forcefully into the deck a few centimeters from Ramsey's boots.

The end of the rope was tied to a huge crossbow at the Hydra's bow, which approached them from the right.

"Fire!" They heard Hydra's Captain shout even over the roar of the waves. Several guns aboard the ship exploded in a volley.

The blast nearly smashed the mast in front of the crew standing at Ramsey's side and caused severe damage to the people.

Ramsey pulled his sword up, turning white with rage.

"What the fuck are you waiting for?! Fire!" He roared.

* * *

"Damn wind!" Sel shouted to Alesei, angry the arrow had missed its target.

At this point, Hydra's sickle blades cut into Cadelia's hull. Crew staggered on their feet.

"Come on, gentlemen and ladies!" Captain Englehon called. "Boarding!" Part of the crew and all the highlanders set off to the other ship with a battle cry.

Then Cadelia's cannons crashed.

The Hydra, much smaller, positioned about halfway along length of the larger ship, driving the blades that held the two ships together. Each of the bullets launched by Cadelia missed the masts, only grazing them without serious damage, but both the captain and Sel knew that the next volley would fix the mistake.

The surprised highlanders automatically covered themselves.

"Come on, ladies!" Cried Nat. "Attaaack!"

Everyone broke up. With more or less skill, they grabbed the ropes and climbed onto the enemy unit.

A sailor with an earring in his ear helped the zealous alewife and, as if they had participated in such skirmishes for years, they stood on the deck with axes ready for battle. There were more sailors in Cadelia, so it was hoped that some support would be provided by the abductees when they could be released.

Sel jumped on deck just as Ramsey, furious, severed the rope from the arrow that nearly killed him.

Their eyes met.

"Caddy?" The smuggler turned towards his chosen one.

"Yes!" She replied stubbornly. "This is Nim's successor."

Her disgust was so great that she did not use a more offensive word at the moment.

"Take care of your baby boy and I'll take care of this here!"

"No!" She replied. "You finish what you started! Three years ago you should have killed him, but you blew it! I'll kill this punk!"

He looked at her, then at the approaching Sel, who made his way through the fighting.

He smiled crookedly.

"As you wish, sweetheart!" He called, then turned to the crew at his side.

"Force the door!"

With the help of a hammer and a few solid kicks, his order was fulfilled.

At the base of the stairs, the kidnapped were standing, ready to fight to the death.

Ross was standing among them.

Ramsey smiled again.

Sel's heart filled with fear as he realized who Ramsey was going to fight with, but he had no way of stopping it.

Ross's mother stood in his way.

Alesei was already around, but still fought a few opponents.

Cadelia drew her sword and, with a battle cry, launched herself into battle. With the sword donated by Queen Constance, Sel countered the attack.

If he had thought for a moment that Ross's mother would be a weak, drunk opponent, now he was out of his illusions. Apparently, she hadn't been idle in those years with Ramsey.

She was skilled with the sword.

The fight was fierce.

Cadelia watched his movements carefully, refusing to be carried away by loathing and hatred. She pursued her goal confidently and relentlessly.

Accustomed to rocking at sea, she took the moment he lost his balance to slash him in the face.

"You won't be so pretty anymore!" She said sarcastically.

Ignoring the blood from his slit cheek, Sel pressed his sword against it. Cadelia's next swift movements cut open his chin and the skin on his chest. He cursed under his breath one of Alesei's favorite curses.

"Are you getting nervous?" She sneered. "Come on, lady, the sharks are waiting for your carcass!"

He pretended to be really losing his temper. He waited until, smiling in satisfaction at his apparent fury, she made a mistake. It cost him some strength, but the effort paid off. Confident Cadelia charged at him, convinced that she was going to kill him in a moment.

Then, to her amazement, he managed to counter, which brought him closer than she had expected, and slapped her face until she staggered and fell.

Before she could pull herself together, the tip of his sword touched her throat... She glared at him furiously.

She spat at him contemptuously. No fear.

In Sel's soul, grief and anger battled with justice. Cadelia allowed Ross to be beaten so that scars would remain for the rest of his life. He ran away from home because of her.

She had failed him and hurt him more than Sel's own mother...

"It's been too long!" She screamed at him. "You have no balls! You are not a real man, you are just pretending to be one! You are a poor substitute for a man! Ross always chooses worse wimps than himself! You and Nimm are so alike! Maybe you can fight, but when it needed, you have no balls!"

"Nim?" Sel wondered.

His predecessor...

"You're wrong," he replied grimly, raising his sword to the blow.

"Seeel!" Alesei yelled suddenly next to him. "Do not do this!"

Cadelia smirked. Evil, sneaky woman ready to abuse her child. The one that caused Ross's previous partner's death.

Cruel and ruthless.

Sel didn't want to hesitate anymore. Or to wonder...

Alesei stopped him at the last moment, and the alewife Mikela suddenly lunged at the fallen Cadelia and wrapped chain around her neck.

"It's..." she gasped as they struggled with each other, "for you to finally shut your mouth, bitch!"

Cadela's face reddened as she fought for air. The over-tightened chain almost deprived her of it.

The alewife dragged her to the center of the deck, where there were already a few trapped, then tied her up.

Sel looked around. They were gaining an advantage.

But Ross wasn't here!

He looked at the broken door leading to the hatch.

At this point, the Hydra fired a second volley. Cadelia's deck shook, the windows in the captain's cabin quivered. One of the masts broke and almost crushed the fighters with it. The guns were deliberately aimed more upwards to cause damage in sails.

Sel started for the door.

* * *

As Cadelia crossed sword with Sel, Ramsey stormed below the deck to scare the kidnapped, leading the men behind him.

But the desperate highlanders, knowing that they were in a trap from which they might not come out alive, if they did not act together, fiercely defended themselves. Some of them tore the weapon of the opponent, hitting them with fists or slamming foreheads against the bridge of the opponent's nose. The women lagged a bit until the men got their weapons, which was unexpectedly easy enough. Maya struck one of the sailors with her sword as he was going to drive a dagger into her fiancé. Mikela, the alewife made her way upstairs, where an agitated sailor dragged one of the women, then slit his throat. They both shared their weapons and joined the fighting on board.

Taking a cursory glance at his men during the fight, Ramsey saw that they suddenly lost their zeal again, as if fearing their opponents. They gave up too easily.

"Sons of the dog!" He yelled at them, trying to get them to order. "This brood is confusing you! Kill them!"

However, contradictory feelings completely confused the sailors. The fear of the captain's anger and the fear of the captain's retribution made them feel completely lost. The highlanders took advantage of this opportunity.

But they did not protect their sorcerer enough.

With a battle cry, Ramsey strode toward Ross, who was holding a sword in his hand. The blades screeched malevolently. The smaller Ross had a hard time countering the attack of a strong opponent, in addition skilled in all fights, which cannot be said about Ross.

"Mommy says you were naughty!" Ramsey brought his face close to his.

"This time there will not be a spank!"

The fear of Ramsey's words made Ross shivers down his spine and he mingled with sweat. His body remembered punches and kicks. The mind knew cruelty well.

"Ross!" Oliver called to him. "You are not alone here!"

Maybe he want to say that his friends are also here? Or maybe that he is responsible for the fate of his companions and must not give up?

Maybe both.

He said nothing more, absorbed in the fight with the freed sailor, the same to whom he had given orders just hours earlier. Ramsey thought fleetingly that she would deal with him later in thanks for Cadelia's interest. As long as the other is still alive.

For now, he relished the fear of his opponent pressed against the wall.

He could see the fear in Ross's eyes.

Ross understood the full meaning of his friend's words. Help was coming. People need it.

He can't give up.

It's easier to think than to do. Ramsey was much stronger than him.

Belatedly, Ross regretted that he hadn't put in too much training.

"Caddy is dealing with your other whore right now, sweetheart," Ramsey smirked venomously. "Luckily, the last one in your life. If you listen, you might hear him dying squealing like a slaughtered pig! Almost like Nim."

"Nim..." Ross replied with effort, "he wasn't screaming. He died like a hero. Sword in hand."

"He killed himself because he was a coward!"

"He did it because your guys wanted to give him a cruel death. He would rather kill himself than die in agony before my eyes!"

Ramsey watched him with quiet satisfaction, waiting for the tears to come.

"You get haughty," he remarked, with a mixture of appreciation and mockery at the same time, as if such a thought had never even occurred to him before. "If you weren't a whore, maybe I'd make a man out of you."

Ross looked at him, wanting Ramsey to read the contempt in his eyes with all his might. He was trembling with the effort. The use of power and weakening after the action of the poison severely weakened his strength.

This time he could lose. He will not get out of death as he has done before. He could feel it.

"It's over, Ross," Ramsey said with odd composure, confirming his fears.

"The end will be whatever I want," said a voice.

Ramsey felt the sword touch his back. Ross looked over his shoulder.

Sel was one step behind his tormentor. He was covered in blood.

Ramsey's face tightened with anxiety and anger as he realized who the voice belonged to and as he saw his opponent's reaction.

"Caddy!" He shouted to the deck. "Caddy!"

"She won't hear you," Sel said softly.

Ramsey looked around. It was only now that he noticed that his men had been defeated, and it was oddly quiet outside. The fight was over.

Ross watched the despair in Ramsey's gaze, his face turning red. The hands trembled like an old man. There was a gleam in his eyes.

He really loved his mother.

"I'm the captain of this ship, son of a dog!" Ramsey roared to everyone present. "I want a fight! If you want to take the ship, you have to defeat me first. Otherwise I swear by all the demons of this and every other world that I will come back here as a ghost and torment you until you all hang on the rope! You're not gonna fuck me like a ram here! I'm Ramsey Taren, Captain of Cadelia, and I demand a fair duel!"

The crew defeated by the highlanders shouted with appreciation, cheered by his words. It was the captain they knew. Their captain.

The angry highlanders began to protest.

Sel looked at his lover pressed against the wall.

He saw his desperation and weariness. He could only imagine how the other felt.

He raised his head a little to say loud and clear:

"Agreed. There will be a duel!"

Everyone fell silent.

Ramsey smiled in satisfaction. Ross's heart almost stopped.

"Sel, I will fight!" He shouted. "It's my business!"

But Ramsey ignored his words and turned to his opponent. He spat on the floor. Sel stared at him, composed and calm as he had learned through the years of illness.

"You didn't heal to die now," Ross said half pleadingly to him.

"A touching scene, I'm about to cry," Ramsey sneered, at which his people laughed maliciously.

"I said it would end any way I want it," Sel replied calmly.

"And I want him dead."

Sel's tone made even Ramsey say nothing. Ross suddenly remembered the grotesque mask on Sel's face on that fateful day as they rode to aid the healer. A mask he painted for him. Julien once said it was like Sel's second face.

Mask of death.

Oliver, on the other hand, recognized the tone of his voice. Last time Sel had foretold Moren's death this way.

"I loved you..." said Sel then...

"Ross," Sel smiled slightly, dispelling the dark memories. "Don't be afraid, I'll be fine. Don't be afraid."

Sel did it for him.

Ross replied with a smile, soft and tender from the bottom of his heart.

The Jewel glowed with a soft glow.

"Enough of this circus!" Ramsey yelled, charging at Sel.

Sel countered the blow with childish ease. Gone are the days when he was a weak, sick man. Daily training, at first under the supervision of the queen's soldiers, and then on their own, into which even Vivan was eventually drawn into, put Sel in a form he had never hoped to get in his earlier life. This was not yet the peak of his abilities, as he well knew, but Kirian, the commander of the guard, praised him for his skillful use of what he had already learned and for his cleverness at concealing his weaknesses. He trained him with the best, and so did Vivan, giving them a good workout and not allowing them to feel sorry for himself. For their sake, he used to say, though there were times when Sel thought he was starting to hate him.

Now he had the opportunity to see what these trainings were worth.

He did not consider failure. It was not an act of pride or vanity. Sel did not think about defeat. He focused on getting the job done. He did not consider any option other than victory. Ross would break down. Ramsey would never pay for the harm he did to him. Perhaps he would have entered a fight that could only end with Ross' death today.

He had to beat him.

Ramsey sensed his opponent and understood that it would not be as easy as he had anticipated. He felt pleasantly surprised by this. Finally, for a long time, he had found a good opponent, one that he did not expect too much at first. He always had a bad opinion of pussies. They are tearful and cannot fight. Meanwhile, he was first surprised by Ross, who had resisted him three years ago, but lost to his strength. Then his lover, Nim, an archer who had just joined the royal guard. The archer could not win against five seasoned men, unless he had completed training. Nim didin't make it...

Now this one. Caddy said it's some artist who draws pictures; a knight helping old men, a real lady, who will cry when someone push her.

Caddy was blind sometimes. Ramsey immediately recognized that the boy is not timid and trains hard. The woman wanted to see what she wanted, that's all.

Caddy...

He attacked again lunging forward. Sel spun the blade and returned the blow, forcing Ramsey to blockade. The swords rang singingly. As they circled each other, they struck and blocked as people fled sideways.

The older man's experience was making itself felt, but Sel seemed to be hiding an inexhaustible energy under his apparent calmness. He did not allow himself to be provoked into stupid outbursts. Kirian wouldn't forgive him. Ramsey was counting on it. At times the blows were so strong that they vibrated in the wrists. Several people cheered in admiration for Sel's skill and composure. Oliver clenched his hands into fists. Ross's hand tightened on his sword hilt. Alesei stood on the steps next to the innkeeper and judged the fight with a trained eye.

The swords struck each other so fast they blurred in the air. Both opponents splashed with sweat. Ramsey tended to expose his left side, but he made such quick counterattacks with a force that made the bones in Sel's body shake that it was impossible to reach him there.

"Come on, Sel!" Alesei exclaimed. "He wants to tire you!"

Even for less experienced people it has already become clear. Ramsey hoped his strength would help him win as usual. Sel let himself to way up the stairs, never taking his eyes off his opponent. After a while they were both on deck, where the rain was still lashing and the wind was blowing. This allowed Sel's aching muscles to cool down a bit.

Ramsey loved to show off in front of onlookers. It was obvious that fighting on board suited him better. They had more space and more eyes to watch the duel.

Sel had to put an end to it quickly.

They began to circle each other.

"What's up, knight?" Ramsey sneered. "Are you tired? My mistress scratched your face pretty well, huh? Was it good for you to kill Ross's mother?"

"Don't call her that," Sel replied grimly. "The only woman who could be his mother was Valeri. No one else!"

"That old whore?" Ramsey laughed. "I fucked her a once or twice..."

Sel liked Valeri and many of the other inhabitants of the House of Pleasure, who always treated him well and friendly as family. Ramsey wanted to provoke him. He will pretend to give him what he expects...

He leapt forward, marking a blow to Ramsey's left side. Ramsey quickly blocked the blow with retorts. Sel made Ramsey's sword whistle harmlessly in the air and got close enough to slap Ramsey in the face a couple of times.

"This is for Ross," he drawled.

Ramsey wiped the blood from his broken nose and spat. He charged Sel, relying on his unfailing strength, rejoicing at the sight of his enemy's weariness.

Then a voice rang out from behind him.

"Ramsey..."

He would recognize that voice anywhere. He distracted. He parried Sel's blows, now only dreaming of seeing her again. She was alive...

Sel seized the opportunity to end the fight. He cringed and lunged forward, sword pointing at his opponent's chest.

He stabbed him with a strong push.

Ramsey choked and grabbed his hands. He slowly pushed it away from him, drawing his sword.

He fell to his knees.

"Caddy..." he said strangely pathetically.

Sel propped himself up against his sword, exhausted from the fight, and Ross fell to him worriedly.

Cadelia stood up, her hands bound and the chain loosely wrapped around her neck. She broke through to her lover and kissed him tenderly, crying. He clumsily hugged her to him, weakening his strength, and looked at the couple standing next to him.

To everyone's amazement, he nodded respectfully, looking at Sel as if congratulating him on a good fight. Sel refrained from a similar gesture, and the smuggler merely smiled. He lay down, supported by Cadelia, and touched her face with a strange devotion, a gesture that marked real affection.

"Caddy..." he choked out, "put the boat in Ross's hands."

"What?!" She asked shocked. "No way!"

Startled, Ross stared at Ramsey in amazement, unable to speak.

"I said something to you, woman!" Ramsey shouted at her. "Give him the boat! This is your son! He has the right to burn it if he wants to!"

"It's my ship!" She screamed desperately, as if her heart was being ripped out her breasts.

"More important than him?" He asked hoarsely, slowly fading away.

"Yes," she replied, looking her son straight in the eye and holding his accusing gaze.

"You... are... ree-al... devil," Ramsey gasped out before he died.

Cadelia looked at him, hugged him and kissed him one last time. With her tied hands, she managed to close his now unseeing eyes.

Ross felt tears under his eyelids. Sel hugged him gently. The Jewel surrounded his heart with a soothing warmth, and Alesei and Oliver stood beside him. But nothing could comfort him now. Even the highlanders looked at him with sympathy, and at his mother with anger.

Nothing could change her feelings.

Finally, she looked at him, cold and inaccessible. She stood up like a queen, proudly and worthily standing in front of him. Despite the ties, chain, tangled and wet hair, fuzzy makeup and a battered head - that's what she looked like. She looked like a ruler.

"Me, the first officer of the sailing ship Cadelia, bearing my name," she began, "before everyone gathered here, I hand the ship over to Ross Hope, who is here," she stopped, and Ross bit his lip, "and I make him Captain of Cadelia," she finished, putting all the contempt of the defeated. "May you learn to sail it," she added venomously.

Ross thought he might not accept this gift. He could burn it with her. But even after so many years of suffering, he could not evoke such hatred. Only regret.

And sadness.

"I accept the gift, mother," he replied calmly.

Her gaze was indifferent, as if she wanted to show him that all his efforts would be useless.

He knew about it. And like an open wound, the pain continued.

"I'll spare you the trouble," she muttered under her breath as she walked over to the scattered loads. She climbed it with some difficulty and stood on the balustrade.

Nobody stopped her. People only purred angrily or shouted at her loudly.

"Stop her?" Alesei asked.

"No," Ross said softly, agreeing with her in that.

Cadelia looked out over the sea, slowly waning after the storm. Clouds still obscured the sky, and there were no stars.

There were sharks waiting for her below, hiding under ships, waiting to feed.

Death will not be easy as her life was not. She made it like that herself.

And now she has lost her love and her beloved ship. These bastards crashed into its side.

Ross probably will burn it.

He wasted her life and took what she loved. That's how she saw it. He never wanted to do the right thing. Even Ramsey couldn't raise him.

She sighed.

Then she suddenly felt a blow. A brief flash of pain before she could understand what was happening. She looked around and, right in front of her son, saw this beautiful boy, Delen, whom she had previously inadvertently appointed guardian of the abductees.

He lowered the hand in which he was holding something a moment ago.

And suddenly she saw it. It was sticking out in her breast. A bolt head, bigger than the others.

A bolt fired from a huge crossbow.

From the deck of Hydra.

She fell into the depths of the water, dying before the sharks caught their prey...

For a moment, no one spoke. Oliver lowered his head, waiting for the first accusing words. Instead, he felt a hand on his shoulder and a soothing warmth that calmed his pounding heart.

Ross only said in a low voice:

"Thank you."

As if this would suddenly break the shackles of silence among the gathered people who were moved to their core. Standing at the side of her husband found during the fight, the alewife Mikela was the first to shout happily:

"Cheers, Captain Hope!"

All but the imprisoned Cadelia's sailors suddenly united in this joy and cried out after her:

"Cheers! Cheers!"

In the crowd of the freed and their relatives, among the sailors of Hydra and Cadelia, Ross stood surrounded by his friends and accepted a tribute he had never expected in his life.

And then everyone started saying hello and congratulating themselves on winning the fight, enjoying the reunion and their regained freedom. Ross accepted the congratulations, the friendly hugs of the women, and the pats on the shoulder for a while, trying to enjoy their joy, but couldn't. Then, with his permission, Alesei ordered a feast on Cadelia's supplies, taking advantage of the fact that the weather was starting to settle down.

He then embraced Sel and whispered that he had no more strength for anything else.

Sel kissed his forehead with concern and led him to the captain's cabin, where luckily Oliver, having sensed the moment a little earlier, made sure to change the sheets and open the windows. He passed them silently. At Sel's urging, Ross handed over command to one of the men recommended by Captain Noren. They were greeted with good-night wishes, especially the highlanders who had been with Ross from the beginning and expressed their concern and support.

Ross appreciated their kindness, but right now he was fed up with both this and the rest of the day's impressions. He had a feeling of almost incredible emptiness and some kind of inner trembling, as if his soul had been placed on uncertain and cracked foundations.

He felt it was about to fall apart. He will kneel among those happy people who are satisfied with the successful action. It will just start to howl.

And will not stop...

Chapter X

Tenan

Mayene put a hand on the tired Tenan's shoulder. She had dragged him to the grove behind Semerald's and Kirst Kalen's house, not giving him a moment's rest since she had come to him at dusk the previous day. She said it was the punishment for sleeping with another woman, believing his story about the hooker.

In fact, she loved tormenting him. Every reason was good. She did not care the rest.

Tenan looked terrible after his experiences with the bracelet and his late-night frolics.

The shadows under the gray eyes made him look terminally ill.

Mayene loved it when her victim staggered with weariness. Each time she visited him, Tenan would gather strength for the next meeting, sleeping long and eating a large meal, because if the witch was with him, she would not let him eat, drink or sleep. He well knew that depriving him of his strength made her wildly happy. Just as he realized he didn't just feel just tired after her visits. At night, she drained his strength. He could barely concentrate, and it was easy to make a mistake at such moments.

It seemed to him that she waited for his mistake, until he made it, until she finally revealed some weakness that she could drill down at will, just like having sex together, when he was exhausting himself. She was enjoying it. Not if he lived up to her expectations as a man. What she enjoyed most was killing him slowly, destroying his young life and beauty, and most of all the fact that he was fully aware of this terrible truth and that he could do nothing about it. She hoped he would soon see his stupid and unfounded hope, hardness, and strength that had helped him endure finally fade away and be replaced by fear.

Then the real nightmare is just about to begin.

So the first mistake against her would be to show fear.

The second is to oppose it. He learned about it painfully the first night.

Third - show her that he cares about someone.

The morning in the valley was dark. It always did before the sun reached her from beyond the ridge of the mountains. The still omnipresent cold penetrated throughout.

Tenan was trembling. He dreamed of finally being in the house they watched. Unfortunately, given the company he was presently with, the sole purpose of this visit to the household would be murder.

"He sleeps there tonight," she whispered in his ear. He knew he meant a healer. "You'll kill before he wakes up. Let the sight of his body shake them deeply!"

He was silent. If she wanted him to do this, she had to give him a clear order. That's how the curse worked. He was doing nothing wrong of his own free will. When Moren told him to kill Milera, for example, he gave him a rope. It was a clear order: "Kill."

He wasn't going to help Mayene or make anything easy for her. If she wanted his services, she had to order him. Otherwise, he will find a way to get around the curse. It has happened before.

He didn't ask who his target was.

He was afraid of the answer.

"What are you going to do?" He asked grimly.

"Do you want to oppose me? Your eyes are turning blue."

"I don't know what you're talking about," he replied coldly. "I can't see my face and I don't know what color my pupils are at any given moment! Honestly, I don't care!"

Her iridescent eyes flashed, but that meant nothing to him. He couldn't guess her thoughts.

The sight of those eyes had long since left its mark on his memory...

She turned his head to look in the direction she was pointing; as if he were a puppet in her hands, which became more and more painful with each passing day. The back door of the house, leading to the riverside garden, creaked in the silence around him.

"Here's your victim," she whispered in his ear, smiling. "Kill her, Tenan. I order you."

"She gave the order," he thought despairingly as he watched the female figure move towards the river.

She didn't tell him how to kill. She only gave hints on what the body should look like after death. This meant that he could do it in his own way, which is not quite the will of his present principal.

"You will obey when they tell you to kill. Submissive when ordered to torture. Diligent when ordered to hurt the innocent."

"Ah yes, Krispine?" He thought mockingly, skillfully hiding his soul behind a false mirror of white, inhuman eyes. "It all depends on the interpretation of the order...".

Mayene did not say to kill with particular cruelty. She ordered the body to be left in a terrible condition.

He always stuck to details. These were the details that allowed him to survive. It didn't matter to his victims. Probably also for their relatives. But for him, yes. He was desperately trying to avoid cruelty.

He was carefully following his every gesture now. Mayene watched his face.

The trembling stopped. He stopped feeling cold under the influence of emotions.

"You will not free me from the curse," his thoughts turned to Julien with a hint of regret. "Not after what I will do."

It was the end of his hope.

If it is to be so, if all he can do is moderate the sentence - he will do it. They hate him anyway. Julien must forget about her forbearance. She must forget her feelings for him. She will hate him like the others. For good.

He murdered two old servants who loved Julien and Oliver as their own children, they knew them from an early age. So what if he did it quickly and they felt no pain?

He killed Milera on the orders of Moren. What is the significance of the fact that he threw her out the window to spare her friend and husband the sight of agony? Moren wanted Milera to be killed in front of everyone, for example - but he didn't say it outright.

He killed Sel's father before he woke up. The other hadn't even fully realized what had happened.

He inflicted a quick death whenever he had the opportunity to do so.

It was his only weapon against the evil he was commanded to do.

He couldn't argue. When the order was given, his whole body focused on carrying it out. He had no power over it, but he always found a loophole in the curse. It was in such detail as it had happened now.

There was a difference between death in agony and a quick death with defilement of the body.

He spared pain and anguish.

But Mayene is not Moren.

Mayene will get his number.

And then its end will be unenviable.

If Julien hated him, he couldn't let that happen.

He couldn't protect her in any other way. In fact, it would be better for all of them if he died.

He watched now as she returned home from her leisurely stroll, unaware of her fate, before the burst of daily duties. Seme...

She will not be his victim...

He had gathered as much strength as he could. He knew all too well what his plan might end in a moment.

Mayene will kill him.

She stood next to him, like a lover, with one hand wrapped around his waist, pressed against his back, her head resting on his shoulder. He slipped out of her embrace, from the touch of her cold body.

He looked at her.

The dagger of his left hand, hidden under his sleeve, was freed by a clever mechanism as Tenan twisted and plunged it into the witch's belly to the hilt. She gasped in surprise. He knew it wasn't enough to kill her. He found out about it when she came to his bedside the first night. He then cut her twice. It was hard to hit. He did not win, and he almost paid for his achievement with his life. But now he was glad she had lost her vigilance and let him hurt herself. Apparently, she was counting on him being too weak to stand up to her. When she instinctively bowed her head after the blow, he did not wait. He grabbed a lock of her red hair and determinedly cut as much as he could hold.

He was sure that the witch would feel their loss painfully. There was no limit to her vanity in this regard. She loved them, brushed them, and played with them. Although he knew that it would not help him at all, he cut off a large handful of them to deprive her of this pleasure, also for his own satisfaction. He was right.

Mayene screamed a groan, gripping her hand where the hair had grown shorter, as if she had peeled a patch of skin off her head. In the blink of an eye, the clip was blackened and turned to dust.

Tenan took advantage of her astonishment and cut her throat... But the blow did not hurt her. Not even blood flowed.

He got closer and hit more accurately than anyone else. He inflicted fatal wounds on her, and she only smiled maliciously, though she felt the blows.

He was lost.

Hearing the scream, Seme stopped nearby and watched in amazement as the red-haired woman grabbed the young man by the neck and knocked him to the ground as if he were just a rag doll. It was so unusual and so terrifying that at first, instead of calling for help, she froze with horror and amazement. However, she quickly realized who the woman nearby was. She hesitated to decide whether to call for help or save the brave boy Mayene sat on, and after a short struggle in which he was clearly too weak, forces him to kiss him. She noticed with horror how it deprived him not only of his strength, but visibly devastating. Mayene fed on his vitality. If Seme returns home now unnoticed by the witch, perhaps she will survive alive, but there will be no help for him.

She picked up a few stones and threw them accurately at the upstairs windows of the house. The glass shattered in the windows of the room occupied by Paphian and Dinn.

"Hey!" She shouted boldly to the witch, being fully aware that she only had a stone in her clenched hand against her.

But judging by the boy who was wilting, it might be too late in a moment.

Mayene looked up, tearing her lips away from those of the half-dead Tenan. Leaning in this way, she looked like a tiger devouring its prey. Seme's eyes scared her.

"Leave him alone!" She shouted bravely, though her voice trembled at the same time.

The whistle of the arrow interrupted Mayene's grim smile as she grabbed her prey, she rolled with it away from the elven archer, which appeared right behind her. Seme breathed a little as she saw Dinn nod at her and disappeared.

"You did not obey the order, my dear," whispered the witch to her lover.

She looked around carefully and hissed. After the kiss, the wound on the stomach and neck closed and began to heal. Still conscious, Tenan could only look into her eyes, which filled him with dread.

"I'll give you another one," she whispered to him lasciviously. "Only to watch you get tired and die, because you will not have the strength to fulfill it. I'd love to see your brain drain from your ears." She clung to him as Dinn flashed past searching for her, but the magic camouflage hid them too well. "Tenan..." She kissed him on the cheek with a mocking smile. "Go back to the inn. Immediately. I order you."

He made his last effort and spat in her face with contempt.

She wiped her face with satisfaction. She left in an unnatural haste.

His head began to throb with a slight pain. He knew that this would change soon.

At least she withdrew that order. She said, "I'll give you another one." Didn't that mean she would cancel the previous one? For him it was unambiguous.

Dinn heard him first and found him partially submerged in the cold water of the river. Tenan felt cold and damp seep through him, but he barely had the strength to move his hand.

"Dinn!" Seme cried.

"Here!" Dinn exclaimed, hastily pulling Tenan out of the water. "Hold on. Vivan will help you soon," he told him.

"I very... doubt it," Tenan whispered, not having the strength to add a little irony to the sentence.

The pain was getting worse. Seme knelt beside them.

"What's your name?" She asked.

"Tenan..."

"He stood up to the witch," Seme praised him proudly. "He wounded her, but the scumbag stuck to him and her health improved."

"Please..." he couldn't remember the last time he used that word.

He wanted to avoid tormenting death at all costs. Yesterday's meeting with Julien gave him a foretaste of what he was facing. He would rather be killed immediately than die a death like this.

"I have to get back to the inn."

"Hush…" his would-be victim whispered, stroking his head. "We'll take you home and warm you up…"

"I'll be dead," he replied bitterly.

"Actually, I deserved it," he added glumly in his mind.

Dinn frowned, the only one who understood what was happening.

"She ordered you…?" He began, but at that moment came the crack of breaking glass from the upper window and the familiar howl, but much longer, full of pain. Seme jumped to her feet.

"It's from Vivan's room!" She screamed.

"Go…" he told the elf with an effort, feeling the pain in his head growing bigger.

"Forgive me," whispered Dinn as he walked away. "Seme, stay with him. Call for help!"

Seme, though she was very concerned about Vivan, obeyed. She would not have done otherwise. She would not leave the wounded man to his fate.

"People!" She cried, "Peopleee! Come here!"

The houses were not too far apart and after a while they heard calls on the neighbors' farms. Seme kept calling for help until she saw the first coming from her seat.

* * *

It was because Vivan soothing presence that Vashaba put her off guard. Vivan fell asleep feeling safe, relying on her skill. His mood affected Vashaba before she even noticed it. The proximity of the healer enveloped her senses like a warm and soft blanket on a winter night. His presence, smell, touch, even when she put her hand on his to see if it was warm, at the same time guided by a secret longing, put her instincts to sleep. Vivan did not do this consciously. This was how he acted on people when he himself was in a good mood. The elves were no exception, though a seasoned representative of this family should have foreseen that something like this would happen and not be influenced by his influence.

Instead of be awake, Vashaba, soothed by his presence, lay down next to him and soon fell blissfully asleep, holding his hand. Even a scream from outside did not wake her up.

When Mayene burst into their bedroom, Vashaba only had time to turn towards the intruder and open her eyes.

In the next moment the witch grabbed her neck and hit her against the wall with incredible force.

Everything happened quickly.

Vivan, still dressed except for his shoes, was horrified to see Mayene yank Vashaba off the floor and hitting her head twice against the wall with all her might. An unpleasant knock at these blows and a trace of blood clearly indicated that the witch was about to split the girl's skull. He jumped towards the witch, shocked by her speed and the damage she had done in a short moment. He heard Vashaba's pulse fade in his head. He had nothing at hand. The zeal of friends and brother meant that the sword was now useless on the dresser, that is, in this situation, as if at the end of the world. He grabbed a lock of Mayene's hair and tugged it.

"Leave her!" He shouted.

Mayene has gone mad. Again, someone dares to touch her hair! She twisted off his handle and pushed him against a room door that someone was trying to open. The oak door made a hollow noise, and for a moment Vivan felt as if his spine was snapped.

"Where's Vashaba's sword?! Or at least her dagger?!"

"On the bed..."

With a groan of pain, he lunged in that direction. Mayene leapt over to him, sitting on him as she had on Tenan before.

"Don't stood up to me!" She hissed furiously, looking him straight in the eyes. "Do what I say, or I'll turn your whole little town into a bloodbath!"

Outside the door he heard Paphian and Julien calling.

Apparently, Vashaba closed it. The thuds showed that the brother was trying to force his way to them.

"What do you want?!" He asked, staring fearlessly into her amazing eyes. At least he was trying to make it look like that.

"Your power."

"That's what I expected."

"I want life in my womb!" She leaned towards him.

There was a silence, broken only by knocks on the door and calls of a few voices.

Vashaba's heart was beating less and less. Her body lay limp, her arm unnaturally contorted. Vivan felt with his whole being her life fading away with each passing moment.

Mayene waited as if the time of the world belonged only to them, sure of hers. She was staring at him. She sat on him, enjoying the sight of her future toy, with which, in the name of love for his relatives and friends, she would do whatever she wanted. Her body radiated with excitement at the mere thought of it. He could feel it.

In his memoirs, unwanted images of debauchery in the royal castle came to life. His body rebelled, torn between disgust and desire. Mayene's excitement had made him feel unfamiliar feelings that were now both disgusting and lit a fire within him. Against his will, he reacted to physical contact with a woman who wanted him. His own acute senses, especially compassion, tortured him, arousing both craving and disgust at the same time. He was avenged by his inexperience in erotic sensations and the hitherto hidden longing for the closeness of another human being...

The horror of the words spoken had not yet faded into the air when

Mayene added firmly:

"Give me a baby, healer. You will be my husband. Then and only then I will show grace and not murder your loved ones or bring destruction to the town. Got it?"

She gave him the order, always used to being in control no one dares to oppose it. She was sure it would be the same this time. She smiled lasciviously, letting him know that she knew about his feelings. Very slowly, hating her with all his soul for what feelings she awakened in him, he replied very clearly, slowly drawing his words:

"Over my dead body..."

If she had known him better, she would have known that she had made him angry with threats about family and friends, and this, especially of him as a healer who loved people with all his heart despite being hurt, made him capable of extraordinary things in their defense, he did not even suspect.

In addition, she clearly announced to him that she intends to rule his life, and he decided to absolutely never let to this...

He put his hand on her breast, surely, without any ambiguity, consumed with anger, into which he had melted the new sensations that burst through him.

"You have my power, witch!" He whispered ominously.

The heat like hot lava seeped into her and seeped into her lifeless heart. Vivan's eyes gleamed. The shining glow spread through the veins and little veins beneath his skin like a wave. Mayene froze in surprise and amazement, staring at this fascinating phenomenon.

In the next moment she felt incredible energy penetrating her body, spreading through it, flowing where the blood was supposed to flow, and suddenly in the dead body shell that she had to hold on to feeding on someone else's vitality, she felt the power accumulated around her heart. And this...

It started to beat...

She was scared like never before. The healer knew! The healer has discovered her secret!

What is alive can be killed...

She groaned, filled with sudden dread.

"Enough!" She called, but Vivan wasn't going to stop. He wanted to revive her, then to keep alive her beating heart.

Mayene, angry and scared, made up her mind at all costs brutally interrupt this process.

With a force far beyond human capacity, she placed a hand on his, grasped it, and twisted it until the bones crackled. Vivan cried out in excruciating pain. His glow vanished without finishing the work. Mayene didn't stop there. In revenge for his action, she pressed against the broken arm and crushed it below the elbow with her strength, causing another wave of pain within him. However, he managed to take the witch with his good hand and tried again with difficulty. She screamed in terror and jumped to the window, shattering the glass.

Vashaba's pulse was ceasing.

Paphian has almost punched a hole in the door next to the lock.

Vivan half rolled, half fell to the floor and crawled over to the dying girl. He sat down next to her with an effort.

"You asked for it," Mayene hissed, glaring at him furiously.

"I'll find another way."

He saw his sword in her hands. Standing over him, she lifted it up.

Instinctively he covered the injured girl with himself.

She will die in a moment.

He held the unconscious hand of Vashaba, giving her his power, praying that the girl would survive when he was gone.

He was no longer thinking about anything else.

It didn't cross his mind for a moment that he might have acted differently, that he might have saved his life by running away. If Mayene killed him, maybe it would satisfy her enough to leave Vashaba alone. She must live...

She must live.

She showed him a touch of a different world of feelings that he had barely realized before. For her he was not a healer, priest, count. He knew and felt it. He could see it in her eyes. Even at night, he wondered, discovered buried, trampled feelings, destroyed by others in the king's castle, distorted, tainted. Yesterday he looked at it differently. He discovered that it could be different, maybe even... If he could change something about himself...

Vashaba's kiss awakened something in him that he did not even suspect about himself. As if it had been a stone form until now suddenly life was breathed into it. Mayene's physical closeness, so different from what he had known so far, confused him as sensuality began to awaken in his body. Misinterpreting this, Vivan hated himself for his reaction.

Now he mentally pleaded with the God of his beloved grandparents, who was as powerful and great as they had told him all his life, whose symbol was still hanging on the chain around his neck - he merely asked forgiveness for the filthy thoughts in front of Mayene, lest God's anger against him not devoured a girl whose feelings were sincere and pure in their intentions. "Save her. I am begging you... You can...".

Brought up in two different traditions, in the last moments he turned to God, whom he respected on an equal footing with Mother Earth, but who right now thanks to the strong faith of his grandparents and mother, even in the new world, where they came, did not forget about him, he spent to be above all power and magic in this world.

A powerful creature whose power could also oppose a being alien to this world.

Dinn got into the room through a broken window. Mayene turned around at the sight of the elf and quickly abandoned her murderous plan. She flashed past him, slashing his face blindly before he could use his dagger. Pain and fear prevented Dinn from going any further. Blood flowed. He knelt on the floor, touching his face.

Paphian and Kirst finally got inside. At the sight of Vivan and Vashaba, Paphian turned white and knelt beside the wounded.

Drenched in sweat, suffering terrible torments, Vivan was still clutching Vashaba's still hand, fearing that she might fall into death.

Dinn, with a bleeding cut across the left side of his face, reached his sister and the healer.

"Solai," he whispered anxiously, crouching down to stroke her hand, touching her clothes, and removing the beautiful purple hair from her face with tears in his eyes, oblivious to his own pain and the blood that meant everything he touched.

"She's alive," Vivan said, trembling all over his body. "Paphian..." he whispered in low despair. "I have to reset my hand."

Paphian already knew how his brother was being treated. Recently, he had the opportunity to observe it in the capital. He regretted the thought of how much his brother would have to suffer now. Whether he will do it himself or someone will help him, the pain will unfortunately be just as unbearable.

"Don't do everything at once," he sat down beside him. "First, heal it, let it survive somehow, until you recover." Then he turned to the elf, seeing that he had no intention of departing from his sister. "Dinn, you're hurt. Do something about it. Then you'll come back," he tried to calm him down.

Vivan whispered softly to Dinn, unable to control his voice from the trembling:

"She will be safe with me. I will not let her die. Go."

"I'll help him," said Sai, who followed Paphian with Julien.

"Good," Paphian breathed a sigh of relief.

Sai was always composed, she had nerves of steel. He could rely on her.

The woman helped Dinn to stand up and with an innate gentleness led him to her room.

Without a word, Julien brought the blanket and covered Vivan, who was shaking.

"I... I can't. Can't do that," the healer, chattering with his teeth, stammered to his brother. "Her mind is in ruins. It is ruined. If... if... I leave her... like that...

"You won't. You just must let yourself cool down. I wouldn't try to make you feel bad, you know. Vivan..." Paphian embraced him gently without touching his right shoulder. "It's gonna hurt like hell. You may pass out in pain and then she..."

"Yes," the Healer replied softly, looking at his foster uncle and Julien, who smiled faintly for comfort. "I know... But it is fucking hurts!" He groaned.

They felt sorry for him, but there was no way they could help him. Only support. Julien gently stroked his cheek, and his adoptive uncle lightly squeezed the hand holding Vashaba's hand. Vivan felt the tears streaming down his face. If only they knew...

"When will you be ready...?" Paphian asked softly.

Vivan was shaking constantly. He held Vashaba's hand, feeling the life returning to her. He is not finished yet, but if he holds back his healing process, he will suffer for a long time.

"I'm scared," he whispered to them.

Paphian moved closer to him. Julien kissed his sweaty forehead she tactfully left the room, taking her uncle.

There were only the three of them left.

"Just do that," Paphian whispered reassuringly. "You faced an evil witch. You can do it. Then it will all be over."

Vivan snuggled against his brother's shoulder as best he could. He was ashamed of his earlier feelings. He was afraid of the pain.

Paphian's eyes were full of tears. He tried to hide them. He wanted to be a real support for his brother.

"Let her go now," he whispered to Vivan. "Can you?"

"I love you, brother," Paphian whispered to him. "I'm with you."

"I swear," said Vivan angrily, all overwhelmed with regret, "that as soon as I get myself together I'll smash this bitch!"

Paphian, unaware of Vivan's dilemmas, smiled slightly at the words. Usually his brother tried to be aloof.

Vivan released Vashaba's hand. He took a breath as if it would help him do something he allowed the regeneration process to begin. The arm snapped back into place. Immediately after that, the bone below the elbow returned to its former state with an unpleasant crunch and began to heal.

The gathered people inside and out heard a shrill scream that was unstoppable, though Vivan pressed his face into his brother's arms. Julien buried her face in her hands. Sai and Dinn froze in compassion and concern, and Kirst clenched his hands in regret and anger. Seme stopped at the top of the stairs. Before that, she had made sure that Tenan was taken to the inn at his pleading request. His head hurt badly. Seme assumed it was probably from hitting the ground. She felt a little sorry for him for not wanting to take advantage of her hospitality and care, but she softened at the sight of his desperate gaze at his beautiful amber eyes. Now she stood at the top of the stairs, surrounded by neighbors devastated by the suffering of their beloved healer, hiding sorrow and tears in her hands. As soon as he stopped screaming, she ran upstairs to comfort him.

Vivan passed out from pain, interrupting his treatment and treatment of Vashaba. Paphian set him down on the bed and sighed at the sight of Seme.

"You're okay," he noted warmly, and she hugged him tightly and stroked his hair.

He did not hide how much he needed such a gesture now.

Seme bustled about with the wounded. She kissed Vivan on the cheek, woke him up, and quickly administered some ointments and tinctures for the pain, using Paphian and Julien. The hand wasn't fused yet, the swelling was still visible, but Vivan was still stubbornly holding Vashaba's hand in his, wanting to heal it completely. Apparently, it was worse than anyone had the courage to ask, or there was a feeling behind it, slowly emerging in Vivan's heart, and a desire to atone for his sins. Vashaba was next to Vivan. Seme hugged them both warmly. She also took care of the unfortunate Dinn, whom Sai had helped by giving a few drops of the healer's blood. He sat timidly on the edge of the bed, as if afraid to disturb the wounded. The scar was slowly healing on the face.

He felt guilty for coming to help so late. Seme brought two armchairs with Julien, sat the elf and healer's brother in them, then stroked him comfortingly on the head. She surprised him very much with this human gesture. She could see how unexpectedly it pleased him, and wondered when the last time someone had treated him so fondly. Has anyone ever done that?

After a while, Sai sent by her handed them blankets and hot roasted grain beverage for all three of them.

Paphian noticed Dinn leaning towards Vivan and gently as if afraid to offend him, squeezed his hand in thanks. Vivan's lips twitched from a warm smile, though it really wasn't easy for him. Now the healing process for both of them was slower due to his weariness. He was grateful to Seme for the soothing herbal compresses with which she wrapped her healing arm and covered his forehead to reduce the fever. Seme had long known the usual difference between Vivan's above-average body temperature, a pre-fever in ordinary people, and a fever that inflamed his body. He couldn't fool her on that point.

By the time the coffee had cooled down and the anxious family notified by the residents had appeared at the house of his adoptive aunt and uncle, he fell asleep, still holding Vashaba's hand, although her appearance clearly indicated that she was well.

"And who's whose guardian now, Solai?" Dinn thought warmly, looking at their joined hands.

* * *

"Yeah," the innkeeper looked into Tenan's eyes, nodding regretfully.

"She is here with us for a few days. She's fond of you, huh?"

Tenan's supporters briefly told the innkeeper what had happened as he led them to the room Tenan had occupied. He quickly sent one of the maidens for drink, eat, and a bowl of water to wash.

Not to mention his visitor, he examined him closely, genuinely shocked by his condition. First, Tenan had lost a lot since he saw him yesterday. His thick dark hair had faded noticeably and thinned as if he was plagued by some serious disease; like travelers who sometimes came from far away to see the healer.

"And what, Wano?" One of the men asked. "How do you see it? Seme asked me to tell her what's with a boy. She says he saved her from the witch."

The corners of Tenan's mouth twitched slightly at the remark, but the innkeeper, who had already seen and knew a lot, and had settled the rest in his head, adding this and that, showed nothing, other than raising his thick bushy eyebrows as if in thought. Tenan watched him. The kind innkeeper looked at him intently. Finally, he sighed and turned to the questioner and his visitor:

"Tell Seme it's not good. If he is strong, and he looks like that - he will survive until tomorrow. As far as I know the witch has been torturing him since he came, so I don't give him too much hope. We will feed him, warm him and see what happens. Our healer could be help here."

Tenan was not particularly surprised by his assessment. He felt terrible. He was as weak as a kitten, he was consumed by a fever. Fortunately, the headache passed as he took his hand off when he got to the inn.

"So, you say the witch got him once?" The thin man seemed puzzled.

Two of his other companions looked at Tenan with no little interest.

The innkeeper pursed his lips, evidently angry that he had said something. Tenan looked at him with a hint of sympathy. Interesting guy, he looked like a good man.

It is a pity that he cannot serve good people. He could even work at the inn for a change.

He even worked once...

"It's not our business," replied the innkeeper at last. "Give the boy a rest and let me take care of my work. Time is running out. I'll let you know."

He led them out after a short farewell and approached the wounded man.

"Where the hell is this Ryska, for bald devil?" He muttered at the maid, but after a while he brightened, hearing a knock on the door.

Ryska brought everything with the help of a second girl who left after a while. First, however, she prepared lint and water.

"Start here," Wano told her, gently touching Tenan's head, and he hissed in pain. "Big tumor," he said. "You have a hard head. She could break it like a melon."

Tenan silently allowed himself to be dressed and washed. Wano sent the girl away when they finished wanting to talk. He calmly fed the wounded man with a few tablespoons of yesterday's reheated broth. He was not at all scared, although yesterday he witnessed a sharp quarrel between his visitor and his niece Seme and her friend. He knew that a dangerous witch visited him every night. He had shown nothing but meticulousness to make the guest eat as much as he could. Then he wiped his mouth, for which Tenan simply did not have the strength to pretend not to see the irritation in the wounded man's eyes at the weakness. He did all of this in silence, without asking anything until they were done.

Tenan wondered why the innkeeper had chosen to accompany him. Before that, he hadn't said any kind words to him, hadn't even paid much attention to him. He only asked for various services, as is the case in an inn, and the innkeeper passed on his orders to his people. And he paid for the whole week in advance. This was probably not a reason for such a favorable host and good care.

"Who were you supposed to kill?" The innkeeper asked suddenly. They measured each other with steady eyes.

"You're brave because you know I'm dying?" He replied with a question.

"Did you hear the healer is wounded?" The innkeeper said softly. "He might not be on time."

Pale as linen, Tenan looked at him thoughtfully.

"Well?" The innkeeper asked. "Then who was it supposed to be?"

"It doesn't matter anymore," he replied softly. "I didn't do it and that's it. How did you guess?" Tenan asked. "Apart from Mayene visits, no..."

"You're from Moren gang," the innkeeper interrupted him. "One of my guests lived in Wermoda, near you. He recognized you. Everyone there knew what you were doing, unofficially of course."

Tenan regarded him with renewed interest.

"Should I notify yours?" The innkeeper asked. "Just in case?"

"In the event of my death?" Tenan prompted him. "Don't beat around the bush."

"Yes. In the event of your death."

"No."

The innkeeper dipped the rag in cold water, which he held against his forehead.

"Why are you doing that?" He asked him softly.

"Because no one else will."

Tenan thought sadly of Julien. Probably nursing a healer. Life at her side was gone. He was still a prisoner of the bracelet and he was going to die as a slave.

Killer.

"It wasn't always like this," he told the innkeeper, suddenly grateful that he was not alone when his death approached.

"How was it?" The innkeeper asked softly.

"Otherwise," he suddenly felt tears welling up and regret choking in his throat.

"What to write on your grave? What do they really call you?"

"I lost my fate..." he whispered, moved by the brutality of this question painful awareness.

He sighed softly, then whispered:

"Bury me like a dog. I don't deserve more."

The innkeeper understood that nothing could be done for now. He got up, getting ready to leave.

"Son," he said gravely, "something bad has happened to you on this path of life that we all follow. This is how I see it. You deserve a better fate. Don't wait to die here. Fight. I'll be checking in here. And woe to you if I see you give up!"

"Nobody talked to me like that in years," said Tenan, his eyes sparkling.

He couldn't help it. He started to like this man.

The innkeeper looked into his amber eyes, which yesterday did not look human.

"I know a thing or two about people," he said. "I saw a traveler who came here because he wanted to escape from something. Then I found out who he was and thought he was running away from the past. And when he thinks no one sees it, his eyes become as human as they are now. Not for long, because he is afraid to reveal that he is only human. And this witch? We all heard you fighting the first night and you had to succumb to it. Then you came downstairs to us because you wanted to be among people, barely alive and hungry like a wolf. You were afraid of her. You were afraid to go back to your room, but you did come back. As if you were punishing yourself or she had such power you couldn't otherwise. And then there's Julien, Seme's niece.

You care about her, but you want her to run away from you so that the witch doesn't hurt her, right?"

Tenan watched him silently, surprised by his perceptiveness.

"So, I'm like an open book?" He sneered finally. "Pathetic. I'm getting old. Good thing I'm dying now, before I totally freak out."

But his gaze contradicted the words.

"Would you like something stronger to drink?" The innkeeper asked.

"The last cup for a convict?" Tenan asked derisively, but the innkeeper did not care about his tone.

He already knew a lot about what Tenan really was.

"And so it is," he replied, a twinkle in his eye.

"I don't used to drink with strangers. Even when dying."

"Wano," the innkeeper held out his large hand.

"Tenan," he barely had the strength to lift his, but it was better than right after the attack.

"So... Tenan..." the innkeeper smiled. "Are you drinking?"

"I won't say no."

"Sleep now, I'll come over later with some food and vodka while I get things in order."

"I'm not going anywhere," Tenan muttered.

"Certainly not for the other world!" Said the innkeeper. "You look less like a corpse than you were an hour ago."

"Because of your kitchen, good man." Tenan adjusted to the conversation easily, unstoppable by his bracelet.

"Or maybe my delicate hands, huh?" laughed Wano.

Weakened, Tenan smiled weakly.

The innkeeper said goodbye to him once more and left the room.

The smile immediately faded from his face and his heart filled with sadness.

Downstairs, his wife and Ryska were waiting impatiently for the news. Sarana worriedly placed a hand on his shoulder, seeing the power of his despondency.

"You don't have a work?" He grunted as he saw their expectant looks, but that didn't sound very convincing.

Ryska began to wring nervously on the cloth she was carrying. Her large blue eyes were staring at him.

"Is it that bad?" The alewife asked quietly, so that the first few customers in the room would not hear them.

"He's dying, Sarana," he sighed heavily, making Ryska's face twist from crying. She hastily covered it with a cloth and ran to the back room. "I don't know if he will live to see the morning."

"Maybe it's better for him," his wife said softly. "Because if the witch told him to come back here and she would come to him again..."

They looked at each other with regret.

"Such a pretty boy," she whispered. "Young, strong. He had a future ahead of him."

"If only someone would not share his fate now," Wano remarked grimly.

* * *

Even the previous day at this time, Sel had sat here, drawing in the chill of the departing winter the beauty of the fjords in front of him, unaware that the ship he had captured in his drawing had taken Ross with it. In the house next door, an elderly woman was preparing hot chocolate for her guest. These morning visits no longer surprised her. Sel liked her very much. Her husband was starting to dress, shaking his head in disbelief that it was possible to sit in the cold and draw. After a long moment, hearing noises from the house, Sel knocked timidly on the door and from the threshold, along with the hosts who treated him almost like a son, he was greeted by the warmth from the fireplace and the unique aroma of hot chocolate.

Now the door to the hill house was open despite the cold weather, and the fire in the fireplace was extinguished. The chocolate scattered on the table indicated that the can, which was stored especially for the arrival of a well-liked guest, had been knocked out of the hand. Today he was not expected, but the habit of drinking chocolate together in the morning became so much in the people's blood that they dreamed of Sel coming back soon and drinking with them the next time, and then he would bustle around the house chopping wood, carrying water, patching or improving something. And if his friend will be with him, whom he can get out of bed so early, his youthful laughter will warm their hearts again.

It was never going to happen again.

Now there was deathly silence all around.

Two old men, dry as shavings, lay not far apart on the floor.

Mayene knew they hardly came downstairs, and it would be a long time before anyone wanted to see what was happening to them, and this friend of theirs hadn't even been in the kingdom. She lay on the old people's bed, oblivious to the cold she did not feel. She thought about Vivan.

Poor creature, it's the first time a woman has sat on him like that! But he had an expression on his face! You can see that no one has caught him yet, the boy is burning with fever! It will have to be caressed properly.

First, she will give him unimaginable delight, and then he will take revenge for trying to kill her. He will take his revenge, but he will not kill.

Her plan might still be successful. All in all, it is good that it was interrupted. It took her a little out of fear.

It was close. Damn close.

Chapter XI

All the tears
fall down the same way

People were walking around in Barnica. The blacksmith visited
Seme's house with his small squad of volunteers. A few looked
after Seme and Kirst's house. Among the carts of merchants who
hurriedly took their goods from the streets, the calls of mothers,
the screams of children, the neighing of horses, the bleating of
sheep, the cackling of chickens, when everyone hurried to their
homes, or with a gloomy face and ax in hand guarded property, a
living port city that Barnica was becoming again after the plague
and the healer returned, was turning into a fortress. Nothing was
the same anymore. The healer was attacked, and it was time to
arm yourself. Even mothers instructed their children what to do
when they saw a witch. Almost everyone had weapons they could
adapt. Whether it was a man or a woman, the weapons were at

hand. Even the pitchfork could come in handy. Highlanders, even though their chances were slim, did not want to be defenseless.

The hustle and bustle faded away quickly. Silence enveloped the narrow streets, though it was not even noon.

"Tenan..." Julien whispered softly. "Tenan, wake up."

He struggled to open his eyes. It was her. Her inseparable friend stood next to her and innkeeper.

"Only now did I find out that the name of the madman who defended my aunt this morning is Tenan. Before I apologize to you, I need to know one thing..." She trailed off.

"Will I do you good enough when you save me?" He asked hoarsely.

"You haven't changed," Sai remarked as Julien blushed and inhaled softly. "Didn't he tell you you'd be his whore? These were your words."

"They fell from my mouth," he remarked mockingly, though he could hardly speak. "I recognize them."

"Are you going to give him some water or will you let him tire?" Asked the innkeeper, and to Tenan he said, "What has gotten into you?"

"Let him tire a little," Julien said with apparent seriousness. "Apparently, he feels better. Perhaps he already missed that pain when I kicked him in the groin."

Tenan winced slightly.

"I wish you give it to me now..."

"Shhh!" The innkeeper barked. "You do not address the lady like that!

"I don't see ladies here," Tenan remarked, sneering.

"Watch out!"

"Seriously," Tenan whispered. "The goldsmith's daughter and... her friend are not ladies. Although they certainly should be treated as such."

The three considered his words. Sai smiled warmly, because Tenan hadn't called her a whore. The compliment did not escape her either.

"That's how I remember you from the House of Pleasure," her gaze told him.

Tenan was never angry with them. Maybe because Moren liked to punch and punish. Or maybe because no one told him to be different, he was kind to women, in his own way cool and inaccessible, but not brutal and cruel. In the bed, he sought to satisfy himself by pleasing the woman first. He was a great lover, so said Sai's friends. The few he was with. She remembered that even this surprised them a little. Other clients didn't care what they felt. He was having a good time when they too had fun.

She hadn't had a chance to check it out. A ruthless bandit became interested in her and Lena.

"Tell me," Julien mastered her emotions. She had already noticed that Tenan was playing these skirmishes. "You were supposed to kill Vivan?"

Her heart told her an answer, but she preferred to rule out other possibilities first.

"Keep on guessing," he replied softly.

"Please, don't make me play this game..."

"I was about to kill your aunt," he replied deadly seriously.

"Yes. It's true," she said silently.

He had amber eyes again. She noticed it. He was free from the curse, probably because he was dying.

"Why did you say that then?" She asked.

"I wanted you to finally look at me differently, but you still only saw the monster I was forced to be. I was thrown off balance. Everyone's having a bad day sometimes."

"You killed Milera!" She screamed. "You call it a bad day?! Or maybe a bout of bad mood?"

She almost laughed in his face. He was not surprised at this.

"It was Moren's order," he replied. He felt the ground slide beneath his feet.

Sai noticed his depression. However, partly she shared Julien's anger.

"You could have protested," her friend remarked. "Like now." Tenan was silent without looking at them.

"Silva was very devoted to us. She loved us like her own children," Julien felt these words should be spoken. The two servants who stayed with her and Oliver until the end. Blood on the spotless sleeve of Tenan's shirt. "Does your obsession with purity come from your guilt? You wanted to feel unblemished, Tenan?"

He was silent again. This time, however, as the silence dragged on, he finally said:

"I had to do it, Julien. But go ahead! Prove you would be the heroine! Be in my skin for just one day. Do what they say! Only hold on to the bad ones, even if they disgust you. Watch as a friend destroys his best friend, beats a woman unconscious, and does cruel things with her because she reminds him of a boyfriend who doesn't want him. And finally - kill on his orders, torment the disobedient. And pay. Pay for every hesitation, for every show of pity, for aversion to such a life, for longing for freedom, for memories of times when you lived differently. For love not in time. Pay every day with excruciating, skull-rending pain. One day you would pray for it to finally kill you. The second - to finally stop. And your lord, or whatever - your mistress - would laugh at it and relish their power over you. They watched like an animal in a cage. And they were giving cruel new orders because they would know you wouldn't run away from it."

He fell silent, as surprised as they were by his sudden outburst. There was awkward silence for a moment.

Finally, he spoke again.

"Don't you dare save me, Julien. I forbid you! If this tearful story touched something in you, some shitty sympathy, then show me a little respect and let me die here alone. I don't want your help. Just stick one of those skewers in my heart and get it over with! Finish this!"

"You could have done it a long time ago," Sai remarked, trying to stay objective.

But the truth was that hearing the suffering in his voice, sincere and so full of bitterness, she softened more and more.

"No," he replied shortly, looking at her respectfully because she was not afraid to be honest. "I cannot."

Julien perched on the edge of the bed.

She pulled out a vial with half its contents hidden there from behind the neckline of her dress.

"Drink it," she said gravely. "Start all over again."

For a moment he looked at her with his amber eyes as if he wondered if she had understood what he was saying. His eyes were huge now in his overly emaciated face, penetrating right through. At the same time, every feeling reflected in them was perfectly visible to them. He didn't want death, but felt he deserved it. And they, knowing more and more about him, became less and less inclined to punish him.

"If I do, I'll be cursed again," he replied softly.

His tone of voice suggested, "That's what you want, right? Is this how you want to punish me?".

She forget. If she nodded now, she felt as if she had stabbed his dagger right through his heart. Until then, she hadn't realized how attached he was to her. After all, he had been hiding it carefully so far. He even hit her when Moren kidnapped her. Why? What had attracted him so much? She realized that the strength that Oliver emanated was not in her. She was explosive, changeable, a bit naive yet. True, the day Vivan and Ross almost died had changed a lot about her, but was she worthy of the strong affection Tenan had for her before?

Why has she become his hope?

"Why me, Tenan?" She asked.

"You were like fire," he replied. "Strong when it comes to brother. Full of temperament. Full of life."

"Spoiled princess," she added.

"Yes…" he agreed with a teasing smile, "and no. Rather like a female cat ready to jump on Moren with her claws."

"You hit me."

"I'm losing..." he broke off, then started over again. "I was already losing my temper. The monster that I must have been... was taking over me. I'm sorry for that. Sincerely. Apart from Mayene and you, I have never happily hit any other woman, if you understand me."

"You were not told," said Sai.

"I wasn't told," he agreed.

"What exactly does it sound like? This curse?" Julien asked, and the others joined them.

"Anything to do with the bracelet?" The innkeeper asked. "You can see it's magic."

Sai explained to him how the bracelet works. He looked at Tenan, fully understanding.

Instead of answering, Tenan suddenly asked:

"What time of day is it?"

"Almost noon," replied the innkeeper.

"Then why is it getting so dark?"

This question caused a panic among those present. The sun shone brightly and clearly, though Tenan's room was not so bright because of the room's position relative to the star.

"Julien…" Sai whispered.

"I understand. This silence is very eloquent," Tenan said, his voice still confident, not hearing the answer. "I don't think we'll have time to drink anymore."

"Do you see us?" The worried innkeeper asked.

But Tenan suddenly began to say:

"You'll obey when they're told to kill you. Submissive when ordered to torture. Diligent when they make the innocent hurt. You will be the opposite of everything you believed in. You will go into service to bad people and obey them. You mustn't kill yourself. You're not allowed to talk about it. If you show even a hint of good feelings, you will suffer. If you object, you will die in agony. No woman will love the monster you will become, therefore, so that you cannot lift this curse, the spell will last until the sign of love breaks it."

When he finished, both women had tears in their eyes.

"What and to whom did you do?" The innkeeper asked quickly, earnestly. "That this curse has been placed on you?"

Tenan looked at them, fading in their eyes. As if he was already moving away from them. He stared at Julien's face, her eyes, her hair, the sadness on her face.

"Don't cry," he whispered. "It's better this way. What will you tell Sel when he gets back? Your brother? How would you meet Vivan's eyes?"

Julien started shaking her head, contradicting his arguments.

"At least I'll fall asleep myself tonight," he whispered with relief.

"Julien," Sai whispered impatiently. "Are you going to wait long?"

"He will become a slave to this thing again," Julien stared into his foggy eyes. He was losing his eyesight. The amber color was dull.

"I don't think so, girl," said Wano firmly.

She leaned forward hurriedly, uncorking the vial. Though he didn't have much strength, he tried to hold her back by grabbing her hands.

"Tenan!" She screamed. "Stop it!"

"Do not do this to me."

"I will save your life," she argued.

"Hold him?" Wano asked eagerly.

"Are you against me? I thought we were getting along!" Tenan snapped at him as the innkeeper held his hands.

"Our bottle is waiting downstairs."

"A weak argument," said Tenan with anger and regret. "Make a little effort!"

Julien leaned forward even more, and in the sudden silence, as Tenan, guessing her intention, froze with timid hope, she kissed him with a passionate kiss. She parted his lips, touching her tongue against his. She pressed her lips against his, until he groaned with delight, feeling the blood begin to circulate faster and his heart pound like mad. Wano deliberately released his hands from his only after Julien pulled away, breaking the kiss. He had a smirk on his face, as if waiting for Tenan to be reprimanded for his feat.

"And now?" Julien asked, pleased with the result. "Do you believe me?" Tenan stared at her, stunned by the promise that momentarily stifled his gloomy thoughts, then at the innkeeper looking like a satisfied cat, and finally at Sai, whose face was decorated with a smile inviting him to give them a chance and allow himself to help. That kind look finally convinced him. So he looked at Wano with mock reproach.

"Not nice," he said rebuked, capitulating to the forbearance so shown him.

The innkeeper laughed out loud. The women smiled through their tears.

"I have to think about it." Tenan's mouth twitched with a smile as he began to succumb to their mood. "Maybe if you could do it again..."

"Drink first!" She laughed, handing him the vial.

He drank the contents obediently and looked at it silently expectantly. Her heart skipped a beat at that look. She leaned down and kissed him again.

The bracelet clicked suddenly. Its characters faded to almost invisible, and a scratch appeared in the patterns. All four looked at her carefully.

"Not yet," Tenan said finally, when nothing had happened. He felt a wonderful warmth ripple through his body.

"But soon," Julien said. "When all doubts fade away."

He smiled doubtfully.

He felt only a faint twinge of pain. They noticed it.

"It's losing power," said Wano.

Tenan touched the bracelet. His already improving mood was broken. He was replaced by sadness, as if darkness suddenly touched his soul.

They were all suddenly struck with the same thought, albeit for different reasons. What if it happened too late?

"Who put this curse on you?" Julien asked quietly, watching the changes in his appearance due to Vivan's blood. "What does it mean that "you will be the denial of everything you believed in"? You've been told to hurt people, and that means to me that you haven't done it before. Is that true, Tenan?"

"Yes," he replied.

"Tell us about it," she said on behalf of everyone. "Please…"

She touched her hand to his cheek as he wanted to turn his head. He looked at her and then she saw the shadow in his eyes.

"Oh no, she thought shocked. Not that. It can't happen!"

"Nothing to talk about," he began in a seemingly indifferent tone. "Our town… smaller than this one here… has also been attacked by a witch. Kryspine. She ate on human hearts. Of course, she torn them from living victims, and it didn't matter if it was a man, a woman or a child. Especially in children it was…" He broke off suddenly, absorbed by the memory. 'You've never seen… My brother was six years old. He hid under the stairs to the inn my father ran. She found him. You know, what a big hole in his chest... He was so small, and the hole in him and that blood, this..." he breathed spasmodically. "I would have helped, had it not been for the fact that she had nailed my hands to front door earlier. I was gonna be next. She took great pleasure in frightening the children. My brother... was dying before my eyes. Father and several people fought her. They didn't stand a chance, though she wasn't as fast as Mayene, but smart. When others tried to surround her, my father set me free and bandaged me. They couldn't find her for a few days, but I knew she wasn't gone. She needed food. She especially liked the hearts of children, and there were many children with us. I found her hiding place. She defended herself first, that's obvious. But I felt some amok. She begged for understanding, begged, tempted. I was deaf to all of this. As I was tying her up, she began to curse me. Then I made a pile for her in the middle of the town. Alone. Others were even afraid to come near me. I put her on top of it. It was then that she let out the curse. Without thinking, I cut off her tongue to make her remain silent. She couldn't take it off anymore, even if she wanted to. I set her on fire and watched as she burn until the fire was extinguished."

They listened in silence.

"When I finally realized what had happened," he said softly, "and I felt terrible despair, the headache almost killed me. I wrapped myself up in agony until my father advised me to silence everything, all feelings. I would be indifferent. It helped. I realized that I had to leave. They couldn't watch it. I didn't want them to see a curse come true, and I turn into a cold, capable monster. Kryspine's spell was powerful, fueled by her hatred, imbued with her spirit. Then the first master of my fate appeared. I had a real nightmarish baptism that would kill my humanity. I took the opportunity to escape. And that's how I got to Moren. End of the story."

"How old were you then?" Wano asked.

"Sixteen."

At the thought of what Tenan had been forced to do in the service of his first master at the age of only sixteen, Julien felt sick. A wave of compassion overwhelmed her as she thought how he must have suffered caged in a curse.

How much this life could destroy in him.

"How old are you now?" The innkeeper's calm tone suggested that he had already drawn some conclusions.

"Twenty two."

"Six years..." Wano said thoughtfully, nibbling at his thick beard and raising his bushy eyebrows.

He looked intently at the boy, as if he wanted to convey a message to him, or if he realized how much havoc in his soul could have arisen at that time. He looked at Julien with a completely different look, as if sympathetically.

"Tenan..." she said softly, and everyone was looking at her now. "It does not matter anymore. I know it won't be easy, that's all. But that is a thing of the past."

Tenan looked at her with a tremble in his heart.

He wanted to believe it, but the past could not always be simply forgotten. In Barnica itself, there were people he had hurt. He will have to face their feelings.

It will be more difficult than it seems now.

"Well, now we know the ropes" said Wano, seeing his despondency. "And I will tell you one thing: if you want to return to the path of righteous people, I will help you. There is hope for you."

"I will also help you," said Sai. "Because you will definitely need it now. Not everyone forgives easily, even when they hear the truth."

She took his hand gently and squeezed it. Then she looked expectantly at Julien. Tenan could almost hear her thoughts. She had a feeling how much she would have to do to defend and support him. She wondered if she really had the strength and affection to stand by his side, despite his assurances. It did not surprise him.

Finally, she looked into his eyes and smiled gently, and he felt indescribable relief to see her gaze full of determination and warmth. He returned the smile with emotion.

* * *

Vivan woke up with Vashaba's hand resting on his chest. Paphian was sitting on an armchair next to the bed, reading a book with unsticking pages, bound and printed in an unusual way. He was so engrossed in reading that he did not notice his brother's awakening. Vivan smiled slightly. As usual, Paphian took a book with him from home, just in case there was an opportunity to read somewhere. He looked at her more closely. Dark cover with an image of a ring covered with runes on the back, badly glued pages.

He knew her of course, they had been in her possession for several years.

Like the others, it was brought by a merchant on the trail leading through the old forest to the west, a member of a large and armed caravan. For years, Erik, because that was the name of the merchant, delivered parcels at the crossroads to the inn "Under the Playful Horse" from a mysterious stranger. The merchant always claimed to be just a messenger. He made a very nice impression. They liked each other. He asked to be called Erik, but Vivan's mother insisted that it was certainly not his real name. He wasn't Vivan's real father either, because that was what Vivan had asked about once. He was probably his friend, but when Vivan wanted to explore the subject further, his mother and grandparents asked him not to. "This is a closed chapter," said the mother then. "That won't come back. I don't want to hurt Erlond with my memories, to give him a shadow of suspicion that there may be someone else in my life, maybe more important than him, because that is not true.

Your father must have stayed in that world and these gifts are a sign that he has never forgotten us."

Neither she nor his grandparents wanted to tell him why; as if something was holding them back. He tried in vain to learn more.

Each package delivered from time to time, each book thus reminded him of this unsolved mystery.

Paphian shifted slightly, revealing a wooden sill on which stood two pots of flowers. Vivan regarded them closely. The flowers have withered despite the wet ground. Plants had evidently always responded to his pain and suffering this way. Withered. As if his extraordinary power had its source in the power of nature. Seme must have seen them before. Probably everyone was already worried about him.

He looked at the flowers, concentrating his hidden power.

He penetrated their structure, strengthened and filled them.

Slowly, but visibly, they rose, stiffened, and their extraordinary crowns came alive and grew in size, more beautiful than before. Paphian watched them come back to life with fascination.

"I've always liked that trick of yours," he said softly so as not to wake up Vashaba.

He smiled at him as he carefully folded the book.

"Which volume?"

"The second," he winked at him. "You know I hate 1st and I read it a lick and a promise. Too many descriptions."

He looked at him with brotherly tenderness.

"How are you?" He asked warmly.

The question, so casual by the circumstances, made tears well up in Vivan's eyes as he was recovering. Paphian tactfully waited until his brother calmed down a bit after the hard times till arousing so strong emotions.

"It's been better," Vivan whispered, instinctively taking Vashaba's hand. He could feel the warmth of her feelings, now a real relief to him.

Paphian noticed the gesture but pretended nothing unusual had happened. He had guessed some doubts about his brother, so he preferred not to frighten him off with a useless word.

"How's the hand?" He just asked.

"Almost cured. My whole body is sore, as if I had hit a wall."

Well, his power would respond to those in need first. Vashaba looked healthy now.

"You know how much I hate these moments, right?" Paphian asked. "When I have to helplessly look at your suffering..."

"It's better already," Vivan interrupted with the shadow of a smile.

Unexpectedly, both echoes of memories pierced at the same time when words about suffering were spoken. Vivan remembered his brother's despair and his mother's cry on his return home, their grief, anger and helplessness. The suffering of loved ones when they saw him, heard his scream at night and came running to console him. Their pain hurt him. And Paphian remembered the moments when his wounded brother writhed in agony from the burning of the wound on his leg, threw himself in silent terror after the nightmare in the marketplace, and shouted when he had to put his hand up. These memories hurt his heart. He shrunk inside from those pictures. Vivan released the hand of the girl sleeping peacefully behind him and touched his brother's hand, giving him the strength of his heart. Paphian felt relieved, as if someone had lifted weight from his shoulders.

He shook his brother's hand.

Tears streamed down Vivan's face. He wiped it hurriedly with his other hand and sighed, imposing self-control on himself.

"What exactly happened here?" Paphian asked to distract him from the weakness.

Vivan quietly told him everything from the attack on Vashaba, ignoring his feelings when Mayene sat on him, which still filled him with self-loathing, but also the cause of which - the need for closeness - he was beginning to understand. It wasn't Mayene he wanted. He was beginning to yearn for experiences that he had not even thought about before, absorbed in his mission to help others and seeing him as if he were some deity, unspoiled by carnal but very human desire.

The touch of Vashaba pressed against his back made him realize that he had dreamed of this moment of intimacy since the time when he healed the wounds after the incident at the marketplace, and at that time some of his new friends had been linked by love relationships.

When he barely concealed his agitation, he revealed to his brother what Mayene was asking of him, Paphian clenched his hands into fists in anger. And when the story ended with Dinn breaking in and breaking the door, he was silent for a long moment. Finally he asked:

"So you're saying her heart started beating and it scared her so much that she attacked you?"

Vivan nodded, holding Vashaba's hand again as if he still wanted to make sure she was alive and well.

"Your power has grown," said Paphian. "You've never been able to revive anyone before."

"Neither kill by willpower," Vivan added.

"Neither kill," Paphian nodded in agreement.

"It's because of her," said the Healer thoughtfully. "And before that it was about those people," he stopped suddenly, and Paphian saw the fear in his blue eyes for a moment. "In danger, my power grows."

"I bet if you fall in love with Vashaba your power will give you even more surprises. It's not just about the threat," thought Paphian, but said aloud:

"It's the emotions. Strong emotions increase your power."

"You're probably right."

"I don't think she gave up on her plans."

"She was trying to kill me."

"You scared her. She's probably glad that it didn't happen."

They looked at each other in silent agreement.

"Only you managed to do something to her, Vivan."

Vivan wished the words had never been spoken as they meant only one thing.

"Only I can destroy her," he whispered almost silently, felt the weight of responsibility in his heart.

Then he remembered her cruel threats, the death of the tiger, and the attack on Vashaba. Anger rose in him, and it sparkled in his eyes.

"So be it," he said.

His tone suddenly took on a sharpness that Paphian had never heard from him before. It was so different from the previous one that expressed a sense of breakdown, so ominous that it sounded completely foreign to his ears. He had rarely heard Vivan say that.

Every time that happened - he felt shivers. And even the fact that the tired healer had fallen asleep almost after the words had spoken did not soften the impression.

Vivan has already proved that he can be dangerous. He stopped people's hearts.

Paphian once decided that he would be careful never to exceed ccrtain limits.

But now he knew he would have to do it.

Chapter XII

Heart

Lena Beckert touched Paphian's arm lightly, smiling fondly. He loved that smile about her. Subtle, feminine and soothing. Watching her bend over his eldest son, kiss him on the forehead and adjust the quilt over him and the sleeping girl, he felt the love radiating from her as if she were a goddess on earth. He wondered again if there were more such women in the world from which his mother and her parents had come. Grandma also had this subtle dignity. His brother had inherited a lot from the women of this family, which in his case became a real blessing in this situation. According to Paphian's ideas, the healer should be like that. He never allowed his brother to be mocked for his sensitivity and warmth. Although it sometimes seemed to him and his father that the mother, her parents and the first son were as if from another world, not only literally, they never felt inferior or alien to them. Thanks to the warmth in this family, thanks to Lena and Vivan, who bonded them with his devotion and heart, they were always inseparable.

Lena left quietly, closing the door, then went downstairs. Her mother spoke to Seme and Erlon in the vestibule to several people. Hearing his wife's footsteps, he looked at her with warmth in his eyes. They still loved each other very much after the years. It was supposed to stay that way.

Thanks to him, she experienced the most beautiful moments here. Her parents and son found a home there and she found love. Erlon fell in love with a pregnant girl with no title and no fortune, with a person from another world. He never regretted it, although his parents had left him, moving to the property of their second son. They rarely came here. Lena knew that her loved one felt better with her family than with his own, so stiff and haughty. She also knew that her husband still believed in the good hearts of his loved ones, although this faith slowly faded in him over the years. Even the respect Vivan gained as a healer did not bring about the changes Erlon expected. His mother once called Vivan a jester, which amused the king and the people with his tricks, although she admitted it was quite useful. She believed that the healer's power would disappear one day or that he would start to lead a hulking life using his fame. He will be plunging in drinking and debauchery until he squanders his talent. As if Vivan was ever inclined to do so!

All because she witnessed an event at Vivan's birthday.

On that last memorable time, Erlon's family graciously came to their adoptive grandson's birthday and found him dancing on the table with Paphian at the "Under the Unicorn" inn among local youth. It was an open party for Vivan's turn eighteen, almost three years ago. The usual thing is that the young are having fun. Erlon's brother had even more fun of his time.

Nobody expected this visit, as they had not received an answer to the invitation.

Paphian's indignant grandparents turned the carriage back, claiming that it was some kind of debauchery in which their innocent rightful grandson is also drawn, and strangers teach others to behave primitively from their world. This hurt Vivan and his mother's family a lot. Although the idea of dancing came from Paphian, Vivan never had fun like that again. No one blamed Erlon, who was suffering perhaps the most of them all, not being able to bear such treatment from his family. It was Lena's father who dissuaded him from chasing his parents in order to tell them never to come to Jandar again, because he removes them from his heart and life.

"Be better than them," Lena remembered those words well. "You have been brought to us by a heart that they do not have in their breasts. Don't let anger blind you. Life is changeable and who knows if fate will make them pay for this harm one day."

"What if nothing happens?"

"If you deny them, you will hurt yourself," the old veteran replied, "because you have something they will never have. Something we love you for."

Though Erlon's contacts with his real family from that day onwards had been limited to short news and casual birthday greetings, he was grateful to fate for taking his kind advice. The pain was easier to bear because there was a faint spark of hope in him that he could not suppress.

Lena looked at her husband lovingly, and the men accompanying Erlon again in their spirit envied them the power of feelings, which in their everyday lives had been dulled by the routine. Most of them have not even ten years passed from the date of their marriage, and it had already lost its splendor when, after more than twenty years, the countess and her husband looked at each other with devotion.

He apologized them and approached her.

"Still suffering?" He asked, and the highlanders were listening to curious answers in silence.

"The worst is over," she replied, loud enough for everyone to hear, including her father by the window. "He sleeps."

"And the girl?"

Lena smiled as she remembered the clasped hands on her son's chest. However, to the others, she only replied:

"She's also sleeping. He's already cured her."

"Paphian?"

This time, cheerful, knowing sparkles flickered in her eyes. He couldn't resist them, his lips twitched slightly.

"He watches over them..." he said more than asked. She nodded her head.

"Dinn is patrolling the area around the house with the others," he said, while those waiting for him started quietly talk. He glanced over his wife's shoulder.

"I think I know what still worries your father," he whispered. "Vivan wasn't his only concern."

Lena read the rest from his gaze. She turned to meet her mother's gaze, who, guessing what the conversation was saying, nodded slightly.

"God," she said softly. "I forgot about him! I forgot about these people."

"Not for long," he assured her. "It all makes me feel like ages passed, but we've only had one day behind us."

She looked at his face, still young, as if he had turned thirty yesterday, although it was forty-two by the spring. Vivan slowed down the aging process in his relatives. She herself appeared to be the same age as her husband, and her parents, even in their sixties, still looked as Vivan remembered them when he was about five. He and Paphian had not yet succumbed to his power. The healer's power was hidden in this way, protecting his relatives so that they could be with him as long as possible, enjoying good health. The inhabitants of Barnica, although to a lesser extent, also felt his influence.

"Mom," her son said once when he was little. "Is it true that you will die one day?"

"Yes, son," she replied seriously.

"Grandma and grandpa too?"

"Unfortunately, yes."

"Even Paphian?" Asked the little boy seriously, "and Aunt Seme?"

"Yes," she replied. "Because all living things must go away someday. This is how our world was made."

"Any world?" He asked. "Even the one you came from?"

"Anyone with life. Otherwise it would stop changing." He looked at her with childish seriousness.

"But I want you to stay with me as long as possible," he replied teasingly.

She felt tears in her eyes. Erlon hugged her tenderly.

"He could have died today," she whispered to him through her tears, her heart trembling with maternal fears.

"No," he replied softly. "It wasn't that day yet. Not today."

"We have to fight her!" She declared. "Let's not let her hurt our children! Neither friends! Let's fight her!"

"Here is a real highlander!" One of the men shouted.

Erlon looked at her with pride and anxiety over his concern for her life.

"That is our plan," he replied seriously.

"You already know something about... these..." her father said suddenly "...about the abductees? Any new news?"

The men shook their heads.

"Don't worry, Victor," Erlon said to him, a long-established custom to use a name. "Sel will make sure the kidnappers regret the day they realized their crazy idea of kidnapping ours."

He didn't mention Ross on purpose. Vivan's grandfather moved, hiding his nervousness.

"I hope he learned something from his training," he muttered so that everyone could hear.

Erlon smiled slightly, though his concern was already evident on his face.

* * *

"Enjoy the peace of the day," Mayene thought enviously. "The night will not be in your favor."

Suddenly, like a blast, uneasiness touched her. Something was happening.

She peeked out from her hiding place, sniffing like an animal. Her inhuman eyes followed the terrain.

The sun was already heading west. Waterfalls falling from the fjords' rocks sparkled in the softening light. Like the waves on which one and only ship sailed. She hissed angrily. However, after a while her cold face twisted into a smile.

He wasn't on that ship.

The slender and swift Hydra headed for the harbor, followed by her gaze.

* * *

Regardless of the danger, the people of Barnica, alerted by their vigilant guards, waited in crowds for the Hydra to dock. While still on board, the liberators and their saviors greeted each other with loud shouts of relatives and friends. The joy was great. Captain Noren, so enthusiastically greeted, rejoiced with his crew. They managed to bring all the abductees, although a few were injured during the fight, but no one was killed.

As the first wave of joy passed, the townspeople began to look for friends of the healer, as predicted by the newcomers. Among their own, they did not see a good-natured bully, or the mysterious

Oliver, who allegedly pretended to be a beautiful Selena in front of the queen's soldiers, which many did not believe, claiming that such a beauty as the delicate Selena could not be a man. Selena went to the capital - that's what it was said. Oliver has been here before, he was known here. He is certainly similar to Selena's cousin, as is his sister, because they have the same beauty. After all, even Seme had told a neighbor that such mistakes were frequent in Oliver, Julien and Selena's childhood. Children often misled adults in the Rserwer family home with their disguises. Oh, such a game. People still confuse them.

Even if the townspeople guessed the truth, it was agreed that it was not their business, because everyone here liked Seme and the healer's friends, and the story was treated as true until it became so in people's minds.

However, Ross and his friend were most sought after, partly because they were a well-known couple of men in the town, but above all because they aroused sympathy by changing the usual stereotypes with their behavior. Plus, Ross's magic gem made him better, because it had belonged to a healer before.

When inquiries were made about them, the alewife Mikela caught a glimpse of the captain and a few people, then turned to them:

"Come on! You have to tell the healer about everything!"

Then they were quickly told about the morning events. Shocked at the news of the attack on the healer, they got scared. Sooner they went to the house of Kirst and Semeralda.

This was definitely not the end of the dramatic events.

* * *

"We have to get you out of here!" Julien decided. "If Mayene finds out you're still alive, she'll be here again."

The two women looked at him with concern. Tenan looked better now, and his eyes hadn't lost their naturalness, because the pain, as he said, was bearable now. But his appearance still testified to his experiences. Wano said, that now Tenan would have to eat well and rest for a while to return to his former form. He still looked like a skin-wrapped skeleton, and it took more than a healer's blood to change for the better. Although the blood itself definitely accelerated the return to strength and former posture.

"I'll take him to my place," said Wano. "At least I'll make sure he eats."

"You have a family?" Tenan asked seriously.

"I have a wife. The children are grown up and on their own for a long time." replied Wano, guessing what the cured was going to. "I can guarantee you that it'll better at my place than here."

"She will kill you when she fin..."

"Not a word, Tenan!" The innkeeper broke in on his word. "Apparently, the darkest place is under the candle. Haven't heard about it?"

"You don't even know me!"

"Who forbid me to look after strangers?!"

"You are not only risking your life."

"With or without you at home - I risk it anyway."

"You're dead with me!"

"You will be dead without care for sure! Mayene won't hunt you! She attacked a healer!" Wano approached him. "She's about him! Why, Tenan? What does she want from him?"

"Do I look like a fairy?"

"Or maybe she means what she took from you?"

"Do you want to ask her? That's why you are taking me?"

"Think, Tenan!" The innkeeper tapped his temple with a finger, while the women listened to this exchange with interest. "Think! The sun is going down!"

Fear made Tenan glance instinctively towards the window. A sudden hunch made him say aloud:

"She wants to intimidate him."

"His power..." the innkeeper wondered for a moment, then suddenly clapped his hands. "Well, it's time for you! You're about to get a hooded coat and you girls will help me. Will you be able to go with my help?"

"I can handle. I just don't know if I want to..."

"Don't sound like an old man!" The innkeeper scolded him once again. "We're taking you out of here, now! You really have nothing to say."

Suddenly from outside they heard merry cries:

"Hydra came with ours!"

Sai looked at them. Tenan nodded understandingly.

"Julien?" Sai asked, ready to leave.

Julien froze for a moment, making her decision in silence. Finally, she came up to her friend and hugged her:

"Give Oliver a hug from me," she said softly. "Tell him I'll be there soon. Tell Ross. All of them. And be careful."

Sai hugged her tightly, glancing at Tenan surprised by the gesture.

"Julien..." he began quietly, but the girl put a finger to her mouth, thus ordering him to be silent.

Sai kissed her friend and left nodding to the men.

Tenan looked at Julien, who clenched her hands into fists. He felt his heart begin to feel like a heavy weight.

"You think the witch wants to suck the life out of our Vivan?" The innkeeper asked to break the embarrassing silence.

Tenan followed Julien as she returned to his bed. He reached out to take her hand. She looked at him with a mixture of warmth and seriousness.

"Come on," she whispered urgently.

He tried to read her eyes for something more than the fear of the future:

"If it were just for that, she would have taken him instead of me." The innkeeper sighed in concern.

"So, what is this woman about?" He muttered.

"We'll probably find out soon enough," Julien replied, looking Tenan in the eye.

He couldn't decipher the secret behind that look...

* * *

"He's gone," whispered Sai.

A crowd of locals led her to Seme's house. Julien's uncle noticed her coming.

"Julien?" He asked.

She explained to him why her friend was not here, while Seme invited the representatives of the liberators, as they would not all fit inside. The rest, along with the crowd of residents, decided to go to the "Under the Unicorn" inn, near Seme's house, and tell their story there. The yard was quickly emptied.

Seme welcomed Captain Noren, the alewife and innkeeper with their sons as well as Maya and her fiancé as best she could, while the Beckert family gathered around the fireplace.

Sai noticed that Paphian opened the door to the room upstairs and stood leaning against the wooden railing that ran in the square as far as the stairs leading to directly into the living room where everyone was focused. That way, he could see everyone and listen to what was happening inside the room.

Seme was indignant at Julien's decision.

"For our Mother!" She exclaimed. "Has this girl lost her mind? Dear Erlon, ask someone to bring her home with my protector. We're not going to run from house to house like that! There will be plenty of space here. I will not regret taking care of him either. He will be even better with me than at the inn."

Erlon asked that the sick man be brought here from the inn with Semcralda's niece.

"Just tell him," Seme called to the chosen two, "that by refusing to he will offend the count himself!"

"Well," Erlon, long friends of her family, told her on different terms than counts in the entire kingdom. "Thanks for trying to make me a tyrant."

Seme poked him slightly playfully in the side, which she probably wouldn't have gotten away with against any other man of a higher position.

"Speak," he asked the audience to see which would be the first to speak. "What happened to our friends?"

He could almost palpably sense the anxiety of parents of Lena, standing next to him, and her hand on his shoulder.

* * *

Tenan met the anxious eyes of the innkeeper and his wife. Julien remained calm.

"And yet I will not fall asleep peacefully tonight," he said to them with a hint of merriment, hiding his fears, "apparently, it was supposed to be like that..."

* * *

"Have I been sleeping all this time?" Vashaba asked softly, taking her hand away from Vivan's chest, strangely embarrassed.

Vivan looked at her. He wanted to answer her, but the proximity of her eyes and the radiance of her extraordinary beauty made him quite intimidating. She smiled at his gaze.

At the same time, she felt it was easy to scare him off, as if he was afraid that there might be more to happen between them. What was he so afraid of? Probably hurting.

Vivan really was different. He put his heart into everything. A heart that people have hurt so many times. However, his resistance was finally overcome. He could no longer remain indifferent to her.

The innkeeper's voice, coming through the ajar door, broke them out of the silence:

"Ross won't be back today, Count," she said excitedly. "Because of all that happened, because of his frizzy mother, the boy broke down completely..."

Vivan's heart tightened with regret. He sensed it. He sensed that his friend would go through a real nightmare there.

The alewife's voice was swollen with emotion and crying. Maya joined. Both began to tell about Oliver's deception, the terrible condition of Ross after taking the poison given to him by the witch, and the cruel mother of the boy, the ship's captain's mistress, about her terrible words when she beat her own son in front of them.

"This picture will haunt me to death!" The alewife shuddered, tears in her voice. "She blamed her own child for her own harm!"

They continued to talk about the rebellion and how Ross was messing up the heads of the crew; about the fight with the mother, about the match between Sel and Ramsey... Vashaba looked at Vivan, who rose to hide his tears from her. Silently, he leaned against the wall by the door, his back to her. She noticed that he swayed slightly, as if his head were spinning. She got up to possibly support him and felt the same. He took her hand.

The world has stopped.

They slowly left the room and joined the listening Paphian.

"Oliver..." the alewife was just finishing the story. "He probably killed her so that Ross wouldn't think about how sharks were eating her alive for the rest of his life. She gave the ship to her son, because her lover ordered... His words were more important to her than the son. Until she died, he did not hear a good word from her."

She fell silent. Vivan noticed Sai next to his mother. Lena snuggled into her husband's shoulder, then looked at her father. He followed her gaze. Grandpa was barely in control. He could see the regret in his eyes, he felt his despair in his heart.

"What happened next?" His stepfather asked softly, feeling only he had the strength to do it.

"Sel took Ross to the captain's cabin," Maya continued.

"And then, somehow after an hour, while we were still settling what to do with the prisoners and the ship...

* * *

"Sel," Ross said strangely. "I must be sick..."

Sel awoke from the vapors of sleep he was already falling into after taking a drop of Vivan's blood against the wounds inflicted on him during the fight. He came to his senses instantly with anxiety, then touched his lover's forehead.

The fever consumed Ross's body like fire and sweat flooded his body.

"I feel weird," whispered the sick man softly. "I haven't felt this way in a long time..." Sel felt a shiver run down his body.

"Wait," he said.

He sprang up from the bed and rushed through all the chests of drawers, cupboards and wardrobes for medicines. He found nothing.

So he grabbed a jug of water and a few embroidered handkerchiefs, poured water into a bowl, soaked a handkerchief, wiped Ross's face with it, and placed it on his warm forehead.

"Hang in there," he told him softly. "I'll get help right away."

"I recognize that smell," Ross said grimly. "It's her smell." Sel froze, handkerchief in hand.

"Everything stinks of her in here," he said after a moment. "I can't do anything about it. Forgive me." He reached for the vial of blood and gave him a few drops in increasing fear...

* * *

"But the healer blood didn't help," Maya continued. "The disease did not come from the body..."

"My touch would help him," Vivan thought sadly....

* * *

There was no improvement. The fever seemed to intensify.

"Sel?" Ross asked suddenly, looking at the cabin windows on the deck side. "Why is my mother hanging around the windows? Don't let her in!"

Sel was horrified, as if his heart was squeezed.

"But... there's no one there," he replied, his voice trembling.

"Don't let her in!" Ross asked, grabbing his hand. "She wants to come in. Don't let her!"

Sel looked at the windows hesitantly but saw nothing. Ross's hands shook. He removed his hand from his grasp.

"She wants me to die!" The sick man whispered. "She wants me to finally come out of this world! She looks through the windows here..."

"Ross, stop it!" He asked, turning pale.

"This beast entered her house and murdered her relatives," Ross continued, as if he had not heard him. "He left her for fun. He raped her next to her murdered mother... She told me! She has spoken more than once. Why are you alive? Why don't you leave me alone?!"

Ross's breathing was rapid, ragged. Sel felt pain in his healed heart, a familiar pain.

"I'll be back!" He said, touching his frightened, changed face. He left the cabin, desperately searching for the only person who knew anything about treatment.

The horrible words from his lover's mouth rang in his head.

"Oliver!" He exclaimed.

"Sel," he heard his friend's frightened voice. "What happened?" He felt tears choke his throat.

"Ross…" he gasped, and Oliver didn't need to be told any more.

* * *

"Oliver asked for my help," Captain Noren said. "But I only had a few headache potions and a bottle of premium brandy. I handed him everything."

"But first he decided to reduce the fever and ordered a lot of lukewarm water to be poured into the tub, which was probably there for Cadelia's comfort. Then they put a boy there, "the alewife replied. "It helped, and he stopped dreaming. He started apologizing to us for the inconvenience and told us to sail home so that we could come back to our friends. Then he got a fever again. It is true that not so strong anymore, but he was still struggling. He didn't want…" she glanced at Vivan's grandfather, then quickly corrected himself, "to see him like this. Once he wanted to run away to the shore, because we were close, and once he fell into a state of numbness. Finally, in the morning he calmed down. Then Alesei asked Captain Noren to take us home. Here we are."

"They ask to apologize everyone," she added. "They'll be back as soon as they can. Let the boy rest. When a witch sees that he is weak, she will kill him yet. And they don't want to leave him. We didn't want to either, but they explained to us that someone has to tell you everything and help you."

* * *

The ship left and there was silence all around. Only a few of Captain Noren's crew needed to service Cadelia and four friends remained on board.

"I laid an egg," Ross whispered softly to Sel, who was lying next to him, watching the light of the setting sun reflected in the windows. "So fall apart..."

With concern and relief, Sel kissed his forehead at the same time, just warm now.

"Not true," he replied softly, as if afraid he would disturb his lover's fragile peace. They lay in this silence for a while.

"The day came when I needed you," Ross said, his hazel eyes sparkling.

A strand of white hair gleamed in the sun's rays. Mentally exhausted, he looked at Sel, whose heart was pounding with the excess of hidden feelings. Their foreheads touched as they closed their eyes.

And then Ross opened his wider and more alert, suddenly struck by a thought that always, no matter what, pushed him forward. He had a right to a better life. He had a right to be happy, no matter what his mother told him. The more she wanted to destroy him, the stronger he felt within himself not to give up. He did not deserve a bad fate! He has done nothing wrong to anyone.

He has the right to fight for his happiness.

He felt a sudden surge of strength, and with each breath, his dark thoughts faded. He had Sel... Julien... He had friends. So he probably wasn't such a bad person? If it were otherwise, would they have stayed with him then?

The Jewel lightened slightly as self-confidence began to return. He moved closer to Sel, feeling Vivan's healing blood tearing down with his like wine. He kissed him, giving vent to his longing, gratitude and love...

* * *

As the last words died down, Vivan saw his grandfather walking silently out of the living room, rubbing his hands, taking his old winter jacket with him. As if he hadn't seen grandmother's gesture to console him, as if he hadn't seen the eyes of others.

But as he left, he looked back, sensing the presence of his extraordinary grandson.

In his eyes, Vivan - and only he - saw all the pain and despair, also because of what had happened to him. He saw the silent plea to be left alone.

They didn't have to speak. Grandpa knew Vivan would understand. Vivan knew all about his heart. No poses could deceive him.

He nodded in silent agreement.

"Where did he go?" Paphian asked softly. "We have to be careful, Vivan."

"He'll be back soon," replied the brother thoughtfully. "He'll just find the right piece of wood in his aunt's woodshed. He will carve."

"Carve?" Paphian asked, and their family read the word from his lips and calmed down a bit.

Vivan caught a note of jealousy in his brother's tone.

Although Paphian had once gotten a horse carved by his grandfather, he was now quietly envious of anyone who would get another sculpture from his grandfather. He felt a bit like a child who never has enough surprises.

Vivan smiled involuntarily.

* * *

Julien, with the help of the stonecutter Bert, who agreed to pick them up with a friend, helped Tenan off the wagon. He wanted to enter Seme's house on his own feet. Wano promised to take care of the horse.

At the door, Tenan hesitated, fighting with himself for a moment before making his final decision. She understood what he was feeling. He was defenseless in the face of what awaited him. He couldn't hide behind a mask of indifference, and the spell of the curse was almost gone. She also knew well that he did not fully trust her, not believing that she would be able to face her loved ones, knowing his true self so briefly.

Though she refused to admit it, she did not trust herself. She kissed him on the cheek, and Tenan pretended the gesture cheered him up.

He couldn't escape the past.

They went inside, just hearing the end of a sad story. They waited in the vestibule until the healer's grandfather passed them nervously. Then they allowed themselves to be noticed.

"Julien," Seme quickly ushered the three of them inside and hurriedly made room for the emaciated man. "Please meet..."

Seme said aloud to all of them with pride in her voice, "this is Tenan. My protector. This morning he saved my life by risking his own."

Julien and Sai groaned inwardly. They were both happy that, fortunately, there was no full confrontation, although Julien felt disappointed not seeing any of her relatives.

She glanced at the stairs, where soft footsteps came from. Suddenly they fell silent.

Everyone looked at the healer who was frozen at the foot of the stairs, staring at Tenan's face.

Julien told him about her and her brother's history, about Moren's gang. Oliver too.

She also told him how his jewel ended up in Ross' hands and who Tenan was.

In his eyes, they saw disbelief first, then shock when he realized it was all true.

The man whose face he had dreamed of at night since the events in the marketplace, the one whose eyes heralded his death then, was sitting in front of him now, aware that his victim recognized him.

Everything was before Vivan's eyes again. The fear of his own back then began to choke him again. He paled in terror at the sight of the man standing in front of him. He wasn't afraid of Mayene. He was afraid of this man and the memories he evoked in him. The suffering he associated with his face.

Nobody said a word.

It cost Vivan a great deal not to abruptly run away.

Tenan sat there, unable to even move, the healer's fear struck.

The words he wanted to say suddenly caught in his throat. They seemed trivial and shallow.

Vivan sensed his mood. He felt with amazement that the man was as terrified of the meeting as he was, and his heart was pounding as hard and fast as if it were going to pop out of his chest, just like his own. Not because he was afraid of the healer's wrath.

He was ready for it.

What he felt in Tenan's heart surprised him immensely. He was sorry to have caused the healer to suffer, and it was a sincere feeling.

Finally, Tenan moistened his dry lips with his tongue, and he made up for three words, so small and so significant at the same time:

"I am sorry…"

Seeing Vivan ready to flee, he was afraid to say any more. The healer's gaze changed suddenly. As if to say, "Do you realize what I've been through because of you?" However, it soon softened. The tense arms dropped.

They were relieved to see the change in him.

Paphian stopped clenching his hands on the railing.

Tenan felt Seme and the others staring at him, amazed at what had happened. Surprised, Vivan noticed Julien's relieved gaze and wondered when she began to care about this man. She understood his half-accusing gaze, but she courageously kept her eyes on.

He slowly turned and climbed the stairs without looking back until he disappeared into his room.

Only then did Tenan allow himself a soft sigh and looked boldly at the audience.

"Who will be the first to ask?" He asked, giving his tone a hint of irony. Upstair, Vivan hid his face in his hands.

Vashaba slipped after him and hugged him gently. He did not defend himself against it.

Chapter XIII

Assault

"Sel!" Ross gently shook the shoulder of the sleeping lover. "How far from home are we?"

"About two hours," Sel muttered sleepily. "A several dozen miles. I do not remember…"

Ross stood up as he heard the Jewel's call in his head.

"WE MUST HURRY!"

"Where are you going?" Sel rubbed his sleepy eyes, struggling to pull himself out of weariness. "Ross, what's going on?"

He looked at him. Ross' scars showed in the candlelight. He dressed hastily. Sel watched him with increasing concern.

"Say something," he whispered.

Ross finally turned, worried. He sat down for a moment to kiss his lips. He did not have a fever. Sel breathed a sigh of relief.

"We must hurry," said the young wizard of the Jewel of Hope calmly. "Vivan needs me."

"You know it?" He replied. "How?"

Ross took his hand and, wordlessly, laid it on the Jewel, which glowed faintly.

The light intensified.

Sel looked at his lover with a new look, pondering the changes that had taken place in him. It was still the same boy; the one who sustained him in the House of Pleasure, his secret longing. But now life had taken his fate to other paths, and Sel wasn't sure he would always keep up with him. Will it be able to cope with these changes, will it not turn out to be weak and bland?

He loved him with all his heart.

"VIVAN."

Sel froze in surprise. Suddenly he heard a gentle tone inside his mind - neither voice nor music, and to his amazement he immediately understood that this was what the Jewel was speaking.

"Vivan," he repeated excitedly.

Ross's eyes widened in surprise and joy.

"You heard…" he whispered.

He will finally be able to share this secret with someone.

He felt the hair on the back of his neck stands up. He jumped up immediately.

He heard something. Like a distant echo.

"Let's go back," he repeated stubbornly. "Sel, let's go back!"

He almost dashed out on deck, where there were now only two people. The rest were asleep. He hardly heard their greeting. He listened.

Among the voices far and near, he picked up one.

"…I will have to die."

"Vivan!"

The distance was too great for him to take more or convey his thoughts to a friend.

He looked at the sentries. It was the first time he would use his new title and position. He never commanded anyone. Can he give orders to these people? They're probably here to help get the ship into port, nothing else.

One of the sailors dispelled his doubts.

"What orders, Captain?"

There was no mockery or derision in his voice. Just understanding. He knew that the young man in front of him had no idea of sailing or being captain. Even so, he seemed kind to him. As if encouraging him. Ross has, in a way, gotten used to being faced with human unfriendliness, whether because of his orientation or his way of life. And lately it hurt like an open wound, mostly because he was alive. The distrust in him was already entwining his heart, defending itself against the next blows.

"I want to go home," he replied hesitantly, fearing how this request would be received during the night.

The sailor, young-faced, with spiky hair and an earring in his ear, the same one who helped the alewife from the "Under the Stars" inn by the port during the fight, smiled encouragingly:

"Is that what the order is?" He asked.

"It's not an order," Ross said, frightened, but still angry at himself.

Since when he started to be afraid of other people too?! Where has his confidence gone?

After all, he does not have to be afraid anymore...

The sailor did not show that he could see how broke Ross was, even though he looked a lot better than a night ago.

"Captain," he said calmly. "The ship is under your command. Our job as a crew is to obey your orders all the way to the port and beyond if need be. If that was an order, issue it! You're in charge here!"

The words were spoken gently but firmly. The second seaman nodded encouragement to Ross.

From a distance of a few paces, the already dressed Sel watched the course of events in silence.

"I've got a job to do," Ross said silently. This broke his weakness, as did the kindness of those present.

"What's your name, sailor?" he asked the nice blonde, mentally thanking Captain Noren for these people.

"Silas, Captain Hope!" He replied with a twinkle in his eye, stressing the word "captain", pleased with Ross's change in behavior.

"Well, Mr. Silas..." Ross began, "I order the ship to turn immediately to the port of Barnica!"

"Aye aye, Captain Hope!" The sailor exclaimed cheerfully, making Ross's heart skip with satisfaction.

"We are to sail as if the devil was chasing us!" he added.

The sailor frowned slightly, and Ross froze inwardly, fearing he had done something wrong.

"Here's the problem, Captain," said Silas. "The wind is too weak for this speed!"

Ross followed his gaze. Indeed, in such a wind it was impossible to develop the proper speed.

"IT'S NOT A PROBLEM," said the Jewel.

He had that feeling again. He barely thought about it and the Jewel joined with his heart. He felt able to change this. He closed his eyes.

The wind intensified. Silas looked at him appreciatively.

"Is that enough?" Ross asked, opening his eyes again.

"Yes, Captain!" The sailor called and ran to wake the rest of the crew.

Ross listened to his calls below deck. He felt Sel's presence close to him and smiled in relief.

"Captain Ross Hope!" Sel said emphatically. "Sorcerer of the Jewel of Hope."

Ross looked at him, intimidated by the magnitude of the changes in his life in such a short time.

"Finally," Sel said to him, proud and warm in his eyes. "You deserve this."

* * *

"...he must have done it because of her," Julien whispered, taking Vivan's hand. "Now do you understand? Can you look at him with your big, loving heart how much he had to endure?"

Vivan snarled at the door where the man in his nightmares was now. Julien insisted on having a word with him. She didn't want to lose her friend because of her decision. She wanted him to understand. When Tenan told the audience his story, their feelings about him changed significantly, and yet the undeniable truth was that he stood up to the witch, risking his life. He turned from a hero to a jewel thief and a murderer in the service of a bandit. Julien could read from her aunt's expression that she had regretted her hospitality and was sure Tenan had noticed it too. They didn't even get to know him, his true self, hidden under the curse over the years. If Vivan does not notice it either, she and Sai's understanding and a new friendship with the innkeeper will not be enough to motivate Tenan to live. She saw it. She saw a shadow in his eyes, the truth of which he no longer concealed. The same shadow sometimes enveloped Oliver's soul when he had moments of doubt and resentment. She and her parents knew how to chase that shadow away with their love. Here the source of the pain was different.

She also wanted Vivan not only to understand, but also to face his own fear. She hoped it would help him overcome his own nightmares.

Vivan was silent.

Nobody slept at home, and neither was the town. Lamps and candles were lit everywhere, as when important celebrations were held. People were still shuffling downstairs. In a moment, everything will fall silent in silent expectation.

Reeba, the white tigress lay down next to them. Paphian called for her, not wanting his brother to be left unattended for a moment when he and Vashaba had decided to give them both a little privacy. They waited in their rooms.

Standing by the window in the corridor, she looked with a heavy heart at Vivan, whose wounded body she had seen from the terrible cruelty he had experienced in the capital's marketplace. She remembered holding his hand.

She knew that the memory of those events would not disappear. Vivan masked his pain, tried to hide his acquired fear from the crowd so as not to hurt his loved ones. He did not want to be mentioned about it. He did not want to be seen as a patient. But as much as he wanted to move on, the past kept him with it.

And now Tenan appeared like a ghostly apparition, causing him more fear than the unpredictable witch.

"Pain..." he said finally softly. "It's a powerful tool."

He spoke not only about the operation of the bracelet. She looked at him with silent hope. Still pensive, he stared at Tenan's door as if he saw something there what she couldn't see.

"I'm not afraid of him," he said softly. "I know what he feels."

She waited. She knew Vivan could see into people's hearts, and she rejoiced silently at the thought that it had to be confirmed in

Tenan's feelings. Otherwise Vivan would not have accepted his presence so calmly.

"But..." he added after a moment, "it doesn't mean that I'm able to become friends with him."

"I'm not asking you," she replied in a whisper, her heart trembling.

He looked at her without anger, warmth in his eyes. She breathed, wrapped in the kindness emanating from all his form. With each passing day, his power seemed to grow unstoppable. Undefeated. As long as he carried love in his heart, everyone could count on his help.

The crowd of desperate, cruel unfortunates could not kill this love in him.

He hugged her to him with a soft sigh.

"Do you know how difficult this will be?" He asked. She nodded silently, soothed by his warmth.

They remained there for a moment in a silence that slowly deepened.

"Don't let her hurt you like Tenan," she whispered to him. "Promise me."

"How can I promise it?"

"So, promise me at least you'll be careful."

"I promise."

"And if..." she looked into his eyes. "If she wants to come out on top? If you lose?"

He looked at her seriously.

"Then I'll have to die," he replied.

"No!"

"I'm not letting her do this, Julien. There is a greater evil behind it than we can imagine."

"You cannot…"

"Don't tell anyone," he pleaded, kissing her forehead for goodbye, then motioned to the tigress, and she immediately followed him.

* * *

Dinn narrowed his eyes.

You could still feel her presence in the house of the two newly murdered old men. She was here a moment ago. Why didn't he come here sooner? He thought she would stay close to Vivan, so he searched the whole area while she came to where Sel was hanging out, as if she wanted a view not only of the town and the harbor, but of the fjord as well. Does that mean she was afraid of something?

Quickly walking through the snow between the trees, light as a feather, he followed her lead.

There was no frost that night. The snow was softening. Winter was giving way under the onslaught of spring. The first flowers must have been blooming in other areas.

Mayene was one step ahead of him. She was disguising herself. He could feel it. Then he sensed her trick outside the house. This time he was better prepared. He took a handful of golden dust from his belt pouch and blew it forward.

The dust did not settle, but rose in the air, flickering in the falling darkness. Dinn blew again, and then the dust spread over the area quickly and silently, catching the human form...

Mayene attacked. Her massive blow was aimed at his head, but Dinn deftly avoided it. She flashed him, no longer camouflaged, running into town. He drew an arrow and aimed his bow. She couldn't escape him. With his extraordinary eyesight, he could see her perfectly. The bowstring groaned.

The arrow missed its target. Mayene has shown her speed more than once.

He ran after her.

Right in front of the first houses in the valley, she attacked him again. Time and time again. Several quick attacks and vice versa. She scratched his face and hands. She knocked his bow out of his hand.

But he had a dagger.

The blade lodged in her chest where her heart should beat. She grimaced in an inhuman grimace as she pulled it out, then unexpectedly dropped the dagger, almost hurting him.

Just as quickly, he jumped up and leapt at her. He struck, but it didn't impress her, nor did the wound that didn't even bleed. She rolled them both over and jumped up with inhuman agility. He sped up, bounced off the ground and slapped her in the back with both legs. She fell. Wild satisfaction spread across Dinn's face as the witch plowed wet snow and mud with her face. Lunging to his feet, he jumped on her and sat down before she could escape.

Mayene twisted her face in an inhuman grimace again, apparently getting more and more angry.

"Who are you?!" He hissed, holding the recovered dagger to her throat.

"A demon," she hissed.

"Demons are powerful."

"I'm close to that!" She smiled slyly. "The healer child that I will give birth to will give me power over the world!"

"How?"

"And I'll tell you, I'll tell you," she said boldly, their voices drawing the attention of the residents of the houses on the outskirts of town. "It will inherit his gift, giving me strength and immortality. Good and Evil in his blood will give him strength greater than that of his father. I will kill it immediately after birth and eat it to gain this strength. Your healer will be my slave till death, feeding me with his pain, suffering and fear until he begs for death. Then his immortal soul will be mine forever! And you will never stop being afraid!"

Dinn felt a cold fear despite his advantage. Cold ran down his spine. Mayene might be a minor demon as well, but her voice, her eyes the aura around her was already taking over. Fear looked into the hearts of those who live today.

"Yeah," Mayene murmured lasciviously. "I feel it…"

He raised his hand, intending to strike. He knew well that slitting her throat wasn't enough, after all, his predecessor had already tried it.

"Here, use this!" One of the men watching the situation shouted, throwing the Labrys, a double-bladed ax, at the elf.

Dinn caught it in flight by the handle and rose to strike. Mayene seemed to be waiting for it. She jumped up, throwing him off her shoulders. The highlanders, who had already gathered about twenty of both sexes, attacked her with a battle shout. She screamed furiously, turned as if she was getting ready to run, her face twisted in anger at the sight of Dinn and his ax. Her inhuman eyes narrowed. She jumped at the attackers, killing as she possibly could, twisting the necks of those closest to her, and as soon as they backed up a bit to take a different tactic, she attacked the elf. But Dinn was prepared for it. He swung his new weapon, acting with the unbelievable speed characteristic of an elven. She deftly dodged his blows and the people attacking her, throwing a few far back.

To kill the elf, she was ready to destroy everything and everyone. They alternately made sidesteps and attacked. Her endurance seemed limitless. Labrys flashed in the torchlight as it cut the air where the witch had stood a moment before.

One blow finally reached her side.

She screamed in anger as she judged the damage to her body and clothes, and Dinn paused, ax in hand. He wasn't even out of breath. Mayene jumped to him, ready to give him her kiss of death, but suddenly a slender, black-haired girl of an exotic beauty unparalleled in this region appeared next to her, as alien to this land as the elf she had decided to defend. Her unusual weapon glittered, and Sai's long middle spikes pierced the witch's chest and larynx as she delivered quick thrusts in a quick turn over and over again. She pulled them out hastily, intending to strike again, but

Mayene, as hard as steel, grabbed her neck with a quick movement. If it weren't for the fact that she had to defend herself against Dinn, she would have broken the girl's neck. She let go of the prey, throwing it at the surprised elf, whom she had grabbed by his long white hair before he stood up.

"I got you!" She said emphatically.

Dinn knew he was about to die. Mayene kissed him greedily, voraciously, as if she were going to eat him. He felt himself weakening.

Sai aimed at her ear, but the watchful witch blocked the attack. Someone threw his ax at her. She grabbed the ax, releasing the elf, and sprang to the unfortunate woman who had dared to attack her. In the blink of an eye, it took her life, drying a fly like a spider. The highlanders felt fear. Mayene sniffed the air as if feeding on their terror, her wounds healing almost immediately. Everything happened so fast… Their best warrior struggled to stand up his feet. Dazed Sai with the traces of blows rose even slower. Nevertheless, the highlanders took their weapons tighter. They couldn't give up. Mayene winced at their stupid stubbornness.

Then suddenly she felt the wind rise. The gust grew stronger with each passing moment, carrying magic within itself.

She knew the source of this magic…

She looked regretfully at her victims. She can't finish them off now. She must deal with a healer. And, apparently, reinforcements were headed here for these fools, judging by the noises.

She looked at Dinn.

She couldn't let him go.

His protectors were scattered like toys, Sai smashed against the wall of the house. A weakened elf, whose hair was sticky with sweat, fell stabbed by an attacking witch. He was unable to lift the ax. She took discarded sword from the ground.

She loved this feeling almost as much as kissing her victims. They were so vulnerable then!

He drew his dagger, which Mayene threw effortlessly, then lifted him, placed him against the same wall that Sai had thrown on, raised her sword and, with wild, vindictive joy, plunged it into Dinn's stomach to the hilt, pinning it to the smooth surface.

"Not so, so maybe otherwise," she hissed right in his face, leaning in and kissing his sweaty neck. "Your soul is mine!"

For the first time, he looked at her with a mixture of fear and determination, fighting with all his might to stay alive.

Mayene waited, but Dinn was surprisingly strong. Help for the attacked has arrived. They started on her. There was no more time.

"Damn it!" She hissed and broke away from the elf in a hurry, disappearing into the thickets of the nearby forest.

"Dinn..." Sai stood up, swaying on her feet. Blood was flowing from the gash on his head. "I'm coming. Take care," staggering, she reached him almost at the same time as the highlanders who wanted to take him off immediately, to which she reacted sharply: "Wait!" She pulled out a bottle hidden under her blouse. "Drink." She gave him the gift of a healer.

Only then did she let him go. He was placed gently on the ground, waiting for the extraordinary blood to act. Someone put a jacket under the head of the wounded man, someone else brought blankets for him and Sai. She took a sip of blood and felt its soothing effect heal her wounds. The pain in head stopped throbbing.

People separated in a hectic rush. A dozen remained with the wounded and killed, the rest ran to Semeralda's house.

"What are you doing here?" He asked as he regained his strength to speak. "Why aren't you home?"

"I felt unnecessary there," she explained to him. "I joined one of the patrols."

He was silent while Sai handed the rest of the vial to the wounded. One of the women knelt beside them.

"You were extremely brave," she praised him. "Thank you for your help, extraordinary visitor from the forests."

He nodded. She gave him water, examined the wounds healed, and smiled with relief.

"Help you get up?" She asked. "The ground is still cold and it's not good for you to lie here."

"I will help him," Sai replied.

The woman smiled kindly at her and walked away, leaving them water.

Dinn wasn't cold. His body felt a pleasant warmth. The relief as the pain and weakness passed was almost overwhelming. He felt his body moves by his breath, and a restless heart pounding in his chest. He was alive. Gratitude filled his soul. He couldn't find the right words to express his feelings, mostly sublime and moving every sensitive string within him.

HE WAS ALIVE.

He got up by himself, effortlessly, feeling everything in him tremble with emotion. He was so close. So horribly close to not just losing the precious gift that is life. He could still come to terms with that. The thought of what would happen to him next terrified him. He saw his fate in Mayene's eyes, every word she said was true.

Eternal suffering awaited him after his death.

It was enough that he only opened the door to this future, stood close...

It was enough that he was so close...

Suddenly he felt that this vision was beyond his endurance.

Sai embraced him gently. He clung to her, trembling all over his body. He squeezed his eyes shut in mute fear.

His fear made her feel anxious too, though she had never experienced his experiences. She gently stroked his head and back, whispered soothing words, and he stood listening to her voice until his heart returned to its proper rhythm. It took a long time because the fear wouldn't go away, holding him in its claws.

Was that what those she killed felt like? When did evil invade their souls? They were so terribly helpless? His soul stood open and defenseless against the evil Mayene... It was not only terrifying... It was impossible to even describe it.

"Sai," he said to her in a trembling voice, and the girl's heart lurched at the sound of his voice.

This Dinn... so much brave Dinn...

"Yes, Dinn?" She asked warmly when he suddenly fell silent.

"Vivan…" he whispered. "He can't... It can't happen..."

Sai's eyes widened. Though she could only guess what her friend had experienced, she was sure that the evil that had hit him must be stopped.

At all costs.

* * *

It was so easy to say, "I'm going to have to die."

But as he spoke the words, he felt an almost physical pain.

He saw relatives and friends ready to defend him. He heard their voices. He heard his breath. He could feel Reeba's soft fur under his fingers. The town looked so beautiful through the windows in the light of a torch, emanating coziness and safety, as if it had been created under the painter's brush. On his way to his room, he heard voices from his grandparents' room. Grandpa worked diligently on his gift for Ross, arguing with grandmother.

It all made his life meaningful. It suddenly became extremely valuable.

Perhaps he will have to give up all this essence of his existence, the world and the people who surrounded him, precisely in order to die.

Though this thought seemed incredible right now, when he felt so strongly, so intensely, the life pulsating around him and the beating of his own heart...

He went back to the room.

Vashaba was adjusting the blanket that sealed the closed window shutters that had suffered in the skirmish with Mayene. The fire crackled in the fireplace, but there was a slight chill in the room. The shutters were not tight. She shifted at the sight of him, and her red ponytail flashed through the air.

She could read the regret on his face, though he tried to hide it from her.

However, at the same time he secretly wanted her to see it after all. He wanted her to do something that would allow him to somehow come to terms with the vision of his own death.

In his eyes, she saw the silent longing she had been looking for so far.

He needed her.

Her heart skipped a beat.

"Hey," she walked slowly over to him. "Was it that bad?" He glanced back. Julien.

"No," he replied.

He looked at Vashaba thoughtfully, as if he wanted to engrave her face well in his mind. What was he expecting from her? Why did he want to be so close to each other again?

As she slept snuggled against him, he unconsciously felt calm. He longed for this relief. For closeness. Behind that wonderful sense of his place on earth as he held her hand resting on his chest.

Vashaba cared for him in a way he had never dared to dream about. It warmed his heart tremendously. He realized that he wanted with all his soul that her affection would not fade away, because although it caused him pain, awakening him to life, it also gave him strength and the awareness of being loved, which turned out to be the most beautiful feeling he could only observe in others. He was so anxious that she should give him affection. Faced with the specter of death, he was ready to trust her, open his heart and forget about his doubts.

Vashaba had been close to him for three months. She flirted with other men, and loved to seduce and abandon them before the game began for good. She enjoyed their adoration, their excitement. She wanted them close to her, but not too close. He watched it, safe in his world, at first treated by her as an important person to be protected during expeditions. Then a companion, a friend you can trust. He was treated as usual. There was nothing extraordinary about it.

Slowly Vashaba discovered other qualities in him. He made her trust him. Sympathy. She always understood his moods. Like when she knew that his brother's overprotection was a bit tiring for him, there, still in the travelers' camp.

She didn't despair of him when he woke up from nightmares. When they were left alone, she did not bring up this topic. Her calmness and warmth brought him to his feet faster than the care of his mother and brother. He calmed down then, and not even for her, as he did in the presence of his loved ones. He did it because that was how her presence affected him. It seemed so much easier with her. And natural.

Her affection was a blessing to him, though he was afraid to return it. Now he understood that he could no longer defend himself against it. It was developing in him against all resistance and doubts. It was the same with her. And it all started so simply - from mutual respect...

Suddenly he made his decision, filled with desire and longing.

With a sigh, he reached out and took her hand, studying the slender fingers, quivering mentally for fear of how Vashaba would react to the gesture. What will she do when she realizes what this gesture means for him.

She felt the warmth radiating from his hand. His fingers traced her arm, rubbing the skin, and her body responded to the touch. He awakened the senses she had put to sleep, knowing that she could sense them. Her skin burned under his fingers. The body felt a familiar tension, a pleasant excitement, increasing with each passing moment. He looked up, genuinely surprised by her reaction. She smiled inwardly. Vivan really has no experience with it! He blushed as he discovered her thoughts.

His ability to empathy was not making his life easier now...

The tension between them became almost palpable. Their breathing quickened. She sighed inwardly. That way they could stand until summer!

Or, Heaven forbid, their captured imaginations will be enough for their actions!

She wanted to him as he stood so insecure and intimidated.

She slowly pushed him towards the door.

He opened his mouth as he hit it, and Vashaba released all the obstacles at the sight. She would have liked to throw herself at him passionately, but she knew that by such behavior she could scare him off. There was something in him, some wall she felt. Violent passion, albeit for pure reasons, would certainly not help here.

So she kissed him gently at first, and when she didn't feel the resistance, deeper and harder, moving her tongue around his tongue.

He reacted better than she could have imagined. He lost himself in that kiss, giving it back with a passion she had never suspected, driven by a hidden longing and desire to live. As if he were waiting for a sign to vent his desires! She felt her body react to his closeness, as if their clothes did not separate them; fever ignites the senses, and kisses become more passionate and insatiable. Her hands roamed his shirt, her lips kissed his neck. Oh, she could caress him all and feel like a priestess worshiping her personal, sensual god! She already knew where the rumors about the sensual effects of his blood were coming from. If only women could, instead of mothering him, and treat him like a friend, taste this warm skin! If these hens had felt his touch like her, they would certainly understand...

His lips... His hair...

Her thoughts...

Their hands...

She tore the wooden buttons to pieces, wanting to pull his shirt off his shoulders. His smell was intoxicating. The taste of his skin, the touch of his body was captivating. She had a feeling she would burn if she will not be naked in his arms immediately.

"Stop!" He shouted softly, holding her hands on his shirt. "No..." The fear in his eyes reminded her of the reason.

She touched his face gently.

"That's not how you want to remember me," he whispered.

"Don't say goodbye to me!" She warned him fondly. "Vivan Beckert, I forbid you to say goodbye to me, do you hear?" she pulled him to her by the skirt of his shirt. "You cannot!"

He kissed her. The strength of his feelings made her senses deliciously torture.

"Oh," she whispered as his mouth wandered down her neck.

He was a teachable student. An additional advantage in recognizing feelings helped him judge if and how much she enjoyed it. She was sure he would find every sore spot on her body if she let him.

She freed herself with difficulty to try again. With every kiss she overcame his resistance. From the mouth, chin and neck to first one and then the other bare arm, until he succumbed to her caresses and slide off his shirt.

Scars from bites and sharp objects were all over his body.

She froze, struck by the cruelty inflicted on him.

Before he could free himself from her embrace, embarrassed by her gaze, she began to kiss the scars one by one until she dropped to her knees to kiss the lowest one, bringing his inexperienced senses to a boil.

Oh, she could see under the fabric of his pants that he was ready for more.

Much more.

She stood up to see it in his eyes with satisfaction. Oh gods of all worlds! She found a real treasure!

As she tucked her hand into his pants and caressed him, she could almost hear the crackle of the flames engulfing them.

Nothing else mattered. She heard nothing but their breathing and the sound of her own blood.

Vivan allowed her to every caress, bewildered, hungry for more sensations.

Outside the door, they heard his mother's parents leaving the room. Vivan tried to stop Vashaba from being heard in the corridor, but she was ruthlessly moving her hand through his pants. With this delightful torture, she made him hard to control himself, which of course amused and excited her even more. She waited until the steps on the stairs were almost silent. Only then did she pull him to the bed, a gesture chasing away the tigress staring at them, who had moved closer to the fireplace.

"Reeba's looking," Vivan said with a smile, seeing Vashaba react to him.

The double impressions made him dizzy, and at the same time it was so amazing, so intoxicating that it even overshadowed the unpleasant memories of his stay with the king.

"She probably likes what she sees," Vashaba replied and gave him another intoxicating kiss, holding his hands.

She sat on him, rubbing herself deliciously. His resistance faded away, giving way to a huge, engulfing wave of pure ecstasy.

"Another moment," she told him, rushing off her clothes. The sight of her breasts almost made him breathless.

"I'm not sure..." he muttered desperately, seeing her body; feeling she almost tear his clothes off him. The world was spinning. The senses have gone mad.

"You can do it, darling..." she whispered. "I'm sure."

He never felt like this. He was under her. Naked and defenseless. She could do what she wanted with him. He was not afraid of it.

He wanted it.

Vashaba's eyes widened as she saw his imposing penis. And then she whispered with a smile:

"I got hungry."

Vivan held his shuddering breath for a moment as he saw her bend over...

* * *

The fire in the fireplace crackled louder.

Vashaba lay down next to Vivan.

They felt a faint gust of cold wind from the leaky shutters. The tigress grunted angrily.

Anxiety enveloped their hearts.

Reeba snarled again, leaping to her feet. Vashaba felt Vivan's body cool with each beat of her heart. Now they heard voices outside through the closed shutters, a nervous commotion. They looked at each other.

"It's her," he said softly, sensing Mayene.

Her fury and determination. Her lust and cruelty. She was close.

Demon.

There was nothing human about it.

Vashaba hugged him tightly and kissed him as if the world was about to collapse. He embraced her with silent longing, returning the kiss, knowing that he was about to face his destiny. The time has come. Nothing could stop the coming events.

"Vashaba," he said to her softly and quickly, feeling he had to explain it before they left the bed. "I'm not without flaws and I know it. I am different from other men."

"Yes," she said simply.

She looked at him seriously, touching his unusual eyebrows.

"That's why I love you," she whispered thoughtfully.

He hugged her tightly against him, feeling in his soul his whole world begins to tremble in its foundations.

Caring for her and everything that was so dear to him made the fear of death go away. He felt responsible for her life and for the lives of his relatives and friends.

It had to be.

Reeba stood by them.

"Let's go," he said, standing up and kissing the girl's fingertips. They dressed in a hurry.

Instinctively he looked at his shirt. Vashaba shrugged with a smile as he silently showed her the torn material, so all he had to do was shake his head with a spark of glee.

"They'll give me an earful," he muttered playfully at her, checking for the sword and the dagger are at his fingertips.

Then he led her downstairs where her stepfather, mother and brother stood with others ready to leave. Vivan felt faint as he saw his mother with a sword at his side. It wasn't supposed to be happening! When he glanced back, he saw his grandparents, also armed with swords, though he doubted they knew how to use them.

What has Mayene done with this place?!

"Sai went out with the patrol," Erlon said. "I didn't convince her to change her mind."

"Stubborn just like my nephew," muttered Seme, also dressed for the exit. "She asked you to be careful."

"What are you doing?" He asked with a mixture of horror and surprise. "Uncle?!" He looked at the accompanying her husband.

"I'm ready to fight!" She replied rebelliously. "You think I'll be sitting at home idle? Even Julien and that friend of hers have swords, although it won't help him. I'm supposed to be worse than them and sit like a hen on its roost?!"

"You are to survive," he replied with concern.

"I've already thought so, and I won't change my mind," she told him. "You have to defend yours!"

"What will Garen say when he finds out you put yourself in such a risk?" And Peran?"

"Wasted effort, son," Kirst muttered to him.

"The children will understand, Vivan," she replied calmly. "So are you. Why aren't you trying to stop yours? Because you know you can't."

He looked at his family and Vashaba at his side. He nervously stroked the accompanying white tigress.

The aunt was right. Nothing could make them change their minds.

"You are my family too," he said to the woman and her husband. "Do not forget about it."

"You would like to contain the whole world in your heart," she touched his chest where the heart was hidden.

His mother and grandmother smiled lovingly at the words, then looked at his shirt as if on command. The men around, knowing it would come to this, exchanged knowing glances.

Vashaba was sure that a blush had just come across her cheeks as the women looked at her carefully. Vivan blushed.

"Wait a minute," Seme said. "What have you done to Garen's shirt?"

The implicit gaze of those present made Vivan flush even more.

"Aaah..." his grandmother began and fell silent, a bit startled by the vision of what was happening upstairs.

Her imagination perplexed her because it was about her grandson and it explained the sounds coming from his room.

Paphian snorted, amused by the confusion of women and brother. Lena looked at her son and the red-haired girl by his side. She and her husband both tried not to smile. She tried in vain to give her gaze a little bit of parental anger, if only for the sake of her father standing next to him, who was the last to understand. This situation was too much like her own past when she had been dating Erlon without her parents knowing. Instinctively, fearing that the old gentleman's indignation at such behavior would focus on Vashaba, she regained her confidence and now boldly looked into his grandfather's eyes, Vivan stepped forward in a defensive gesture that made the women who loved him tender.

Paphian looked at his brother with pride and a twinge of envy in his heart.

"Where are the times when such things were not happened before the wedding?" The grandfather sighed grumpily, shaking his head in displeasure, although his keen eyesight did not escape his grandson's defensive gesture, which clearly testified to his feelings.

However, he wasn't going to indulge so easily. Vivan has always been an example and his pride, and here is such a thing! It is unthinkable!

"Lost in our old world!" His wife told him firmly, cutting the subject off. "Seme!" she asked her friend. "You have other son's shirts. Give me quickly, before Vivan goes outside like that!" She commanded her grandson.

"Lord Count!" The agitated stonecutter Bert entered the room, for which Vivan was immensely grateful to him at that moment. This one broke the embarrassing situation.

His eyes flickered quickly from Erlon to the healer. "They are carrying a wounded Azylas! Mayene killed some of our guys and cut off his arm!"

"They have that hand?" The healer instinct in Vivan acted instantly, putting other matters aside.

"Yes, my lord! Supposedly in a pot of snow. They are carrying it here!" He replied quickly when asked. "But that's not the worst of it, Count!"

"Gate?" Lena asked anxiously.

"Open, Countess," the stonemason confirmed her fears. "The trolls have come in with a whole pack. They scattered around the city, they'll probably be here soon!"

There were calls outside. The wind whistled through the leaky shutters and doors, gaining strength.

"He's trying to distract," Erlon said glumly.

"Trolls?" Vivan's grandmother turned pale.

"I won't let them come near," Erlon assured her, and she smiled at him hesitantly, gratefully, remembering the old days.

Erlon looked at his stepson sympathetically. Vivan was grateful to him for this concern.

Lena hugged her son tightly.

"Take care of him," Vashaba asked quietly.

Vivan had changed his shirt and pulled on a straitjacket when they brought the wounded man. Several nasty trolls tried to get in after the people. Their attack was repelled by Erlon and Paphian. The group of volunteers that accompanied them ran around the house to see if the shutters and other security devices could withstand the pressure of the beast. The patter of bare feet and scratching resounded in several places.

Trolls climbed the walls. They were looking for an entrance.

Vivan took care of the wounded blacksmith, and Vashaba helped the wounded man sit up. One of his three companions brought a severed hand in a pot full of snow. Due to the presence of women, Azylas did not curse, although he wanted to.

"We let them deceive us, for God sake," he merely muttered. "Only this bum will keep telling mc when he finds out! She climbed on me before I noticed! I wanted to defend Gert, but it happened so quickly. She drained his life. I couldn't help it!"

"It's all right," Vivan reassured him, taking the blacksmith's hand in his hand and pressing it over the stump.

"Can it be repaired?" The blacksmith worried. "What a blacksmith I will be without hand?"

"Just look," Vivan ordered him gently.

Everyone looked fascinated.

For a moment they saw only the changing colors under the skin of the stump and hands. The red line at the junction was visible, but the blood had stopped flowing. Vivan saw with his inner vision as bones, joints, muscles and tissues were fusing. The fingers twitched. Moved by the incident, the blacksmith sucked in a breath.

"Does it hurt?" Vivan asked calmly, absorbed in the healing process.

"No, Count," replied Azylas with awe.

"Of course not," Vivan smirked.

His good mood shared with those present. Vashaba moved closer.

She saw that he noticed it.

The index finger moved visibly. Although they have witnessed this power more than once, they felt relieved and moved at the sight of another miracle. And when the line of intersection disappeared and a happy Azylas proudly showed his working hand, the joy was great.

Gently stroking Reeba, Paphian thought that he would never get tired of seeing the power of his remarkable brother at work. Neither is the joy of the healed.

However, he was most pleased that Vivan ceased to be a priest of good will, distributing the gift to little ones, and finally became a man of flesh and blood, capable of deeper feelings. And that he would remember his grandfather's face for a long time when he realized what his grandson was doing in his room.

This will be especially remembered by him. Like his brother's blush, of which he might remind Vivan one day in more favorable circumstances. He only dreaded that there would be no more memories of Vivan. He could see that his parents were also worried, though they tried not to show it. Their eyes followed Vivan and Vashaba with concern.

Azylas, moved to tears, embraced the contented Vivan and kissed both cheeks, scratching him with his thick chin, then briskly sprang to his feet.

"We have to drive these trolls out!" He exclaimed. "Give me something to fight! I'll clean up right there!" He looked at the fused hand and was a little worried. "Is it holding it up well, Count? It won't let go?"

Vivan laughed, shaking his head in disbelief.

"What to let go, Azylas?" He asked warmly. "You're expecting pegs and nails there?"

"Oh no!" The blacksmith laughed coarsely, infused with the healer mood, and then hugged him again tightly. "Since this is a reliable job, I'll go and tickle the trolls," he took the sword handed to him by his companions. "And you make sure that the witch says goodbye to her life."

For the first time since Vivan had talked to his brother, someone mentioned a duty of Vivan. Knowing that it was not going to be an ordinary fight, everyone suddenly grunted, and the good mood disappeared somewhere.

There were so many things that could happen, so much in danger, and yet he was their hope and the only weapon that could really defeat Mayene.

They knew about it.

And they really loved him.

"Vivan," Azylas began solemnly, suddenly giving up his formal form. "Such stories happen. One hero stands up against evil that wants to take over the world and knows that he can die in doing so. There is always someone standing by him who says: Kill this carcass! And I'll tell you this: Don't forget to get out of this alive!"

Vivan's eyes flashed as he met everyone's gaze. They silently wished him the same.

The blacksmith patted him on the shoulder, then looked at his companions, listening for a moment to the sounds of the gusting wind and scratching around, then after a moment with their silent consent, they nodded goodbye to everyone and went outside.

Immediately they heard his thunderous cries as he cursed the trolls.

Vivan looked back, touched by an unspoken thought as Julien brought Tenan downstairs. He stubbornly avoided looking into his eyes. He was torn between a desire to redress, remorse and self-harm.

Like it or not, the healer sensed resentment and a sense of injustice in him. He knew the cause of these feelings.

Mayene caught up with him before him.

Some noble part of his soul rejoiced at being punished. But a sense of justice triumphed over that thought.

Even so, he did not dare to speak to the man. He could not.

"I'm going out," he announced to the audience.

Then there was a thud and a crash outside. The earth shook to its foundations.

Erlon walked over to the door with a few people to look outside.

"What's going on there?!" He called, seeing a blacksmith and a dozen people on the street.

"Palace, Count!" He replied in horror.

They went outside, concerned about this news. They looked at the nearby hill where their family home was. The panes in the windows cracked with a crash, and the whole palace with them trembled in its foundations. Even from here, they could see the extent of the damage growing before the eyes.

"My God!" Vivan's Grandma cried softly as she snuggled up to her husband. "Our house! Erlon, our home!"

Lena embraced her husband, devastated by the sight of him, silently watching the destruction of his household. The palace finally gave up with a bang, the walls collapsed under the pressure of the roof, and everything they held dear, literally everything they owned, perished under the pressure of the crumbling structure.

The house he knew - ceased to exist...

Crushed by this sight, the Beckert family stared silently at the gloomy rubble.

Tenan, standing at the door, turned softly to Julien.

"Is the rope you tied me with still in my bag?"

Julien thought for a moment, silently deciding that she would not be embarrassed by what they had done with Sai at the time. After all, they had good reason to do just that.

"Wano was packing it. I know he hid a rope there. The bag is in the room by the window."

Tenan assessed his options in his mind. They weren't impressive. Perhaps after the meal Seme had served him, despite his reluctance, he now felt surprisingly better than he had expected. Probably thanks to Vivan's blood, who now stood before him, trying to soothe the grief of his loved ones, but that was certainly far from his recent abilities. He could see Vivan was angry with Mayene for hurting his loved ones.

"What do you need the rope for?" Julien asked.

"I'll grab her. Will you help me?" She nodded, taking his hand.

The hair on Tenan's neck bristled. He noticed Vivan froze, and the red-haired elf took a defensive position, listening carefully.

"Inside!" Vivan ordered everyone.

The shutters, though specially secured, snapped open.

Everyone gave a nervous twitch and went home in a hurry.

As soon as they returned inside Seme's house, the panes of the windows broke, as did those in the palace, and the wind blew through the rooms, extinguishing the candles and oil lamps.

"Everyone talk!" Erlon commanded.

Speakers took turns to be heard, and Erlon silently checked against the state before going outside. Finally, there was silence.

"Julien and her companion are gone."

"Fool!" Seme called. "He doesn't know what he's exposing her to?!"

Vivan ran out before anyone could stop him, and Vashaba and Paphian followed.

Erlon stopped the others, taking a seat by the door.

* * *

"I'm close, sweetheart," Ross whispered as the ship was moving at incredible speed near the port. "I can feel you."

They had already seen the lights of the town, as if a great festival was being organized there.

"We're going ashore, aren't we, Captain?" Silas asked hopefully, toying with his inseparable knife.

Ross exchanged a slightly amused look with Sel and his friends at the eagerness.

"Yes, Mr. Silas," he replied malevolently. "We'll go out."

To Sel's amazement, the sailors clearly enjoyed the news. Alesei grimaced as his faithful dog climbed higher and began barking with short, single barking. Oliver's hands tightened on the balustrade.

Ross reduced the speed of the wind in his mind.

Cadelia began to slow down.

Chapter XIV

Jewel

"Where are they?" Paphian asked.

They ran to the center of the cobbled street. They quickly turned their backs to each other, assuming a defensive posture.

Vivan looked towards the palace, sensing its malevolent presence. The alley was empty, but he was sure Mayene was there.

That she is waiting.

Were it not for the moonlight, darkness would shroud the town like a shroud.

All the lanterns have gone out. Life stopped. The wind faded noticeably.

Somewhere you could hear the cry of a child hidden from the witch's sight, somewhere else a worried horse snorted. In the prevailing silence, the witch stood in front of them at the bend of the alley, leaving the ruins of the palace behind. Her silhouette against the glow appeared suddenly, out of nowhere; dark, silent and motionless.

The sight caused more fear in people's hearts than any of her actions. He shocked with his ominous calmness, arousing more anxiety than previous violent attacks.

Vivan knew Mayene was doing it on purpose. Precisely to increase fear and panic in people's souls. She managed to achieve her goal because no one dared attack her.

Finally, as her silent presence became almost unbearable, she moved. To everyone's surprise, she did not move rapidly towards her victims, but walked slowly, imperious and confident. Though Vivan couldn't see her face, he was sure she was looking directly at him. His hair bristled on the back of his neck. He felt Paphian and Vashaba's hesitation but controlled himself.

Vashaba, reassured by his composure, reached for an arrow and drew her bow.

Paphian drew his drawn sword.

Mayene was getting closer with each passing moment, she was walking firmly. A dozen or so meters in front of them, a sudden movement and a clatter of hooves distracted them. That on the left side of the stable a horse ran out, carrying two riders on its back: Tenan and blacksmith.

Mayene paused to examine her victim, who took her time to flee, deliberately pushing herself up in front of her eyes.

On the other side, Julien, on Aunt Seme's white gelding, passed the house, Sel and Ross's carriage, until she was outside the gate just as Mayene turned her head toward her. Then she dropped the rope, and the blacksmith grabbed it tightly, wrapped it around his healed arm, and grabbed the other's Tenan's doublet, which was holding the reins.

The center hung for one brief moment between Vivan and Mayene, as if separating them.

Vashaba raised her eyebrows in appreciation.

A string of elves.

The horses moved towards the palace.

Vashaba released the arrow before Mayene could interrupt the riders, thus gaining a moment of surprise for them, which allowed them to hook on the witch's neck in an unusual maneuver, to find themselves behind her back, missing each other a little, which was helped by Tenan's excellent riding skills and breakneck for a blacksmith a way that had to tilt dangerously to swap the ends of the rope to make it obediently reach his outstretched hands. The length of the rope was deliberately uneven. Julien caught the shorter end as she lay down on the horse's back. It was a circus maneuver, designed to surprise and dexterity on both sides.

But it has undoubtedly paid off.

The noose tightened around Mayene's neck, knocking her to the ground.

The horses stopped.

Mayene, with an arrow through her heart and a noose around her neck, lunged furiously. People were slowly peeking out of the windows and doors to see the whole thing.

"Kill her!" People began to shout.

She gasped furiously at the sight of Vivan walking towards her. She tried to crawl away as the crowd gathered around her.

Vivan held her firmly, kneeling down. He looked at her fearlessly. He wasted no time on unnecessary words. His eyes glittered. The silver lines broke from those eyes to his face and neck, flowing down. Mayene narrowed her eyes angrily. She looked around quickly for something to distract him. The victim must be close.

The shutters of all the windows slammed. The horses were frightened by the bang.

She found it...

Twice as painful, even triple...

She giggled maliciously, surprising the healer. Her laughter made the voices around her go silent.

The gelding lifted his front legs, taken in horror. Julien released the rope to hold on tightly. Unexpectedly, the horse sped forward, and Mayene's malicious, cruel mind guided him sideways, up against the walls of the buildings, right at their protruding roofs and signboards.

Against all instincts...

"No!" Tenan exclaimed in horror, urging his horse to help the girl.

Vivan froze in horror.

The horse galloped straight to the protruding ornate signboard of the best tailor in town.

Julien's head was thrown back from the blow, and the unfortunate animal, unable to stop in the rush, stumbled and fell with a loud whine, crushing the girl with its weight...

Mayene pushed the devastated Vivan aside and before he grabbed her again, she fled, ripping the rope from her neck. She plucked the arrow out and jumped on Paphian. She stood behind him, one hand wrapped around his neck and brought her face close to his ear. Vivan hastily stopped the people who wanted to pounce on her, for he saw the demon's long split tongue slide out of her mouth, touching his brother's face.

The tongue moved like a separate being, pointing at Paphian's ear...

"Well, well," she said with a hint of mocking appreciation. "I have to admit, you have imagination! Do you realize that both of them are now dead because of your stubbornness, right?

Vivan's eyes gleamed.

"She's dead," Mayene said with satisfaction.

Tenan's desperate scream came from behind her.

He felt a chill sweep over him. He trembled in fear, feeling the pain and despair not only of that man, but his own, burning like fire. Julien... Oliver...!

* * *

Oliver fell.

Pain was tearing him apart. It was so shocking that he couldn't even make a sound.

He was unable to move.

He was surrounded. He heard the voices of his friends. He was shaken frantically, something was shouted at him.

He knew about it all.

His brain registered sounds and images, but he himself was incapable of any reaction, he stopped responding to all stimuli.

The picture was blurry.

The voices began to sound like the incomprehensible gibberish of a madman.

The pain was the worst...

Infinite... Bursting something important in him. His personality, sense of being, love. All his "me."

Wrecking every feeling he had ever experienced and kept in his memory.

It wasn't physical pain. It deprived him of everything he was, of his being, existence and psyche. He tugged at his memories, digging his claws into them, tearing to the foundations of his soul. He was destroying what made him what he was. He tore off fragments of images and thoughts, rendering them meaningless and causing him great, bottomless despair. He was falling into this nightmarish abyss. Lost. Disappeared.

And the pain was getting worse.

He wanted to scream, at least hear his own voice, terrified of the emptiness consuming him. He fought for it with all his might. To get away!

Get away!

Julien...

* * *

"Oliver!" Sel shouted at him. "Oliver, say something! Can you hear me?!"

Ross felt his eyes start burning dangerously over him.

Sel was shaking his friend, hugging him, speaking, threatening and pleading. Others watched in silence, deeply shaken.

Oliver just fell...

Then, slowly, the light in his eyes grew dim, he didn't answer. He didn't even react when Sel gave a slap him.

Like a puppet whose strings have been cut off...

Ross touched his lover's shoulder, struck by the loss of Julien and the terrible, slow agony of Oliver:

"Sel..."

"Shit, Ross, don't say that!" Sel hugged his friend desperately. "This can't be happening! I can't lose them! Julien is not dead!"

"Sel…" Ross whispered, trembling all over.

"Don't use your power on me!"

"I did not want to…"

"What's with you?! Julien called you her brother, you know that? Do you know?!"

"I..." Ross gripped his hair desperately. "You did not say…"

"You want to kill him, right?!"

"No!" Ross exclaimed, frightened at the mere thought. "He saved my life!"

"But you already thought…!"

"Sel!" Alesei shouted at him, unable to hold out. "Ross didn't say anything! Shut your mouth, dammit, or apologize to him right now! He already experienced a lot!"

Sel realized he was overdoing it. He pulled the devastated lover to him. He hugged his free hand tightly, cradling his face against his neck.

"Forgive me..." he whispered to him. "I did not want to."

"After all these years with Moren..." Sel's voice was filled with anger mixed with despair. "After he struggled with him... how much they both had to endure by this..." he struggled with himself for a moment, as if he didn't want to name the thought yet. Painful but true. "That son of a bitch almost took everything away from him!" He blurted out angrily, and Ross looked at him with a mixture of sadness and pride. "It can't happen! They cannot die! Can not…"

"Lord," Silas said hesitantly on behalf of the crew. "You have to finish him off. It's over. That's what it is with the twins." He bravely stood Sel's glare amidst tears. "He's gone."

"Stop, damn it, repeating that!" Sel shouted at him, making Ross cringed in his own despair.

He loved Julien just as she put it. Like a sister he never had. A confidant in misfortune when they both suffered.

He would like to think that he will not believe her death until he sees the body. But he already knew a thing or two about the twins. It had to be true...

Suddenly, Oliver awoke from this strange numbness and looked around consciously. His eyes locked with fear and determination on Sel's face.

"It begins..." Silas' companion grimly remarked, with the ring tattoo on his face.

Oliver gripped Sel's clothes tightly and hissed in a pleading voice:

"Kill me!"

Sel froze, struck by his words. The tattooed man pulled his dagger from his belt and handed it over, saying:

"If you are truly his friend... do what he asks you to do! It will be much worse soon!"

Sel gave him a murderous glare. Ross couldn't stand his lover's suffering and the loss of his friends. But he felt that the sailor was telling the truth. Oliver looked as if sensing his hesitation.

"Ross..." he asked desperately.

Now everyone waited for his decision. Even the dog licked his hand. Alesei put a hand on his shoulder, and Silas looked hopefully at his captain.

Sel pleaded him in the mind not to do so.

Are they all crazy?! How could he decide someone's life?! But it was enough for him to meet Oliver's eyes. Trembling with emotion and pain that caused him more suffering than anyone present could ever imagine. He remembered Julien crying. He remembered how she had felt the blows being given to her brother. He remembered her state when she was almost losing her mind in despair. He saw. He saw the fear. The despair that was but a spark of what was happening now in her brother's heart.

He could see her gaze in his eyes, begging to end his agony. That he would not leave them in their need...

"ROSS," he heard a jewel suddenly. "I CAN DO IT. YOU ONLY HAVE TO WANT THIS!"

For a moment he didn't know what the jewel was trying to tell him.

The mind, disturbed by despair, was not thinking clearly.

"What?" He asked, unaware that he was asking out loud.

"Captain?" One of the sailors heard the voice.

Everyone looked at each other.

Oliver's hand tightened on Ross's, pleading, insistent.

"What are you talking about?" Ross asked his jewel, and the people around him agreed that the captain was mad.

Only Sel looked suddenly with a gleam of hope and touched his hand as well. Absorbed in what the jewel was trying to tell him, Ross looked at his surroundings somewhat distractedly.

"HURRY UP," said the jewel.

Oliver closed his eyes and pursed his lips in anguish.

"YOU CAN SAVE HIM."

Ross met Sel's astonished gaze. He heard it too.

"How?" He whispered, while Oliver began to turn restlessly.

He felt the answer frightened him.

"ONLY WE CAN DO THIS. ONLY ONCE," replied the jewel.

"What's happening?" Silas's other companion asked.

"The captain is talking to his rock," Silas explained, as if it were the most ordinary thing in the world.

The tattooed man lowered his dagger.

"CONNECT YOUR SOUL WITH HIM."

Ross paled.

"No!" Sel said firmly, shaking his head no. "It's too dangerous! I do not agree! Don't do it, you hear?!"

But Ross realized that further delay would mean even more suffering for Oliver or immediate death.

"Julien would like it," he whispered.

"No," Sel hugged him tightly. "She wouldn't. You don't have to prove anything to me either. Please…"

Oliver opened his eyes and looked at the man with the tattoo. He held out a pleading hand. The other nodded.

Ross knew Oliver had had enough and wanted to end his torment.

"I'll be fine," he tried to give his voice enough power to convince himself, remove fear.

"I agree," he mentally replied to the jewel.

"No!" Sel cried desperately, but the jewel was already shining with all its power. Everyone except Sel backed up quickly, and the dog hid behind its master, watching the situation from hiding.

Ross felt as if a great door had opened in his soul. He closed his eyes fearfully. He heard voices around him, saw good and bad souls. He felt as if he was dying, and good and bad gathered around to clap his soul.

Everything was so immaterial... It was as if somewhere nearby, as if he was surrounded by an invisible barrier.

Ross, he heard a warm voice suddenly. "You're crazy".

"Julien!"

He smiled in his mind. He felt sadness overwhelm him. "I love you for that, little brother," she whispered somewhere close to him.

"I will always love you too," he replied. "Little sister," he added warmly.

He felt her sadness.

"Tell me," he asked her.

"Tenan is alone," she whispered.

Then she was gone.

He did not have time to think about this information, strange for him, because he heard a familiar voice:

"Finally it is your turn" he heard malicious joy in his mother's voice.

"I'm not dead."

"I've prepared a special place for you," she hissed in his ear. "For people like you."

"I will not follow you!"

"Are you sure?" He could almost see her smile.

"Leave him alone at last!" He heard Oliver's voice suddenly.

And then everything went quiet.

There was only them.

"Ross," said Oliver. "I don't even know what to say to that. What you did..."

"The most important thing is that you will live," he interrupted seriously.

"I SEPARATE YOU," they heard the jewel. "ONLY LIFE WILL CONNECT YOU."

"Thanks a lot," Ross replied sincerely.

Oliver smiled slightly at him, without eyes. There was only great regret....

* * *

He opened his eyes.

Sel held him with one hand while his other was around Oliver. Like when Ross made his decision.

Seeing him awake, he looked at him closely before kissing his temple.

"How long it took?" He asked consciously, and Sel breathed a sigh of relief.

"A moment," he replied with tears of emotion in the corners of his eyes. "Just a moment. You crazy..." he said fondly.

Ross looked at him with warmth in his heart.

Someone grunted significantly, so he glanced at his surroundings. His humble crew did not know where to turn their eyes now. He smiled indulgently.

Oliver woke up. He sat down with their help without a word. Everyone watched him closely. He waited for his head to stop dizzy before looking at Ross and Sel. He gave them the shade of a smile Ross had just seen. He took Ross's hand. For a moment he hesitated, not knowing if he was grateful for the brave gesture or if he wished it otherwise. Then he looked at him again. He remembered matching these two thanks to the past, in the eyes of Sai... In her sad smile. Her slender body. Dark, jet black hair. He remembered Ross's comment as the Jewel announced that only life will bind them. His smile widened at the memory. Ross returned it lightly, guessing his thoughts. He felt Oliver's hand tighten on his. He returned the embrace firmly in the quiet agreement of souls.

They didn't say a word.

Alesei helped Oliver to get up, then they let him go without a word. After a while, he retired to the captain's cabin. They knew that was what he needed.

Ross felt weird. He felt as if he were in two places at once. It was a new and utterly strange experience for him, as if a part of him were now not too far away, only in the captain's cabin, but still seemed further than usual. He couldn't name these feelings. He was torn. Maybe that was the right word? For he felt strangely stretched and uncomfortable.

"Ross?" Sel was concerned about his confusion.

Ross felt panic begin to seize him. This state was not normal for him. He never felt like this. It was quite an unpleasant feeling.

It seeped into his intimacy with every moment. Good thing the jewel separated their minds. If he could still hear Oliver's thoughts... God forbid, if in addition Oliver could now hear his...

Sweat spilled over him.

The crew watched him anxiously. The tattooed man shook his head pondering.

"Ross, talk to me!" Now Sel was concerned. "What's happening?!"

Ross could hear his own troubled breathing.

"It's nothing..." he said with difficulty. "I need to get used to..."

It was easier said than done. There was something in it. Something foreign. The feeling was terrible. How was he supposed to deal with it? He grabbed the jewel around his neck desperately. Sel released him anxiously.

"Help me..." Ross whispered.

The jewel glowed slightly. The door to the captain's cabin swung open. Oliver was with him.

"It's nothing, Ross," he told him in a low, calm voice with a hint of sadness. "It will pass."

"How would you know?" He asked with a hint of panic. Oliver touched his shoulder.

The shocking sense of being torn is gone... Ross breathed a sigh of relief. He looked at his new brother gratefully.

"You see?" Asked Oliver with a sad smile.

"Captain!" The steersman called suddenly. "We're mooring right now!"

Ross nodded silently. He was curious when he would get used to the title he had been given. He stroked the happy dog who wanted to lick him very much.

He took a deep breath.

"Do what you have to!" He called to Silas, to which Silas nodded. "I'll look for Mayene."

Oliver looked at him with a mixture of appreciation and dread. Ross thought silently. He's been doing things lately that he would never have suspected. It was as natural for him as breathing. It is as if it was created for them. Despite the dangers that came with it, he accepted it. It was his life. His new, real life. Both he and Oliver looked towards the port. Sel smiled slightly at that.

After a moment, Ross leaned against the railing and closed his eyes. Alesei smiled crookedly at Oliver, hoping that his friend would give the witch an unpleasant surprise. The man sighed softly, trying to postpone his regret to the future. He hadn't gone far, but he couldn't take possession of him now...

Sel looked up as he saw the silhouettes on the nearby shore.

"Where are you?" Ross whispered.

Through the streams of voices and thoughts, he finally found her. He discarded the angry thoughts lest she sense them, and slipped into her mind like a snake.

She was standing with Paphian in her hands.

Sel saw people coming up the pier. Among them he saw Sai and this silent elf. He gestured for them to stay where they were and to remain silent, pointing to Ross. He was sure that the survivors had already told something about his abilities.

He was right.

Meanwhile, there was a discussion on the shore.

"Here's what happens now," Mayene said to the healer. "You give yourself to me voluntarily or it won't end with this."

Vivan was silent, watched by the people.

"It looks pathetic," crossed the witch's mind. "They see one woman against the crowd. Plus I took that bastard." She looked at Paphian with disgust.

"Don't do this, Vivan!" His brother shouted at him.

"I have another idea," replied the Healer calmly. "Let him go."

"Not stupid. I'd take my burden off... Wait!" She wondered almost immediately. "Why would I do that?"

"Why would I do that?" She asked mockingly. "To make it easier for you to kill me?"

"He squirms all the time," she thought mentally, though Paphian hardly moved.

"Take me if you want it so badly," Vivan replied. "And let him out." Something was wrong, she felt it. And it wasn't the healer's decision. That's to be expected. He is sure he will use his power. Well, he will make her change her mind...

"Don't fidget!" She hissed angrily in the ear of her victim, who only moved slightly.

These people! They surrounded her on all sides! It won't be easy to get away from here. They won't let her out without a fight.

Vivan noticed the witch looking around anxiously, frowning. A moment ago her cold self-confidence was frightening. But now...?

"Come to me!" She ordered, but her tone lacked the firmness she had so far.

As if she was in a hurry. She was still looking nervously at the people who, sensing her fear, surrounded the witch and their healer more tightly. This was not the way Mayene, whom Vivan had met, acted.

"Ah, damn it!" She yelled impatiently at Paphian. "You're worse than a baby! Stop fidgeting!"

Paphian hardly moved!

Her behavior began to seem strange, even to the highlanders.

"Vashaba," Vivan whispered softly, not looking at the girl.

She drew her bow again. He raised his sword. People approached slowly. Whoever had crossbows and bows prepared as well.

Mayene felt a strange fear. They surrounded her. And she had that fool with her!

With him, she will not run away anywhere!

In a moment they will attack her, and she has no room for maneuver because of him. They will nail her!

She cursed ugly.

Why the hell did she take him for?!

And why is this healer looking at her so strangely?

His eyes are disturbing. He will surely surprise her with something!

She must get rid of this garbage!

"You're in my way!" She hissed in Paphian's ear.

The next moment she did something that went against her previous actions.

She pushed the man away with all her strength, without hurting him.

Paphian collapsed onto a cobblestone street. At that moment, Mayene realized she was acting weird... as if... that fear of people! After all... No siree!

"Come here!" Vivan held out his hand hurriedly, helping his brother to his feet. "Stand behind me!"

He raised his sword as a sign.

Mayene sniffed. And suddenly her iridescent eyes flashed.

"The Jewel Sorcerer!" She hissed angry, but at the same time worried that she was so easy to approach. Vivan sensed her fear.

She looked around. He signaled to attack.

They surrounded her and chaos ensued, but the healer already knew he had lost this encounter. He was right.

Mayene was gone.

"What happened?" Paphian asked incredulously.

"Ross is back," Vivan replied.

"The Jewel Sorcerer," his brother understood quickly. "She's afraid of him." Vivan remembered her behavior from moments ago.

That's why she organized the kidnapping...

Touched by recurring grief over the loss of friends, he hugged his brother tightly. Paphian understood that. More than anything else in this world, Vivan loved his family. They were his life. His shield. His essence of existence.

After a long moment they both looked at the direction where Julien had died.

With the help of the others, Tenan released her body from under the horse. The unfortunate animal had to be finished off. He was walking now with the girl in his arms pressed against his chest, mute and dead. Her dark hair was moving in the breeze. The eyes were already closed. She looked like she was sleeping in his arms now. Had it not been for the tears on his sad face, perhaps some of those gathered here would still have hoped that it was so. That it is a dream in the chains of night, not of death. But tears of despair cannot deceive anyone. The world will not stop for them, but will allow them to flow so that they touch a tender heart.

Vivan's gaze met Tenan's. For the first time, they no longer looked at each other with dislike. Vivan walked over to them. His gaze shifted quickly to Julien, who Tenan was clutching in his hands. He couldn't look at him anymore. He could no longer keep his eyes on him without feeling the fear and guilt at the same time that he couldn't forget it so easily. He didn't want to forget easily. The harm done to him was painful and immensely overwhelming. He, this man, was related to her. It was causing him pain. Not physical. It hurt his feelings with memories. Though he had changed now, thanks to his gift of compassion, and he knew it, that did not invalidate those events. Neither the nightmares associated with them. Vivan didn't know if he would ever think otherwise.

He did not know that thanks to his big heart, he was already starting to think like that...

He touched Julien's face.

Nothing.

Emptiness.

No pulse, body cold. There were no eyes fixed on him with sisterly eyes. There were no more words from the lifeless lips. Not love. Not understanding.

He touched her hand, which that night, as he lay crushed by human cruelty and pain, kept him alive and hope.

They will never even have a word with each other again. He would never feel the soothing touch of her hands...

His eyes welled up with tears.

Through regret and pain, he felt the sadness of those present. The despair of that man who silently held her in his arms like a treasure.

She loved him.

Quickly, so that no thought would make him change his mind suddenly, regretting it, he touched Tenan's shoulder.

He pulled it back.

Everyone watched intently. As he stepped back to let him pass, the murmur of voices suddenly disturbed the mournful silence.

Something unusual has happened. Many of them had heard the story of Tenan passed by word of mouth throughout the town. There were those who wanted to rebuke the healer for rash kindness. Many felt mixed feelings. But everyone was now looking at Vivan with warmth in their hearts. It was the healer they knew.

They waited for his final decision.

They silently lowered their weapons and headed for Seme's house...

At the sight of her niece, Seme, who waited anxiously outside the house, began to wail with despair. Her voice penetrated Vivan's soul. In a sense of defeat and immense regret, he followed the mourners into the house. There, Tenan kissed Julien before laying her carefully on the table among the large crowd.

Vivan clearly felt his pain and loneliness.

What had convinced the healer for good came straight from the despair of his heart, proving to Vivan that Tenan had really changed. He did not sense any falsehood or hypocrisy in his behavior. No trace of the old calculation.

All people were strangers to Tenan. Many of them learned the story of their first meeting with a healer. Almost no one believed the curse on him. Though his breakneck maneuver with the horses had helped him somewhat warmer his image, as did genuine despair, they were still wary of him.

Vivan knew what would actually allow Tenan to gain favor with the townspeople.

He looked at the dead girl.

She used to hold him in her arms all night so that he would not go away to embrace death.

He couldn't do it for her, but he felt what her heart would please now.

Seme despaired as she held Julien's hand against her. Kirst nervously stroked the hem of her dress, not looking at any of them.

Nobody paid any attention to Tenan. Seeing the enormous mourning of the Julien family, they almost forgot about his existence. Some even began to simply ignore him, and seeing Seme taking his presence indifferently (too absorbed in despair now paying no attention to anything else) took it as a sign. They began to press against him, forcing him to step back. They wanted him to leave. At first he stood dumb, as if absent, completely indifferent. He allowed them to do so. However, when Julien's body began to obscure him, he awoke anxiously. Without hesitating, he reawakened his old fervor to find himself with her again. He did get the first few malevolent looks.

Vivan noticed it. He sensed the moods, so he could easily catch the emerging hostility. At this point, he also met the default gaze of Vashaba and his mother.

He had to change that.

People parted in front of him as he walked to the table.

He touched his adoptive aunt and uncle's shoulder, giving them relief.

Then he walked over to Tenan.

He felt everyone was watching them. But he wasn't doing it for them.

Tenan looked at him, and suddenly, as if searching for a modicum of understanding in him, he extended his hand towards him, on which, in Julien's words, was a bracelet.

He held it in his hand now.

"She said…" he choked out, overwhelmed with emotion. "She said… kiss me, Tenan," he shook the useless bracelet in front of Vivan's eyes.

"Kiss me…" he repeated like a mantra in a whisper.

Vivan took a breath and approached him with a tremble in his heart. As if Tenan was just waiting for it. It was enough for the healer to slowly spread his hands in an inviting gesture, and in the next instant, Tenan cried out in his arms, protected by his touch from human dislike, which had melted toward the healer kindness and understanding.

Vivan closed his eyes. He felt relieved as if a heavy weight had been lifted from his shoulders away.

* * *

"Sai…" whispered Oliver in the darkness of the cabin, when she cooled down a bit after hearing the news.

She brought him here, seeing what condition he is in. She hugged him tightly, shedding silent tears, but at the same time happy that he was safe with her. That he is alive…

"Yes, Oliver?" She asked softly.

He silently cuddled up to her, which told her more than any words…

* * *

"Do you feel her?" Alesei asked quietly.

"Barely," Ross replied. "She walked away. She's out in the woods, which is practically anywhere."

"May she lose you somehow?"

"No," he shook his head confidently. "I got her mark. I will always find her."

Alesei breathed a sigh of relief, and then Ross added quietly:

"And she will always find me..."

He felt the cold seep through him. He tucked himself closer in the blanket Sel had brought.

"We have to go," he said.

He felt an overwhelming sadness at the thought of what they would find there.

Chapter XV

Expectancy

Joy mixed with regret accompanied their greeting. Of course, they were hugged warmly, there were also tears of emotion and lots of warm words addressed to them. Even the survivors and Captain Noren and his crew appeared at the news of their return. Ross greeted everyone in front of the house next to the carriage, not to disturb the peace of the deceased. Their return was celebrated with great joy, congratulating Sel and Alesei on a successful rescue operation with the participation of the captain, who picked his up at the Under the unicorn Inn, where it was temporarily decided to place Count Beckert's family and their friends until the windows in Seme and Kirst's house were replaced.

Vivan hugged Ross tightly, not hiding his emotion, as did his friend.

"I'm sorry you've experienced so bad things," he whispered in his ear. "What I was worried about was how you would take it."

When regret suddenly reappeared, Ross was unable to say the right words. So he clung only silently to his friend, letting him warm himself with his soothing, healing warmth.

It took a long moment to hand it over to Sel and Alesei, allowing himself time to cool down before delivering the most important message.

He noticed that Vivan's grandparents were not present at this greeting.

He felt a pang of regret in his heart. Why did he count that maybe he could change something? If he were also among these people, that would be enough. Ross understood perfectly well that some things take time. Also the fact that although this thought was painful for him, some things will never change. But when it came to Victor, he had hope... He was clearly wrong.

He sighed inwardly, not looking at Sel, who probably noticed it as well.

"I have to tell you all something!" He cried when they finally stepped back. "There's someone else with us. And I think this news will bring you some comfort!"

As per the established plan, he, Sel and Alesei moved to one side, and the modest Cadelia crew to the other, as if they were clearing a way. The crowd stood behind him, except for the Beckerts and Seme with her husband, who stayed in front of the gate, anxiously looking for the guest.

When Sai and Dinna were recognized walking on either side of the hooded figure, the crowd boiled.

Touched by a premonition, Seme came to meet the people walking, folding her hands on her breasts. Vivan recognized the newcomer. He barely held himself back from revealing his secret, overwhelmed with a mixture of relief and joy.

He looked for Tenan standing in the doorway of the house. The other, sensing his gaze, broke away from his reverie to look at it as well.

The healer smiled through tears as Oliver pulled back his hood and showed himself to his aunt. At first she froze with surprise, then embraced her surviving nephew, flooding him with tears of joy and kisses. Kirst, more reservedly, joined them. Vivan found Vashaba's hand. He noticed Sel discreetly kissing Ross on the temple as if congratulating him on something, but before he could think about it, Seme exclaimed:

"But how?! Child, how did you survive safe and sound?! I know... everyone knows what it's like with twins!"

Oliver looked at Ross with a sad smile, who instinctively straightened as everyone's eyes began to linger on him.

"Thanks to him, Aunt," he replied gratefully, making the crowd rustle. "I live because of him. And the Jewel of Hope. Although now I don't know whether to be happy or to cry. I know one thing: the love that created this jewel allowed Ross to save my life today. The jewel could not have gone into better hands. It had to be you, Ross. Julien knew it too."

Ross, bemused by the kindness surrounding him and embarrassed, looked down.

People approached him.

They patted him on the back, talking kindly for a long time before slowly going back to business.

"The second time they pat you like that," Alesei remarked. "I'm starting to get jealous." Sel only smiled thoughtfully.

"Do you want to see her?" Seme asked tearfully, dispelling this sublime mood.

Ross hugged her tightly, causing new tears of emotion.

"Yes," he replied warmly.

"Yes, aunt Seme," she said in his ear. "Oliver explained to me when people surrounded you. You're part of our family now, Ross. This is your home. And your friends."

"Seme..."

"Yeah... Oliver usually talks to me that way too. Ok, if you insist! But from now on I'm an aunt to you, and Kirst," she indicated her husband, who shook his hand, "he is your uncle. Our boys who will be coming home soon, your cousins. You are not only a friend, but also a brother of Oliver, and so you will be treated in our family! Understand?"

"But..." she got upset.

"But what? No talking, Ross! You are ours and end of the story! Come on now! If Julien knew... Oliver!" She hugged her nephew spontaneously, as it was in her nature. "Be strong now! You have to go through it! Come on!"

Ross gestured for her to be joining, remaining with Sel, Alesei, Vivan, Vashaba and the rest of his friends in the now deserted square. It was dawn. Tired people decided to go to their homes. It was evident that, despite the confusion, Erlon had not forgotten about his responsibilities. He was still discussing organizational matters and assigning people to tasks when Vivan looked back at him.

"Did you hear what I heard?" Ross asked his lover, his head confused.

"We all do, Ross. As we all do," Sel replied with a fond smile, glancing over to where the nice old men who had welcomed him with such kindness were probably on the hill.

Suddenly he missed them, pleasantly touched by Seme's kindness. He thought he'd like to say hi to them at last. Certainly waiting for some news.

If he looked at Dinn now, he would have noticed his sad gaze fixed on him.

"You hear, Julien?" Ross asked softly.

The jewel glowed warmly on his chest.

* * *

Unnoticed by Vivan and his friends, Tenan returned to the "Under the Unicorn", feeling, despite understanding the healer, like a homeless dog.

He left Julien with her loved ones, feeling completely exhausted and empty himself.

Wano hugged him and patted him until it pounded.

"I have your room," he told him, but Tenan shook his head.

"I'll lie anywhere but not there," he replied. "Even on the floor behind the bar."

"I thought so too," Wano replied, nodding his understanding.

"That's why your things are already in my house, and Sarana made you a warm bed and a bath. I was hoping you would like to take advantage of our hospitality."

"And you keep yours!" Tenan purred, but now without conviction.

"Tenan..." the innkeeper said amiably, pushing him slightly towards the exit. "Go."

"I won't be here long," he told him. "I'll leave as soon as that bitch dies. Tomorrow at the latest," he added vengefully, a twinkle in his eye.

"And where are you going to go when it's all over?"

"Ahead."

"What if I told you I have a job for you? Would you help me?" Tenan looked away.

"It's too late for that, Wano," he replied grimly. "There is no future for me anymore."

Wano grasped his hand, in which Tenan was still holding the bracelet.

"And this?" He asked, pointing to the item. "It does not mean anything?!"

"Nothing."

"Fool! You are going to waste her love thinking about death!"

"She's dead! And me too, Wano!" Tenan shouted. "You may not see it, but I'm already dead too! Nothing's keeping me here anymore! Nothing! Only revenge!"

"You can start living anew!"

"I can't do it alone!" Tenan yanked out of his grasp. "Not now."

"And your family? The one you left behind?"

"I have been dead to them for a long time. Nobody cares. And when the man I killed his wife meets me tomorrow, maybe I'll let him do whatever he wants with me."

"And there is one?"

"Sel, a friend of the healer."

"He had a wife?!" Wano was surprised involuntarily. "But…!" He came to his senses quickly under Tenan's gaze. "It was an order, wasn't it?"

"Whatever," he replied indifferently.

Wano really sincerely regretted that Julien, or at least his wife, was not here now. They would certainly have been better in this situation.

"Don't show yourself to him yet," he advised.

"There'll be a funeral over the next day," Tenan said.

"I'm not gonna listen to you."

"Shit!

They fell silent.

"You can't avoid it, you have to go in," Wano said finally. "Did you hear?"

"I knew you'd say that," muttered Tenan.

* * *

Ross had assured his friends that they would know about Mayene long before she set foot in town. Though he sensed that she was testing his abilities with various camouflage spells, he knew that her attempts would be unsuccessful. There was one primary reason Mayene had failed in any way to fool the Jewel. Love was the driving force behind the Jewel's power, and it was undeniably present in Ross's heart as well. It was a feeling Mayene wasn't capable of, so she couldn't even breach it.

Of course, she had considered a plan to sneakily poison the wizard's thoughts, making him unsure of his partner's love and the truth in his friends' showing of affection. She wanted him to feel insecure, cheated and rejected.

The problem is, Jewel, and therefore Ross, knew about every single idea she made. Ross didn't want to tell anyone about this. The unease her thoughts had aroused in him, he would not let him sleep peacefully for a few hours in the morning, because if something could really hurt him, it was it. Eventually, when Sel genuinely concerned about his condition, he told him about what Mayene was up to.

"You see," Sel said to him. "The very idea has poisoned your thoughts and made you restless." And that's what she means! Don't give up on her. You know me. You know our friends. I sailed for you, and they showed their feelings for you, even yesterday," he squeezed his hand. "Your hand is cool," he observed anxiously.

"I'm cold," Ross replied, indeed cuddled up to his ears in the quilt. "Ever since I touched her, I'm still cold. As if it was taking away all my heat."

"The demon," Sel thought, "absorbs heat. Yesterday they mentioned something about it."

"Cut yourself off from her," he asked, hugging his back and hugging him.

"I can't," said Ross. "Thanks to that I know that she is far away now."

"Do you feel weaker?"

"No. Only sleepy."

Sel closed his eyes.

"Better?" He asked after a long moment.

He felt Ross's skin, even through his shirt, grow much warmer.

Still, he waited anxiously for an answer.

"Much better," said Ross sleepily.

Sel waited for his lover's breathing to shift to a steady rhythm of sleep.

"Are you vigilant?" He mentally directed the question to the Jewel.

"YES" was the reply in a characteristic, melodious voice.

Sel didn't close his eyes anymore.

* * *

Dinn was grateful to Vivan for the restored peace. He did not believe that he would ever fall asleep again. Paphian with suspicious enthusiasm decided to accompany him to the room designated by the innkeeper. Of course, he could not deny himself the pleasure of not winking significantly at his brother when the siblings did not see. As always, he was incorrect in this respect.

Oliver and Sai were taken under wing of aunt, so Vivan had no chance to get to his friend. He was not satisfied with that. After all, his touch soothed his nerves, but here Seme decided that she would be fine on her own.

They exchanged only knowing looks, which reassured Vivan. Oliver apparently took it easier thanks to his relationship with Ross.

So he and Vashaba were the last to enter the designated room.

The sight of the beautifully carved bed and the subtle interior design made them realize that the innkeeper had welcomed them with a room for newlyweds or wealthy couples. Instinct prompted the former. The old truth was that rumors traveled quickly. One of the men accompanying the healer's stepfather in defense of the home of Seme and Kirst had too loose tongue. Maybe even all of them. It was certainly a sensation to hear that Vivan, the great healer, had slept with a woman. He imagined the curiosity of the inhabitants at the funeral of the murdered.

It depressed him.

He felt terribly tense, irritable and sad at the same time. He was angry about his own slowness when it came to fighting Mayene. If only he were faster...

"Ross said Mayene was far away," Vashaba said gently at the sight of his somber expression.

She walked slowly over to take his hand.

"Come on," she whispered, looking at him gently.

Vivan stared at her with a wounded animal gaze. Yes, she sensed what he thought.

"I wanted to give you a soothing massage," she explained warmly. "There are relaxing oils here. Wano cares about the guests in this room." She touched his face. "I wouldn't do anything against your will."

"Sorry," he whispered, kissing her cheek. "I think about so many things at the same time..."

"I know."

He allowed himself to be led to the bed. With a hint of hesitation, she reached for the buttons on his shirt.

"I'll take it off," she said, still calm.

If only he could, he would have tensed even more. Her heart squeezed.

"For massage," she reminded him.

Uncertainly, he let her undo the buttons and take off his shirt. Before he fell into a larger anxiety, she ordered him to lie down on her stomach, then she prepared the oils. Then, in the glow of the oil lamps, she saw the scars on his back.

She would be lying if she said the sight had ceased to shock her.

She has little desire to kiss every scar, erasing it forever if she could.

She felt tears welling up under her eyelids.

He shifted uneasily, which reminded her that he was perfectly aware of the emotions of others.

She reached for one of the bottles.

Using this oil would certainly make Vivan relaxed and amenable to caressing, so she didn't even hesitate. This was what he needed, though he did not realize it.

She warmed the fragrant oil a little in her hand and gently smeared it on the skin of his back, shoulders and neck. Then she began the massage skillfully and effortlessly, letting the oil penetrate his scarred skin and his scarred muscles.

He sighed with relief, surrendering to her hands. The tension was gone, but she added some oil to relax him even more.

Slowly her hands, following the hidden desire and longing, began to touch him more subtly, sensually. The eroticism of these movements, their apparent slowness, and her fingers reaching under the trousers' fabric, as if in passing, did not escape Vivan's attention, decisively distracting him from his gloomy thoughts. She waited, massaging wherever her hands could reach. Will he be angry with her innocent tricks?

"Take off the rest of your clothes," she told him, then quickly corrected herself, feeling her heart speed up at the thought. "I mean... take off your pants, just your pants."

Their eyes met as he carried out her command. She tried very, very hard to look innocent, but she didn't think he was fooled. However, he did not protest. Apparently he wanted to know what will be next.

He lay down on his stomach again, and Vashaba's mouth felt dry. She started the massage again, but this time she was bolder. Under her underwear, she could feel his soft skin on his buttocks.

As she began to massage his thighs, reaching higher and higher, she heard a soft groan and shaky breathing.

Good.

She felt vibrations between them. Vivan's body responded to camouflaged caresses. His hands tightened on the pillow.

"What are you doing?" He asked softly, feverish at her touch.

She felt a tremor at the sound of that voice and her body felt a feverish thirst. The oil intensified their emotions. Slowly, starting at the roots of her hair, she showered him with gentle kisses. She heard his rapid breathing and the soft moan that made her torment him eagerly with the sensuality of her kisses and the touch of her hands.

She loved it when he succumbed to her so.

She took off her clothes, followed by his fiery gaze, then forced him to roll onto his back. She sat on him and leaned over, letting him caress her. His hands were touching her breasts, his lips were burning with kisses. She tautened under his touch.

Finally they removed the last obstacle and she let him in...

They found themselves close to each other, face to face, bound inextricably, connected intimately, moving slowly. She pressed against him, pushing him as deep as she could.

He looked at her touched and trembling with emotion. It took her breath away from that look. They paused, savoring this moment of absolute bonding.

He seemed to see more than passion in his eyes.

They shone.

They moved slowly in rhythm until they were fulfilled at the same time. A moment later, Vivan hugged her tightly against him, trembling as she was already sure, not only because of the exhilaration experienced, but also because of hidden emotions. She couldn't see his face anymore.

She felt a piercing sadness that quickly faded her memory of the joy of fulfillment, as if they were together for the last time.

She felt the bumps and dimples of the scars on his back and sides under her fingers, a testimony of the evil people had repaid for his kindness.

He did not allow himself to meet his eyes. He just hugged her tightly in silence.

"Don't say goodbye to me," she whispered to him in the quiet anxiety of her heart.

He did not answer. It made her even more sad, as if she had already lost him, though he was still there, so warm, so soothing. Unusual.

"I love you," she breathed feelings into those words, despite being against herself.

Then he kissed her fervently, hard, torn by the feelings she was so afraid of, even though her heart already sensed the separation.

* * *

Sai looked at the figure sitting in the rocking chair facing the window.

The blanket slid off her lap in the gentle, weak rhythm of the motion of the furniture skids.

"Glad you came," said the innkeeper's wife. "He hasn't slept for a moment. He do not want to eat. Maybe you can at least persuade him to have tea," she whispered conspiratorially and added even more quietly, leaning to the girl's ear, "Better he not be there. A terrible row breaks out. The funeral is not a good time for such things. They should both be entitled to grief. When will the ceremony take place?"

"Tonight. Unless Mayene interrupts us," Sai replied equally softly.

"We all need to rest."

She looked at Tenan sadly. He didn't even notice her coming. On the one hand, he looked better, the effects of the witch's kiss were not so visible, but on the other hand... he was a vivid reflection of her beloved Oliver, whom she had just put to sleep, giving him a calming tea at his request. He was so excited and exhausted that he could barely stand on his feet. However, he could not sleep, therefore he asked for help. This, in turn, was certainly needed now also by Tenan, whose amber eyes were filled with suffering.

She did not envy him his present fate. He had nothing. He had nothing to hold on to. The only person for whom he put himself in danger - died. It's good that at least Vivan forgave him in front of everyone. He knew it would help Tena new to win people over. But there was also Oliver.

And Sel...

She came up to him quietly. Light stubble appeared on his sunken-eyed face, with visible shadows under his lower lids.

She adjusted his blanket.

He looked at her, surprised to see her, as if he didn't expect to see her again.

How could he think that way after what he had told them?

"What are you doing here?" He asked softly and a bit too sharply. "You should be with Oliver. He definitely need you. Certainly more than me.

"He sleeps."

"You came for one last talk with a convict?" Sai put her hand on his.

"I came because I can cry with you," she said, and the tears, as if induced, ran down her cheeks. "My grief would hurt Oliver. He is already suffering. Alesei means well, but I don't want his consolation. I don't have a friend to talk to anymore. And this is the second time in such a short time... This emptiness devours my hearts. Today only you can understand me. You and I have a past that we don't want to remember. We have lost those we still love."

"I'm a murderer."

"You were a slave, Tenan. You remember Ramoz, right? I was his slave. Me and Lena. You and I already know this pain."

He squeezes her hand. He got up and embraced her gently, feeling that was what she expected. He must have been waiting for it too.

They were just silent for a moment.

"I'd like to see her, this one last time," he said softly as their emotions drained.

"Come on," she took his hand. "Nobody can stop you from doing this."

Seme was not pleased with his arrival. She reluctantly let him into the small room where the shutters had already been repaired. It was bitterly cold. Julien's pale body was dressed in a white gown. She was lying on a long bench. Her face was calm, as if she was asleep. Long, dark hair fell over her shoulders. The hands were folded over the chest.

Tenan leaned over and placed the broken bracelet in his hands. He placed the last kiss on the lips of his beloved...

* * *

Dinn saw Sel come down to the dining room. He quietly asked the innkeeper to send a meal to his room. He walked over to the builder before he returned to the second floor.

"Sel," he asked as gently as he could. "I have to tell you something..."

When he finished, Sel was silent, unable to utter a word.

"The neighbors have taken care of them already," he added quietly. "They found a letter at home for you. They probably wrote it just in case something happened to them." He pulled an envelope out of his pocket. "Gunter and Maria had no children. Home is yours if you want it. I know this will not soothe your loss at all, but you may be comforted by the fact that they love you as a loved one, so much that they gave you their only fortune."

Sel thought bitterly that this love had only brought them a terrible death.

"Someone died again..." he began softly, his voice filled with regret, and stopped suddenly.

Dinn stared at him, not quite understanding what he was thinking. He didn't know his whole story. He just hoped desperately that his guesses weren't true. If so, the fate of these good people's souls would be as Mayene wanted him to do. Sel would break down from despair.

If this turns out to be true, the death of the witch will help them. He didn't tell Sel about his suspicions.

"Tell Ross I went to the carriage," Sel said with difficulty, keeping himself under control before he left without any outerwear, regardless of the cold.

So Dinn went with a heavy heart to the room where Ross was sleeping, but found Vivan's grandfather at the door. Now he couldn't deliver the news. He did not want to spoil this special moment. He knew from Paphian how much anticipated this meeting was. So he went away.

Ross was sleeping restlessly. He did not hear a discreet knocking.

He dreamed that he was at the House of Pleasure with a client who wanted his services. He refused him, but the client insisted. He was insistent. Sleazy. If Sel saw him... He didn't want to fuck with the client. He wanted to be with Sel. But there was still something pushing him away from him. Finally Sel looked at him as if Ross had just cheated on him, though he did his best to get away from the leering client and leave the room. Then he left him. And he still couldn't get out, he couldn't escape!

"ROSS," he heard the Jewel. "WAKE UP! IN DREAM YOU TRAVEL BETWEEN DIMENSIONS!"

Suddenly another voice entered his word...

"I GOT YOU!!!"

This voice could not be confused with any other. Mayene burst into his sleep, shaking him deeply. He was scared because he was in no way prepared for it. In addition, the nightmare had upset him.

She sent it to him! A brief flash of thought was enough to make him understand. This...

Someone moved his arm hard enough to wake him up. He heard her say his name insistently:

"Ross! Wake up, son. Come on!"

His eyes snapped open, gasping for air. To his amazement, he met the concerned gaze of Victor, the healer's grandfather. He was probably the last person he expected to see now. He didn't even greet him then! He didn't even come! So why did he do it now?!

Although it is not actually the time and place for these discussions. He ripped it out of the witch's tentacles and was grateful to him for it.

"My God!" The old man said in spirit, but not with his body. "What did you dream of?"

Ross felt a cold shudder. He was still overwhelmed by the paralyzing fear. He couldn't help it. He felt distressed by this nightmare and Mayene's being forced to sleep. He was barely in control, so he preferred to keep quiet. He cringed, wrapping the quilt half consciously, unable to move anything else. Victor took his old, otherworldly canteen from the inside pocket of his coat and handed it to him quickly.

"Here, drink!" He ordered shortly, opening the bottle, concerned with his condition. Ross accepted the canteen he knew by sight, but never got the chance to taste its contents, and took a long sip. His throat burned hard, as if it was consumed by fire, until he choked and tears filled his eyes.

"More!" Victor encouraged him. "This is our Polish vodka! You haven't tried anything like this before in your life, have you?"

Ross shook his head no. But obediently, he took a second sip. He could feel the burning effect of the alcohol warming his insides, which was not so bad.

His head brightened.

"More?" Victor asked hopefully, but Ross vigorously returned his manner, shaking his head.

"Please, don't…" he just choked out.

He felt better, and the horror of the nightmare he had lived had faded somewhat, though the fear that Mayene was still in his mind, holding him in her clutches, remained.

She did it. She really succeed.

"SHE'S NOT HERE. SHE CAME BY A DREAM HERE. THE SECOND TIME I WILL BE AWARE," the Jewel assured him. "SHE WILL NOT GET YOU ANY MORE. I WILL NOT ALLOW IT."

He closed his eyes in silent anguish, feeling something inevitably bring him to the breaking point. It got more and more difficult. Time and time again he was hurt painfully. It was more and more difficult for him to get up from the next blow, and his heart, still sore after being thrown away by his mother, continued to bleed, sensitive to any harm he inflicted.

Plus, this cold. Constant cold, ever since he touched Mayene's mind... Something very bad had happened to him. He could feel it.

"It's all right," Victor hesitantly leaned forward to stroke his hair with fatherly tenderness, to his amazement. "It's over now. It's just a dream. It's gone."

He spoke to him until Ross calmed down. Gently, with concern like never before. Deeply moved by this, Ross wished this moment would never pass. He rested mentally, feeling the sincere concern of the old veteran, devoid of prejudices at last.

"Say something," the healer's grandfather spoke to him after a long moment. Then he looked around for Sel, surprised to not feel his presence. He was not there. He missed him painfully, thirsty for his touch.

"He'll probably be back soon," Victor said, seeing the young man's gaze wandering around the room.

Ross was confused and recovered a little, now for completely different reasons. Victor would be shocked to see their tenderness. He took a giant leap forward with this caring, fatherly gesture, making him feel like he accepted him, just as Ross had always dreamed of accepting. Though he didn't openly admit it before the kidnapping, Ross felt that the old veteran liked him, but it was still hard for him to just switch and accept the difference in his world.

But he tried. He and Sel knew that they had to be gentle, without pressure, if they were to gain his friendship and acceptance. Tender gestures would not help, certainly not in his presence. Victor must have seen Sel come out, therefore he came, although it also took a certain courage on his part.

He didn't know what he might find here.

"I thought I'd see you," he told him now, sitting on the edge of the bed. He pretended not to see how completely surprised Ross was nervous about his visit and checks to see if he is wearing a shirt. As he recovered from his nightmare, his heart raced again as if it were about to spring out of his chest.

"I'm glad," said Ross softly.

Victor looked at him with a serious look.

"You dreamed your old life," he half asked, half said. "You were talking in your sleep."

He would give a gold ducat to find out what he said and what Victor thinks about him now. He could read the enormity of embarrassment from his face after these words. So he said calmly:

"I didn't come to judge you here, Ross. Whatever was, is behind us." But it was evident that he was thinking about what he had heard, so Ross felt anxiety.

Victor exhaled loudly. He looked at him warmly.

"Sel's gone somewhere," he began to explain, clearly ending the topic. "Thought you were alone, and mine woman is busy with Seme... So we can talk. Well, we didn't see each other so far, right? They all took you so that there was not a moment of peace after the whole clash. But I saw how Seme took you into the family. You are surely glad, huh? Now you finally have a normal family. Now you don't need to sit with me anymore..."

"Mr. Victor…" Ross began after he cooled down a little.

"There aren't any misters here and they haven't been. I told you, but you insisted yourself that it was not appropriate!"

"Sel says so..."

"Then stop it too, Ross!" Victor looked at him nervous.

Ross was a bit scared.

The old gentleman did not like being accused of being rude. He allowed Ross to call himself by name but not Sel, hence Ross's strange reaction.

"Don't sulk on me about such crap on me," Victor waved his hand in front of his face. "Understand? You're too smart for that!"

"Yes, sir," replied the Wizard obediently, but without flattery, pleasantly tickled by Victor's words. There was a moment of silence.

"I was worried," said Victor. "They didn't want to tell me what was going on, but I heard something from Lena. About your mother."

Ross looked away.

"And those people who were with you... they told everything. Mikela cried." Tenderness for the alewife rose in Ross's heart.

"You have scars," Victor remarked softly. "She ordered to kill you."

Emotions were still too fresh for Ross to be distant from the past. He felt a burning sensation under his eyelids.

"You want this whole ship?" Victor tactfully pretended not to see his emotion.

Ross nodded with conviction that had its origin in the past.

"What do you think about Seme? Are you glad that she made you part of the family? Yes," Victor said. "Too bad she was the first." Ross, surprised and agitated, looked at him.

"Since you have a ship," he suddenly pulled out the bundle he was hiding behind his back, "you probably want to have wind in your sails. You'll go somewhere far." He unwrapped the mysterious package, and a touched Ross saw a hand-sized miniature of Cadelia, somewhat inaccurate, but recognizable. "Well, the winds must be favorable to you, so I thought that if I gave you this..." Victor put the little ship in his hand, and Ross felt a choking in his throat, "you will have enough of this wind and you will remember about us in your traveling. It could be such a talisman. And that I will be waiting here..."

Victor's voice finally broke with emotion. "And now I will listen to you when you tell me about your strange world and miracles. And I'll be proud of you."

Ross looked through his tears at the wooden galleon, still painted with the fresh paint he could feel under his fingers. He took him tightly, as the most precious treasure, and then he embraced Victor, moved to the limit.

After hesitating for a moment, unsure how to act, Victor returned his hug.

"I was hoping you wouldn't be mad at me," Ross said softly.

"What would I be angry about?" Victor was surprised, releasing him from his embrace.

"About my sickness at the ship," Ross replied uneasily. "You would never have acted that way."

"Rubbish!" Said Victor, half angrily, half surprised by this idea. "Everybody has it sometimes that he can't take anymore. At least I did."

"Really?!"

Victor looked at him seriously.

Ross understood the look and didn't ask any more questions. He knew the feeling behind it. It was still in his heart.

He looked at his little ship.

"Will you still call him Cadelia?" Victor asked.

He shook his head slowly. He remembered the previous moments before he met his current friends. When he felt in the depths of despair that someone cares about him. Just when he had given up hope. He felt the thought of her warm his aching heart. The world began to take on colors again.

"I will name it after the name of the woman to whom I owe my life. Valeria. I called her Valeri..."

* * *

Vivan was hugging Vashaba against him. She slept so soundly. Reeba was dozing so quietly he barely heard her. There were sounds of bustling and talking from outside the door. People gathered for a meal. He heard the voices of his mother and stepfather. The innkeeper urged one of the girls. Grandma reproachfully asked Grandpa why he went to Ross himself and didn't wait for her. There was no joy and laughter. Just muffled conversations.

Today was the funeral of the murdered.

Julien's funeral.

He felt hot tears streaming down his face. Regret squeezed his heart like a vise.

It choked the throat.

However, it was not the funeral that was the reason for this...

* * *

Ross walked over to his lover in the twilight. The wind was rushing through the broken glass of the carriage, moving the several drawings scattered on the table.

"Dinn just told me," he confessed quietly.

Sel hugged him. He felt his body tremble despite the fact that Ross dressed warmly and pulled on the cloak. Apart from the despair that tormented him, fear overwhelmed him. His lover was exposed to contact with a witch. He was afraid for his fate.

"Are you cold?" He asked with concern.

He thought Ross would try to downplay it, but he just whispered,

"I just have to take it. Do not panic."

Something about his movements, something in his gaze, disturbed Sel even more. Like when Ross looked at the dead woman and her child lying in the street as they drove through the plague city on their way to their new home.

"He's on the verge of endurance," he realized suddenly.

Kidnapping... A nightmare confrontation with her mother and her lover... Her rejection... Sickness... And then the unexpected kindness of so many people. And finally the death of Julien, the merging of souls with Oliver. And Mayene...

Ross has been going through a constant mood swing ever since he was kidnapped. He would despair once, then rejoice after a while, then fall into despair again, and then feel joy again. He shouldn't be fighting Mayene right now. He should get some peace and rest.

He hugged Ross tightly, desperately helpless, filled with fear and love.

"I can't lose you either," he whispered in his ear. Ross's eyes glistened with tears.

"You won't," he assured him warmly. "I can handle. Don't worry. That's not the first time."

Sel was silent, so he added softly:

"I'll take you on a Valeria cruise later. I'll be the only captain in these waters who has no idea about sailing so you can't miss it. Silas promised to stay and assemble a crew for me."

"Valeria?" Sel asked, stepping back.

"Would you prefer it to be named after you?" Ross asked hesitantly.

"No, I wouldn't do that to you," Sel replied silently.

"I'd have a few ideas about Valeria's appearance," he told him with a hint of a smile. "Could use some improvements as well. Of course, if you allow."

Ross sighed.

"Great," he replied, trying to align his thoughts with the ideas. "Because I hate her gilding. They are completely tasteless. And a bit old-fashioned."

"You got it."

"Great Mother!" Sel thought. "He really wants this ship!"

"Take care of the captain's cabin, too," Ross added as if casually, but his face took on that unsettling expression again.

Sel nodded, watching him silently.

He silently promised himself that he would try to find out from Alesei and Sai how Ross coped after running away from home when he recovered from being almost beaten to death. What gave him strength then? Ross was his strength. If he breaks down after what he experienced, he will give up too. He lost someone he had liked again. Without it, he could not imagine his further life. He could feel the darkness in the lover's heart, although the latter tried very hard to show that everything was fine. But it wasn't.

Too much has happened.

* * *

The ground was muddy. The snow is almost gone. Alesei, hand in hand with Azylas, helped the inhabitants to prepare the graves and collect the stones. The dog held on to its master as if sensing something, and when the master reached for him with his hand, he licked him anxiously, as if afraid that the master might leave him.

"You named this pet yet?" Asked the blacksmith when they were done.

"Dog!" Alesei cried simply, and the animal came up to him again. He stroked them tenderly.

"I see," the smith replied laconically.

"He already has his name," said Alesei thoughtfully. "Except I don't know it. It was given to him by people killed by the plague. I will not change it. Maybe someday it will come back to him."

The blacksmith pondered the words as he looked at them.

The hill, which is also a local cemetery, was filled with inhabitants. Everyone came to the funeral. Songs were sung. Hands were held. The same despair was shared. There was something really extraordinary about it: so many people had gathered, ready to support each other in sorrow. On behalf of all, Vivan appeared before the crowd and gave a short farewell speech amid crying and overwhelming sorrow. People expected this from him and he didn't disappoint. His speech gave hope that this time evil would be stopped once and for all and that no one would ever suffer again. Witnesses to the clash with the witch near the port looked at Dinn and Sai, remembering how close the elf would have died despite his bravery. Neighbors of Gunter and Maria were warm towards Sel. Sai pointed to Ross, Tenan hidden under a hood, who kept aloof. Someone patted him on the shoulder reassuringly. Ross hugged his sad friend, eyes full of tears. Alesei tried a little to show all of them his support with discreet gestures.

Seme was sobbing softly against her husband.

Oliver stood by his sister until the last songs had died down, then dropped to his knees without a word, ignoring the mud. He remained in that position, nodding slightly in silence, staring from her body to face and eyes closed. After a while, Ross joined him in brotherly pain. Oliver seemed to be torn by emotions looking for an outlet with a great bang. Ross could sense these emotions. Like Vivan, concerned about the despair within them.

At one point, Oliver, no longer in control of himself, pulled a dagger from his belt and swung it straight at himself...

Everyone froze with horror.

Sel, the crew who had accompanied Ross so far, all who knew about soul mating froze in horror. Sai slumped to the ground in front of her beloved on the other side of the tomb, pleadingly extending her hand. Sel sat down next to her.

The dagger in Oliver's hand shook dangerously.

Ross looked at him with strange composure, though he was now suspended between life and death. Nobody saw fear in him. This was what Sel was the most terrified of because it confirmed his fear that Ross was too close to the emotional edge now.

"Vivan..." Victor whispered to his grandson.

Vivan silenced him with a wave of his hand, knowing full well how close Oliver was to the abyss. Every gesture could provoke him to act recklessly.

Oliver looked only at Julien.

An ominous silence gradually enveloped everyone gathered.

Vivan looked at Sel. They exchanged glances.

"Ross," Sel said in the silence, his voice trembling with tension.

Ross looked at his lover and in his gaze Sel saw nothing but love. No sign of fear or hesitation.

Yes, he was preparing for the worst. He let the Jewel soothe him.

"Just look at me, okay?" He whispered to him. "Only me."

"Why don't you stop him?!" He asked in horror. "You can do it. You and the Jewel!"

"Okay," said Ross, trembling, his face pale.

Many of their shared memories passed through Sel's mind. From the first time to the stay at the House of Pleasure and the present moments. He was burning with anxiety. One move from Oliver and he would jump at him over Julien's body. He could see Ross out of the corner of his eye. He felt the tension in Sel, he could see it in his eyes. He was staring at him, but his mind was somewhere suspended, far away.

Oliver looked up at Sel, waking from his trance.

Then his gaze slowly fell on Sai. Then both Sai and Sel saw a flash of awareness in Oliver's eyes.

Finally, following his friend's gaze, he rested on Ross.

Slowly he understood what was happening. He threw the dagger aside.

"A bond..." he whispered. "Ross... I'd give you a terrible death. Why didn't you try to stop me?!"

Ross quickly embraced him without hesitating, hiding his relief. The almost tangible tension is gone. Oliver took a deep breath, as if he had suddenly freed himself from a great burden.

Ross hid his emotions by closing his eyes.

"It's okay," he said gently. "I know you wouldn't do that."

Chapter XVI

The final fight

Night came and Mayene was still gone.

They knew perfectly well that the witch was delaying to scare them completely, but after all these events, fear did not enter the hearts of the waiting people, but rather grim anger and a desire for revenge. They wanted her to finally pay for all the harm done. Even if they feared death, they did not show it. The healer himself said during the funeral speech that Mayene made a mistake in thinking it would be easy for her to control him and Barnica. He has no intention of giving up, and the people here have proved that even cruel death cannot crush their courage.

* * *

Dinn did not tell anyone about his experiences. Nobody but Vivan and Vashaba. Tenan, who also knew about the threat, did likewise. Though the truth was not known, people felt in their hearts that they were fighting for more than their own freedom and the life of a healer. They were determined to fight, even if it was the last thing they did. For the whole future was at stake. And the future of their families.

Without a healer whose life harmonized with theirs, their future would be like that of other people, and if Mayene made him a slave to her own desires, this future would not be enviable. The existence of Barnica in its present form as a bustling port town, where people hardly got sick and grew slowly old, depended largely on the healer. He drew the strength and power of his gift from their sincere love and affection. People really loved him, for which he gave them his willingness to help, good, warmth. And security. His suffering and death would be really painful for them. They would herald their own doom.

They had to defend themselves at all costs!

Dinner in the great hall of the Under the Unicorn Inn passed in silence. Apart from the Beckert family, their friends and the innkeeper with his wife, there was no one here. Seme returned to her home with her family. Oliver was not fit to social life now, so he even missed the dinner they all ate together. He couldn't be with anyone but Sai right now. So he asked her to apologize to everyone on his behalf. He slept most of the day anyway.

Erlon, tired of his duties, spoke little. He was awake while others went to rest, overseeing many things, from organizing a collective funeral, collecting belongings from the remains of a palace, to setting up a volunteer guard in the city and dividing responsibilities in helping the families of the murdered. Lena cuddled up to him with concern. She couldn't persuade him to go even a little rest now. He wouldn't listen to her. Everyone had a feeling that Mayene would be back in town. He rested his head on her shoulder. However, when Vivan approached him to give him strength, he dismissed him gently.

"Save yourself," he ordered him.

Vivan refused to yield. He felt he had to take care of a few things.

Alesei's dog walked over to him and licked his hand. He stroked it thoughtfully. Even the animals sensed something. Reeba was staring at him from her position in front of the huge fireplace. He looked at everyone despondently. His mother shook his hand in a gesture of encouragement. He loved her motherly look that had seen so much. Like now.

"Anna," Victor turned quietly to his wife.

Vivan's grandmother looked at him fondly, kissing him on the cheek. Then she looked questioningly at Ross. Everyone in attendance immediately picked up on it. He shook his head. She frowned. Some other came back from this unfortunate journey. There was less of the energy he had had in him. Well, he's had a hard time going through it, including the unfortunate return here.

Mayene left a mark on him.

At least he wasn't so cold anymore. Vivan took care of that.

Now they were talking to each other in low voices. After a while, Ross stood up.

"We'll be back soon," he told the audience.

Vivan stopped Vashaba, who wanted to follow him. So she sat down next to Anna, worried and not very pleased.

"They have a common world," Anna tried to calm her down. "Similar powers, same amulets, only one magic. They will be back soon."

"Did you notice," from the first meeting they called each other, "that they have something else in common?"

"What do you mean?" Victor was concerned immediately.

They both figured out what he was thinking for Ross's sake, his reddening slightly from nervousness.

"Old and stupid!" His wife said. "What's on your mind too?!" Sel looked at them curiously. Like Dinn.

"What are you talking about, Vashaba?" The healer's mother asked.

"About the scars," Vashaba replied. "They both have them."

"Yes, we know, but..." she began, but Vashaba cut her off with a shake of her head.

"Sel," she said to her friend, "supposedly during the fight with Ross's mother and Ramsey, you were hurt. So it was said. Is it true?"

He remembered perfectly well how Cadelia had cut him on the chin and cheek, as well as her malicious comment.

"Yes," he replied.

"Where?" She asked.

He told her about the cuts.

"There's no sign of them," she said softly.

Everyone looked at him with increasing interest.

"Vivan and Ross have kept their scars," she explained her guesses. "They reflect their souls. If they wanted them not there, they would have disappeared. But they are because they've been deeply hurt and don't want it to be forgotten. Their wounds on the body healed, but those on the soul - no..."

* * *

"Ross..." Vivan began as they found themselves in an abandoned room with only the inseparable tigress sitting next to it. "I know how we can beat her."

He laid out his plan to him, trying to remain calm. The more details he revealed, the more frightened Ross was in his heart. He started shaking his head before Vivan finished speaking.

"No!" He replied eagerly. "I don't agree to this!"

"Help me! This is the only way!"

"You cannot do it!"

"Ross, listen!" Vivan gripped his shoulders. "If she wins, if she survives and prevails, everyone will suffer. Sel, Vashaba, Paphian, our families!"

"Yes! I know!" Ross replied forcefully. "But this plan... Your way is..."

"Please!" The healer interrupted him gravely.

Ross paused, thinking about what he heard. Vivan went to the window. He pretended to be watching the town's dormant streets lit by torches. However, in fact he waited for his decision...

"Okay," Ross finally replied, with a heavy heart. He walked over to him and hugged him tightly, saying:

"Remember I'm here."

"You need to be. She's gonna want to get both of us. If something happened to me... then you will be everyone's only hope. Understand?"

Ross nodded his head in agreement, still holding him in his arms.

"You cannot die..."

"Look after them."

He hugged him tighter, nodding silently before loosening his grip hesitantly.

"One more thing..." said the healer, trying not to let his voice tremble. "Tell Sel, Paphian, Dinn and Alesei about it. Not anyone else, not everything. They would not agree. Get them out of here. All of them. Let them know as little as possible, though they must know a little. They deserve it."

"And Vashaba?"

"I'll tell her... At the right moment. Don't tell her how..."

"How far will you go?"

Vivan went numb. The question sounded harsh, but Ross's gaze seemed gentle.

"Yes," he replied.

He read sympathy on Ross's face.

"And how far will you go, Vivan? That's what I need to know."

The healer looked at his friend seriously.

"As far as needed."

* * *

Through the window of the sumptuous bridal room, Vivan watched the ruins of his house. The glow of oil lamps and torches illuminated some of the ruins of the palace. Erlon ordered whatever could be saved to be moved to utility rooms. Some items had already been moved while they were resting here. That's good. Maybe it will cheer up his family.

Over dinner, he saw Paphian touch the book thoughtfully underneath the doublet. He probably wondered if the other two volumes of the trilogy had survived. He had himself several favorite volumes, the fate of which was uncertain. In one of them, the protagonist was called the Cat, just as Oliver in Wermoda was said to be called. And he also led a double life. In another, the hero suddenly became the chosen one with a purple aura, the only one with whom it would be possible to defeat the archdevil himself...

He gave in to such contemplation. He didn't want to think about those things anymore, nor about his future. He wanted something to finally start happening. But the moments passed and Mayene did not show.

She was tormenting him.

She tugged at his nerves with the silence.

Vashaba kissed him lightly on the temple. She watched with him. Her eyes watched his face anxiously, as if sensing something she was afraid to even think about. She must have wondered what he had secretly talked to Ross about.

He loved her for this concern. He felt sorry for having to hurt her.

The lights were turned off in the houses. The streets were empty. The first frost-free night passed in total and apparent peace.

Reeba stood up before they heard footsteps and a soft knock on the door. Vashaba walked over to open them. Vivan touched the soft fur of the white tigress, knowing what he would see next.

Ross nodded to both of them with deathly earnestness. Behind him he saw Sel, Paphian and Dinn.

"She's coming," he said shortly.

"I'll wait here for her," he replied calmly.

They both looked at each other with a heavy heart. Together they carried this burden.

"I'll be around," Ross said. Vivan nodded.

"Are you sure?" Ross asked as he stepped inside.

"I'm not sure of anything."

"I will stay with you."

"Then she'll kill you. We must have a background, remember? We settled it." Vashaba became concerned.

"How that is: you settled?! What did you settle?! Vivan?"

"If anything goes wrong..." Vivan continued to stare into his friend's eyes, lacking the courage to look at her. "You know what to do..."

"Paphian?" Vashaba asked. "Sel? Can you tell me what's going on?"

"You must go with them," Vivan ordered her.

"Solei (little sister)," said Dinn. "Nimas ale gann (He must do it)."

"Tu let da! Nah, binn ate bost! (Don't say a word! I don't want to listen to you!)" She shouted, "Ami eno Kilinn! I'm his Keeper!" she switched to a common language.

"I will not fail again!" She cried, staring passionately into the healer's eyes. "I will not let you down!"

"Vashaba..." he began, but she gave him a sudden hard cheek.

He paused, holding Paphian back.

She grabbed his shirt, agitated and moved by her act. Her red, loose hair gave her the appearance of a fireball. She touched her gently slapped cheek, which had turned purple.

"It's nothing…" he tried to calm her down. She was shaking with emotion.

"I'm not leaving you with her!" She said hoarsely.

"You will die..." he tried to convince her.

She hit him in the chest with her fist, not too hard, but firmly.

"Shut up!" She ordered him firmly with a hint of despair.

"Solei," Dinn said softly. "We must go. She gave him an angry look."

Vivan took her chin. Angrily she broke free from him, so he tried again once. They could not part in anger. He kissed her tenderly. She gripped his clothes tightly, as if she weren't about to yield, kissing him back. There was some kind of desperate passion in it.

Involuntary witnesses of the kiss could not take their eyes off them.

These two did not want to part with each other, although the reasons for each of them did not quite harmonize with each other.

Dinn felt he had to intervene if Vivan's plan was to succeed.

"Let's go now," he extended his hand to his sister.

She did not take her eyes off Vivan's eyes, as conflicting feelings fought an internal struggle.

Ross was sure his friend's hidden desire now was to go with them and hide from the witch.

Most of all, Vivan wanted to live!

In the end, however, reason won out. He slowly released his beloved, letting his brother take her away from him. They said goodbye to him with a sad look.

Paphian hugged his brother tightly.

There was nothing else he could say.

"Vivan..." Ross embraced him last. "I'm around. Remember."

"Get out now," he replied warmly.

"Make sure he doesn't come near," Vivan instructed.

"I will," Sel replied. "Don't get yourself killed."

Vivan listened to their silent footsteps. The inn was deserted. Everyone had abandoned her except him and the tigress, who clearly did not intend to leave him in need.

"Reeba," she looked at her severely. "Come out. Come on!" She ignored him. Only one ear moved nervously.

"Reeba, don't be stubborn," he ordered her.

The silence of the night was suddenly interrupted by a familiar roar that he had never expected to hear here. From outside he heard a dog barking. He looked around just as a green shape flashed before his eyes. He paled.

"The dragon!" The innkeeper's wife called. "It's a dragon!"

"Hide!" He ordered the tigress quickly, while there was an ominous thud and crack outside.

The dragon destroyed everything in its path.

Reeba finally obeyed her master and slipped out the open door. Vivan heard his own rapid breathing. His heart was beating like crazy.

She sent a dragon on his people!

There were screams and crackling of flames from outside. The dragon breathed fire. He looked around. The fire has already consumed some of the houses. People were hiding… Some were drawing bows and crossbows.

They were not scared of the beast.

Fire hit the inn building. It had ripped a huge hole in the roof from a tail hit. Everything trembled in its seat. The inn's door and windows rattled. The ones from the room hit the wall until it burst. How could they be any obstacle for a witch?!

Mayene suddenly burst from above amidst the smoke, and her malevolent steed roared to announce their arrival in the town. The flames of the blazing fire crackled as she stopped just outside the room.

She rose from her crouching position. Her inhuman eyes were focused directly on him.

Chills ran down his spine.

Demon.

Powerful and malevolent again, she regarded him with a slow, appraising gaze.

"Stop the dragon," he said to her, showing no fear. "I give up.

I'll give you what you want."

She tilted her head.

"Only now?" She asked. "And just like that?"

"You've killed a lot of people."

"Come on, come on," she shook her head with a smile. "You are so concerned about it?! Bullshit," she said, stepping over the threshold. "What are you hiding there now, huh? Any surprises again? Or maybe some horse?" She looked around contemptuously. "You're so still. I can't see anything here. No bows, women, ropes. Nothing! Boredom! What did you get up here this time? You will not tell your future wife?"

She laughed hoarsely.

He could feel a malevolent aura tightening around both of them, pressing into his mind like poison. An evil like he had never met before was emanating from her. She was unscrupulous.

Cold seized him.

She circled him, watching everything, hardly paying any attention to what the dragon was doing in the town.

"Why don't you stop him?" He asked after a moment, following her with his eyes.

"It's too late for that!" She suddenly shouted into his face, as if she were giving him a sharp reprimand. "Now you have realized what I can do?!"

"You wanted a baby," he replied, though the words barely passed his throat.

She stood in front of him suddenly, and he knew. Ross was carrying out their plan...

Mayene's gaze told him that she wanted to fuck him in any way she could think of.

He expected this.

She took him firmly by the chin. He met her eyes with determination.

"You must obey me absolutely," she demanded firmly.

"Stop the dragon. Keep the deal," he replied with difficulty, referring to her earlier words.

She growled angrily.

"Agreed," she said reluctantly. "But no other combinations. Complete, slave submission."

Her cold words and touch made him tremble. She liked it.

"You eat when I allow, you sleep when I allow. Understand?"

"Yes," he answered quickly.

She looked at him lustfully. She loved such submission. He knew about it. Ross used her likes and dislikes to fuel these thoughts.

By the neck she dragged Vivan to the bed he had shared with Vashaba. She pushed him at them unceremoniously.

"The dragon!" He reminded her, clenching his fist with determination.

She grimaced impatiently. The sound she made had nothing human in it.

There was a sudden silence outside.

Mayene looked at the bed's ornate carvings. She used magic. Wooden branches trapped Vivan's hands.

"You won't use your hands," she told him ironically.

She sniffed him carefully. Then she sat on it to better lean in, sniffing again.

"Ah," she realized after a moment. "You've fucked someone on that bed before. I should make a reservation that I want to be your first. Stupid, stupid mistake. A wasted opportunity! Well…" She tore the shirt over his chest with a quick, violent movement, making him twitch nervously. With sick fascination, she examined the numerous scars on his body.

"So you already know what it is like," she said coldly. "But you can forget about it. It won't be like this with me."

Yes. It will be much worse…

"So much suffering…" She smiled lasciviously, running her long fingernail over the unevenness of the skin. "So much delightful pain…"

"Come on!" He urged her mentally, fighting the fear. "Have fun, let's get it over with."

She dug her nails into the scars, urged on by Ross's fueled desire. She began to move them slowly, creating a bloody mark on the healer's body. He groaned softly, which only increased her excitement.

"You don't like it, huh?" She asked.

"No," he replied truthfully, while she gouged bloody furrows on his body, moving her hands with pleasure.

Vivan's breathing quickened. Pain shot through him, taking his breath away.

Mayene wasn't just scratching him with her nails. She was doing something that made the impression much more pronounced. It evoked nightmarish associations in him.

He swallowed nervously as she stopped. Her iridescent eyes flashed.

"Oh, he's so cute," she thought wildly. "It will be a pleasure to destroy him."

Unknowingly she bit her lip.

"I want to try," she thought suddenly, somewhere on the verge of consciousness. "I want to check what he tastes like."

"If only she wouldn't come to her senses," Vivan thought, watching her face anxiously.

Sitting on him, she leaned over, wanting to touch the bloody marks with her tongue. She ran it slowly over her lips, lasciviously. Just a little. A little...

He held his breath.

She sighed with delight before she began to lick the drops of blood in a slow, sensual movement, running her hands over his body with more insistence, smearing the bloody marks.

He was a sacrifice on her altar.

He pressed his lips together, breathing hard.

Managed to.

She was going to have a heat.

"It tastes great," Ross thought meanwhile, as he sat hidden in the abandoned house of Gunter and Maria. "Like pure fear..."

Sel had covered him with everything he could and lit him in the fireplace, but Ross was shivering from the cold. Cold sweat poured over his body. Vashaba watched his face anxiously, sitting so that he could not see her. She gripped her brother's hand tightly. Paphian leaned his hands on the window frame, unsettled and anxious. He preferred not to look at Ross. Though he and Vivan had not revealed what their plan was, they all felt it would not be easy.

Nobody said a word so as not to distract the wizard.

Paphian tried to think of his mother and father who hid with their grandparents in the inn by the marina. You couldn't see what the dragon was doing from here. Everything seemed to suddenly come to a halt.

Ross focused on his task. Mayene had to be persuaded to lose herself in her sick play. He could barely bear himself for what he had to do. It was sick. And bad. Very bad.

Sel carefully pulled a handkerchief out of his pocket, gently wiping the blood that ran from Ross's nose. The one with closed eyes in concentration did not react to the gesture.

The jewel shone.

Time passed slowly. Midnight is past.

He waited for a sign.

"With each passing moment," he whispered finally to the others, "she made me feel more and more ill..."

He needed a moment to rest. Sel met his tormented gaze.

"You know what she does?" He asked softly.

"All too well," he replied, avoiding the eyes of the others. "Her aura... Her thoughts... He saw it through Mayene's eyes, but Vivan wouldn't let him do anything."

Not yet.

Thanks to her greed, his blood seeped inside her, changing them, building, enhancing the experience. It flowed like a wave...

"Ah!" Mayene shouted, dazed, excited to the limit.

She looked at the healer hungrily, wondering what she wanted more right now - whether his body or his blood. Both, if only she could... Her sinister, inhuman nature chose her favorite pastime, but in a different way than before.

She lunged at him and stuck her sharp teeth into his neck to taste more. She sucked greedily, overcome with the desire to possess everything in him, absorb everything, and destroy it. Eat!

"He will kill me!" He thought in horror, feeling his heart pound, as if it wanted to pop out of his chest.

She was draining his blood every moment, shortening his life! And yet he had to...

"No!" He struggled desperately. "No, hell's bells! Leave it! You will kill me!" She jumped up and sat on him. His head was buzzing.

"A kiss," she whispered dreamily.

Horror seized him by the throat and the hair on his head rose.

"No..." he only managed to groan.

Their lips met. Kiss of death...

Ross opened his eyes, but he didn't seem to see anything in front of him. He saw the souls of the people Mayene had killed swallowed up by her, despairing, moaning. He inhaled loudly.

She ate their souls!

And now she kissed Vivan. He could smell him as if he were right next to him. His thoughts. He resisted. Mayene wouldn't be that easy with him. He didn't let her take his life. He was strong.

But it was only the first kiss, and it weakened him severely.

Ross sprang to his feet abruptly.

"Ross!" Sel called. "What are you doing?!"

"I go there!" He shouted frantically.

"Can you imagine that I just let it happen?!"

"She'll kill him!"

"First," Sel suddenly approached him, "she wants to fuck him! Don't interfere, asshole!"

Ross froze in surprise. He looked at his lover in horror painful amazement.

"You forgot to protect your loved ones, sweetheart," she hissed at him in her voice, moving Sel's lips.

The jewel glowed instantly before Ross could get his thought into focus. The glare almost blinded them.

Sel staggered. He fell to his knees, clutching his head. When he lifted her up, he saw two bloody tears. Dinn immediately joined him and helped him to stand his feet.

"Sel?" He asked anxiously.

"She was inside me..." he whispered, his face white.

"I know," Dinn replied seriously.

"It's okay," he whispered, while Sel nestled against his shoulder, shocked by the rape of his soul.

Anger sparked in Ross's heart from his love for Sel. She hurt him. Contaminated. Possessed.

The jewel fully shared that anger.

"She said then," he said emphatically, "that I could be more powerful than the foundations of the earth. Well..." The jewel glowed an intense red, "I'll make that the earth will tremble at her feet, and she will love me so much that she will agree to whatever I make!"

"You can't kill her," Sel whispered.

"No," Ross replied, kissing his forehead tenderly. "But I already know what to do." Suddenly he was no longer cold. He felt an extraordinary power within him, as if he could move mountains.

It was an unusual, overwhelming feeling, as if he was trapping his mind in a cage and now finally releasing it.

He felt that he could do so much.

Because of love.

Nothing could stop him!

"We're going with you," Paphian said, Vashaba standing at his side.

* * *

The dragon stopped in the market square, crushing all the deserted tents of travelers.

Something has changed. Suddenly he awoke from a strange dullness.

Why is he here?

What is he doing among the people?

They brought him here. They have weapons. They wanted a dragon?!

They treated him like a toy. Oh no, he won't get fooled around like that. He will show them the danger of his anger!

Chapter XVII

Dragon

Tenan ran straight in front of the dragon a few yards away and aimed his bow with great precision, slowly tightening the string. The dragon has put up the travelers' tents in the marketplace. Now, overcome with anger, he began to demolish houses and catch people.

Tenan wasn't going to let him do that.

He released an arrow.

It bounced off the hard armor without hurting the dragon in the slightest.

He cursed softly, pulled out the other, drew his bow, and released it again.

This time it was precisely stuck in the neck, which really wasn't an easy trick. The dragon did not stand in one place for a moment. Many axes, bolts, and arrows missed their target this way.

"Good," Tenan said to himself.

The dragon seemed to hear him or the arrow enraged him, for he looked directly at the impudent archer with large green-blue eyes. He opened his mouth.

He wanted to breathe fire.

At this point, a missile flew out of nowhere and hit it right in one of the blinds. He roared angrily, cocking his head and covering the sore spot with his paw. He could no longer see the archer who looked around for his protector.

Oliver took the second stone out of his pocket and without hesitation shot the slingshot into the beast's other eye as soon as the head was on his side.

There was a roar again, and the furious and sore dragon began to twist and roll blindly, crashing into houses. The ground trembled underfoot, and there was a roar again and again as the stone walls cracked.

Surprised, Tenan waited until his and Oliver's eyes met. He couldn't believe what he saw.

His amazement became all the greater when he realized that he recognized him.

And yet he helped him.

Uncertainly and respectfully he nodded to say thank you.

Oliver replied the same.

A scream distracted Tenan. The long-haired girl screamed as the dragon threw the young boy into one of the houses with a stroke of his paw. The thump and the open gaze of the young man left no doubt. He died on the spot.

"Maya!" Exclaimed Oliver when he saw that the girl stopped, shocked by what had happened.

The dragon did not wait. He was about to drag her off the square with his tail. Tenan ran to the girl and dragged her to the pavement with him, just below the dragon's tail.

Oliver ran courageously past the beast's paws and helped its victims to stand up.

"Thanks," he said shortly, looking seriously at the former pursuer. "Are you OK?" He asked a girl he obviously knew.

She just shook her head, looking at him, then at the dragon, peering down the streets converging in the marketplace.

"Brother?" Tenan asked anxiously.

"Love," replied Oliver for the girl, and she hugged him despondently.

"Let's go from here!" Tenan commanded, seeing the dragon turn back. All three escaped to the ruins of one of the houses and hid from sight the beast.

"He's going to rise," she informed them, then her gaze followed the motionless body in the marketplace.

"Don't look," Oliver asked softly, drawing her to him.

"Where's Sai?" Tenan asked.

"Do you know each other?" Oliver's cold tone even caught Maya's attention.

"Julien bring me into contact with her," Tenan chose quickly one of the options he could think of to avoid confusion.

Unfortunately, this answer was not enough for Oliver.

"Ah, yes," he drawled. "Maya, please meet Tenan," he introduced the situation maliciously. "He's a thug and murderer who killed Sel's father and his wife, as well as our devoted servants!"

Maya looked at Tenan in horror.

"He killed Sel's father?! And a wife?!"

"Wonderful…" Tenan growled. "So why did you save me?"

"Because I'm not like you!"

"He was cursed," Maya said. "He had to do it."

"Are you telling such fairy tales people now?!" Oliver exclaimed. "You rotten apple!"

"Calm down!" Maya snapped. "The dragon rises. He doesn't need to hear us!"

So there was a tense silence, which lasted until the dragon flew from the marketplace towards the harbor.

"Just don't fight here!" Maya threatened. "I saw the bracelet in Julien's hands at the funeral. She has ended the curse with love, right?" She looked at Tenan.

"Yes."

"What the fucking love?!" Cried Oliver in amazement, trembling with anger. "My sister would never love a murderer!"

"And with a love like mine is now lying on the stones! True!" Maya sobbed violently, shaken by her own loss. "People saw him cry for her! That she told him to kiss her, they said! Because a kiss of true love will destroy any spell! Each! Only death can not be undone. There is no help for this…!" She broke off suddenly and hid her face in her hands.

A terrible fear burst from her breasts.

Surprised by her despair, they were at first silent, not knowing what to do, helpless in the face of her suffering. And then Maya jumped up suddenly, and before Oliver could stop her, she ran to her fiancé's body and knelt beside him.

Shocked by the overheard words, Oliver fell silent. Maya's parents appeared at the marketplace, concerned about their daughter's fate. People rushed to look for the buried, cries for help and crying of children were heard.

"I did not understand that," whispered Oliver at last. "She told Ross: Tenan is alone. He didn't understand either. And she was really worried about you..."

Tenan froze.

Oliver looked at him with painful eyes.

"Sai is watching over my aunt and uncle. They are with Vivan's family. I came to help... I didn't want to wait in the hideout..."

He didn't want to wait and sit idly. Yes, Tenan showed up for exactly the same reason.

Oliver sighed and stood up. He looked at the distraught Maya, who was holding her lover's head in her lap. Both families, hers and the dead one, had already surrounded her, trying in vain to ease their grief.

"I'm a fool," he said. "Without her, I feel so incomplete. Somehow angry at everything. I put the life back to me at risk. The life Ross gave me. Sai is probably out of her mind. I should be with her. Not here. And I keep trying to do something, I still miss something. I don't know what to do to quell this pain, Tenan. I don't know what to do to silence this regret. Fool…"

The feeling was also no stranger to Tenan. He had similar feelings. He got up to stand beside him.

"I shouldn't be here…" whispered Oliver, looking at Maya.

Carefully, fearing rejection, Tenan put a hand on his shoulder.

"If you like," he said softly, "I will accompany you on your way back."

He did not intentionally use the words, "I'll walk you back." He did not agree that he had acted foolishly. Oliver was not a stray child or a dog, but a lost, unhappy soul, doomed to share its existence with someone else. He did not ask for such a fate. He didn't deserve a severance pay. They both left with the same urge, seeking relief in their pain. A perverse fate, however, decided that only one of them had the right to do so, without putting others at risk. Only one had the right to decide his fate.

Oliver looked at him with utter sadness.

Tenan would have liked Oliver to accompany him, but they knew fate had arranged their cards differently…

"DRAGON! THE DRAGON RETURNS!" Someone suddenly shouted, and at that moment they heard the roar of an approaching beast.

They both looked at each other surprised as at the command.

"Well," Tenan observed sarcastically, "it seems time's up."

"Funny," remarked Oliver in a similar tone. "I thought of the same thing."

They looked at Maya and her family gathering in a hurry. They did not want to leave the dead body.

"Tenan," said Oliver solemnly, "this does not mean that between us..."

"Yes, I know," he interrupted firmly.

Nevertheless, they looked at each other differently than a few moments ago, though neither of them would admit that a change had taken place.

They ran to help in unison.

* * *

"Ross!" Sel cried as they ran through the alleys, trying to avoid the dragon at all costs. "Vivan forbade you this! He didn't want you there!"

Ross replied with only a brief glance with much meaningful eyesight. Vashaba drew an arrow from her quiver as the dragon staggered over the marketplace wider circle, passing near them. She pulled the bowstring and released the arrow.

Accurately.

She noticed them.

Ross looked at Vashaba reproachfully as the dragon roared and headed straight at them. Alesei cursed ugly.

The dragon breathed fire that they barely escaped from.

However, as he started looking for them, something distracted him. A man ran down the street below him, and Sel gave a nervous twitch when he saw him. Just behind him was Oliver, who saw a group of friends.

Tenan released the arrow with great precision, straight into the dragon's throat, which spun in pain above them and crashed with a crash between the group and the two shooters. He jerked his head up, angry with the archer, ready to pursue him until his last breath. His teeth clapped dangerously close.

The fearless Tenan, who was also driven into danger by some determination, pushed aside Oliver standing next to him, costing him precious time for his own escape.

The dragon caught him with its teeth.

The arrow he was holding in his hand was aimed straight in the eye, and Vashaba hit the base of his neck.

The dragon roared painfully, thrashing its tail in all directions, damaging the walls of the still standing houses. He moved his wings desperately, feeling his end, but nevertheless did not want to let go of his prey, which he clearly intended to drag with him into imminent death.

Each clench of his jaws caused a wave of new suffering in the archer. Shocked by this sight, the people waited with fear for the beast's agony at last will come to an end.

At last the dragon fell, and the wounded Tenan, with the help of Oliver and Alesei, slid from his motionless maw straight onto the pavement.

Oliver hurriedly examined the injuries. Abdomen, chest. Tooth marks.

Fang wounds.

After the injured man's behavior, he guessed that he was aware of the gravity of the situation.

However, he didn't seem to care.

Hurriedly, he reached behind his collar to grab a chain from the end of which hung a small bottle of Vivan's life blood. Tenan recognized the gesture and held his hand.

"You don't have to…" he choked out with difficulty.

"You are mad," said Oliver shortly.

The bottle was in his hands, and the rest of its valuable contents flowed down the wounded man's throat, against his resistance. He had to swallow. Too many viewers have flocked in here from all sides.

"As stubborn as she was," Tenan muttered afterward.

There were many questions on Sel's lips, but Ross, who wanted to get to Vivan as soon as possible, refused to let him ask even one of them. Seeing that Tenan would only feel better from now on, he nodded to Oliver and left the crowd without waiting for the rest.

So there was nothing for Sel to do but follow him as quickly as possible.

He also saw how a clearly concerned innkeeper from the "Under the Unicorn" inn was kneeling down by the wounded and Oliver. Apparently, he and the murderer were friends already, which was really beyond Sel's mind.

Suddenly he met Tenan's gaze.

Sel's eyesight turned cold.

But then he turned his back to the wounded man and walked away. Even so, Tenan knew it wasn't their only meeting.

The worst is yet to come.

He felt a touch of darkness.

Wano saw the shadow in his eyes that Julien had been so scared of before.

Now it was he who felt scared at the sight, and the scene he witnessed appeared to him from a new, gloomier perspective.

It wasn't courage that pushed Tenan to fight...

"Ross was here," Tenan observed. "He is going to a healer, I think."

"Yes," replied Oliver thoughtfully, waiting for him to recover while Ross's friends hurried out of the crowd.

"So, you have a fifty-fifty chance," the healed man noted. "Either way... you might die. Anytime. Even now."

Oliver looked at Tenan seriously. There was not even a trace of amusement on his face.

"Does it bother you?" He asked.

Wano pretended not to hear them. The crowd slowly became interested in the dead dragon, sensing personal matters between them.

Tenan mentally relished the pleasant, soothing warmth that spread over his body and the strength returning to him. He was silent for a long moment.

"Yes," he said finally, not looking at him.

Surprised, Oliver did not take his eyes off him. He could feel his gaze.

Chapter XVIII

Help me

Kiss of death…

Vivan felt his strength draining out of him, his hands faint with exhaustion, trapped in the carved branches.

Mayene, absorbed in this kiss, forgot herself for good. His blood had so much power, so much power his touch had in it that suddenly her purpose, which was to beget a monstrous child, was void. A tremendous urge over which she had no control prevailed: to take everything she could from him.

Insatiable.

Hypnotic.

Absorbing it completely.

There was nothing more important. Until she was satisfied with it, she cared for nothing else.

He realized that there was no longer any hope for him.

Even when she finally tore off her lips, he knew it was too late. Weakened, he felt that she was unbuttoning his pants in a hurry, as if she hoped that despite what she has already done, the healer will still have the strength to do anything.

He desperately thought that if he did not interrupt her now, Vashaba would see him with his pants down under a dead, almost naked old witch, and nothing would erase the sight of her from her memory. Not from her heart.

He didn't want this.

So he had to do what was necessary.

Mayene's hand dove under his underwear.

He closed his eyes...

Only a portion of the enormous life-giving force that illuminated his gaze and penetrated the blood appeared on his face. He almost had no strength for such a powerful dose. He hoped that what he gave her would be enough to enliven her heart, since the blood had helped prepare the rest.

A powerful impulse shook Mayene's body: a desperate dose of power she had not suspected until recently in herself. One and only.

It contained everything.

Mayene's heart beat slowly until it caught the right rhythm.

The healer's heart slowed rapidly, barely having the strength to resume his work. Vivan was dying...

"WHAT HAVE YOU DONE?!" She screamed, waking up violently from amok. "YOU...!" Her passion turned to pure anger in the blink of an eye. The hands clenched on the neck of the imprisoned Vivan, his face contorted in inhuman cruelty.

"You thought..." she screamed, wheezing as the healer fought futile under her grip for a breath of air, "that the human form would take away my power?! I had her before I became who I am, you goddamn virtuous misfit!"

Vivan struggled for his life, but weakness and lack of air quickly deprived him of his strength.

The only thing he could was fail, having Mayene's face twisted with anger as this time she was definitely taking his life.

Someone else will have to...

Then a white shape flashed before his eyes, and the witch screamed in pain, knocked off the bed to the floor.

Reeba, he thought gratefully.

The white tigress was trying to get to the neck of Mayene, whose human form apparently lacked the remarkable strength used so far. The fight between the faithful animal and the human could only end in one way, as Mayene soon learned. Scratched, wounded, however, she fought a ferocity that could be envied by many men on the battlefield. Her kicks were particularly strong, one of which kicked the white tigress away.

Mayene stood up with a tiger clawed neck. The blood finally flowed from her wounds. Scratched all over her body, in torn clothes, dangerous despite her injuries.

The tigress snarled and jumped onto the bed, ready to defend her master. She prepared to pounce while Mayene looked for something to defend herself, feeling the effects of her injuries.

Vivan gasped for breath. His regenerative abilities were running out, as was his entire body. He didn't have the strength to complete the work because he couldn't breathe freely, and that certainly didn't help his concentration. The effort tormented him terribly.

The tigress was watching the witch cautiously as she walked away from the bed in search of a weapon.

Through half-closed eyelids, Vivan could see her analyzing the situation, wanting to weigh the victory on his side, but there was nothing he could do about it. He could feel her anger. After all, an ordinary animal could not just disturb a future ruler of the kingdom.

It was beyond her mind.

"Thanks to your body," she hissed at him, "I'll live forever. Since that's how you played it, I will keep it and feed on you until there is no trace of you left and your power seeps into me for many years. There is always a way…" she whispered vengefully at the end, looking into the tigress's eyes.

Only Reeba stood between her and Vivan and her new plan.

"They can't kill me," she snapped.

A smile curved her lips as she felt the healer's blood circulate within her, healing her wounds in front of Vivan's eyes. Her smile was lascivious, as if something extremely exciting was happening to her. In a way it was like that.

His weapon turned against him…

He could see the satisfaction in her eyes as she saw the expression on his face.

"Mayene," they heard suddenly a calm, but unusually imperious voice, "sit down!" It was as if he was talking to a dog, not to a dangerous witch.

Vivan looked at the entrance in amazement.

Ross, so different than before. The friend was serious and firm. He stood on the threshold, with a gesture confirming the order.

It was as if he was looking back into his former life, dominating an insecure but willing client. Although Vivan had a vague idea of what this kind of frolics might look like, they were completely alien to his nature, but looking at Ross, the same Ross who listened to his grandfather with cordiality and patiently and kindly chase away his nightmares, he could also imagine its other side. The dark one he sometimes mentioned to him when he wanted to lose oneself in the decadence of the House of Pleasure, to suppress the inner torment of the ordeals.

Only Vivan and the two dead women who took care of the tortured boy knew about it. Thanks to his extraordinary senses, from which nothing could hide, he knew no painful past. Even Sel hadn't been privy to it, believing it would be better to forget it.

At least Ross thought so.

Until one day Cadelia showed up in town...

However, he hadn't had time to remind him that he shouldn't be here according to their plan, because something extraordinary had happened.

Without a word of protest, without even trying to fight, Mayene, as she stood, fell to her knees and sat on her heels!

Vivan saw in her eyes a similar surprise to her own behavior.

However, the will quickly won, although in her voice they both heard the fear before it could fully regain control.

"Wizard!"

Vivan renewed his efforts to keep from losing consciousness.

Ross hurriedly glanced at him, and the image was etched hard in his memory. The bloodied healer lay tied in a strange way on the bed, barely alive, and beside him stood a white tigress on the bloodstained sheets, alert and ready to defend her master. Her sides and muzzle were also scarred, probably by Mayene's sharp claws.

It was worse than they had both predicted.

"YOU HAVE NO POWER OVER ME!" Mayene said emphatically, drawing his attention as if she wanted to convince herself as well as him.

She stood facing him, looking into his eyes.

In the next moment, the entire inn building shook as two powers clashed in a struggle of one will against the other. Mayene spread her hands. Reeba lay down on the bed next to the healer, prudently not wanting to attack now, because the witch, using magic, could defeat her. She waited for the right moment, like a real good hunter.

Ross tried to penetrate Mayene's mind, but Mayene was stubbornly resisting him. Sweat beaded on his brow. He knew that losing taint to destruction not only himself. He still remembered the image of the enslaved Sel with the eyes of Mayene and the mortally wounded Vivan lying on the bed.

He couldn't lose this confrontation.

Mayene tried to penetrate his mind and he tried to penetrate hers. It also cost her unexpectedly a lot of effort. So much that for a long moment she couldn't even move.

The walls of the inn began to crack, pieces of the roof fell to the ground.

"Vivan!" Vashaba shouted desperately, whom Sel and Paphian stopped from bursting in.

The gathered residents watched the building with horror. Wano gripped Tenan's arm tightly as he watched what was happening in the inn. His wife hugged Riga, a kitchen maid for whom the inn was the only home she had ever had.

Oliver felt dizzy.

"I'll get you both to hell!" Mayene hissed furiously, and the inn shook violently.

Some of the walls began to fall apart. The ground around her opened in several places, revealing deep fissures. They all backed up quickly, and some hid under the stables' rooftops as violent lightning thundered overhead and dark clouds obscured the dawn glow.

Reeba decided to take advantage of the fact that the witch's entire attention was seemingly focused on Ross and attacked.

Mayene with a careless movement of her hand made the tigress's body toss back and struck the window and it burst open, letting in the cold air still carrying the last breath of winter.

Cold penetrated right through the half-undressed Vivan. He swallowed with less pain.

The sharp air finally rushed into his lungs freely, and icy chills began to shake his body.

Reeba lay down, unable to move from the excruciating pain. Vivan felt her suffering, though he could not see her. He felt sorry for the brave animal.

"Your hair is turning white!" Mayene noticed meanwhile, watching Ross's auburn hair quickly fade in streaks to white.

Ross gritted his teeth. The jewel glowed incessantly red, fueled by concern and love of its owner, so that no one from his relatives would be hurt, even if he himself had to pay for it.

The hair soon turned snow white.

Ross felt himself losing strength, and the building he could sense thanks to the jewel with all his body was about to collapse under their feet.

He redoubled his efforts.

"Tenan..." Oliver staggered, feeling the weakness engulfing him and the darkness before his eyes. Tenan turned just in time to see Oliver collapse to the ground. He grabbed him at the last moment. The small man was not heavy when he took him in his arms.

"Oliver!" He called to him, drawing the attention of Sel, who paled at the sight.

Oliver lost consciousness.

"Come!" He felt a gentle touch on himself and saw the mother of the healer. "We'll carry him to a safe place!"

"Nowhere will be safe for him now!" He replied glumly. She agreed silently before waving her hand.

"What about Oliver?!" Seme, who appeared in the crowd a moment earlier, worried. "Tenan?!"

It was the first time she had spoken to him directly, but he didn't have time to think about it.

Sai appeared next to them and touched the unconscious lover with concern.

"Ross," he told her, following Sai.

"I know," she replied.

"Vivan..." Ross did not dare to look at his friend. "I can't kill her with my power. I don't have a sword."

"I know," Vivan croaked with difficulty.

It's time.

He had enough strength for it.

What could he be thinking about now?

What can you think about in such a short time? About life? The thought hurt more than the wounds he had inflicted. The image of Vashaba, his mother and his relatives were a torment for him.

About the death that awaited him?

He wasn't ready for it. He couldn't think of it or accept that it was coming.

He closed his eyes.

He was mentally inside the body of Mayene, who was already looking at Ross in triumph.

"You know," Ross said to her. "You've lost a long time. As soon as you set foot in this town. Just when you thought about getting rid of me! Then..." the jewel glowed an intense red, fueled by his emotions, "when you killed Julien with your tricks! When you killed Gunter and Maria! Once you broke into Sel's mind!" He shouted the last words, then quickly subdued his voice: "Don't you dare move without my consent!"

Mayene's smile froze into a grotesque mask.

She couldn't move from the spot! The order sounded like a bell in her head. The primal fear of some unimaginable punishment he might inflict on her had suppressed all reflexes. It crossed her mind that she shouldn't think that, had almost beaten him in the end. A moment ago, she almost had him in her hand!

But now she had no power over him.

He, by virtue of his love for Sel and his friends, had absolute power over her. And the jewel was in full agreement with him.

The white-haired Jewel wizard's dark eyes pierced her through. They held in place.

She should defend herself. Resist him. But she was scared to death.

She was afraid of the power of those feelings that emanated directly from him, and to which she never had access because she couldn't control it. She could never make them out of herself, therefore she could not be the perfect witch. She reached into the power of hell, hoping that the other, the dark side, would allow her to win.

It was much easier to go on the dark side when a person was born without the ability to warm feelings, unfinished, against all norms and rules. It was enough to succumb to these influences.

She needed even a child just to gain power.

She loathed something she couldn't understand, loved to destroy it.

Death took all those who had affection.

Death should meet this male whore.

Death would be the end of the sweet healer.

"All that good heart of yours is worth shit," she said. "You should die in agony on the ship!" She cringed at the words, as if she expected him to punish her for it. "The good are the weak. They are rubbish. They first dies in the belief that they are heroes for the cause. Ordinary rubbish that needs to be crushed and trodden down. What good has your goodness brought you, asshole? Where did you get through it? Were you good? And that one?" She nodded timidly and viciously at the same time, like someone who knows there is no longer any chance of surviving. "How would he end up at the market in Vermoda? Why are you still doing this? Do you want to please them? What was bothering you?! You are sucks, not the chosen ones! They fucked you up, they tortured you, and you keep licking people! Why?!"

She was afraid, and yet she couldn't help but utter the words.

She couldn't understand why they hadn't followed a similar path to hers when people had betrayed them.

Ross approached her, full of imperious dignity.

"We are not succumbing to anyone," he replied seriously. "We only listen to our own heart, it is our own choice. They cannot deprive us of it. Because they are our strength. Yes, we suffered by people, that's true. But they also taught us love and sacrifice. And friendship. I pity you. You don't even know how much you've lost. Evil is too easy, and only fools always go the easy way. Sometimes you have to work hard to appreciate. Sometimes you just have to endure it to fight for yourself. You didn't feel like it."

She froze.

She felt a pang of jealousy. Or even, perhaps for the first time in her life, a sense of regret? She didn't want this. Her face twisted in a desperate fight against his will.

The crackle in the air came not only from the breaking boards.

Ross felt he had to use all his strength against her will. So possessively she sought to overcome, break his will. He had never had to fight so desperately, not only for power, but above all for his own existence, and only with the strength of his mind. When he lived with his mother, each day was survival, and constant vigilance was sometimes the only weapon. He had to be alert as when he was afraid of an unexpected attack.

And that was literally exhausting him mentally.

The witch wanted to take over him.

He was weakening, not used to such a fight yet.

He looked at Vivan once more, to incite his will, to inculcate the sight of his tormented friend into his mind. In order to constantly remember that she is not fighting to prove her strength, but that she will never be able to harm anyone again. But, though he tried his best, not trained to play such a hard game, he succumbed to her pressure. His body, tired with the constant tension, was beginning to give up.

When she sensed a weakness in him, she smiled.

He resisted her, but it cost him more and more. His head was bursting with pain, as if someone were squeezing it with great force.

"Ross..." Vivan whispered, touched by his torment.

Mayene held out her hand, and a magic-drawn stone from the inn's wall dropped into it. Powerless Ross could only watch as the hand moved towards him to deliver a punch.

He defended himself until the last moment.

The blow knocked him to the ground and severed the bond. Pain shattered his skull. He grabbed his head with both hands, groaning. At the last moment he noticed that she was moving towards him, ready to split his head with that stone or do something much worse.

"You won't know my kiss," she said to him. "I'm too disgusted with you!"

"No!" He began to back away from her, crawling. He wanted to gain time to get up, but he felt light-headed. "You're afraid of me!" He hissed, driven by pain and anger.

She laughed contemptuously.

Vivan clenched fists. One more time. This one time!

"Drop it!" Ross called.

He had the feeling that his own screaming would kill him, but it worked.

Mayene threw the stone away!

He almost screamed with joy. But angry at herself and confused, the witch screamed furiously and looked around. Her eyes fell on the stand by the fireplace, where the poker hung...

Vivan's gaze followed her, and for a moment he held his breath in dread... He must help him!

Mayene held out her hand while a sore Ross held his on top of his head where the blood was oozing. Despite his daze with pain, he saw what she caught this time. His heart skipped a beat with fear. Poker. Poker again!

Mayene looked at him with satisfaction, both hands hugging the object. She took the first blow...

Ross cringed involuntarily, knowing that if he could, he wouldn't have time to get up.

He knew exactly what would come next.

He was wrong.

"No," Mayene said, "I'm not going to hit you with this!" She swung at the show, her face an expression of unimaginable cruelty. "I'm going to do you pleasure with it..."

He turned pale at her words with fear.

Everything that had happened to him so far was no worse than what was about to happen.

Even Ramsey hadn't thought of giving him such a death.

And he would never allow ex-clients to have such sick fantasies.

"And then I'll screw it..." She grew serious, ready to act.

"Put that down," he said, but his voice was not sure. Fear had already taken his hold over her.

She did not obey this order. Terrified, he almost begged her for mercy, but he gritted his teeth quickly.

He was lost, but he would not hear him scream. At least as long as he can stand it. The jewel flashed brightly as Mayene leaned over.

"Vivan…" he whispered to the healer, saying goodbye to his friend.

Vivan closed his eyes and clenched his fists in one last desperate gesture.

Mayene staggered. Her eyes darkened. Her breasts exploded with an enormous, crushing pain... In the blink of an eye her face turned blue, her face twisted in disbelief, and her lips changed color. She turned to the dying healer, eyes widening. He should be gone by now!

He had stopped her heart by the strength of his will, as he had done in his rescue attempt a few months ago, amidst bloodthirsty people, overwhelmed by hopeless despair.

He squeezed it with a large, invisible fist.

She had no time to do anything.

She fell to the floor, struggling for her life in vain. She still crawled up to him, reaching out her hand. She wanted to strangle him, crush him, and drag him to the grave with her. But here her time has finally ended.

She died at his bedside, one last tug grabbing his hand, once severely torn by others. She used her long fingernails to cut through his skin, as if she wanted to destroy at least this: a symbol of his gift, which could also bring ruin. Her unusual iridescent eyes gazed at the gates of the opening hellish abyss with no longer seeing eyes.

It was over.

Ross crawled over to her. He touched to make sure she was already dead. Then he pulled himself together and, an angry tug, grabbed her hair. She did not react. She fell like a puppet with its strings cut off.

"She's dead," he said quietly after a moment. "Finally..."

Everything around calmed down instantly. The inn froze as if waiting.

He looked up with an effort to look at the injured Vivan.

The healer's eyesight faded. He was still alive, though he had little of this life left.

"Vivan…" Ross whispered, pain in his heart.

Vivan looked at him with difficulty. The corners of his mouth twitched from trying to smile, as if he wanted to cheer him up, to cheer him up after the act of violence.

At this point, there was a loud crack. The whole building of the barely holding inn began to crumble with a bang...

"Ross," Sel whispered despairingly. Vashaba pressed against his shoulder. Dinn took her hand.

The tigress raised her head in its last breath to look at the source of the unusual noise.

Then she put it back down and closed her extraordinary eyes forever while the world around her cracked and thundered...

There was a wail around the ruins.

Sel, Paphian, and Vashaba began working their way through the rubble in unison before the dust settled, calling for their loved ones. They heard silence, but they did not lose hope.

The floor where Vivan's and Vashaba's room was located was still covered with what was left of the attic and roof of the until recently beautiful highlander "Under the Unicorn" inn. It was terribly dangerous and difficult to get through there, but they kept on trying.

"Over there!" Sarana, the innkeeper's wife, called to them. "I can see the chimney, and it was right above the fireplace in their room!"

Paphian followed her gaze and noticed him too. Now he was working desperately to get there. Dinn stood on the boards beside him as if he weighed as much as a feather. He was helping Vashaba upstairs.

The elves were light when they wanted it.

"Dinn!" Paphian called to him.

"It's dangerous!" Vashaba shouted. "We will go!"

"I'm not going to stand and wait!" Sel muttered beside him.

"Stop!" Stonecutter Bert shouted at them, standing by the rubble. "The elves are right! Here you have to be smart! It is all just sticking together! It'll bury you all alive!"

"There is Vivan!" Paphian shouted.

"And the Wizard! Yes, Count, I know!" The stonecutter agreed calmly. "But if you go on, you'll be dead and so are they! This is how I feel it!"

"You have to gradually! Tools are needed," his friend agreed.

"Harness the horses to the carts!" Exclaimed the innkeeper from the "Under the Marina" inn, who was here with his three sons. "Pull back logs!"

"I'll talk!" Bert the stonecutter said. "Everyone has to obey!"

"What shall we do?" Erlon, who had arrived with the family, asked him.

The stonecutter looked around at the crowd. The survivors of the kidnapping and their defenders stood in one group as if they had colluded. Rescued recently by a healer, including the blacksmith Azylas, they stood against. The rest - in the middle.

Paphian dragged the reluctant Sel with him, mentally agreeing

the words of the stonecutter. The dead won't help anyone.

However, the real sensation was caused by Oliver, who appeared among the crowd in the company of Tenan. Though he was pale as linen and didn't look very well, he had inspired hope among the people by his coming, especially in Sel's heart.

That's why he insisted on coming here.

He felt that his presence would be needed in this situation. For if he was still alive, it made sure that the Jewel Wizard, Captain of Valeria, though still Cadelia, whose humble crew was also here, was alive too. So maybe a healer...

For that moment, Sel forgot even what he felt at the sight of Tenan, he felt so much joy.

"Take hammers, axes, choppers, ropes and whatever!" The stonecutter exclaimed. "And listen, then we'll do this..."

* * *

"Ross..."

"Yes, Vivan...?"

"Help me…"

"I cannot move!"

"I know," the Healer said softly. "I feel it. Legs, hands..."

"What about you?"

For a long moment he didn't get any answer. But he felt that his friend was still alive. The jewel had assured him of that too.

"I'm dying..." Vivan replied finally.

Ross closed his eyes as tears rolled down his cheeks. He sensed it.

He had known it would be so since he saw him wounded on the bed.

"No..." he said, desperately wanting to chase away this future, stop time, stop events.

Anything as long as this doesn't happen...

"Please..." Vivan spoke with difficulty, his voice hoarse, "for other help."

He already knew what he was going to hear, so he shivered with suppressed despair.

"Help me go," his friend asked softly.

"Vivan..."

"Ross..." Vivan's voice suddenly broke. "Believe me, I don't want to do this! I don't want to die..."

"So fight!" He shouted to him. "Do you hear these voices? They are coming for us! Hold on!"

"I don't have the strength..." Vivan croaked with difficulty.

"Please!"

"I'm so tired..."

"If you close your eyes now - you will die! Can you hear me?! Vivan?!"

"I'm cold..."

"Please don't give up," he said pleadingly. Silence answered him.

"Vivan?" he couldn't even see him from his place, there were so many boards and stones.

"You too?!" He whispered regretfully. He felt the sorrow of the Jewel.

"Vivan?!" He exclaimed. As long as he is talking to him...

He called for him twice more before he finally heard a weak voice:

"I am here..."

The tears kept flowing from Ross's eyes.

"I was on the other side for a while," Ross said. "Back when I helped Oliver. Julien was there."

He didn't know if Vivan was still listening to him.

"She'll definitely come out to meet you," he assured him through tears. "I know that what you fear most is that you will be alone there. You will not be. She will be waiting for you there, I'm sure. You won't be alone, can you hear?"

At last he heard a soft sob.

"Only for us you have to wait a little," the tears almost choked him.

He paused. He heard voices above him. Help was undoubtedly coming.

"I didn't tell Vashaba that I love her," he heard his friend say. "It's because... my God!" He interrupted suddenly. Through the noises outside, Ross heard his muffled groan. After a while, Vivan calmed down a bit. "It's because... for me..." he spoke the words with difficulty, "I mean... I love her... tell her... more than life... forever..."

Ross was calling for him constantly, but Vivan didn't answer anymore. Despair burst through the survivor's breasts with muffled sobs.

"He's still alive, isn't he?" He asked Jewel anxiously.

"YES," said the Jewel. "HE HAS A STRANGE DREAM. BALANCES BETWEEN LIFE AND DEATH."

Ross sighed heavily and looked up for familiar voices.

He, too, felt a bitter cold. Blood was dripping from the throbbing gash on his head.

Mayene's lifeless body lay beside him, closer now than before. Her eyes were fixed on him as if she was still watching him.

Somewhere in his psyche, the rift grew deeper from this dead one of hers gaze. He was afraid of her gaze, though there was nothing she could do to him, and at the same time he genuinely hated her for all the wrong she had done.

He looked away with an effort.

Worse than these thoughts were the others that formed in his mind as he looked at her. The ones he didn't recognize. So different, foreign. Terrifying. It was some other part of his nature - dark, different, for which nothing mattered but demon self-pity and retaliation. He was afraid of this darkness, its destructive power. She would take from him what he was until now and what he was loved for. He would rather get out of this dark trap now. He preferred not to look at Mayene anymore. Don't be left alone with your own thoughts. As long as Vivan was with him, he kept his thoughts focused on him. He was gone now.

He was left alone, and he no longer had the strength to fight his own demon hidden in his soul. He had nothing to hold on to.

"They're coming for us," he whispered to himself to break the silence around him and the dead witch.

"DO NOT LOOK AT HER," said the Jewel. He clung to his voice like a drowning razor.

"Talk to me, please," he whispered to him. "Do not leave me."

The jewel enveloped him with its warmth of feelings, glowed in the prevailing twilight, filling his heart with hope again. He felt the darkness leave him.

He was himself again.

"ROSS," said the Jewel. "SEL IS JUST ABOVE YOU."

He smiled weakly.

"And Vivan?" He asked.

He wished the Jewel would tell him.

"HE HAS NOT LEAVED US YET," said the Jewel.

Beneath the ceiling beam that held his hands, he clenched them into fists with silent hope.

"REST," the Jewel told him gently.

* * *

"They fell all the way to the basements," Paphian remarked.

"Be careful with those boards!" The stonecutter Bert called to them. "Get your head on your neck!"

"Ross…" Sel whispered frightened, touching the fallen man. "Paphian, look at his hair!"

"Nasty gash," added Paphian, watching the cut in his snow-white hair. "He's stuck. He could be seriously injured."

"Ross, can you hear me?" Sel patted Ross gently on the face.

The wounded man opened his eyes with difficulty and looked at him half-conscious.

"It's you..." he croaked with difficulty. Sel smiled slightly.

"Disappointed?"

Ross tried to smile back, but only winced in pain.

"You have a broken head," Sel explained to him. "Do you hurt somewhere else?"

"Legs... Belly... Hands..." Ross began to list, to which Sel hastily pulled a bottle of Vivan's gift from behind his shirt and held it to his lips.

"Drink," he whispered. "What would happen if we hadn't it...?"

Ross obediently obeyed his instructions. A concerned Sel kissed him with concern in forehead.

"And Vivan?" Ross asked. "Did you find him?"

Paphian was just looking through the rubble where his brother might have been. At first glance, it didn't look good. He couldn't even see a scrap of free space.

"He was there, wasn't he?" He asked Ross, who was slowly recovering. "Did you hear him?"

"Yes."

There was the sound of planks being pulled away from above, a little further away.

Bert asked to find another way.

"There was a bed by the window," Paphian remembered. His voice cracked at the end of his speech. "Was he on him?"

Ross didn't answer right away. Paphian knew Vivan would use a way to deceive Mayene, though he did not know the details. Still, he guessed the truth.

"Yes," he replied after a long moment.

Paphian's eyes fell on Mayene's lifeless body they had found together with Ross.

For a moment it looked as though Paphian was about to kick her. They had never seen such a fierce, cold anger on his face before, especially when his eyes ran over her half-naked body, covered with a torn, colored, as usual, bloody shirt.

"I interrupted her," he felt he had to tell him. He did not want to see this stubbornness in him. "Nothing happened."

Paphian looked at him, or rather looked at his snow-white hair seriously.

Then he glanced at Sel. Apparently, they both had to come to the same conclusions, for Sel came up to him and put his hand on his shoulder.

"We'll find him," he whispered.

Ross was given a gloomy look away. Paphian regarded him anxiously.

He opened his mouth to ask a question. Then they heard Vashaba's voice from above:

"Vivan!" She exclaimed. "He is there! I can see him..." Her voice broke suddenly.

Paphian felt anxious.

She called Vivan, but they didn't hear his answer.

* * *

It was hard to break out of this strange state.

As if he had a long and hard way to get home. It would be much easier to give up, but he knew that one thing he couldn't do. Some force was pushing him towards the light. It took a lot of effort. So much that he was almost exhausted.

It finally dawned on him that he felt warm.

Soothing warmth.

He was so cold! He froze in the ruins of the inn.

This heat did not come from fire.

Someone was hugging him, warming him up.

He was holding his hand.

Two beings. Behind him and in front of him.

Soft, down-filled bedding.

Quiet breaths.

A gentle kiss.

Vashaba!

And behind him...

Paphian. Paphian and Vashaba kept him warm under the soft, gorgeous duvet. A fire crackled in the fireplace somewhere nearby, and the two of them were getting hot.

They both held his hands, which hurt mercilessly.

He felt so heavy! The skin on his chest and abdomen stung him, but tolerably. He smelled the herbs.

An herbal dressing on the hands and somewhere in front, on the body. Dressing around his neck.

But when he wanted to speak, it hurt. It must wait.

Slowly, as if they weigh too much, he opened his eyes.

In a darkened room, the first thing he saw was her beautiful face. And a wave of purple hair revealing the elf's pointed ear.

As if she sensed that he was looking at her. She woke up.

He loved her wonderful green eyes, which widened as they met his gaze. First, full of disbelief, and then indescribable joy.

He tried to smile, but even his facial muscles would not listen to him, he was so exhausted from returning to the world of the living.

Because he was alive, right? He was looking at her now, so he had to live...

She parted her full lips as if to say something. But then she glanced at Paphian sleeping behind him, and in order not to disturb the moment with his awakening, she gave up her words. Her eyes glistened with tears of secret happiness.

He had barely managed to tighten his fingers on her palm, lightly, but every movement, every gesture was important to him, although it cost him a lot, because it made him realize that he was alive. That and seeing her were worth every effort. She shook that hand silently, moved carefully, and kissed him first on the cheek, then on the forehead, then finally to his mouth. It felt as if she had breathed strength into him with that kiss. His blood began to circulate faster, his muscles reminded him what they were for, his eyesight brightened, and his touch was fully back. The mortal pallor was replaced by the usual blushes.

He didn't have the strength to really kiss her yet, but at least he could cling to her, hug her happily, contemplating this moment of silence.

He began to tremble, and then she hugged him tighter, awakening Paphian, his face lit up at the sight of the conscious Vivan.

Then he felt a tender touch that he could not confuse with anything else, it was so dear to him. Mother sat down behind Vashaba to see his face. She ran a tender touch through his hair.

Seeing that he was very weak, she approached him herself to kiss him on the cheek, as she had done in the past. They both hugged him to each other, and Paphian even adjusted the duvet on his back to make his brother really warm, although he could see that it was much better.

This genuine love and concern of others acted on his heart like a balm, although it also aroused the fear that he would lose it all, that he would not be able to hold on to them.

Everyone embraced him, happy for his return, sensing this fear in him, and Vivan clinging to Vashaba's body held her hand very tightly, fearing that he would not stay with them and would fall somewhere in the bottomless blackness, cold and empty. It was only when the trembling had stopped that he calmed down under their touch and fell asleep exhausted, reassured by their soothing words of assurances that the evil was over and would not come back, and that everyone was waiting impatiently for him.

He fell asleep listening to their voices.

And he felt so good with it...

* * *

Once it was certain that the healer would survive, the overjoyed residents set about repairing the damages. Ross and Captain Noren engaged their crew in rebuilding the Under the Unicorn Inn, and Count Erlon was again busy organizing work in the Barnica.

This time, a large canteen was set up at the market place under a makeshift tent, where the workers ate their meals. The supply and food point was led by the same women who did it during the plague. Tents were erected for those who did not have a roof over their heads. Most of the families from damaged houses found temporary accommodation in Seme's house and several others, as well as in the Under the Marina inn.

The most important and real event for the inhabitants, right after the witch's defeat, was the burning of her body at the stake on a small beach by the port. There was no person in the town who did not want to see such a spectacle. People cursed her, not only for the evil she had contributed to, but also for the harm to the healer she had almost killed.

Ross, who was being greeted everywhere now as a distinguished guest, stared at the funeral with grim thoughtfulness, thinking about how much Mayene had changed in the hearts of these people, how much anger she had instilled in them that they had not realized before. He hoped that when the emotions subsided, life in this place would return to harmony and to the peace that sprouted here just after the plague.

He longed for peace in his life, promising himself that as soon as they finished helping with the reconstruction of the Barnica, they would remake Valeria to go on a cruise. He liked the prospect of swimming in the calm waters of the endless sea.

Even the storms did not scare him. It was a major change in his life that finally gave hope for a better future alongside Sel with Alesei, now open to everything, and his Dog.

It was the future that attracted him to itself, cried out with a sweet voice. He smiled at these desires with irony. For it seemed to him that completely unplanned and unconsciously, his mother had just instilled in him this love of sailing, which she had not expected at all. Even in his eyes, Sel could see the surprise at times. The beloved was still amazed, though he did not say it, why Ross had such great sympathy for the ship that his mother gave him with such contempt and reluctance, and why he was so drawn to sailing. Why should it be otherwise? The ship was not to blame for the fact that it was commanded by vile Ramsey, and it was Ross's responsibility that, with Sel's help, he remodeled Valeria so that even a tiny trace of its previous owners would not be left. Then she would become his beloved, dignified Valeria, who warmed in him the greatest memories of the gloomy period in his life.

He could even see her in his mind. Sel painted her in a painting, flowing on the waves, and Victor borrowed from him the wooden miniature of the ship, which he had previously donated, to return it to him, in every detail similar to the future Valeria, upon hearing about the planned changes. Silas had assembled a crew of trustworthy people for him, and the captain of Hydra in his spare time taught him the art of navigation and sailing commands. Especially the latter, Silas liked to follow. He gladly assisted in this, and laughed kindly with Captain Noren at his mistakes.

Sel, on the other hand, learned cartography in preparation for future expeditions, and sketched his ideas for improvement on both Hydra and Valeria. They did not spend much time with Ross during this time, except at night, because Sel's help was also necessary for the stonecutter Bert, who commanded like a captain the construction works in the town under the watchful eye of Count Erlon.

As a result, architecture changed throughout the town, as Sel's designs and roof solutions, based on observation of the life of residents in winter, were quite popular. Even the palace, which was planned to be built at the end, already had new solutions in its designs, including a water system, and its little prototype was installed by Sel in his family home.

While working on the inn, Sel met with Tenan from time to time...

Their contacts were limited only to mutual observation. Neither of them wanted to be the first to start the conversation.

Slowly - as Sel observed with amazement - a friendship between Tenan and Oliver grew, also thanks to Sai, whom Tenan treated as a dear friend. Of course Ross had told him about the curse, the bracelet, and how she was finally left with this man, but as long as Oliver finally understood how awful Tenan's position was when he was Moren's right hand, and love lifting the curse had to be one another, and so strong as to help create the Jewel of Hope - Sel have not as open-hearted as his friends. In his memoirs, this man was still his father's murderer, and therefore will never be able to communicate with him. And the murderer of Milera, who was devoted to him and loved him, despite his faults and the threat of his imminent death.

He couldn't forget what had happened. Nor was he sure he would ever do it.

Ross did not interfere in his decisions. He did not avoid Tenan or approach him for Sel's sake, but he agreed mentally with Oliver. However, in this case he did not want to take any side. He had known Tenan from his stays at the House of Pleasure, and had seen both his good and bad sides there. Looking at it more objectively: there were times when this or that situation could be played out differently than with the hapless Reniel, a poor girl so similar to Oliver, a toy in Moren's hands. He once attracted too much attention of the bandits who took the brothel in defense of Valeria, his guardian. He could not endanger himself more for others. But Tenan had the opportunity to ease her fate several times. However, pleased with the fact that impulsive Moren focused on the slut, he did the same as the rest of the gang.

Probably a noble act towards Reniel would cost Tenan a lot as well, but Ross had no idea of that...

Ross had not witnessed the pain killing Tenan when Sai and Julien came to him. Sai never told him about it.

Tenan made no effort to put pressure on Sel. He was just living his own life, hoping he would stop hating him so much in time.

There were no simple solutions to this situation. Only time could help here.

For the time being, he enjoyed the friendship and cordiality he gained for him, the innkeeper Wano and his wife, as well as the sympathy of the inhabitants, who quickly made a romantic and tragic background to his story.

Only his heart remained full of longing. The mouth remembered the taste of not that last kiss, but that sensual in his room. He missed her painfully.

He saw that Oliver too. He had often seen him at her grave.

Dinn regained his composure when one evening he heard a story by chance through the window of one of the houses.

Grandma was telling the longing little girl about her mother, arranging her to the sleep.

"I dreamed about your mother yesterday," she told her warmly. "She asked about you. She said she loved you very much."

"And what else did she say?"

"Remember what your dad told you? Your mother was defending this white-haired elf who fought the witch."

"Dinn," the girl said softly. "Leni says his name is Dinn. I heard it."

Dinn smiled warmly.

"She also asked about him."

"And what did you tell her?"

"What I should. That he is safe and sound. And she said: Tell him we're free now. Our souls are no longer in danger. I have to tell him when I meet him."

"What does that mean?"

"Someday I'll explain. He will understand for sure."

"It's good, isn't it?"

"Yes, honey," said Grandma. "This is very good news."

"Thank you," Dinn whispered softly to the deceased.

A sudden breeze brushed his face in a gentle caress.

* * *

Every day the inhabitants of Barnica would leave gifts for their healer in the dining room of the Under the Marina inn. Someone brought delicious food, someone else brought warm woolen blankets or vests. Others handed out tidy surviving books from the palace library, herbs to improve health, a quilt, hand-carved figurines... If it were spring, the inn would probably be flooded with flowers.

Every day they asked about his health.

The innkeeper would not let anyone except the inhabitants, the count's family and his friends upstairs, where the healer's room was located, and sometimes using help of his own sons when it was asked too insistently. At first he only let his family in, making an exception only for the Jewel Wizard, whom he did not intend to refuse after living through Cadelia and everything that happened there. Everyone kidnapped with him at that time was shocked at the sight of his new hair color. He bound them together with his heart. Through his nightmarish experiences with his mother, they always welcomed him warmly and treated him kindly. He also liked them very much, as if they all had some strange bond.

"He is still too weak for constant visits," the innkeeper patiently explained to the rest of the people, when he had to let the chosen ones upstairs next to them.

He was proud that his care was helping Vivan to heal, though it was certainly Vashaba's love that mattered most. And the care of loved ones.

He made sure that none of the guests spoke about the planned surprise for the healer, hoping with the blacksmith Azylas and other originators that this gift would bring Vivan more joy than sorrow.

They had carved two white tigers in the marble. In memory of their courage. After all, these wonderful animals gave their lives for him...

* * *

Vivan stood by the window, invisible from the outside thanks to the densely woven patterns on the curtain.

After a few days, when the weakness caused by the loss of blood had passed and his innate ability to regenerate with the immense love that had been shown to him returned, he finally rose from the bed. Mayene's sharp claw wounds didn't heal quickly, and her hands were rubbed to blood, when he tried in vain to protect himself from suffocation, they still stung him, but at least he could speak again. Mayene's handprints became faint.

He watched the familiar world begin to change before his eyes and thought that he might never see it...

"What are you thinking about?" Vashaba asked quietly, hugging his back.

He took her hands and wrapped them around him, though she tried to prevent it so as not to offend him. She didn't want her hands to move around the bandages under her shirt. But Vivan chose to endure the pain rather than give up her touch. Since he woke up, she knew that he was constantly looking for an opportunity to feel her with him. As if he was afraid that without her he would lose all support. He needed a sense of security.

She kissed him softly on the back of the neck, where she could still see the fingerprints as if they had hardly disappeared. She would always see them there.

"Look," he said softly. "When summer comes, many things will be completely different."

"You didn't think about it," she thought, but did not repeat the words aloud. She listened to his calm breathing. He radiated again wonderful, soothing warmth she loved so much. She missed his touch. It had been two weeks since he first got up on his own, but they were still not together.

Wounds did not heal quickly, not least because they were inflicted by the incarnate demon. It was she who discovered this mystery of suffering.

"When will you leave the room?" She asked gently.

"Tomorrow," he told her. "I cannot wait. I want to see it all!"

So far he has not come out, because it was good for him here. Alone when everyone thought he was still too weak. He wanted time to recover among people close to him. Calm his own thoughts.

"Do you know how much they are waiting for you?" She asked cheerfully. "Have you seen all these gifts? They missed you."

And then she quietly added:

"I missed you..."

Vivan turned slowly to her. She lowered her gaze, intimidated by his gaze, which was unusual for her. He reached out, scarred from chafing and Mayene's sharp claws. He carefully lifted her chin.

She shuddered at his touch. The heat penetrated her body like a wave.

"Vivan..." she began to say, because she felt that she would no longer bear this tormenting longing.

He kissed her passionately, impassionedly. She kissed him back with delight, hugging his body, wrapping her arms around him. As if that kiss was the spark that set her on fire.

"You're hurt..." she whispered, full of remorse for reacting to him like that.

He showered her with kisses as if he were consuming the same fire.

"I'll be careful," he whispered hastily in her ear.

They slowed down once they were in the bed. Slowly, filling each other with mutual closeness, gentle towards each other, they shared their passion, love and trust among themselves.

Only those moments were important, so full of undisturbed harmony and happiness.

And when he fell asleep, she watched over him. His guardian, ready to ward off bad dreams. She woke him up when he dreamed that the furious Mayene wanted to strangle him again, and when like Ross, he dreamed that the inn was collapsing, burying him alive.

As it had happened incessantly since that fateful day.

She was his guardian.

She chased away bad dreams with her voice.

And love.

"Inen min, Kalen..." then she said gently, "sleep well, my love."

* * *

By the time they left the inn the next day, they found a small package at the door of the room.

Inside was an intricately carved tree. An oak painted white, each leaf of which was a work of the finest art. This is the most beautiful grandfather's handiwork Vivan has ever dealt with.

There was a little note from Victor between the branches:

Vivan, you are our courage.

Our life.

And our strength.

THE END

ACKNOWLEDGMENTS

A few words of acknowledgements.

Magdalena Marków, for the map and constant support for the Healer.

To my friends.

Agnieszka - my FrodoSam, always...

Renata - for being ready to answer the most bizarre questions.

Damian for memory.

Daniel for... growth :)

And the family, especially children.

Friends I have met since the time of the first part.

Katarzyna for comments, Adrian for sympathy.

Marta Bilewicz for the review and sympathy for my protagonists.

All bloggers and readers for their reviews and comments.

Thank you.

.